I0588361

INFINITE PIECES VOLUME 2

Infinite Pieces
Book 2

STERLING & STONE

STERLING & STONE

Copyright © 2025 by Sterling & Stone

All rights reserved.

No part of this book may be reproduced in any form or by any electronic
or mechanical means, including information storage and retrieval systems,
without written permission from the author, except for the use of brief
quotations in a book review.

The authors greatly appreciate you taking the time to read our work.
Please consider leaving a review wherever you bought the book, or telling
your friends about it, to help us spread the word.

Thank you for supporting our work.

INFINITE PIECES VOLUME 2

Just Another Dead Girl

SEAN PLATT

Just Another Dead Girl

SEAN PLATT

AVA WOKE.

And she was cold.

Not the kind of cold when you've kicked off your blankets in the middle of the night. No, this was meat-locker type cold. Not that she'd ever spent any time in a meat locker. But she imagined this was how you'd feel. A cold that got into your bones and made your teeth chatter.

One problem.

She couldn't see where she was. So she didn't know why she was cold. Just that she was.

The air carried the faint scent of disinfectant and something else — something sickeningly sweet that she couldn't quite place.

She sat.

Hit her head on something metal.

The resulting sound clanged all the way down into her brain.

What the actual fuck?

She raised a hand. More cold. This time, it was metal.

Above her. Below her. Beside her. Even her skin was cold. Because she was naked.

But she couldn't remember why.

In fact, she couldn't quite remember the last thing she was supposed to remember. And she was certain there was something between the time she left home this morning and her waking up here.

A crisp sheet lay over her body. At least, she was grateful for that. And there was a string around her right toe.

She didn't like it.

Made her toe feel weirdly claustrophobic. If toes could feel such a thing.

Time to assess.

She was cold. Lying in a metal box. Had something tied around her toe. Could remember fuck all about the day before.

You're in a morgue, bitch.

She knew she was right. Not that, at 16, she had much experience with morgues. She was drawing on all those TV shows that her mother used to watch before she left Ava and her father.

She shimmied down and kicked the end of the drawer.

Thud.

Thud. THUD.

Okay. Obviously, that wasn't gonna work.

She bunched her fingers into a fist and bashed the wall. Was it a wall? Side of the drawer? Who the hell knew. She banged it anyway.

But all she got was metallic reverberations drilling into her skull.

And bruised knuckles.

She gave up.

"Hey! Anyone out there?"

No response.

"Help!"

Nothing.

"LET ME THE FUCK OUT!"

Nada.

Goddamnit. She supposed eventually SOMEONE would open the drawer and let her out. And then she was gonna find whoever put her in here and swap spots. See how they liked it.

Unless she wasn't in a morgue.

What if it was a crematorium?

Panic.

"LET ME OUT. LET ME OUT. LET ME OUT —"

The door at her feet opened. She sat. Hit her head. "Fuck!"

She fell back. A blast of fluorescent light hit her eyes. The metal slab beneath her groaned when it slid forward.

"Jesus Christ," said a girl on her right, with a halo of tight black curls framing her face. She held a cloth bundle in her arms. "If you're trying to wake the dead, I've got news — they're already up."

"Fuck you," Ava said, clutching the sheet to her chest.

"You didn't think you were gonna get burned up, did you?" A second girl on her left asked. She had a shock of electric blue hair falling in her face.

"Of course not," Ava said.

Blue hair shrugged. "I thought so when I woke up here. But then I didn't smell gas. So I knew I was gonna be okay."

"Who the fuck are you?" Ava asked.

Blue hair gestured to herself. "I'm Mary. And that's Zahra."

Zahra plunked her cloth bundle on Ava's chest. "Get dressed. We've got places to go."

Ava stared at her. "What places?"

Mary smiled. "The dentist."

AVA WORE an oversized T-shirt that reached her knees and read: *Save Water, Drink Beer.* It had a moose sitting next to a cooler full of Pilsner. The jeans fit better but they were too long, so she'd rolled up the cuffs. A pair of *Team-Bride* flip-flops completed her ensemble.

Was this some kind of hazing ritual?

Only she couldn't think of anything she needed hazing for.

Mary and Zahra told her they'd wait outside the morgue. That was fine with her. She wasn't planning on seeing them again.

But after a quick search of the room, she realized that was the only exit.

There was a phone on the wall. But there was no dial tone.

She exited into the hall.

Mary jumped to her feet. "Ready?"

"I'm going home," Ava said. "My Dad will be worried sick about me." *Assuming he was sober.*

"After the dentist," Zahra said.

Ava was beginning to get pissed. No, she was WAY past pissed. And verging on irritable. "I don't need the dentist."

"Trust us," Mary said. "You do."

"That is if you want to find out how you wound up in the morgue," Zahra said.

Ava glared at her. "Was it you?"

"All will be explained at —"

"— the dentist's," Ava said.

Mary beamed. "Exactly."

Ava looked up and down the hospital corridors. She didn't even know what hospital she was at. Let alone WHERE.

"After I go to the dentist, you'll take me home?"

"Of course," Zahra said.

Mary glanced at her.

Ava chewed on her thumb. *What was she supposed to do?*

"Well?" Zahra asked.

Fuck it.

"Let's go."

~

AVA FIGURED that since none of them looked old enough to drive, she might be able to ask their driver where they were.

But they wound up walking to the dentist's office.

They went out a back door, so she still wasn't sure what hospital she'd turned up in. To be honest, it mostly looked abandoned. Windows boarded over. Large metal gates around the property.

And it was late.

What the fuck kind of dentist's office was open in the middle of the night.

Ava stopped. "Am I being trafficked?"

Mary looked horrified. "Of course not!"

"Then what's this about? The last thing I remember was —"she broke off. Frowned.

"Yes?" Zahra said, her mouth twitching in an almost smirk. "Please tell us."

Ava glared at her. "Never mind."

They resumed walking.

Ava kept her eyes on Zahra's back. She was certain the girl knew she couldn't remember. But how? She wanted to ask.

But for the first time since she'd woken up in the morgue, she felt nervous about hearing the answer.

AVA FOLLOWED Zahra into the dentist's office.

A receptionist sat behind the counter. Her name tag read: Sarah.

She looked up and smiled at them when they entered. "Welcome back, girls."

"Uh huh," Zara said. She proceeded through the door into the back of the office.

Mary, however, stopped for introductions. "This is Ava. Ava, this is our receptionist."

"Hello, Ava."

Ava forced a smile. "Hi."

Sarah waved her hand towards the door Zahra had taken. "You can go on through."

"I really don't need a check-up," Ava said.

Mary snagged her arm. "Come on."

Ava sighed and went with her.

Was she being kidnapped? Was this some reality show prank? She stopped in the doorway. *Maybe she'd finally gone insane.*

"Come on," Mary said.

Ava followed her down the row of rooms to the last one on the right. Zahra was seated on a dental assistant's chair. She patted the client chair.

"No," Ava said.

"Suit yourself," Zahra said, leaning back and putting her feet on the chair.

Mary stood in the doorway, looking anxious.

"Alright, spill," Ava said. "I'm here. Do your worst."

Zahra fiddled with a dental pick. "You're dead."

Ava blinked.

Huh?

"What?"

"Zahra," Mary said. "We talked about this. Making it easier on the girls."

Ava was still staring at Zahra. "Dead?"

"Or, if you prefer, deceased. Passed. Over the rainbow bridge. Kaput. Six feet under. Shall I go on?"

"No. Dead is fine," Ava said. "Only it's not true. Because I'm standing here."

Zahra reached behind her for a hand mirror. Held it out to Ava. She took it. Weird. It wasn't like a mirror at all. Because the face in the glass wasn't hers.

And then she realized it was. Only she wasn't her.

Ava dropped the mirror. It shattered on the floor. "What the fuck. Where did my face go?"

"I told you," Zahra said. "It died."

"My face did not die," Ava said.

"It did. Along with your bones. Eyes. Feet. Heart. All of it. Dead."

Ava stared at her. Then turned to Mary. "What is this bullshit?"

"It's true," Mary said. "You died."

"Then how am I standing here?"

"It's because you're back. You're what we call a Dead Girl."

"Okay, I've had enough of this." Ava stepped towards the door. "I'm going home."

"Don't do that." For the first time, Zahra looked serious. "It'll only cause more harm than good."

Fuck that.

Fuck them.

She'd had enough bullshit this evening.

"See you later." She brushed past Mary and headed back to the reception.

Sarah smiled when she entered. "That was quick."

Ava grunted. Made her way outside. Half expected Zahra and Mary to follow her. But they didn't. She tried to get her bearings because she was thoroughly confused. A truck barreled along the road towards her.

She ran out to flag it down.

Right when it reached her, a raccoon waddled into the road. The truck swerved to avoid it. Lights flashed bright and —-

~

AVA WOKE.

And she was cold.

Not the kind of cold when you've kicked off your blankets in the middle of the night. No, this was meat-locker type of cold. Not that she'd ever spent any time in a meat locker. But she imagined this was how you'd feel. A cold that got into your bones and made your teeth chatter.

One problem.

She couldn't see where she was.

She just knew that she was fucking cold and —

Goddamnit.

Not this again.

The door at her feet opened. The metal slab beneath her groaned when it slid forward. Waiting for her, once again, were Zahra and Mary.

Zahra dropped the bundle of clothes on her chest and headed for the door. "Meet you in the hallway."

Ava shook out the shirt. This one had a cartoon woman in a straw flower hat. *I Love My Husband Almost as Much as Wine.*

"Where the fuck do you get these clothes?"

Mary pointed to a box on the other side of the room. Lost and Found.

~

AVA SAT on the dental chair.

Sideways.

Just in case they decided to try to knock her out with some laughing gas. "I'm really dead?"

"'fraid so," Zahra said.

"How?"

"We don't know the details," Mary said. "But it wouldn't have been … natural."

"Not natural?"

Mary shook her head.

"Like an accident?"

"Not really," Mary said.

"Jesus Christ," Zahra said, decorating her fingernails with toothpaste as though it were nail polish. "You were fucking murdered."

"Zahra!"

Ava stared at her. "By who?"

Zahra shrugged. "Dunno. Dad, boyfriend, uber driver, science teacher. Take your pick. It's not important."

Ava snatched the toothpaste from her hands and threw it across the room. "It's important to me!"

"Zahra's been dead second longest," Mary said. "So she forgets what it was like."

"If I'm dead, how come I'm here?"

"Because you're a Dead Girl," Mary said.

"It sounds like a cult," Ava said.

Zahra laughed. It sounded genuine. Mary glared at her. Zahra covered her hand with her mouth. "Sorry."

"It's not a cult," Mary said. "It's a sisterhood."

"Which sounds exactly like what a cult would say," Ava grunted.

"Zahra, you explain," Mary said.

Zahra licked the paste from one of her nails. Grimaced. "As Dead Girls, we are destined to die repeatedly in order to inspire men."

Ava blinked. "What?"

"Exactly."

"I'm supposed to die to inspire men. Sure. Like Jesus?"

"Yeah," Zahra nodded. "But with more daddy issues and less carpentry skills."

Ava laughed.

"And the only people who will recognize you from one life to the next are your fellow Dead Girls. To everyone else, you'll appear as a completely different person each time."

"Every time? How many times are there?"

Mary gestured to Zahra. "She's over three hundred."

Ava's mouth fell open. "You've died three hundred times?"

"Over."

This had to be some kind of joke …

"But … how? Why?" Ava asked. "Who decided this was a thing?"

Zahra shrugged. "Dunno. Just the way it's always been."

Mary nodded. "We die, we inspire, we come back and do it all over again."

"And I'm not allowed to go back home?"

"It's not, NOT allowed," Zahra said. "It's just usually too painful."

"Good," Ava said, sliding off the seat. She went out to reception. Waited for Sarah to look up. "Where's Chestnut Street?"

Sarah pointed east.

"Thanks."

And out Ava went.

~

SHE'D WALKED for over an hour before she started to recognize her surroundings. But as soon as she did, she started to run.

Ahead was the overpass, then the exit to her neighborhood. The crosswalk would be just ahead.

She crossed beneath it. Heard a loud bang and turned back.

A car had broken through the cement barrier of the overpass and was coming right at —

~

AVA WOKE.

It was cold.

"FUCK."

~

AVA LEFT the morgue wearing a shirt that said: *I'd rather be screwing.*

"I'm beginning to think this is deliberate," Ava said, looking down at the cartoon man wearing carpenter's gear.

Zahra grinned.

But once they left the hospital grounds, they didn't go left; they went right. She stopped. "We're not going to the dentist?"

"Nope," Mary said. "We're headed to Zander's art gallery."

"For what?"

Zahra glanced at her. "Wine and a showing. Why do you think?"

"I think we're all under 16, and we won't be allowed entrance."

Zahra pulled a compact mirror from her pocket. Flipped it open and held it out. Ava checked her appearance.

"Why do I look like Betty White?"

"You're not that old."

Ava grunted.

They caught a city bus and made their way downtown.

Zander's Art Galleria (God, could it be more pretentious?) was located at the edge of the art district. Inside, it was all white walls and long rows of track lighting.

And it was packed.

The three of them made their way up, and a bored student dressed all in black opened the door for them. Zahra gestured for Ava to enter first.

The paintings were a riot of red, splattered across multiple canvases in patterns that were too chaotic to track.

A placard next to the first painting read: *Semi-Permanent* by Marcus Jeffries.

Ava sure as fuck hoped they were semi-permanent. Because these paintings were bad. Mediocre at best. "I came, I saw. Can I leave now?"

"But you haven't seen all your paintings," Mary said.

"My paintings?" Ava said.

Zahra nodded. "Marcus was the one that ran you over."

Ava blinked. Looked closer at a painting. A raccoon covered in blood. "He killed me?"

Zahra nodded. "The second time. He's already being called the next Jackson Pollock."

Fuck him.

"Where is he?" Ava asked.

Mary pointed to a gaunt man surrounded by art enthusiasts. He was dressed in black. The mirror image of the student who had opened the door.

She marched over to him and poked him in the chest. "Asshole."

Marcus recoiled. "I beg your pardon."

"You killed me, you fucker."

"Uh —"He glanced at the other guests.

But Ava didn't give him time to respond. Instead she walked over and grabbed the painting of the blood-spattered raccoon. Yanked it from the wall. Tried to tear it into pieces. No luck. So she walked to the entrance. "I'm taking this with me."

"Ava!" Mary looked worried.

"Stop her," Marcus said. "She's stealing Trash Life!"

AVA DARTED outside and down the stairs. The painting was large and cumbersome. It caught between her legs, tripping her. She went flying onto the road. A manhole cover was missing. She tumbled down into the sewage and —

AVA WOKE.

"Son of a bitch."

～

AVA YANKED the *It's Beer O'Clock* t-shirt over her head.

This time Zahra didn't leave while she dressed. Instead she scooted around the morgue on a gurney, using a mop for propulsion.

"You've done this over three hundred times?" Ava asked.

Zahra nodded.

"Who gets you out?"

"Steph and Bella."

Ava stared at her. "There's more like us?"

Zahra rolled her eyes. "Of course. There's hundred of Dead Girls"." She stretched out the "s" so it sounded like zzzzzz.

"And when do I get to meet them?"

"Dunno," Mary said. "But Margaret wants to meet you in ten minutes."

"And who is Margaret?"

"The dentist."

Ava swallowed. "Am I in trouble?"

"Dunno."

"How many times have you had to go to the dentist?"

Mary smiled, standing proud. "Never."

Ava turned to Zahra. "You?"

She shrugged. "Over three hundred."

～

WHEN THEY ARRIVED at the dental office, Zahra and Mary declined to go inside.

"You can't be serious," Ava said. "What about sisterhood?"

"It's you she wants to see, not us," Zahra said. "We'll wait for you here."

Ava glared at her, then stomped inside.

Sarah looked up and smiled. "Exam room three."

Ava growled, then stopped. It wasn't Sarah's fault she was here. She turned back. "Thanks. Sorry if I came off grouchy."

Sarah laughed. "You're good. Go on in."

Ava made her way to the third room and entered. A stern-looking woman in her fifties, wearing a lab coat, sat in the dentist's chair.

"Take a seat, Ava."

She did. "Am I in trouble?"

"No. Why?"

She shrugged. "I feel like I got called to the Principal's Office."

Margaret rummaged through a cupboard. "You want some toothpaste?"

Ava blinked. "For what?"

"Your teeth."

"No, I'm good," Ava said.

Margaret nodded and closed the cupboard.

"Wait. Do I need to brush my teeth? I mean, I'm dead." Ava widened her eyes. "Unless I'm not?"

"No, you're dead," Margaret said. "And you don't need to brush or floss or mouthwash. Although some girls find it helps to maintain a semblance of their prior life."

"So, who are you? Head Dead Girl?"

Margaret laughed. "You can call me that."

"What do others call you?"

"Their dentist."

"And why do we need a dentist?"

Margaret smiled. "That's exactly what I'm here to tell you."

~

"THERE ARE TWO RULES," Margaret said once Ava got settled in the dental chair. "One. I give you the name of a man you are to inspire. Two. You figure out how to inspire him."

"Inspire?"

"Yes."

"What do you mean by that?"

Margaret mimed hanging herself.

"You mean die?"

"Well, yes, but it's rather a touchy subject, so we find inspire a better word. And the bloodier and more violent and painful, the better. Anything less, and inspiration won't take."

"Is this a fucking joke?"

"Language," Margaret said. "And it's no fucking joke."

"Well, it's stupid."

"It's the system."

"And what man came up with it?"

Margaret's face remained impassive. "I am certain I don't know. The rules have been in place for as long as anyone can remember. Even Joan doesn't know their origins, and she's been with us the longest."

"So, what if I want to opt-out? Quit?"

"You can't."

"Say's who?"

Margaret's expression hardened. "This is who you are now, Ava. There is no way out."

"There's always a way out," Ava said. She grabbed the dental drill, switched it on, and drove it into her neck.

∾

AVA WOKE.

∾

MARGARET PRODUCED a slip of paper from her pocket. "Shall we continue?"

Ava grunted.

"Your first assignment is Daniel Anders. Musician. Find him, inspire him, you know the drill."

Ava plucked the paper from her fingers. "Ha, ha."

Margaret blanched. "My apologies. I didn't mean to suggest —"

But Ava was already gone. She stepped out of the office and — where the fuck was Mary and Zahra? She went back in. "Uh, Sarah. Where are Mary and Zahra?"

Sarah looked down at her appointment book. "They're out on assignment. Do you need them?"

Did she?

"Nope." She looked down at the paper. "I'm good."

She exited, crumpling Daniel Anders' address in her hand, then tossed it in the nearest bin.

She didn't need it 'cause Ava was going home.

∾

AVA STOOD across the street from her home.

Staring.

The once wild jungle of weeds and dandelions that had been their front yard for years was now a manicured expanse of emerald grass. The peeling, sun-bleached grey home had been painted with a fresh coat of cheery yellow paint.

For a moment, she thought her father might have moved.

But no, that was his F150 in the driveway, the bed filled with cardboard boxes.

Then the front door opened, and her father stepped out. He was clean-shaven, and he carried another box.

Ava couldn't remember the last time she'd seen him without his usual scruff or holding anything other than a bottle. And the way he moved. His shoulders seemed lighter.

Her throat tightened.

Was he happy she was gone?

The front door banged open again. Another figure emerged. Ava's eyes widened in disbelief. "M- Mom?"

It couldn't be.

They hadn't spoken in years. In fact, she could still hear her mother's last words. "I'm never coming back."

But there she was.

She'd been broken-hearted when Ava decided to stay, hoping she could help her father get sober. She'd begged and pleaded. But Ava had her father's stubbornness.

Her father stopped half way to the truck. And her mom added her box to the top of his. Then she turned around and went back inside.

Ava's shock turned to anger.

What the hell was going on?

And just how long had she been... gone?

She marched across the street.

"Hey!" Ava waved her arms.

Her father set the boxes in the truck bed, then turned around. "Can I help you?"

Could he help her? No, where the fuck have you been?

And then she remembered. He wasn't seeing her. He was seeing someone else.

Ava opened her mouth to explain, but the words never came out. A deafening crack cut the air, followed by a blinding flash of light.

Pain exploded through every nerve in her body, and then—

DARK.

"Oh, come on!" Ava said. "Seriously?"

The drawer slid open.

"Rough day?" Zahra asked.

"What the hell just happened?"

Zahra handed her a fabric bundle. "Lightning strike. Pretty rare, but it happens."

"There wasn't a cloud in the sky," Ava said.

"As I said, rare."

Ava glared at her.

"Margaret's mad," Mary said, her large eyes looking worried. "You weren't supposed to go home."

Ava slid off the metal bed, letting the sheet fall away. "Margaret doesn't get a say."

AVA RAN FASTER.

Her house was just two blocks away now.

She heard a growl. Glanced back. A massive dog with foam dripping from its jaws crawled out of the bushes and scampered after her. Ava ran faster. "Good boy."

METAL.

21

AVA SCRAMBLED OVER THE FENCE. Maybe the way to success was going in the back door. She heard something electrical snap.

Looked up.

A power line fell towards her in a shower of sparks.

COLD.

AVA WALKED.

Careful to avoid any obstacle. Crossed the street only when there were zero cars. She was two houses away now.

Alert for any possible sign of interference.

It was now or never.

She stepped off the curb.

Something hit her on the head.

"A TOILET SEAT?" Ava said.

"Uh huh," Zahra nodded. "From the space station."

Ava glared at her. "Sounds like something from a TV show."

This time when she stepped out of the morgue and into the hospital hallway, Margaret was waiting for her.

"What the fuck?" Margaret said.

Ava looked down at her shirt: *Warning: Fart Loading.* "I agree. This might be the worst yet."

"I am not talking about the shirt," Margaret said

through clenched teeth. "I am talking about Daniel Anders."

"Who's that?"

For a moment, Margaret looked like she wanted to put Ava back in the drawer. "Who is that? The man you supposed to be inspiring."

"Oh, right."

"Only you seem to be determined to go home."

Ava pointed. "Zahra said it wasn't against the rules."

"Hey!"

"It's not. Because it's impossible to go home. You'll just wind up dead. Those we've left behind have moved on."

"But I haven't." Tears pricked her eyes. "I want to see my dad. My mom."

Margaret walked over and hugged her. "I know. But it's impossible."

For a moment, Ava resisted. But it felt good to be hugged. She tried to imagine it was her mother holding her. But she couldn't quite get there.

"You weren't murdered for nothing, Ava. You have the potential to inspire hundreds. If not thousands."

"Of men." The words were dripping with disdain.

Margaret obviously chose to ignore her tone. "Exactly. So why not embrace it?"

Ava stiffened. *Why not embrace it?*

Why not, indeed.

She pursed her lips, a plan forming in her head.

"Alright. Give me Daniel's address."

Margaret looked shocked. "You don't have it?"

Ava shrugged. "Must have burned up when the lightning struck."

～

THE ADDRESS for Daniel wasn't a house but a coffee shop.

Bean There, Done That.

Ava wasn't sure how she was supposed to recognize him when she entered. She just did. He was seated in the window, hunched over his laptop, eyes on the screen.

There was an empty chair opposite him, so she walked over and sat.

It took him a minute to realize she was staring at him. But finally, he looked up. "May I help you?"

"No, but I'm here to help you."

He looked confused. "With what?"

"Your music."

He stiffened. "You know my music?"

"Sure do. It's awesome. Amazing. I can't get enough of it. You should write more."

His eyes narrowed. "Did my sister send you here?"

Ava blinked. "What? No. Why?"

"Because she's the only one who has ever heard me play."

Shit.

"Look, Daniel," she said, leaning in and lowering her voice. "I'm trying to inspire you."

He recoiled. "You know my name?"

Double shit. Maybe she had been too forward.

Ava pointed to the barista. "I heard him call it out."

Daniel turned his cup around. Scribbled on the side was: *oat milk latte, extra hot.* She met his eyes and shrugged. "I guessed."

Daniel closed his laptop, got to his feet, and collected his cup. "Have a good day."

Ava got up. "No, wait. Please. I just want to talk."

He headed for the door.

She followed him out.

As soon as he spotted her, he broke into a jog. Cutting across the road towards a high-rise building that was under construction. Ava tried to follow, but the light turned red. When he got to the other side, he stopped, turning back to make sure she hadn't followed him.

Which was the exact moment a cement block from the half-built high-rise fell on him.

～

FOR THE FIRST three seconds after the cement block splatted Daniel Anders into a pancake everything continued on. And then someone screamed.

Eventually, Ava was jostled by others wanting to get a front page seat to *Man Squashed by Cement Brick!*

But Ava didn't need to watch.

She also didn't know what to do.

She went back into the cafe and sat. Until someone next to her hissed and pointed to her face. She went to the washroom and checked the mirror. There was a spot of blood on her unfamiliar cheek. Daniel had traveled in death.

She wondered if she had.

And why the hell she hadn't looked into her own death. That was weird. Even now, trying to hold onto that thought felt difficult. Like it was evaporating into the ether.

She had no idea where to go.

Not to the dentist's.

God, what was she supposed to tell Margaret?

She wiped her face and exited the cafe. Then started walking. And, of course, her feet took her home. She stopped mid-block, looking around for whichever unseen force was watching her. "I don't want to talk to them," she said. "I just want to SEE them. And then I'll leave. I promise."

She waited a moment.

And when she didn't wake up in the morgue, she decided that she had permission to proceed. She walked up to the front window, resisting the urge to bolt inside.

But she was going to be true to her word.

She peered inside.

Her father's face was red. Drinking again. Or not. He paced. And then her mom stepped out, arms waving about.

They were arguing.

She stepped towards the door.

And then her dad collapsed on the couch. Head in his hands. Her mom went and sat beside him. Pulled him into her arms, cradling him. His shoulders shook. He was crying. And Ava knew it was because of her.

He was sad she was gone.

Tears pricked her own eyes.

And she caught her reflection in the window. Even if she were to go inside, she wasn't Ava anymore.

She turned around and walked away.

Might as well go see Margaret.

Get the lecture over with.

THE DOOR of the dentist's office banged closed behind her.

Sarah looked up. Her smile faded instantly. "You better get in there."

"Number three?"

Sarah nodded.

Ava headed into the back of the office and walked

along to the third office. Margaret exited just as she neared.

"What. Did. You. Do?" Margaret ground out through clenched teeth.

"What do you mean?" Ava asked. Although she probably wasn't going to be able to play innocent for long.

A familiar head popped out of the room.

"Hi."

It was Daniel Anders.

"Oh," Ava said. "*That*."

"Yes, that!" Margaret said, marching to her and grabbing her arm. Dragging her down the hallway. "What the hell am I supposed to do with him, Ava?"

"I don't know," Ava said.

"What happened?"

Ave gesticulated. "He just died."

"That was supposed to be you."

"I get that," Ava said. She was starting to get pissed. "Maybe he took one for the team."

Margaret glared at her. "That's not how it works."

"So now what?" Ava asked.

Margaret pinched the bridge of her nose. "I don't know. I'll have to consult with — well, I'll have to consult."

Ava stared at her. "There's someone above you?"

Margaret ignored her. Slipped a piece of paper from the pocket of her lab coat. Held it out. "Your next assignment."

Ava took the paper and gestured to Daniel. "What about him?"

"Look after him," Margaret said, stalking off.

Ava planted her hands on her hips. "Why me?"

"He's your Dead Boy."

∽

THEY MADE their way through reception, and Ava handed the paper to Daniel. "You better hang onto this. I tend to lose them."

Then they exited the office right when Zahra rounded the corner.

She stopped short, and Daniel bumped into her.

Zahra stopped too, eying Daniel. "Who's this?"

"Dead Boy," said Ava.

Daniel glared at her and held out his hand in greeting. "Daniel Anders."

Zahra eyed his hand as though she'd just seen him sneeze in it. "Daniel Anders. Why is he dead?"

Ava shrugged. "Got to him too late, I guess."

"He passed his expiration date?"

"Something like that."

Daniel crossed his arms. "I'm not sure I appreciate you discussing me like I'm a can of tinned tomatoes."

"Why not?" Ava asked. "You kinda were."

He glowered at her.

"What did Margaret say when she saw him?" Zahra asked.

"That she needed a consult."

"Oh, you really did fuck up," Zahra said. "She's only ever asked for a consult once before."

"When was that?"

"Long time ago."

"Shouldn't we be going?" Daniel asked, waving the slip of paper at her. "Don't we have an assignment?"

Ava glared at him, then walked over to Zahra, lowering her voice. "I've got a question for you. You ever wonder how you died?"

Zahra crossed her arms over her chest. "That kind of thinking never leads anywhere good, Ava."

"It's when you said maybe it was father. What if it

was?"

Zahra shook her head. "No. It's not him."

"How do you know?"

"Because you remember him."

"And?"

"We never remember the ones that kill us. Probably to keep us from going back and getting vengeance."

"We can do that?"

Zahra shrugged. "Maybe."

Ava took a breath. "You did that."

Zahra looked sad. "I don't recommend it."

"Why?"

"It left my mom without a daughter. And a son."

"Fuck." Ava hugged her. For a moment, Zahra was stiff. Then she relaxed, but only for a second. Then she was pulling away.

"Thanks."

Ava nodded, gestured to Daniel. "Come on, we got work to do." Then she started walking. When she got to the end of the block, she stopped and turned back.

Zahra was still watching after them.

AVA STOPPED in front of the house.

Her father's truck was gone. He was out.

"Is this our assignment?" Daniel asked. "Because the address doesn't match the paper."

"Fuck the address," Ava said, walking up the driveway. A box of bottles sat next to the garbage can. She bent down and picked one up. Artemis Tull. And it was still full.

Huh.

"What's wrong?" Daniel asked.

"Nothing. Let's go inside."

Ava walked to the front porch and found the plastic stone hidden in the flower pot. It had a false bottom. She dumped out the key.

Unlocked the house.

And entered.

The familiar smell of her father hit instantly. Her whole body relaxed. She was home. She walked to the closet and opened it. Took out one of his coats and slipped it on, smelling the sleeve.

"This is your house," Daniel said.

Ava walked into the living room. He was standing in front of the wall next to the window. A bunch of newspaper clippings had been taped there. *Teen Murdered, Body Dumped in High School Parking Lot.*

Teen.

Her.

Ava pulled the clipping and read. She'd gone to the school dance with her boyfriend, Steve Messenger. They'd had an argument, as witnessed by several friends. Messenger reported that she didn't want a lift home. Said she'd walk. So he left her. Four hours later, her body was discovered by a man who was walking his dog.

Daniel was looking at a photograph of her with a teenage boy. He was dressed in a football uniform. A large Eagle on his chest. "Are we supposed to be here?"

Ava ignored him, and plucked the photograph from his hands. Compared it to the one in the clipping. Steve Messenger. She didn't remember having a boyfriend.

A flash of cold slid down her spine like a knife.

We never remember the ones that kill us.

Steve. Steve had killed her.

She looked up at the wall. There was another news article. Steve had been taken in for questioning a third time. His photograph had been circled with a pen.

Several times. A yellow sticky was in the center of the wall.

Eagles versus Guardians. Plus, a date. Today's date.

Her father wasn't going to do anything stupid, was he?

She glanced at the coffee table. An empty holster sat there. Fuck.

"I don't think this is our assignment," Daniel said.

"No, it's not," Ava said. "I'll catch you later."

Then she headed for the door.

"Where are you going?" Daniel asked.

"High school."

AVA ARRIVED at the high school to find the parking lot packed and crowds of people streaming toward the football field. She glanced over the crowd, spotting a familiar face. Callie. Her former best friend.

She was with her parents. Holding tight to her mom's arm. She looked sad.

Ava stepped towards her, then remembered.

Callie wouldn't recognize her.

Besides, she was here to find her Dad. But why? Steve. That's right. She thought he was going to kill Steve.

She made her way into the school.

The smell of it, the memory of classes, of bells and tests and teachers all came flooding back. She understood why Dead Girls weren't supposed to go back to their other life. It was overwhelming.

She walked along the hallway, peering into classrooms, running her fingers along lockers. Reading posters announcing dances, study sessions, lost textbooks. The next classroom she looked in, she stopped.

Her father was seated inside.

A bottle of whisky on the desk before him. Along with the gun and his phone.

She put her hand on the doorknob, waiting for lightning to strike. But it didn't. So she opened it and went inside.

Her father looked up, straightening, wiping his eyes.

"Are you okay?" Ava said. For a moment, she was scared he'd recognize her voice. But it sounded different. Even to her own ears.

He opened his mouth, then gestured, unable to talk. His head dropped again. Ava walked over and pulled up a chair. Sitting next to him. Then she lay a hand on his shoulder. It took every ounce of willpower not to throw herself into his arms. "You look … sad."

He sniffed. "My daughter … she was murdered. I'm not handling it well."

Ava's throat tightened. "I'm so sorry."

"Don't be." He reached for the gun, then his hands dropped into his lap. "I came here to kill the little shit that did it."

"And have you?" Ava asked.

He laughed. It was brittle, bitter. "Nah. Cops picked him up about an hour ago. They finally got enough evidence to arrest him." He gestured to his cellphone. "Just got the call."

Ava felt her shoulders sag. Relieved. "That's a good thing, isn't it?"

He cleared his throat. "I guess so. I just — all I can think about is my baby dying alone. All by herself. All scared."

Ava took his hand. She couldn't help it. It was warm and strong. Like she remembered. "She wasn't alone."

His eyes flashed. He tried to pull his hand away. "I fucking know that. That bastard—"

"No, no, that's not what I mean. I'm not talking about *him*. I'm talking about you."

Her father met her eyes. "What do you mean?"

Ava's fingers tightened on his. "I know that in her final moments, her thoughts would have been on you and Mom. Her mom. So you would have been with her. Even if you weren't physically there."

Her father cleared his throat. "You think?"

"I know," Ava said.

He gave her a wobbly smile. "Thank you. That means a lot."

Ava squeezed his hand. "Is there someone I could call for you? Take you home?"

He wiped his eyes. "Already done. Just waiting for her now."

There was a quiet knock on the door. Ava looked up. Her mom stood there. She bolted to her feet, dropping her dad's hand.

Her father got up and gestured to Ava. "She was helping me."

Her mom smiled. "I heard. I got here a few minutes ago, but I didn't want to interrupt."

Her father turned to her. "Thank you —?"

"A- Abigail," she said.

He gave her a hug. Then released her and walked to the door. A moment later they were both gone.

Ava sat.

A minute later, her mom appeared at the door. "Is that — is that my husband's coat?"

Ava looked down at it. "Yeah, sorry."

"No, no," she said. "You keep it."

Ava swallowed. "Thank you."

"Although, maybe I should dispose of those two

things." She gestured to the gun and the bottle. Ava nodded.

Her mom entered and collected them. Then she paused. "Do I know you?"

"I don't think so," Ava said. "Take care of him, will you."

Her mom smiled. "I will."

And then she was gone. Leaving Ava alone. From outside, a loud cheer came from the direction of the football field.

AVA ENTERED the dentist's office.

Daniel was seated in a chair. He jumped up when he saw her. "Hey, Ava. I don't think my mission went quite as planned."

Ava ignored him, walking past Sarah without greeting her. The receptionist's smile was gone. In fact, she looked downright pissed. Ava made her way through to the back office. A line of men stood waiting to get into number three. Jesus, why was it so busy?

"Psst."

Ava turned.

Zahra and Mary were watching from room one. Ava walked down to them.

"This is all your fault," Mary said.

"What did I do?" Ava asked.

Zahra stopped mid-floss and gestured to the line of men. "We all decided to stop dying. And every single target showed up as a Dead Boy. The entire system has ground to a halt."

Ava blinked. Then turned to Mary. "Even you stopped?"

"I was peer-pressured."

Zahra rolled her eyes.

Ava gestured to the line-up. "So they're all —"

"Yep," Zahra nodded. "Dead Boys."

"What's Margaret got to say about it?"

Zahra shrugged. "Dunno. She came out of her consult and has been hiding in the bathroom ever since."

Ava made her way past the line-up. "Excuse me."

The boys shuffled to the side.

Ava reached the bathroom and knocked.

"Go away." Margaret sounded like she had been crying.

"Open up," Ava said.

The lock clicked.

Ava opened the door and stepped inside. Margaret was seated on the toilet, her eyes red and puffy. "What's going on?"

Margaret gestured to the sink. "I got the next set of assignments."

Ava picked one out of the sink. It was slightly damp. *Zahra.* She pulled the next one. *Mary. Ava. Joan. Sadie. Clara. Helen.*

"Huh?"

"You're all supposed to kill yourselves."

"Okay. I mean. I've done it before."

"Not like this," Margaret said. "Not when Management wants it."

Ava set the paper down. "What's the difference?"

Margaret's cheeks look hollow. "You don't rise again. This is it. The end."

"How do you know?"

"It happened once before in '66. Clean slate. Except for me."

"Why?"

Margaret sniffed. "The Dead Girls went on strike back then as well."

Ava crossed her arms. "Who's in charge?"

Margaret stiffened. "I can't tell you that."

"Why not?"

"It's against procedure."

"You think if I burn this place down, they'll come and talk to me? Or maybe I go destroy the morgue. Or how about —"

"Sarah."

Ava blinked. "What?"

"It's Sarah."

"Sarah's in charge?"

"But you don't understand what she's like. She can —"

Ava was already gone. Out the bathroom and past the Dead Boys to where Zahra and Mary were waiting for her. Then out into the reception area.

Ava walked over to Sarah and slapped her palms down on the counter. "I would like to talk to management."

Sarah looked up at her. "I beg your pardon?"

Ava smiled. "You heard me."

Sarah stood, rising taller and taller, transforming into a grotesque creature that was half shadow, half flesh.

"*Clever girl,*" she said. "What can I do for you?"

"You can die," Ava said.

Sarah laughed, smoke expelling from her mouth, eyes, and nose. "I think not. As a Dead Girl, that's your fate."

"No," Ava said. "It's yours. Because when I said I wanted to talk to Management, I didn't mean you."

Sarah stilled. "Pardon?"

Ava bared her teeth. "I meant MANAGEMENT."

The door to the street opened. A tiny woman who looked to be in her sixties entered. She carried a leather handbag and wore shiny Mary Janes.

"Madam," Sarah said. Her hands came out in supplication.

But the woman ignored her, turning to Ava instead. "I'm here, girl."

Ava turned. "You've been watching me."

"I watch all the players," she smiled. "What is it you want?"

Ava pointed to Sarah. "Can we fire her?"

Zahra's eyes widened.

Mary shuffled behind her.

"Now, wait a minute," Sarah said. But that was all she got out. Because she exploded. A shockwave of dark energy shot through the office, shattering windows and blowing Ava clean off her feet.

A second later, it was over.

Blood and guts dripped from the ceiling.

Ava spat out a half a toe.

Then she stood. Daniel coughed. Zahra picked a chunk of intestine from her hair. Mary still cowered behind her. Margaret appeared in the doorway. Spotted the small woman and paled.

"Games-Mistress."

Ava glanced at her. "That your title?"

"It is. Although it's hardly fitting. I run the board, not the games. And it's been some time since anyone has asked to end one."

"There are more games?" Mary asked.

"Oh yes, many more." The woman nodded. "But Sarah's appears to have run its course."

"It's over?" Margaret asked.

"It is."

Margaret smiled, then dropped into one of the chairs, looking exhausted.

Ava glanced at Mary. Then Zahra. "So what happens to us?"

The woman smiled. "You can take the life you currently have and live, dying naturally when your time comes. Or ..."

Zahra headed for the door. "See you."

Then she banged out and was gone. A second later Mary ran after her. Daniel followed shortly after.

But Ava hadn't moved. "Or?"

"You become a demon yourself and set up a game of your own choosing." Ava glanced over at Margaret. Her eyes were closed. She wondered if she was asleep. "Well, my dear," the Game-Mistress asked. "Have you decided?"

Ava smiled. "I have."

Mikey Franklin is Not "Not" Gay

CAMERON STONE

Mikey Franklin is Not "Not" Gay

CAMERON STONE

IT'S AN AMAZING DAY WHENEVER CHRISTINA AGUILERA wakes me up by telling me just how beautiful I am in every single way. Except the world does, indeed, hold me down.

Well, most of the time.

Almost all the time.

Okay, every day.

It's not like I don't try to make it better. I do. I really do.

But it's your parents, you know, and it's not like you can just go ruin their day because you feel like it.

Look at me, dumping all of this onto you. Like it's your business. Like you really care.

But maybe you do. Let's see if I can give you some insight into where I'm coming from.

The morning starts at 6:30 am, when the "Dirty" diva herself, Ms. Christina Aguilera, wakes me from my beauty sleep. From there, it's a struggle to start the day off right with a ritual of taking care of myself through skincare, a little bit of spontaneous yoga, and some power poses in front of the mirror. The divas themselves, from Madonna to Beyonce to Dua Lipa, watch over me as I practice. Posters and pictures cover the walls. My parents think I want to be a performer when I graduate. They think I'm going to hit the stage and be a leading man in a Broadway play.

I mean, I wouldn't mind, but I'm not that good at acting.

Most of the time, I feel like I'm half-convincing, playing the part of a straight son in a family of suburban white folks.

Beyond the divas, I have blue walls because that is what boys have on their walls. I still have medals from the championship Little League games I played in. The allure was the way the pants made my ass look, but sure, it was kind of fun, too, I guess.

The baseball bat I used to win the championship is encased in glass on my wall.

I'm just kidding.

I fucking sucked.

I was on the team because my dad knew the coach. I was the best bench warmer the team ever had. I could run fast, but had a habit of throwing the bat whenever I swung at the ball. I was a hazard to the team. Both teams, actually.

The parents would all laugh except mine. They groaned and told everyone that the little ginger kid who got the home runs (his name is Harry, by the way) was their son.

That's why I pose in the mirror. To find that inner strength that these fine ladies on my wall all have.

And only the most fierce poses will do. I walk like I'm Tyra on the runway, taking a fierce step, eyes forward like I could burn the world down with my stare. Let everyone

know, but really my room, just how fucking lucky they are
to have met me. That to gaze upon me is a gift to them.

The girls all want to be me or be my bestie.

The boys?

Well, that's more complicated.

I'm always interrupted mid-wardrobe change by my
mother calling me down to breakfast. "Michael! Your eggs
are getting cold."

Fortunately for me, t-shirts and jeans never go out of
style. I go for a tighter fitting blue shirt with a slight rip in
the neck hole. My mom hates it, but I refuse to let her fix
it. It's mine and I like it that way.

Besides, it's that one conversation piece that everyone
needs to have when they go out to present themselves to
the world. I can't go with blue or pink hair. And there's no
way my mom will let me wear pink or baby lilac nail
polish. So, I go for this as my refuge. It's nothing and
everything all at once.

Mom taps on my door just as I'm finished pulling on
my socks. They're rainbow, from red at the toes to purple
just below my knee. It's a look that dares to scream, "I'm
here, and I'm queer," if you bother to look hard enough.

Today, I'm not taking any chances. Not a single bitch is
going to misinterpret shit today.

Because I'm here. And I'm queer.

"I'm coming, Mom."

What I meant to say is, "I'm coming out, Mom," but
it's one baby step at a time. Baby girl needs to walk in heels
before she can work the catwalk.

"M'kay, honey." I can hear her footsteps disappear.
Back into the kitchen, I presume.

I check myself over in the mirror again and again. The
shirt is a size too small, but it makes my shoulders look

great. The rest of me looks like a flat board, but that's neither here nor there. It's the style. The fashion.

I open the door, and my mom is halfway down the stairs. She turns around and looks at me. "Is that shirt too small for you? You should change."

"I'm fine, Mom." I grab the handrail for support. I'm not going back in my bedroom.

"You really should. It's too small. Please don't tell me the 90s are back again." Mom refuses to continue going down the stairs. She's blocking me from life and self-expression and my food. My literal cupcakes, rainbow with a whipped cream cheese frosting and party sprinkles for good measure.

What's the point of doing rainbow and leaving out the sprinkles?

"Mom, we're going to be late. I'm fine."

"And it has a hole it in."

She acts like she hasn't seen it before.

"Mother, can we go, please?"

Mom keeps her eyes on me. She wants me to feel each judgmental little thought she has. Those thought worms digging through my skull to the one part of my brain that's bigger than every other part: the part that feels shame.

I let go of the railing but seize it again. "I'm not going to change. I don't know what else to wear."

"I can do your laundry."

"No!" I scream it at her, but it's a reaction. Honest. Nothing meant by that. It's just that at a certain time in a young man's life, you do your own laundry. It's for my — and her — protection.

She holds up both hands in surrender. "Fine, no laundry. Do it when you need it."

"I will."

"Okay."

"Okay."

We lock eyes. She recognizes the fact that she lost this battle, but she'll win the war. Mom will make sure of it. "Well, let's get to school, shall we?"

I follow her down the steps. The further we go, the more I start to wonder if the shirt is too tight. Is someone going to say something? Something that's going to make me regret everything?

Thanks for the gaslight, Mom. It was starting to get a little dark in here.

The cupcakes are already in a plastic container, sealed off from the rest of the world with its translucent cover. All I see is white frosting and bits of red and blue through the sides.

"Thank you for getting this together, Mom." Every time she pisses me off, there's something like this she's also done. I would say this is manipulative if I had more evidence.

Once in the car, the cupcakes rest on my lap, and I pray that each speed bump and stop sign doesn't send them flying. That me grabbing for the "oh shit" bar on the side of the car doesn't loosen my grip too much.

In between stop signs, Mom eyes the plastic dome that covers the cupcakes. "Why cupcakes?"

"Just a sweet treat for my friends."

She nods with a smile that tells me that although I can't see in her head, I know something's cooking in there. And my mom's not exactly a Michelin-star chef. Whenever she's cooking—plans or recipes — it usually comes out a disaster and an incomprehensible mess. Mashed potatoes with Chinese food. We're talking about cuisines that have no reason to be together.

The classics are a classic for a reason, is what I'm trying to say.

But Mom? She's the creative one in the family.

I should put "creative" in quotes because that's exactly how you should interpret it. Creative, as in, her mind doesn't know what else to micromanage now that I'm old enough to do my own laundry. She's the type of person who cleans my keyboard and mouse, getting in between the buttons and crevices with a toothpick.

Not that Dad is much better, but he's not questioning my choice to bring homemade baked goods to school.

"Is that even allowed anymore?" Mom says. "I thought you had to label everything."

I show her an index card I planted on the bottom of the tray. "It has all of the ingredients."

"You made it from a box."

"We made this from a box," I remind her. "And some substitutions that I found on TikTok."

Mom nods at the correction. "Right." She says it loud enough for me to hear it. The next "Right" is just under her breath. She thinks I can't hear the tone, but there's a tone. There's always a tone.

She pulls up at the school at the end of drop-off time, and it's like torture. I'd rather have someone stand above me, dripping water against that spot between my eyes with a plastic syringe, than suffer this. The silence— at the risk of being cliche about it — is so totally silent. It's *A Quiet Place* quiet, like our lives depend on it.

Mom nods at me and smiles.

It's off. It feels so off.

I don't know why, but I want to apologize, even though I'm not sure what I did wrong. Was it because I didn't say she could do my laundry? Because I corrected her about the box of cupcake mix? Was I too quiet?

Maybe she sees the rainbows and the girl friends — *not girlfriends* — and she already suspects and is mourning the loss of her dear child. And I'll come home to a bag of my stuff, wrinkled and stinky, and she and my dad will be sitting on the couch. The only words will be "How could you?" and "You're not my son anymore."

My stomach hurts just from the thought.

Someone behind us honks, and that's what breaks the silence. Finally, something louder than all of this doubt and shame I'm feeling over God-knows-what.

"I'm sorry," I blurt out.

Mom says, "It's fine."

But I don't know what's fine, and I don't know what I'm sorry for.

Another honk.

"Mom," I begin. I don't finish. Mom taps the side of her cheek for the kiss goodbye. I give her a peck on the cheek and realize I'm too old for this. But guilt is a helluva drug.

Door opens. More honking.

I step out and glare at the people behind us while Mom hands me the cupcakes. "Have fun, Michael. Be good. Learn lots."

"Thanks, Mom. You, too." I close the door. And no, I don't know why I said that.

Taylor and Charlotte come running. This time without the tackle. They see the cupcakes and immediately, it's "Can I have one?"

Charlotte doesn't even ask. She just grabs the container and opens it up, her hands gripping the silver foil wrapper and she looks at me, eyebrows, drag queen high on her forehead and she says, "What?"

"Nothing." I roll my eyes. "Take one. You already touched it."

"They are for us, right?" Charlotte already has half the wrapper off the cupcake.

Taylor takes one and peels hers off slowly. She's methodical and surgeon-precise, while Charlotte takes more of a "bull in china shop" approach.

Taylor and Charlotte look up almost at the same time.

"Rainbow?" Taylor says.

"This is so cool," Charlotte smiles. "How'd you do it?"

"Actually," I say, "it's easy to do. Just time-consuming. What you do is portion the batter out into six bowls and then drop in a bit of food coloring."

White frosting lines the corners of their mouths before I can even finish the explanation.

I sigh. "Were they at least good?"

Charlotte licks the frosting off her fingers. Most other straight guys would be losing their minds over it.

"Okay, guys. I have something to tell you," I say.

Charlotte goes to reach for another cupcake. Her eyebrows are still so high, but that's her way of asking a question.

I take a cupcake out and hand it to her. "Look, I'm gay."

I try to pose a little bit, shifting my hips to the side and trying to be more feminine. Trying to be light-hearted. Not be so serious. But immediately my attempt falls flat.

"You can't do that," Taylor says. "You're lucky no one is recording this, or you'd be dragged online."

"Why?"

Taylor takes a second cupcake. The precision of the layers isn't as pretty as I want them to be. From the outside, all of the colors take on a light brown color from the heat. Inside, though, the colors shine bright, and I feel like the yellow blends in with the green and orange a little too much.

"Because you can't be straight and make fun of those

coming out videos like that," Charlotte says. "It's insensitive. People really struggle with this kind of stuff."

Tell me about it. I'm struggling right now.

Most people, gay people, my kind of people, fear not being accepted. My fear right now is their refusal to accept it. I stand up tall. I walk with my shoulders and not my hips. I love pop music and divas, but no one knows about that because they've never been in my room. I wear T-shirts and jeans; I look for sneakers and collectible shoes. I don't work out, and I don't really enjoy sports. I don't really have the gay voice thing, either. At least not from what I hear.

But that's not a gay thing, necessarily. I'm more in the "I lack any real athletic bones in my body" camp of boys.

Charlotte finishes her cupcake, licking her fingers. Again. "Your mom sure can bake, though."

"Can she?"

Charlotte nods.

"I'll be sure to tell her." I step away from them but leave the plastic cover off my cupcakes. I will offer one to anyone who asks. When we enter the school, students approach, wanting to try one. "Hi," I tell them. "I'm gay, have a cupcake. Hi. Have a cupcake, I'm gay, by the way."

The students who actually take them? Not a single fucking one listens to me. Like, no one hears a single word from me. They see cupcakes, and they ask for one. There are so many of them asking for a cupcake that I might as well not be here. I might as well be a plastic stand in a supermarket, holding these things out and letting the world take take take…

When the tray is empty, I toss it into my locker and move on to my next class.

And, of course, it's him, I see first.

Again.

Chris.

But I don't have time to study him because our teacher, this small blond thing with short hair and thin lips, hands a stack of paper to the first student and says, "Take one, pass it around." Her big, owl-like green eyes make you feel like she's always watching you, even when she's facing the opposite direction.

The paper in question is an outline for the next documentary. What we're supposed to do is fill it in while we're watching what she shows us. It's her way to make sure we're actually paying attention. But really, we'll just wait for Aaron to finish before we cheat off of him. It'll start with Chris, who will send it over to Ian, who sends it over to Rachel, who sends it over my way.

And Ms. Bowbel? She's clueless as to what's really going on. Or she doesn't care.

Neither would surprise me.

The lights go down low, and the documentary starts to play.

But ten minutes later, I haven't filled out a single line. I hear the movie. I just don't know what's being said. My eyes only see Chris's jawline. The green eyes and brown hair stand out, even in the darkness of the room. My pen sketches a line for his jaw, hard thickness at first, then lightening to match the soft curve of his chin, letting the line smoothly wander upwards until it slides out to create the soft curvature of his nose. Another thicker stroke from his nose bone up to his forehead. His eyebrows are thin, but they work. Large eyes and skin that glows with the green and black and browns of the documentary.

Ms. Bowbel walks up and down the aisles, hands behind her back. She scans each of our papers, stopping when she gets to me. Then she taps the edge of my desk and says, "Good job."

I don't have a single answer on any of the blank lines. The margins of the paper are littered with body parts. Not like that. His body parts. His shoulders are in the lower right corner. His profile, specifically his nose, is in the lower left. Along the right margin, a long, slender sketch of his bicep down to his knuckles. It's not picture-perfect, but it's close.

Ms. Bowbel looks across the room, clever enough that no one really catches what has to be the quickest glance in the history of ever. She looks back down and says, "You're good."

If you could see me through the darkness, my face would be one giant patch of red.

At the end of the period, she asks us to turn in our worksheet. My worksheet is bare. Nothing there except for the sketches along the sides and corners. My hand shakes when I hold it up to her.

She looks at me, looks at the paper, then back to me and says, "If you need more time, you can have more time."

"Thank you."

"Don't mention it." She smiles at me. The rest of the class exits in a thick group, leaving me alone with Ms. Bowbel. "It really is good. You should consider art."

"I don't know that my parents would be..." I falter, not knowing what to say.

"This is Chris?" she says.

I can't keep myself from shaking. Manage a nod.

"It's spot on. You have an eye for drawing." There's a pause, and then she smiles. "Or an eye for —"

She doesn't finish the sentence. She knows it doesn't need to be said. And I hope to God that she will never say it out loud. Finally, she breaks the awkward silence. "Don't be late to your next class. I'm all out of passes."

The hallway is about to clear out, with about two minutes left until the next bell.

I hand her my paper and escape.

Ms. Bowbel knows. And I wanted someone to know. In fact, I'm so fucking happy that she knows.

But also, please don't tell anyone. Please, please, please don't tell anyone.

I pull my phone and bring up Taylor. And then I type: "I have a secret."

I hit send. And I leave it at that.

The suspense will fucking kill her, but I need to do this. They need to know.

WE EAT at the outer reaches of the campus. During lunch, we can pretty much do whatever we want, as long as we're not hiding out in a classroom or in the hallways. And even then, the teachers turn the other cheek. Or their eye. Or something like that.

Taylor is the last to meet us at the table because her class is at the other end of the campus. The art wing, with the ceramics and studio art classes. Taylor's not exactly a creative person. Not in a traditional sense. What she does is more like an open interpretation of art. If she knew what expressionist art was, she'd say that's what she did so we'd take her seriously.

As usual, her hands are bright pink from the soap and hot water that she uses to take an extra layer of skin off every time she has art class. She holds up her hands, which look like fleshy pink gloves, and says, "We were working with oil paints again."

She forks out a few bucks, slaps them onto the table, and starts to pick food off of Charlotte's tray. It's chicken tenders with pureed mashed potatoes and brown gravy with skin thicker than a drag queen in a small town in Alabama.

Taylor takes a tender and tears off a small hunk of it. Stringy white flesh hangs from the corner of her mouth when her blue eyes meet mine. Of the entire group, she's the only one of us that's had a boyfriend, let alone a relationship, period. She's incredibly religious on the outside, but deep down, she's bragged about how many times she's gotten drunk and showed us selfies of her right after she had an orgasm.

What I'm trying to say is bitch is nasty, and I'm here for it.

Charlotte notices that something is going on between me and Taylor, but she's not quite sure what. Her eyes dart between us. But honestly, there's not much else to look at.

Behind me is a solid brick wall. To my left is a metal gate, then more brick wall, then a wide open metal gate painted green. That's one of the school colors. If you were to believe the sun-faded signs on the walls, it would look like green, white, and purple. The purple used to be black once upon a time. On spirit days, some of the kids still wear purple as a way to mock the stupidity of not replacing these signs.

"What's going on here?" Charlotte asks.

Taylor pulls out her phone, strings of dry chicken slowly being sucked into her mouth with repetitive chews. She pulls up her phone and flips her fingers around the screen from one side to the next so fast she must be going on muscle memory. I don't believe she even sees what she's actually doing.

Then, she shows her phone to Charlotte.

Taylor looks at me, a quiet smile on her mouth. Her lips shine from the grease.

Charlotte mumbles, "A secret. What the hell does that mean?"

Taylor slides over next to me. Her knee touches mine, and her hand grips my thigh. Then she leans in. "Alright, Michael. What's your secret?"

My heart beats, thumps, thunders under my chest. In the deepest memories of my head, Christina sings that I'm beautiful in every single way. I get that familiar warmth that I felt a few hours ago in first period.

Taylor taps my knee with her finger. "So?"

"So what?"

"What's your secret?"

I gulp. There's nothing to wash down the fear with. My own food is a sandwich and a dry granola bar that I found buried in my backpack. Mom dropped them in there. More of her crossing boundaries.

"Please tell us," Charlotte says.

"Remember the cupcakes?" I ask.

"You baked those after all?" Charlotte slaps Taylor's hand. "I knew it. See? I told you he baked them."

"No," I say. "I mean. Yes, I did. But that's not the secret."

"Then what is?"

I put my head down on the table. I sigh so deeply that I end up breathing in some sour smells of dried ketchup, and I don't even know what. I don't want to know what.

"Homosexuality," I say. I raise my head up. "I'm gay, okay? I'm actually gay."

Taylor laughs immediately. "No, you're not."

"But I am. How are you going to say that I'm not gay?"

Charlotte tries to hold back laughter. "Because, look at you. You don't look gay. You don't sound gay. You don't do this," and she flops her hands around with the limp wrist stereotype.

"Don't do that," I say. "That's kind of fucked up."

Taylor says, "What do you care? You're not gay."

"Oh, for fuck's sake." I stand up from the table, my palms against the surface. "I like dick."

"See?" Taylor says. "What you need is the right girl."

My knees can't take it, and I collapse back onto the bench. "This is impossible."

"It's not funny," Charlotte says. "It's tragic. I mean, the cupcakes and the video and this secret confession. You're trying a little too hard to be relevant or popular or something." Her eyes widen and she looks under the table, beside the table, between my legs. "Are you hiding a camera? Are you filming this? You're not going to go viral for pretending to be gay."

I just shake my head, rolling my forehead along the tabletop. "Why would I do that?" My words are muffled through the wood.

"I don't know. Because you think it's funny."

Taylor chuckles. "Because you're a middle school boy."

"Besides, it's not like you've had sex," Charlotte says. "You're not gay because you can't compare. You don't know what you do like or don't like."

"You're insane. The both of you. You're insane."

"You don't wear nail polish. You don't do your eyebrows. You don't do anything effeminate."

"You're basing this off what you've seen on TV?" I ask.

Taylor comes to my defense. Or at least tries to. "Okay, so Michael's right. You can't just base what you think you know about people from TV."

"It is reality TV," Charlotte says.

Taylor taps my shoulder. "So there's that."

"This is ridiculous."

Charlotte sits on the other side of me, and she puts her hands on both sides of my face. She lifts my head up from the table, staring at me in the eyes. Brown eyes against white skin, she says to me, "I can prove it. I'll introduce you to the right girl. Or girls."

"You think you're the right girl?"

Charlotte lets go of my head. "Don't tell me what I said or didn't say. I didn't say that."

Taylor repeats, "Yeah, she didn't say that."

"But she meant it."

"I did not. Mean it, I mean."

Charlotte sees from my face that I don't believe her. Not that it matters. I can already see what she's thinking. Her eyes shift around me, glancing at everyone. Measuring them out. Assessing.

This bitch, she's already looking around for girls to introduce me to.

I'm saved by the literal bell.

There's nothing to be done here except to just let go and realize that Charlotte is going to do what Charlotte wants to do.

Taylor, on the other hand, kisses me on the cheek and says, "I'll talk to you after school, okay?" She sounds sad, somehow, like the tone of her voice is apologizing for something she didn't even say.

AT THE END of the day, I'm outside waiting for the girls to arrive. Taylor comes out first, but she's busy talking to an Asian kid I don't recognize off the bat. And then he turns to face me.

It's Ethan. I've seen him around. He's a senior who came onto the Mr. Maple Ridge fundraiser stage wearing a

Speedo. The girls—and some boys—all wooed and catcalled.

Ethan loved it. He also won because, well, sex sells. Even if the sex wasn't real actual sex. It was skin. Lots and lots of skin.

Taylor stands there long enough for Ethan to lean in and kiss her on the cheek. And then Taylor sees me and waves for me to come over.

I approach, holding my hand out to Ethan. "Hi."

Ethan laughs. "How old are you?"

I put my hand down. Message received.

He points at me, though. "You're that Mikey guy. The one that everyone says is trying too hard to be gay."

"Trying too hard?" I say. "How do you try too hard?"

"That's just what people are saying," he says. Then he waves to Taylor. "I'll text you later."

Taylor blushes. Actually blushes. And then he walks away.

"That's cute," I say.

"Him?" Taylor says. "You really are trying too hard."

"No, I mean that you're blushing." I lean in. "You like him."

She blushes further. "I do not like him."

"You don't don't like him."

She glares at me. "You need to stay out of other peoples' business."

"Sure," I say. "Okay."

A line of cars appears at the drop off and pick up location. My mom's in there somewhere. I don't even see her at first, she's so far behind.

Taylor says, "I need to get to work, but if you want to talk later, let me know."

"I'll be fine. I have a lot of homework."

Taylor nods, waves, and walks off. "See you tomorrow. And if you end up making more cupcakes, I won't say no."

Mom's car inches closer. She's maybe five cars down the line. The sun casts short shadows along the ground.

And then Charlotte shouts out my name, waving her hand in the air to flag me down. "Mikey! Mikey!"

Mom gets closer and closer.

Charlotte runs up to me and says, "I got something for you."

What she has is a piece of paper. It's white except for the faint shadows of black marker all along the inside of it. Even from a few feet away, I can tell that the paper is covered with random, sporadic writing.

She's out of breath by the time she reaches me. One hand rests on my shoulder, and the other holds the paper in front of my face.

"Here," she says. "Take it."

I do.

Charlotte looks like she won first prize in a cross-country meet. "I did it."

"You did what?"

"I got you names." She taps the flimsy edges of the paper. "And numbers."

All girls.

"I don't want names and numbers."

Charlotte stares at me. "If you want to find out if you're really gay, then this is your chance."

I want to rub the paper in her face, hoping that the pen somehow smears against her forehead and her cheeks. I want area code 425—whatever, whatever — to be tattooed on her skin as a reminder of just how obnoxious she is. This is her hope. Not mine.

Taylor's car honks like a pathetic baby duck. "Come! On!" she screams.

Charlotte ignores her, but something comes flying out of Taylor's passenger side window. It clinks against the cement sidewalk.

"Did that bitch just throw a fucking fork at me?" Charlotte shrieks. She presses a hand against her chest in that self-righteous kind of way.

"My question is why she has a fork in her car," I say.

Charlotte holds a hand up to my face, and it's my sign to shut the fuck up.

So, I shut the fuck up.

Then Charlotte's face softens, and she jams the paper in her backpack. Then she takes my head into her hands and kisses my cheek. "Alright. We'll talk with new numbers soon. I have just the person in mind."

And then she's gone.

I sit on a concrete bench, which is really just a block of cold gray leftover sidewalk that has somehow been shaped into a block beside the grass.

I still can't see Mom.

She's probably busy trying to sell the last of her spare time to buyers who want her expert knowledge on gluten-free cooking. No one in my family is gluten-free, by the way. Mom found a cookbook and a person who can set up a website, and now she does webinars all the time. She loves the word webinar as much as dogs like hearing their own name.

The cupcake carrier lays nestled between my feet.

People stare at you if you have food. It's like stray pets, only worse. Humans, at least, should know better. Most of the time, we don't. But we should have a sense. As I sit, I have to find something to do with my hands, so I play with the rainbow wristband on my left hand. Flip it inside and out, turning it from one side to the other. Spin it around like it's a hula-hoop along my bird-thin wrists.

Then, Asshole Number One comes up and sits next to me. He's not just any regular asshole. He's a special asshole. Maybe the most popular asshole, and not for any reason you'd expect.

It's Mathias. His shirt is so tight I can see whether his belly button is an inny or outie. He shifts his blond hair to the side, green eyes peeking out from under the stray bangs, and he extends one side of his mouth into a smile and a dimple. His lips seem pink and glossy, but maybe that's just the sunlight.

"Here," he says. His accent isn't as thick as his parents. Some rich Dutch family that migrated here because taxes were too high in the Netherlands. At least that's what Mathias's twin sister loudly announces to whatever audience will pay attention to her.

Mathias's hand is full of cash. I see fives and tens folded up, but there are too many corners for me to count just how much he's holding.

"What's that for?" I ask.

Mathias looks down at his hand. "I thought you were selling brownies?"

I laugh. "You want brownies? These aren't, like, special brownies."

"If you made them, then I think they are special. So what are you selling?" He shifts his weight over toward me.

"I wasn't selling anything. I was giving them away."

Mathias hands over the cash, pressing it against my chest. His hand lingers a little too long as if he's somehow feeling me up. "If you want to take the money, I'm okay with it." He looks down between my legs, then at my knees. "Those the brownies?"

"Cupcakes," I say. I lift the container and raise the lid. "But it's empty. Everything's gone."

"That's a shame." When he sees that I won't take the

money, he pockets it but keeps eye contact with me the entire time.

Not that I minded.

He sees that I'm playing with the rainbow bracelet and nods knowingly. "Ah. You were the boy handing out the rainbow cupcake."

I shake the container. "Was being the operative word."

"You talk smart," he says. "I like smart. Not enough smart people here." He looks around, pointing at some of them and muttering, "Dummy, dummy, idiot" under his breath.

"We're not all stupid," I say.

"We?"

"Americans."

He nods and smiles. "I've been here long enough to know that, yes, not all of you are stupid." He smiles at me, showing more of his teeth. Pearls so white that I refuse to show my own.

His green eyes sparkle as he squints, trying to block out the sun. When he sees me looking back, he doesn't move. Instead, he watches me study his face. Mathias' shirt is unbuttoned up to the middle of his chest. As far as the staff is concerned, it's a European thing, but I have my suspicions. His burgundy slacks sit low on his hips, giving me a glimpse at the name brand of his underwear. He smiles at me, and his smile is everything.

It's my stars, my sun, my moon.

He sees me studying everything about him, and he says, "You like?"

I cough into my hand. "What?"

"The rainbow cupcakes were a statement, right?" He leans in closer and smells like peaches and blueberries. "I've seen the YouTube videos, too. They're cute but unrealistic."

I shove the cupcake carrier between my feet, covering it with my backpack to hide it.

Mathias presses his hand against his chest and laughs, chin upwards, throwing his head back. It's all so fabulous and showy. But it feels real. Or real enough.

"It's funny you say that," I say.

Mathias watches my shoulders go up. "Honey, it's fine. No one will hear you." He presses down on my thigh. His fingers are gentle and warm. He smiles through half his mouth. "You're tense. You need to calm down." He scoots a little bit further away from me but crosses his legs at the ankle. "So, you didn't answer my question."

Which one?

"I'm waiting for my mom."

"You don't drive?"

"I have a drive," I say.

He laughs.

"I mean, I don't have a car, but I can drive." I wait, looking up as I imagine the right word order. *Yep, that sounds right.*

Mathias parts his pink glossy lips and says, "That was perfect."

The words spin around in my head, side-to-side, until he says, "You're not really interested in girls, are you?"

He's impossibly close to me. Our toes touch, and his left hand touches my elbow. My mouth goes numb, and words just don't exist in my head right now.

"Or at least that's what I heard," he says.

"They're cool." I nod, biting my lip. I try to lower my shoulders and play it cool. It's not working. My stomach gets tense, my chest tightens. Everywhere that he touches, tingles.

"They're not cool," Mathias says. "Not at all. Sometimes they can be hot, though." He produces a makeup compact from his pocket and glances at himself in the mirror, falling in love with his hair and his eyes. "My sister gets a lot of glances. Lots of people think she's hot. Good thing we're twins, right?"

"Twins?"

"We look alike. Mostly. I have the better genes."

I nod, swallowing. "Yeah."

Mathias takes my shoulders into his hands, looking at me and holding me like he's a father about to instill some deep, harsh truths about The Real World. "Is it true?"

"Yes." I don't know what I said or what was true, but I wanted him to hear whatever he was looking for. A dimple teases me on his left cheek.

"I thought so," Mathias says. He takes his hands away. My body feels colder with him so far away. He pauses. "You are out?"

It's not until my lips are on his that I realize it was a question and not a command. He grunts in surprise but laughs while his lower lip is in my mouth. Then he pulls away and says, "Whoa there, cowboy."

"Sorry," I say. I wipe his saliva off my mouth. "I should go."

"No," Mathias says. "I liked it."

"I have to go."

"You have some glitter and makeup here," he says. He points at various parts of his face. I can't keep track of it all because I'm seeing the sparkle of his eyes, the dimple, the sharpness of his jawline. I take a step back, and he grabs my shoulder. "But I think you answered my question."

"Can I ask you a question?" I start trying to scrape away some of the golden glitter and makeup.

"Shoot."

"Why do you do this?" I wave my hand over my face, open my hand, then close it as it reaches my chin.

"In American sign language, that means perfect or beautiful," he says.

I blush.

"But if you're asking about the makeup and other accoutrement. It's simple: I like to look pretty, and I'm comfortable looking pretty." He turns his head away, looking up to the sky with his hand flared out under his chin. "You like?"

"I do, but it's just so—so different."

"I am different."

"Yes, you are." The words come out of my mouth like a whisper. I try to get up, but he grabs my hand. "I have to go," I say.

"No one saw a thing," Mathias says. "As good-looking as I am, even I can't command attention all the time." His magnetic smile pulls me closer. We're next to each other but not touching.

I feel like I want to cry, staring at the cupcake carrier between my feet.

"If you're out, then why do you feel like you need to run?" Matthias asks.

"I want to be out, but no one believes me."

He pats the small bit of bare chest exposed by his unbuttoned shirt. "Really? It's plain as day to me."

I laugh, but there's a hidden worry. "Really?"

"It's not a bad thing," he says. He pulls at the tail of my shirt. "Not every straight guy wears shirts this tight. This is almost asking someone to offer you poppers and take you to a club in the early 2000s."

I nod.

"You don't know what poppers are."

I shake my head.

"Aw, a baby gay." He clasps his hands together, holding

them near his head. His eyes sparkle even more. Think wannabe mothers at a baby shower.

I don't have to use my imagination to know what that means.

"If you're going to be mean, I'm leaving," I say and start to get up. He grabs my hand this time, his fingers wrapping around mine. I have to ignore just how soft his fingers are. How smooth his skin is as it rubs against mine.

"Don't," he says. He stifles his laughter, but just barely. "Please don't go. I've just never seen one in the wild before."

"When you came out, did anyone believe you?"

"My mom was waiting for me with a rainbow cake," he says. "My sister was convinced I wasn't effeminate enough to be gay. My dad denied it, and I didn't have friends, so that point is moot."

"My friends refuse to believe it, and my mom and dad don't know."

"Have you told them?"

"My friends? Yes."

He looks at me and blinks twice.

"My parents?" I roll my eyes. "No, I haven't. But it's not like I didn't try."

"So you said, 'Momma, Poppa, I prefer the company of men.' Just like that?"

"No one says that."

He pulls back. "Well, I'm not no one."

I laugh. He laughs. And then we're both laughing until he stops and opens his emerald eyes, wide and big like real crown jewels. "If you're going to be convincing, you have to convince yourself."

My phone dings and I take a peek, though I feel rude. And annoyed. Because it means I have to stop looking at this beautiful, beautiful boy in front of me.

"If it's your mother, you can go," he says with a smile.

"It's my friend, Charlotte."

"Does she believe you?" He gently lays his wrists on his knees and lets his hands just hang off the edge. His nail color takes on the sun's sparkle.

"No, she doesn't." I pause. "What do you mean she?"

"Honey," he says. "You're gay. If you're gay, you have a girl best friend. I don't write the rules. I just enforce them."

I look around. "Where's your girl best friend?"

"Andrea killed her years ago." The motherfucker doesn't blink. He doesn't even smile.

"You're kidding?"

He laughs. "Of course, I'm kidding. Killing is my dad's business. Not ours." He puts his arm around me. I tense up.

"Andrea, is your sister?" I ask, standing up.

He joins me and nods. "Why?"

We walk closer to the pick up circle behind the school. The line of cars has started to thin out, but there's no sign of a white Hyundai Sonata anywhere.

"What's your last name?" I ask.

"There's only two Andreas in the whole school," Mathias says. "If she's brought up in conversation, it'll be my sister."

"I think Charlotte is trying to set me up with her," I say.

"That's a poor shame. That girl will fuck you, eat you up alive, then spit you out. The worst part is you'll be coming back for more."

"I'm not even straight."

"Then why is your friend trying to set you up with my sister?"

We stare at each other for a moment, cars driving by. Even the herd of students has thinned out. It's me and

Mathias and the kids who are practicing for their math clubs and their spring band performances.

"I dunno." I take a peek at my phone again. Charlotte has texted me a name and a phone number.

Mathias peeks over the edge of the phone and he laughs. "That's her number. She is trying to set you up." He releases his arm from my shoulder. "You're considering it?"

I shrug. "I dunno. I'm wondering if maybe all of these people are right. Maybe I'm wrong. It's just me, after all."

"No one knows you better than you. But if you want to make everyone else happy, go ahead."

"It's sort of what I do," I say.

Mathias sticks out his lower lip. "I'm so sad for you." He looks from side to side, taking a peek around every little corner of us. "If you're going to do this, and let's be clear, I don't condone dating my sister—but if you do, then take this gift and pack it into the back of your mind."

"What gift?" I say.

He leads me to the end of the wall, before the open walkway between the 2400 wing and the 2500 wing of the school. It's barren except for a long walkway with doors that lead to both wings. But by now, even teachers have fled the campus.

Mathias looks at me.

Then I grab both sides of his head and pull him to me. We kiss again. His body actually softens up, but his breathing is so loud and hard I can feel the warmth against my cheek.

I moan, then pull away. "I'm sorry."

"Don't be." He wipes some of the glitter off my face and says, "I'll see you around?"

"I'm not straight," I tell him.

"Anyone who kisses me like that can't be straight. And it'd be a crime if he were."

I can't not smile as I pull away and slip through a door into the 2400 wing. I wander into the bathroom for a few minutes, staring into the mirror just above the sink. I'm squeezing the ceramic like I wish it was Mathias's bicep.

Then I turn on the taps, gathering water in my palms and splashing it against my face. My chin drips water onto the edge of the sink, and the splatters wet my shirt.

And yet, I smile. Water drips from my face and my cheeks are red like I just ran a marathon. But I'm also smiling like I won the marathon. My heart races but I'm cucumber cool. As chill as a Britney Spears ballad.

My phone vibrates and vibrates and vibrates.

"What, goddammit? What?"

When I check, it's Charlotte. She sent me three instances of "You get that?", then four repeats of "WDYT?"

I send back, "I think this is a lot to ask."

When I leave the bathroom, there's a blond woman standing in front of me. She's in a skirt that only comes halfway down her thighs. She's Norwegian originally, so her blond hair and dark red lips create an intensity that you just don't see here in America. She wears makeup at school like it's a photoshoot. I remember in middle school when girls would wear makeup so thick it looked like they were applying to clown college. And there are hints of that, but it's just done…better.

It's stage makeup.

Where all the world is a stage, and she's the only actor in it.

The rest of us? We're the audience taking her in. We should be so fucking lucky to be her. We should count our blessings and thank God herself that we got to witness the being that is Andrea Bergmann.

She's gorgeous, but not for me.

Her brother, on the other hand, I start to wonder where he is.

"You're here," she says. "Good. Mathias said you were leaving."

"I was, um," I check my phone to pretend it's my escape route. "I mean, I am."

"But you're not going to now," she says. "Now that you've met me."

She extends her arm. Her hand goes limp. I take it and shake it, but the grimace on her face indicates this is the wrong protocol. Was I supposed to kiss it? Curtsey? Where's the handbook for situations like this?

"You're a strange one," she says.

"You talk like your brother."

She laughs sort of like an evil villain, throwing her head back so I can see her hair flutter behind her. "You mean he talks like *me*. Besides, I'm the one with better genes," she says with a smile.

I raise a finger to tell her that her brother already said that, but she lowers my finger and says, "I need your number if we're going to go out." She looks at me, up and down, then down and up. "I hear you haven't been dating long."

"What else did Charlotte tell you?"

"That you desperately need my help."

"For what?"

She shrugs. She glances off to the side, down the hall-way. Then she turns back to me like she has all the time in the world. "I was hoping you could tell me."

"I don't know what she told you and why she told you any of that, but it's all a lie," I say.

"It wasn't a lie. I can see it on your face." She grabs my chin and turns my head from side to side, checking me like I'm up for Best in Show. She even starts to put a finger between my mouth to show my teeth.

When I pull away, she's offended, like *I* did something wrong.

"What was that for?" she says.

"I'm not a fucking pony. Don't check my teeth like that."

"You'll do," she says. Andrea hands me her backpack, which is this little pink pack that has to be half the size of her total back. It looks Japanese, with buttons all over it.

"This isn't even heavy."

Andrea starts walking, looking over my shoulder to see that I'm keeping up. "You have a lot to learn if you're going to make this work."

"Me?"

She says nothing, just motions slowly with her "come hither" fingers. Her walk is slow yet sexy. She's a music video vixen hoping that all the cameras are watching her all the time. "Come. Follow me." She takes a few more steps and stops. "And call your mother."

"Why?"

"Because I'm taking you home."

"Shouldn't the guy do the driving in the relationship?" I say it jokingly, but she's not looking at me.

"So you already think this is a relationship?" She laughs. "Good, good. Then you'll need to earn your keep." She snaps her fingers. "I want to get home before my brother gets home."

"Mathias," I say. Perhaps with a little bit more enthusiasm than I should have.

She smiles, tosses her hair. Walks outside towards her car, which is a pink Audi. I didn't even know they made pink cars. Everything lights up when she taps her finger to the car door. "It's not the best car, but it suits my needs."

We get in. Even the seats have ass warmers. Thin lights trace the surface of every part of the car. They glow orange at first, then shift to blue as she starts the engine.

"Buckle up," she says, "I'm not a very good driver."

I check my phone and text Charlotte: "Thx."

Then I text my mom. Tell her I'm getting a ride from a friend.

Charlotte sends back a smiley emoji and the world just doesn't get it.

It doesn't get me.

My only hope at this point is seeing Mathias, the boy who I actually want to know. But if I want to prove to Taylor and Charlotte that I'm gay, then I have to see this through to its terrible end.

After all, it's the only way to find out if I'm gay or not not gay.

Pass Me Da Mic

BREA BOLTON

Pass Me Da Mic

BREA BOLTON

Tonight was it.

The most coveted rap battle night of the month.

Kids everywhere had dropped what they were doing to be at the club and witness the next possible Jay-Z or Eminem. And headlining the whole event was reigning champ and local superstar Theo McClain, a self-proclaimed rap genius and 100% violent con artist. I shivered at the thought of being in the same building as him, let alone having to share a class with him at school.

I maneuvered through bodies, packed together, before spotting Dre at a table in the middle of the room. He stood with another group. I didn't know who they were, but I could see Dre. He wore the same clothes as the others: polo, baggy jeans, and a fresh pair of shoes.

I frowned, marching over to him and tapping him on the shoulder.

He turned quickly, then widened his eyes as though shocked to see me. He leaned down, whispering. "Mo, what are you doing here?"

"Coming to get your ass. Daddy would kill us if he knew you were here."

Dre shook his head, "I can't go home, Mo."

He motioned over to the crowd. I looked up to see who he was pointing at and saw the one person I dreaded. Theo, talking to a group of guys. He wore a fitted cap and a gold chain with a big golden Jesus hanging from it. But he hadn't noticed me yet.

"I already told these guys I would hang," Dre said. "They're gonna get me signed."

"Signed for what?" I asked. "Juvie?"

"Mo has connections in the music business. My rapping's gonna take us out of here."

I shook my head. "Nope. Your grades are going to take you out of here. Time to go home." I tried to pull him away, but he resisted.

"Look, give me 30 minutes, okay? Then we can go home. Dad never needs to know."

Even though I was only two years older than him, at times, he felt more like my son than my little brother.

"No."

"Please, Mo. Just 30 minutes."

I caved, sighing and dropping my shoulders. "Okay, but don't let nobody know I'm here. I'll sit at the bar and wait for you—30 minutes, no more."

Dre lit up, smiling, before I left him.

When I arrived at the bar I took the first available stool. It gave me a clear view of Theo and his gang with Dre. I was keeping my eyes glued to him. Because there was no way I was letting my little brother get wrapped up in the wrong side of life.

I had my back to the bar, but the bartender still made his way over.

"What you drinking tonight, little lady?" He asked, his graying beard getting in the way of his words.

I turned around. "Water. With ice,"

He smiled at me. "Sober night," he joked.

"Sober every night. I'm only 18," I said.

He set the cup down in front of me so that I could see the cup was clean. Then poured in the water.

That was something you had to worry about in this club. If somebody was going to slip something in your drink, it would be here. When he finished, he walked away, and I took the water and sipped it.

"You better be careful talking like that; you might get thrown out of here." A voice said next to me.

I turned slowly, praying it was somebody I didn't know. It was a woman I'd never seen before. She had straight-back braids, no makeup, and was dressed just like one of the guys. Underneath her left eye was an old scar, long healed.

"I know what I'm doing," I said, turning away from her. She looked like the kind of trouble I didn't want to get into.

"All right then, my bad," she said, holding up her hands. Despite her outward appearance, her voice was syrupy and sweet. "I'm Sienna, by the way." She moved her hand over to shake mine. I looked at it for a quick second. The rings on her finger glistened, and her short nails were perfectly manicured.

I took the hand slowly and shook it. "Mo."

"Mo," she said. "Shit, I think I've heard about you."

I shrugged, "Couldn't have heard too much because I haven't seen you here before."

She shook her head, "No, I'm new. But my cousin is Terrence, and his friends know you."

I rolled my eyes at the mention of Terrence. I knew he was probably here somewhere, surrounded by a bunch of girls, getting their numbers and throwing down his immaculate game. We didn't cross paths too much. I was standoffish, and he didn't want the challenge of trying to talk to me. Typical guy.

"Yeah, I know Terrence, but he knows nothing about me." I said, "And neither do you."

She held up her hands in defense once again. "Hey, I don't want no trouble. I'm just saying I've heard of you before. They didn't tell me how pretty you were, though."

I rolled my eyes at her, looking back over to where Dre was. I was done letting Sienna distract me.

But just as my eyes hit the crowd, they met the one person I was hoping against hope I wouldn't see.

Royalty.

ROYALTY'S brown eyes locked with mine. It was a deadly game, a tug-of-war. And then a devious smile spread across her face. I wanted to jump out of my skin and run, but I forced myself to stay while she approached, a girl flanking her on each side.

All three were dressed scantily; they were arm candy at best.

"Well, well, well. Monique Day shows her face in public," Royalty said in a sing-songy voice.

I rolled my eyes. "I ain't scared to be out here."

"You should be," Royalty said. "What are you going to do if Theo catches you? Do you think he's just going to let you walk away without tearing you to shreds?"

The girls to each of her sides laughed.

"There ain't nothing Theo can do to me," I said. "Our past is done."

Royalty shook her head. "Then why are you here, a freestyle night of all nights? It's not like you're drinking."

"I'm here for Dre," I said.

"Dre doesn't need a babysitter," she said.

"He does. He's only 16, and he's not about this life." I could feel Sienna's eyes watching me.

"Well, it should be an interesting night," Royalty said. "Will we see you up there?"

"Absolutely not," I answered.

Royalty laughed. "Of course we won't. You don't have the chops to join in. When was the last time you rapped something? Eighth grade?"

The girls laughed again.

I rolled my eyes. "I've been studying, getting my grades straight for a good college. You know there's life outside of rapping, right?"

"That life you want to run away from, right?" Royalty said. "Or is it gonna lay you down just like Theo used to?"

I wanted to say something rude and unforgivable, but I just got up and walked to the bathroom, pulling up my hood.

"Hey, wait," Sienna's voice followed.

I turned around as soon as I got in the door. She came in, closing it behind us. "Hey, they didn't hurt your feelings, did they?"

I shook my head. "No, I just don't like to get into fights publicly. It was going too far." I walked over to the sink and washed my hands.

"Well, you must be some kind of great rapper the way you have beef already," Sienna laughed.

"I don't rap," I said. "Not like they do."

Sienna raised an eyebrow. "So what, you like a smooth jazz spoken word kind of girl?"

"No, I just dabble."

"Well, you should definitely get on stage then, show these suckers what it's really about. They must be terrified of you if they're trying to get you to stay off," Sienna said.

"I didn't come here for all that," I said. "I just came here to find my brother. And I don't even know you like that. Why are you worried about it?"

"I'm not. I'm just saying this place seriously lacks some talent, and if you have some, you should show it off. Don't let whoever that is, Theo," she said, "take home the crown just because you don't want to get down."

She laughed at her own rhyming words.

I rolled my eyes. "I'm not letting Theo take anything home. I'm not in this," I said, drying my hands. I walked around her to exit the bathroom. But before I opened the door, I heard the announcer call all freestylers to the stage. A hush fell over the crowd while people made their way up. I didn't want to be out there right when they were announced. I waited a moment, then snuck out. Sienna was right behind me, slightly shielding me from the crowd. I was thankful, but she didn't have to do that. This wasn't her situation.

I returned to the bar, happy to see Royalty and her goonies had walked away. With any luck, they'd stay gone. I sat back down as the three people on the stage — Theo and two other boys —traded the mic off and decided who would go first.

The two unknowns went against each other first; their raps were fire, but it wasn't competitive like it should have been. The boy with the mohawk was knocked out, and Theo was the next to take his place.

He walked up there, calm as ever, taking the mic. "Hey, yo, let me show you how a real player does it."

The crowd was hyped, clapping and yelling. He was holding up his pants to keep them from falling down. They flipped a coin, deciding who would go first. The other boy won, and his verse was the same as the first time. I could tell he had rehearsed it, and so could the crowd. They responded with weak applause when he finished.

Then he gave the mic to Theo. There was something about Theo in this music, even though he was the most despicable kind of human. His lyrics were legit when he started to rap. He spit a verse so strong that the crowd went wild, and I was even a little put off by the reception that he got.

A man — the bartender I had spoken to earlier — walked on stage and held up Theo's arm in victory. "Looks like we have a clear winner here tonight, folks. Drinks on the house for Theo."

I looked over to where Dre was and saw him cheering, too.

Theo took the mic back from the bartender. "Hey yo, hang on. I got one more person I want to battle," he said, looking out with his hand over his eyes to block the spotlight. I knew it would be over as soon as his eyes met mine. If I wanted to run back earlier, now I wanted to evaporate.

"Hey, Yo, Mo, make your way to the stage. I can't be the winner if I don't roast your ass," Theo said. A second later, the spotlight shone down on me. The crowd turned to see me sitting at the bar, my hood down. And they were silent.

"Oh shit, Mo's here?" I heard whispers from the crowd, and cold shivers made their way over my skin.

"No, I'm not here for that," I said.

"Hey, don't be a coward," Theo said. "I'm calling you

out. Are you going to choke in front of all these people? Again?"

The crowd laughed.

"Again?" Sienna asked.

My heart beat out of my chest, and my palms were sweaty. Before I knew what was happening, I got off the bar stool and walked to the stage.

THE BRIGHT LIGHTS on the stage were hot against my skin, and I immediately started sweating. I looked out over the sea of faces, spotting Dre in the crowd. He looked both worried and excited. And then I saw Sienna walk over and stand next to him. For some reason, she didn't feel like a stranger anymore. She felt familiar, and I anchored myself to her when she smiled and nodded, telling me everything would be alright without actually saying it.

The bartender walked over with the microphone and held up the coin with his free hand. "Who is going first, heads or tails?"

Theo looked at me and sneered. "Heads."

The bartender flipped the coin, and it fell, hitting the wooden stage hard. I didn't look. By the crowd's reaction, I knew it landed on heads.

"Alright, Theo's up first," the bartender said. "Let's go ahead and get this started."

He smiled and motioned for the DJ to start up a beat. The music started slow, but then the crowd got into it. I shut out the noise and let the beat vibrate in my chest.

Theo stepped back from me, raising his mic, and then: "Ayo, she thinks she's all that/ better than us/she's a queen caught in the slums/ college apps got you buggin'/ hating on me cause I'm thuggin'/ but you can't get on my level even if you wanted/ The streets are my kingdom/I'm a lion amongst hyenas." Theo rapped.

I stayed focused on the crowd, watching them cheer for each dagger line.

"Fresh waves getting paid/ bank account full like Benzino/ your raps on welfare/ dirt poor no childcare/ trash man daddy should spin the block and take you there." The beat went off, and he finished, smirking

The crowd went crazy for him, letting out deafening cheers.

"Alright, Mo, do your worst," he said, passing me the mic.

The bartender looked back at the DJ again and nodded. I stood there frozen. I had so much I wanted to say, and, at the same time, I couldn't say anything. I opened my mouth, and no words came out. I looked at the crowd and immediately thought, this will be so embarrassing if I choke.

I have to say something.

I looked at Theo. He seemed so pleased with himself, just like he always did. He was taunting me; he wanted to tear me down again, and I couldn't let him. So, I did what I do best: I started rhyming:

"It's funny you should mention the dump/ since the only way your getting bread is picking up cans/you're just a lightweight thug with gumption/ got no drive/ the only way you're moving is aside/ and damn straight I'm a queen in the slums/ its better than being a peasant looking after you chumps/."

The words flowed slowly at first, but then I picked up momentum: "You ain't never caught beef unless you're on the grill/I'm out here hustling my shit is for real/ whole time I'm quiet holding in how I feel/ whole time you watching just pass me the deal/ Yall still think I'm playing though/ heart ice cold like I'm made of snow/ I don't see nobody who can say I'm broke/ cracked up but not counted out/I'm just laying low/."

I couldn't hear the crowd anymore. The words echoed in my head, blocking out all other sound. But I could see them out of the corner of my eye, jumping for each hit I delivered. None were aimed at Theo, but I tried my best to stay on topic. I wasn't a rap artist; I was just someone with something to say.

"And maybe I'm real again like Pinocchio/ I can feel again, let the record show/ I was buried alive, but I survived, and now I'm back like Messiah/can't step on my pride/I'm ready to fly/Delta can't take me higher/ You thought you could kill me, but that was a decoy/It's time to get ready for jets/It's time to deploy/ dropping the bombs/Yeah, I'm nuking the beat, boy/ rhymes in my head and wings on my feet, boy."

When the beat cut off, I kept going. I was on a roll, and like I said before, it's hard to stop once I start.

"Whatever, you can't catch me/ just watch your mouth when you see me because I could get nasty/ you had your chance to see me, but you blew it /9th grade's got to be feeling stupid /And for the record, it was you who called me out. I was chilling/ I hate that I stepped out and became the new villain."

And then I finally lowered the mic.

The sweat glistened on my forehead. I could feel it vibrating on my arms, the backs of my hands, my palms, every inch of my skin.

And then an enormous eruption of applause and cheers.

Everyone jumped up and down, even Dre. He was barely contained, smiling so wide at me, throwing his hands up in celebration.

"Alright, well, we have a clear winner here. Theo dethroned himself," the bartender laughed, grabbing the mic and my wrist and holding my hand up like I was a boxer who had just won a prize fight. Theo narrowed his eyes, leaving the stage quickly.

I couldn't help but feel this was the start of the trouble I had avoided for so long. "You know the reward, alcohol on tap tonight for Miss Mo."

The bartender smiled and let my wrist go.

I turned and ran off stage in the opposite direction of Theo. I needed to get some air. I walked straight out of the club and out into the night.

"YO, MO, THAT WAS CRAZY," Dre said, running out of the club behind me. He threw his arms around my shoulders. "I can't believe you got up there and did that," he said, shaking me.

It still hadn't fully registered, what had happened. And the air was now only beginning to return to my lungs. "Yeah, that was wild."

"Man, my sister's a queen right now," Dre said, doing a stupid little dance. Everyone on the sidewalk looked at us and kinda laughed.

A moment later, Sienna walked out after us. "Hey, that was dope." She held up her hand to give me a fist bump. I did, and she blew it up, but I didn't bother.

"Thanks," I said.

"You gotta teach me some of your techniques some-time," she said, smiling. "Maybe over a milkshake or something."

I cocked an eyebrow. "Are you asking me on a date?"

Dre stopped his dance and fell back, watching the

interaction between us. Suddenly, I felt a little embarrassed.

"I mean, if you wanna call it that," Sienna said. "Or we can just call it hanging out if you want. That's cool, too."

I fished out my phone and handed it to her. "I don't mind if we call it a date."

I watched her enter her number, then took my phone back and put it in my pocket. People started to file out of the club and go their separate ways. I looked over at Dre.

"We should definitely get back to the house. If daddy comes home, and we ain't there, it's gonna be both our asses."

Dre frowned, "We haven't even been gone an hour yet."

"This is all you get," I said, pointing to where the car stood at the curb. "And you're lucky I don't whoop your ass right here in front of everybody and God. Now go get in the car."

Dre frowned and grumbled something under his breath I couldn't quite make out. Before heading towards the car, I looked at Sienna.

"I'll see you around," she said.

I nodded. "See ya."

Sirens started up somewhere in the city, and moments later, flashing lights sped down the block. That was our cue to leave. Everybody sprinted out in all different directions, laughing with their group. The cops swerved and picked only a few people to chase down in their car. I ran past them just before they got out and started pinning kids to the pavement.

Another reason I didn't want Dre out here.

Dre was waiting at the passenger door for me, looking nervous. "Come on, let's go."

I quickly unlocked the doors and we jumped inside. Started the engine and we took off around the corner and out of sight of the club. More police cars passed us, heading towards the club. I bet it was all cleared out by now. Even one cop car in the hood can clear a room full of black folks.

I drove expertly but slowly in the direction of home, ensuring I wasn't causing undue attention to myself. We wanted to get away, but we didn't want to get in any more trouble by getting a speeding ticket. Or worse. When we reached our house, the block was quiet. The sounds of the sirens were distant.

I pulled into the driveway, parking in my usual spot in front of the garage.

"So, you're not gonna tell Dad, are you?" Dre said. He was speaking in a low voice. And I knew this was something that really worried him.

"I really should," I said. "But won't. Although you got dish duty for the whole month."

"A month?" he pitched his voice.

"You lucky I don't make it two, and don't ever do this to me again."

"Even though the night went great?" he said, "Come on, Mo. You almost fully redeemed yourself."

I frowned. "Redeemed myself? I don't need any redemption. I didn't do anything wrong."

Dre nodded, "I guess. After all, it's just a freestyle night at a bar. I don't know why people try to make it bigger than what it is."

We both got out of the car. He stood still, looking up at the sky. The moon was shaded just a sliver on one side. I stopped and took it in with him.

"Someday, we're gonna find out what's up there," he said.

I smiled. "Well, first, we need to find out what's down here."

He smirked, walking to the front door. "We already know what's down here, heartbreaks and 808s."

I couldn't help but laugh, following him inside, shaking my head.

Country Musical

KATHRYN COTTAM

Country Musical

KATHRYN COTTAM

"SEAT'S TAKEN." HARMONY LOOPED HER FOOT AROUND the leg of the empty chair opposite her at the table and held it in place.

The girl – Harmony didn't know her name, mainly because she didn't care – peered over her glasses. She had one hand on the back of the chair, the other balancing her lunch tray. "But no one's sitting here."

Harmony gestured to herself. "I am"

The girl looked confused and pointed across the table at her. "But you're there."

Harmony shrugged. "I might change my mind."

The girl shook her head and walked off, looking for another empty seat in the cafeteria. Harmony turned her eyes back to the sheet music she had been reading – 24 Caprices by Paganini – it was her favorite. She ran the sound through her head, fingers twitching in time with the notes.

"Jeez, you're such an asshole."

Harmony glanced behind her. A boy sat at the next table over. He had obviously been watching her. His blonde hair fell in his eyes, and she thought she recognized him from English class. Luke Something.

She met his eyes. "Me? I'm the asshole?"

"Yeah." He took a sip of orange juice. "Would it hurt you to be nicer?"

"Why? What's wrong with wanting to be left alone?"

"You're the new girl. It'll be a long three years if you treat everyone like that."

"Not for me," Harmony said. "Besides, after today, you won't see me again."

He raised his brows in curiosity.

But she wasn't about to explain. And then the bell rang, signaling the end of the lunch hour.

Harmony smiled. It was almost time to get out of Timberline High School and this goddamn small town. And back to where she really belonged: New York City.

EVEN THOUGH HARMONY only had to sit through English and Biology, those two hours felt like a week. She was beginning to think that time moved differently in Tennessee. Or at least it seemed like that. Harmony might have been in Cottonwood Glen for just under three months but sometimes it felt like she'd spent her whole life here.

After school finally let out, she grabbed her knapsack and violin case and walked down the block to the corner store. It sold everything from nylons (who still wore those?) to candy and magazines in brown paper bags.

She'd told Bo not to pick her up. That she was going to a friend's house. And he'd bought it. Her Dad was an idealist that way. Couldn't imagine that the daughter he'd uprooted and forced to leave the only home she'd ever known wouldn't have made friends here.

Fuck him.

The cab she'd ordered between classes was waiting in the parking lot. She walked over and got in. "Bus depot."

The driver stared at her. "Your parents know you're going there?"

She looked him in the eye. "You gonna drive me, or do I need to walk?"

He sighed. Reversed out of the parking spot and turned into traffic. She glanced out the window and spotted Luke on the sidewalk. He met her eyes and waved. She gave him the finger. Then she faced forward, plucking at the straps of her knapsack. She forced herself to stop. She wasn't nervous. Not about going to New York. Just about getting out of Cottonwood Glen.

She'd tried it twice before and failed. This time it had to work. It just had to. She didn't know how much more country jamboree she could take.

"You play?" the driver asked, gesturing to her violin case.

She eyed him. Wanted to say: *No. I carry it around for the hell of it.* But she really needed this ride. "Got a concert in New York."

"What's your favorite song to play?"

Song?

She didn't play songs. She played music. Sonata No. 9 by Beethoven. Violin Concerto in D Minor by Sibelius. The Last Rose Of Summer by Heinrich Wilhelm Ernst. If there was such a thing as God, she would exist in the sublime beauty of those pieces.

She ignored the question. "Are we almost there?"

He pointed out the window. A large sign stood at the

side of the road, Bus Depot, written on it in scrolling letters. He pulled up to the curb. She paid him, cash.

"Have fun at your concert."

She got out and slammed the door behind her, looping the violin case over her shoulder and walking inside the building. It hadn't changed much in the eighty years since it'd been built. Large ornate clock on one wall (still ticking the time away), wooden benches, art deco lights.

Harmony made her way to the bathroom. Once in the stall, she changed from jeans and a t-shirt to a thrifted business skirt and jacket. Then she rolled her hair into a bun and added a pair of specs (non-prescription glass). Once she'd peed and washed her hands, she applied makeup with a heavy hand.

Then she studied herself in the mirror.

On the one hand, she looked older. On the other, like she was playing dress-up. Oh well, it would have to do. The point was to look old enough not to draw suspicion as to why she was traveling alone. And she felt like she'd succeeded in that.

She stuffed her jeans and t-shirts in the knapsack and went out to the waiting room, taking a seat in the far corner away from people – her favorite place to always be – and took out her phone. She pulled up Adele. Thought about texting her to say she was coming, but she might try to talk her out of it.

Especially if she knew she hadn't told Bo.

No, better to wait until she got to New York. She looked at her Dad's messages. There wasn't a whole lot of communication between her and him. *What time will you be home? I'm gonna be late, can you start dinner? Don't wait up.*

He probably wouldn't even miss her.

Okay, the last two attempts he came after her. But

surely, this time, he'd let her go. Even be relieved that she was finally out of his hair.

A staticky voice came over the PA. *New York City.*

That was her.

So long, Cottonwood Glen.

It ain't been nice knowing ya.

THE BUS WAS NOW an hour outside of Cottonwood Glen, and Harmony began to relax. She'd done it. Yeah, there were nineteen more hours to go. But she'd actually made it out. She turned and smiled out the window.

It was the first time in a long while that she felt anything akin to joy.

And then she noticed the bus appeared to be slowing. She couldn't see why, there wasn't a bus stop. The driver was simply pulling over onto the shoulder of the road.

Then she heard a male voice in the back. "Cops."

Harmony froze. They couldn't be here for her, could they? She had been so careful, buying a prepaid credit card from the corner store and using the computer at the library to purchase her bus ticket. Not telling a soul that she was leaving.

The brakes hissed. The bus rolled to a stop.

She pressed her nose to the window.

The driver got on the PA. "We'll just be a moment, folks."

Harmony was torn between hunkering down in her seat, pretending not to exist, and looking out the window. Her curiosity won out. She spotted the cop first. And then —

Fuck.

The man accompanying him was Bo. But how —

Luke.

He must have reported her. Goddamnit, why had she given him the finger? Because she had to be a little shit, that's why.

A second later, the bus doors wooshed open.

The cop got on board. Looked at the scattering of passengers. It wouldn't take him long to inspect everyone's ID if it came to that. "We got a Harmony Ward on board?"

Silence.

Harmony waited a few seconds and then got up, pulling her knapsack and violin case from the overhead compartment. Then she walked up the aisle towards the front, keeping her eyes on the floor. She didn't want to see anyone watching her, wondering what was going on. Did they think she was a murderer fleeing the scene of a crime?

Or, more likely, a stupid juvenile delinquent delaying everyone's journey because she was a selfish runaway asshole. She stopped in front of the cop.

"You Harmony Ward?"

She hitched her knapsack over her shoulder. "No, I just got up because I felt like a walk."

He frowned at her. "Your Dad's worried sick about you. He's here to take you home."

Harmony resisted the urge to snort. Bo was not worried about her. More like inconvenienced. Dads that worried about their kids didn't go no contact with them when they were seven years old. Didn't miss their ex-wife's funeral, leaving their kid to handle it alone. Didn't reappear only when that kid's life went to shit.

The cop shuffled to the left, letting her off the bus first. Maybe he thought she might run back to her seat, and he'd have to haul her out.

No, she wasn't about to make that much of a spectacle of herself.

Much as she wanted to.

She hopped off the bus.

Bo's jaw was clenched so tight she was worried he might break a tooth. "Get in the fucking car."

"Aye, aye, Captain." She walked along the side of the bus. No doubt everyone was still watching. She hated that. Wished she were invisible.

Bo's shitty truck was parked behind the cop car. She opened the passenger door and got in, putting her knapsack in the footwell. Then she buckled up, drawing the violin case into her lap. She held it tight, needing its comfort.

The bus pulled out onto the road, driving away.

Bo stood talking to the cop for a few minutes. She imagined their conversation: *So, sorry you have a shitty kid. Yeah, I do everything for her, but she just doesn't appreciate it.*

Fuck them both.

She stared out at gentle green hills. It was pretty alright. It just wasn't New York. Her eyes burned with unshed tears, but she would not cry. Not in front of Bo.

He returned to the truck and got in without saying a word. Seconds later, they were making their way along the highway. At the nearest crossroad, he pulled a U-turn, driving them back toward Cottonwood Glen.

Finally, he glanced over at her. His jaw was still tight. "What the hell did you think you were doing?"

"Running away. I thought that was obvious."

He gripped the wheel. "You said you'd give it a try."

"I did."

"Three whole fucking weeks."

"I still tried."

He hit the indicator, pulled out and around a semi

carrying chickens. The birds were all crammed into tiny little cages, spitting feathers. She wished she could release them.

"You run away again, and I'll send you to one of those Wilderness Therapy Camps—"

"—they abuse kids there, you know."

He sighed. "Harmony."

"You'd do that to me? After all I've been through?"

He didn't answer.

And that was the end of their conversation.

They were silent all the way back to his trailer.

HARMONY SAT at her usual table in the corner of the cafeteria, picking at her banana muffin and running through Liszt's B Minor Sonata in her head. A shadow passed over her, and a minute later, Luke pulled out the chair opposite and sat.

He grinned at her. "Thought you were running away."

"I tried."

"So you actually went through with it."

"I always do what I say I'm gonna do." She brushed crumbs from her fingers. "Besides, I'm not talking to you. You ratted me out."

"That was Mr. White, actually. He was in the corner store and saw you getting into the cab. Thought it looked a bit hinky, so he called your dad."

Harmony eyed him.

He laughed. "You don't believe me?"

"I dunno. I don't know you."

He flushed a little. "You could."

She refrained from rolling her eyes. "I'm going back to New York."

He raised his brows. "You're gonna try again?"

"Of course."

"Stubborn thing, aren't you?"

Harmony froze. Stubborn. That's what everyone called Gwen. Even Bo. That last argument her parents had before separating had been a doozy. And Bo had used the words stubborn-as-fuck against Gwen more than once. But when was stubbornness a failing? Harmony viewed it as a gift.

She got up, gathering the remains of her muffin. "You know nothing about me."

Then she walked out of the cafeteria and down the hall, dumping her muffin in the closest garbage can. Above it was a large bulletin board with various school notices, including an advertisement for the High School Hoedown Showdown in Nashville. First prize: five thousand dollars.

She yanked it from its staples.

Read the small print:

• All participants must be under the age of 18.

• Each participant must be currently enrolled in a high school or an equivalent educational program.

• Teams are to be a minimum of four students (no upper limit).

• Teams can choose any country music song from the past 80 years.

• No pre-recorded backing tracks. The performance must be live.

Harmony's eyes strayed back to the five thousand dollar prize. That was get-out-of-town money. And really, how hard would it be to win in this place?

∼

AFTER SCHOOL, Harmony walked back to Bo's shitty single-wide trailer.

As soon as she arrived, she texted him: *Home.*

It was what she'd agreed upon to get out of being sent to Wilderness Therapy. Too bad they didn't have that kind of thing for parents. Bo could probably use a good dose of it. She unlocked the door and entered, going straight to her room.

She got out her laptop and opened the internet. The home page brought up YouTube. Always and forever, Gwen's performance of 24 Caprices at Carnegie Hall.

She got out her violin case, unlatching it, and reached for the bow. Then she adjusted the screw at the end to tighten the horsehair. She grabbed a block of rosin and ran it along the strands, ensuring an even coating. When that was done, she set the violin on her shoulder, nestling the chin rest beneath her jaw, heat tilted into position. Her hand found its place on the neck, fingers hovering.

Then she adjusted her grip on the bow – tight enough for control, loose enough for fluid movement – and drew it across the strings, warming up.

She closed her eyes, each stroke becoming more precise.

And then when she was ready, she opened her eyes, reached out and hit play on the video.

Gwen's playing was relentless. The notes tumbled over each other like they were living creatures. Short bursts of staccato one second, smooth legato the next, her transitions as seamless as breathing. Harmony joined in. She wasn't as polished as her mother – she knew that—but one day, she would be.

A lot of others couldn't keep pace with Gwen.

But Harmony could.

And she did.

Until she heard a door slam.

Then she dropped the bow and hit pause on the video. She walked to the window and spotted Bo's truck parked outside in the driveway. She hadn't heard him pull up.

A second later, he knocked on her bedroom door.

"What?" she asked.

"That you playing? It sounded good." His voice was somewhat muffled by the door.

She looked down at the violin. "No. YouTube."

Silence.

And then: "I'll get dinner on."

"Okay."

She waited until she heard him in the kitchen, then she put her violin and bow back in the case. She snapped the latches closed and placed the instrument on its shelf in the closet. She went to her desk, got out her books, and started her biology homework.

She left Gwen's video playing but hit mute.

That way, whenever she looked up, her mother was still with her.

WHEN IT WAS DINNER TIME, Harmony went out to the kitchen and sat at the table.

Shepherd's pie. Again. It was the only thing Bo really knew how to cook. But at least it wasn't spaghetti. That had been a disaster.

Before he could dig in, she set the poster for the High School Hoedown Showdown on the table and slid it over to him.

"What's this?" She didn't answer; she just let Bo read it. "You forming a band?"

She took a bite of potato and swallowed. "Thinking about it."

He forced a smile. "That seems like a good idea."

"Only I want to make a deal."

He froze, fork halfway to his mouth. Then he set it down and rubbed his hand over his face. "Go on."

But she could tell he was already irritated. "If we win the contest, I get to go back to New York. But in the meantime, I promise I won't try to run away again."

He sighed. "And what are you gonna do in New York?"

"Stay with Adele. Study violin."

He shook his head. "You can't. She's your teacher, not your parent."

"Then come to New York with me."

"Jesus, Harmony, we've discussed this. New York wasn't good for me."

"No, the booze wasn't good for you."

Bo bunched his hand into a fist and slammed the tabletop. The silverware jumped, and she froze.

"You don't give a shit that you've destroyed my career," Harmony said.

"You're sixteen goddamn years old," he said. "You don't have a career."

"But I could. Playing violin is all I ever wanted."

"No," he said. "It's all Gwen ever wanted. She pushed you to study with Adele when you were far too young."

Harmony bunched the High School Hoedown Showdown advertisement into a ball and chucked it at him. It bounced off his chest and hit the floor. "Why do you hate me so much?"

He recoiled as though she had hit him. "I don't hate you, Harmony."

She got up, pushing back her chair. "But you hated Mom, and we're exactly the same."

"Come on, kid—"

She ignored him, making her way to her bedroom. She entered, closing the door behind her and locking it. A minute later, he knocked.

"Come on out, Harmony. Finish your dinner."

"I'm not hungry."

She heard him grumble something but couldn't make out the words. She got out her phone, pulling up her contacts, scrolling to Adele. Then she dialed. It rang through to voicemail.

"It's me. I'm working on a plan to get back to New York, I promise." Her voice broke. "I miss you."

Then she hung up.

Gwen was still playing in silence on the laptop.

Harmony walked over and flipped the screen closed. Who was she kidding? Gwen was dead and scattered to the winds. Even if she went back to New York she wasn't going to find her mother there.

She fell onto her bed, burying her face in her pillow.

～

WHEN SHE WOKE the next morning, Bo had already gone to work. He probably didn't want another mealtime confrontation. Most likely, he was as sick of them as she was.

He'd set her place at the table. Bowl, spoon, glass of orange juice.

She poured out cereal, added milk, then spotted the High School Hoedown Showdown poster next to her placemat. It had been flattened out. And written across it in pen was: *you have a deal.*

Harmony sat back in her chair. Checked the poster

again. The ink was fresh, it smudged against her fingers. An unintended grin lit up her face.

She couldn't believe it.

Bo had actually agreed to it.

For the first time since arriving in Cottonwood Glen, she was excited to get to school.

~

TODAY, she didn't even bother with the cafeteria at lunch. Instead, she went straight to the art room and got a piece of poster board and a thick black ink marker from Mrs Saunders. Then, she made up a poster of her own:

GOT TALENT? *Wanna make five grand? Looking for bandmates to join me in the High School Hoedown Showdown. Meeting at 3pm in the southwest corner of the cafeteria.*

HARMONY STAPLED it to the bulletin board where the original advertisement once hung, then went to class. As soon as the day was over, she made her way to her usual corner in the cafeteria. Once there, she waited, chewing on her nails. It was an old habit from childhood. At least until Gwen coated them in some kind of chemical compound that tasted horrific. That had been all that was needed to stop Harmony from chewing her nails.

Now, she watched as a few kids passed through the cafeteria. Most of them looking for a friend. Or beelining it to the vending machines for a coke or a bag of chips.

By three-thirty, she realized no one was coming.

Three-forty-five confirmed it.

She left the cafeteria, walking back to the bulletin

board. Her poster was gone. Someone had torn it down and tossed it in the garbage. She unfolded it to see *BITCH* written across it in all caps.

Well, fuck whoever did that.

She marched right back to the art room.

Mrs Saunders glanced up at her. "I'm about to leave, Harmony."

Harmony pointed to the poster board and pens. "I need five minutes."

Mrs Saunders sighed, then looked at the clock. "Go on then."

Harmony grabbed her supplies and then wrote up another poster.

LOOKING *for bandmates to join me in the High School Hoedown Showdown. I know I suck as a person, but I don't suck at violin, and surely some of you idiots wanna win $5,000. If so, meet me at 3pm in the southwest corner of the cafeteria.*

ONCE SHE FINISHED, she hung it on the bulletin board and dragged the garbage can to a new location. She could do this again and again. Until she got what she needed. Stubbornness.

In the end, it took three more posters.

But then, Friday afternoon, Luke appeared and sat opposite her once again. She eyed him. "What do you want?"

He held his arms wide. "Is that any way to talk to your banjoist?"

She pursed her lips. "You play banjo?"

He pretended to strum. "Sure do."

"And you have experience playing live?"

He grinned. "Every Tuesday at Southern Comfort."

"What's that?"

"Local diner. They have an open mic night. If you actually tried living here instead of running away, you might actually know that."

She glared at him. "Ha ha."

"So I'm hired?"

She hesitated. Did she really want him in the band? Maybe not. But the goal was to win the money and get the hell out of Cottonwood Glen. "As long as you're telling the truth that you can play."

"Oh, I never lie," he said.

Harmony leaned back in her chair. "We still need at least two more musicians. Know anyone else?"

He raised an arm and gestured towards the door.

Seconds later, three girls their age entered the cafeteria. "They didn't wanna join if I didn't get the gig. We're a package deal."

Harmony clenched her teeth. Was she that unlikeable?

Luke grinned and made introductions. "Tanisha. She's a vocalist. Gonna give Aretha a run for her Grammy count one day."

"You know it," Tanisha said.

Then Luke pointed to the other two girls. They looked similar. Almost like twins. "Jenny and Jessa. They already have a band, the Fiddlers Three. But they're willing to give you a chance."

Harmony took a breath. Willing to give her a chance? Gwen had been one of the top violinists in the world. And her talent flowed through Harmony's fingers. Luke was just trying to goad her. She wouldn't let him. "Fiddlers Three? Where's the third?"

Jessa laughed. "She quit. But we liked the name, so we kept it."

"So, you're all in?" Harmony asked.

"Let's get something clear," Tanisha said. "We're not here for you. We're here for the money. A thousand bucks each if we win this thing."

Harmony nodded. "Yep."

Luke and the others exchanged looks. "Alright then, let's get registered."

Harmony opened her laptop and pulled up the registration page, filling in all their information. Then she paused. "We need a group name."

"How about *No Strings Attached*?" Luke said. "After all, this is a one-time gig."

Harmony glanced around the table. No one protested. So she put her fingers on the keys and typed the name in. Hit enter.

Silence filled the cafeteria.

"Now what?" Jessa asked.

Everyone looked at Harmony. She shrugged. "We play."

~

AND THEY DID.

Everyday at three p.m., after the bell rang, they gathered in the English classroom (Mrs. Givens didn't seem to mind), pushed the desks aside and practiced.

Tanisha chose the song.

You'll Find Your Way Home.

At first, Harmony refused. Thought they were making fun of her. Until she discovered it was a country-classic. Won awards and everything.

The notes were simple enough. But it wasn't working out like Harmony expected it to. Given her experience, she had thought she would be taking lead. Instead, she found herself struggling to keep pace. Mostly because Luke kept tripping her up.

For the third time, Harmony stopped, holding up her hand.

Tanisha rolled her eyes. "Not again."

Harmony pointed her bow at Luke. "He's not sticking to the notes."

Luke glared at her. "And you're too rigid. We're playing country, not Beethoven's greatest hits."

"Do you wanna win this thing?" she asked.

He raised his brows. "Do you?"

Jenny touched her shoulder. "Just try relaxing a little. Focus less on the notes and let the strings drive the rhythm."

Harmony set her jaw, raised her bow, and rested it against the strings.

Jessa looked at her. "Ready?"

Harmony nodded.

They went again.

Tanisha's voice was about the only thing that sounded right.

This time, it was Luke who broke off first. "You're still too tight."

"Listen," Harmony said. "I studied under the best concertmaster in New York–"

"We aren't in New York," Tanisha said. "We're in Cottonwood Glen. And Luke's right. We're not playing Mozart or Beethoven or Puccini. We're playing country. And right now, you're the weak link. So get better, or you're out of the band."

Harmony flushed. She would be out of the band? This was her fucking group. She clenched her teeth, turned on her heel, and walked to the door.

"You quitting?" Tanisha asked.

"Taking a break. I need some air."

Harmony made her way down the hall to the exit doors and stepped outside. Walking over to a curb and sitting, laying her violin across her lap.

Harmony was the weak link?

Adele – even Gwen – would have laughed at hearing that. Her playing wasn't weak, just misunderstood.

She heard the door close behind her. A minute later, Luke sat next to her. She glowered. Why couldn't people leave her alone?

"What do you want?" she asked. "I said I was taking a break."

"Yeah, but you really came outside to sulk."

She glared at him.

He grinned. "I'm betting not too many people have told you your playing sucks."

"I don't suck. I study under Adele."

"Ah yes, One of the top teachers in the world. You've already said that ten times."

"Hardly."

"Alright, twelve."

"Shut up."

For a moment, there was silence between them, and then he nudged her. "If you loved being her student so much, why are you here?"

She opened her mouth, then closed it again, fingered her bow. "It wasn't my choice. My mom died."

"I'm sorry."

"Why?" Harmony sniffed. "You didn't know her."

"No, but I couldn't imagine losing my mom at this age. What happened?"

Harmony set her jaw. She didn't want to cry. "We were eating dinner. She stood up. Said her head hurt. And then she fell. That was it. Dead of an aneurysm."

STERLING & STONE

"Jesus," Luke said.

Harmony rubbed her thumb against the neck of the violin. "All I want is to do well for her. And my dad agreed that if we won, we'd move back to New York so I could continue to study."

Luke was silent for a moment. "Then, can I give you some advice?"

Harmony stiffened. Then, she forced herself to relax. "Okay."

"Country's all about the story, expressing emotion. If you try and stay in control of the strings, the music won't like it. The judges will sense you're trying to front. You're gonna have to relax and let the notes breathe. It's more about the feeling than the precision."

"Let the notes breathe?"

He nodded.

She chewed on her lip for a moment. "I'm not sure I know how to do that."

"Well, I know who can teach you."

She eyed him. "You?"

"Hell no," he grinned. "But you're in good hands with the holy trifecta. Dolly, Reba, Patsy. Watch them. They'll teach you all you need to know about country."

AFTER DINNER, Harmony went into her room and put her headphones on. Then she sat at her computer and played the video that Luke sent to her.

The holy trifecta.

Uh-huh.

Harmony didn't get any further than Dolly because when the singer walked on stage—sequins, rhinestones, and bright, bottle-blonde hair piled high like a crown—

something shifted in her. It wasn't just Dolly's presence; it was the way she carried herself. Like she'd walked into a room full of old friends and not into a venue where everyone was a stranger.

How did she do that?

Dolly's smile lit up the arena, and she stopped before the microphone stand, her guitar resting on her hip. She tilted her head and smiled. She hadn't even started to sing, and she already had the audience in the palm of her hand.

And then she opened her mouth.

And boy, could she sing.

She belted out song after song, and the whole time, she seemed to be having fun.

Luke, Tanisha, Jessa and Jenny were right. If this is what country was, Harmony was the weak link. And they were gonna lose if she couldn't adapt.

But that felt dangerous.

The vigilance, rigidness, and focus that she had to demonstrate in each lesson with Adele was essential to her craft. Panic rose in her throat. If she let it go, would she be able to find it again?

Then she thought about her deal with Bo.

If they won, she got to go back to New York.

She knew she could find the hardness again. The competition. The edge. It lived and breathed in Adele. Working with her had never been fun. What it had been was productive.

Harmony looked back at the video.

Dolly was exiting the stage.

She hit replay.

~

"WELL, GODDAMN," Tanisha said when the music died away. "Somebody found the little bit of country in their soul."

Harmony grinned. They had the classroom windows open, and a light breeze blew in. The sun warmed their faces. For some reason, it was the happiest Harmony had been since leaving New York. "I had a good teacher."

"Luke?" Jenny asked.

"Hell no," he said. "I gave her a lesson in Dolly."

Jenny and Jessa crossed themselves in unison. "She's the source, the story, the song."

"Y'all are weird," Harmony said.

Tanisha nudged her. "And you're starting to talk like us."

Harmony rolled her eyes, placed her violin back in its case, and snapped it shut. "See you all tomorrow."

Tanisha laughed.

Harmony grabbed her case and coat and walked outside. Luke jogged along behind her. "Want a lift?"

She glanced over at him. "You live in the opposite direction."

He flushed a little and shrugged. "I don't mind."

She stopped and studied his face. "Look. I appreciate it. But I'm not looking to get involved with anyone in Cottonwood Glen. I'll be gone soon."

He eyed her. "You're really sure we're going to win."

"Of course," she said. "Aren't you?"

He shrugged. "Never won anything before."

"That's because you haven't worked with a professional."

He laughed. "And that's you?"

"Sure. Why not?"

He waved. "See you tomorrow, Harmony."

She watched him walk off. It bothered her that he

questioned whether they were going to win. They all had to believe it, or it wouldn't happen. That's what Gwen used to tell her: *Believe it. Believe it in your soul. Otherwise, you'll be a nobody.*

And Gwen wasn't about to let her kid be nothing.

~

HARMONY DOUBLE-CLICKED ON THE INTERNET.

Stood for a moment, staring at the frozen image of her mother on YouTube. Then she closed it.

Pulled out her music for *You'll Find Your Way Home.*

And then she closed her eyes, began to play. When she reached the end of the first verse, she heard guitar.

Same song.

But she hadn't been playing that music online.

She opened her eyes. The sound wasn't coming from her computer. She dropped the bow, walked to her bedroom door, and flung it open.

Bo sat on a stool at the kitchen bar, holding his guitar. He forced a smile. "Been a while since I heard you play. Guess it made me think about picking the guitar up again."

For a moment, she didn't move.

He lowered the guitar. "Sorry, didn't mean to interrupt."

Harmony raised the violin and tucked it beneath her chin. Raised her bow and continued from where he left off.

Bo froze, then a second later he got the guitar back in position, fingers moving in rhythm. He was stiff, unpracticed. But he knew the tune.

For a few measures, the two instruments seemed to chase each other, weaving in and out, playing tag in the open spaces between the melody. Harmony bent a note, and the guitar followed. Bo shifted his chord, and Harmony echoed its change. Around and around they went, letting the music guide them.

Harmony heard the words in her head: *The moon finds the night, and the sun meets the day,*

You'll find your way, just like they find their way.

Bo stopped –

Got up and walked to the front door. Exited, letting the door slam closed behind him.

Harmony stopped.

What had she done wrong?

She didn't think she'd missed a note.

Had she sung the words?

Had that pissed him off?

Gwen used to walk out on her as well. Whenever she'd made a mistake. Whenever she wasn't good enough.

Harmony let the bow fall to her side, went back to her room, and kicked her door closed.

You'll find your way.

And she would. Once she got back to New York. To Adele. And away from Bo, who had no fucking idea of who she really was or what she was capable of.

NO STRINGS ATTACHED NO LONGER PRACTICED in the English classroom. Mrs Givens had moved them to the gym.

Now, the music of *You'll Find Your Way Home* filled the auditorium.

Mrs Givens stayed with them though, marking papers and exams while seated on a bench at the back. And when they would break or restart, she'd applaud.

But they didn't need her applause to know that they were good.

It was apparent.

Students had now started showing up to their practice sessions and lingering in the doorways.

Harmony and the others would sit together at lunch every day and review their practice sessions. Were the strings overpowering Tanisha's voice? Did they need to pull back? Push harder? Let the music lead?

They parsed every note.

Reviewed every bar.

They didn't sugarcoat anything. The music had to be honest – as did they – even when it stung.

"You know," Jenny said. "Maybe we should stick together when this is all over. Keep playing. We're kind of magical."

"Can't," Tanisha said, pointing to Harmony with the microphone. "She's headed back to New York."

"Oh, right," Jenny said. "I forgot."

Harmony shrugged. "Doesn't mean you four can't keep going."

Luke nodded. "I'm game."

Tanisha shimmied over to Jenny and Jessa. The four of them leaned in, hands extending forward, knuckles meeting. Then, their fingers unfurled, wriggling outward in sync like they were dancing in the air. "To No Strings Attached."

They all grinned.

Harmony felt left out.

~

IT WAS close to midnight by the time she got home. The

trailer was dark. But Bo's truck was in the driveway so he had to be in bed.

She hadn't meant to be this late. But it was the last Friday before the competition, and Mrs Givens held the gym open for them until nine. Then, the five of them took Luke's truck and went for supper.

They'd wound up celebrating how far they'd come in the past few months. Not with alcohol, but with strings. They'd broken out their instruments in the parking lot and put on an impromptu concert.

By the time the evening ended, they had an audience of a couple hundred. And Harmony had never had so much fun.

She went to her bedroom and put her violin on its shelf in the closet. Checked her phone. And froze. She'd missed a call from Adele.

Shit.

She dialed into her voicemail. And within seconds, her instructor's familiar voice filled her ear. "Harmony. I hope you've been practicing like you said you would. Because I've got you an audition with Manuel Garcia."

Manual Garcia.

Her stomach lurched into her throat.

Holy fuck, holy fuck, holy fuck.

He was the world's best conductor. At least to Harmony. He could make or break any musician's career. She didn't bother listening to the rest of the message. She simply exited out and dialed Adele. It rang twice before she realized the time.

Just after midnight.

Shit.

"Harmony?" Adele said.

"I'm so sorry," Harmony tripped over her words, "I just realized the time. Were you in bed?"

Adele laughed. "Of course not. I knew you'd call when you got the message."

Harmony smiled, happiness flooding her veins. "I've really missed you."

"You still got your fingers on 24 Caprices?" Adele asked.

"Of course," Harmony said. It was a little lie. But she wasn't about to tell Adele she hadn't played it in two months.

"Good," Adele said. "Because you need to be in New York next Friday. Get Bo to make the arrangements."

Harmony stiffened. "Next Friday?"

"Is that going to be a problem?"

"No, no problem. I'll make sure I'm there."

"Saturday two p.m. Carnegie Hall. But I don't want to go in raw. So come Thursday so we can do some last-minute training."

Harmony nodded. "Yeah, okay."

"Let me know when you arrive."

"Will do."

Adele rang off.

Harmony dropped onto her bed.

Fuck.

～

"WHAT'S WRONG?" Bo asked at breakfast the next morning.

Harmony poked at the pancake on her plate. "Adele got me an audition with Manuel Garcia."

Bo set his coffee mug on the table. "Holy shit. Congratulations."

"Thanks."

"Why the long face?"

Harmony mashed her pancake beneath the fork tines. "It's next Saturday. And Adele wants me to come on Thursday to practice."

"Tell her you've got another commitment."

"I can't. She won't understand. It's just—" She broke off, shrugged.

"It's just what?"

"Country music."

Bo leaned back in his chair and rubbed his jaw. "Then I guess you've got a decision to make."

She slouched in her chair. "I know."

Bo watched her for a moment, but she didn't dare meet his eyes. She was too nervous. Didn't want to see the disappointment in them.

"Look," he said. "Whatever you choose, it's up to you. But I'll support you either way."

Harmony blinked. "What do you mean?"

"If you want to go back to New York and play for Manuel, I'll take you. If you want to go to Nashville for the competition, we'll go there. But you're the one that's gotta tell me what direction to drive."

"And if I choose New York," Harmony asked, "what am I supposed to tell No Strings Attached?"

He shrugged, got up, and started clearing away the breakfast dishes. "Seems to me the answer is in the name."

"ARE YOU FUCKING KIDDING ME?" Luke asked.

Harmony stood in front of the others. They were seated on the edge of the stage, staring at her.

Harmony sighed.

He threw his hands wide. "What was that bullshit you told me that you always do what you say?"

"I do," Harmony said.

Tanisha looked irritated. "Except when it comes to us."

"Can't you tell him you're booked?" Jenna asked. "Request a different audition date?"

"It doesn't work like that," Harmony said, clutching her instrument case to her chest. "It's Manual Garcia. It's rare to get a first shot at playing for him. Let alone a second or a third. If I say no, that's it. And Adele will never speak to me again."

Luke rolled his eyes. "And we wouldn't want that, would we?"

Harmony flushed. "No, we would not."

Luke snorted. "You know, she's not your mother, right?"

Harmony flinched. It would have hurt less if he'd hit her. And he must have known he fucked up because he immediately reached out to touch her. "I'm so sorry, Harmony. I didn't mean—"

"Fuck you," she said. And then she ran towards the door. She heard Tanisha call her name, but she ignored her. Pushing open the exterior door. She realized she'd left her knapsack behind. But she didn't care. She wouldn't need it again. Not in New York.

It didn't matter what anyone else said. Gwen would have wanted her to take the audition. It was what they had been working towards before the aneurysm. Day and night. Practicing, practicing, practicing. In the hope that one day Harmony would be better than her mother.

Now she had that shot.

And she was gonna do whatever it took to nail that audition. Play until her fingers bled if necessary. Harmony ran all the way home, and thankfully, Bo was still at work.

She went straight to her room.

No Strings Attached had simply been a distraction.

She kicked her shoes off, threw her coat on the bed. Then unlatched the case and pulled out her violin.

Then she opened her laptop.

Changed the google home page from Dolly back to Gwen. 24 Caprices.

She hit play.

Positioned her violin beneath her chin. Rested the bow against the strings. And then pulled the first note to life. Her bow ricocheted against the strings, this time daring Gwen to keep up with her. By the time she finished, she was exhausted. She hadn't missed a single note. Her playing was loose and carefree, not at all like her previous sound.

She'd never played with such ease. Such perfection.

And never felt worse about it.

HARMONY SAT in the passenger seat of Bo's truck, chewing on her thumb. She had to do something; otherwise, she was going to jump out of her skin.

They were headed north. By tomorrow night they would be in New York. She blew out a breath, readjusted her position.

Bo glanced over at her. "You okay?"

No, she wasn't okay. Neither Luke, Jenna, Jessa, nor Tanisha had talked to her at school that week. They hadn't even sat at her table. Not that she blamed them.

She ignored his question and asked one of her own. "How come you stopped playing?"

Bo braked. "When?"

"You'll Find Your Way Home," she said. "You walked out on me."

He applied the gas, his fingers tightening on the wheel.

"Felt like when I used to play with Gwen. She didn't always play classical. Guess it kind of overwhelmed me. I wasn't always a failure as a father, you know."

She studied his face. He had more lines. More gray in the hair. He'd aged in the past year. "But after you and Mom broke up, you never came to visit me in New York. Why not?"

He shook his head. "I came for each of your birthdays."

"That's a lie."

He shook his head. "Nope."

"I never saw you."

"Gwen wouldn't let me in the apartment."

"Bullshit," Harmony said.

He clenched his jaw. "She told me if I left, I was to never come back. I tried. But Gwen – your mother – she was stubborn. Wouldn't let me see you."

Harmony stared at him.

Gwen wouldn't have done that to her, would she?

She always seemed rather tense on Harmony's birthday. But she figured it was because Bo had forgotten it. Not that he was trying to see her.

Bo glanced over at her. "I didn't hate that you played violin, Harmony. I just wanted you to still have a childhood. Gwen's mom controlled her career from the moment she picked up an instrument. Day and night, she was at the strings. Never had friends because she didn't know how to make them. Everything was about the music. All I wanted was for you to be the one that chose that life."

"I did choose," Harmony said. "And I could have stayed in New York with Adele and continued my training."

"I asked. Adele didn't want you."

Harmony clenched her hands into fists. "I don't believe you."

Bo fished his phone out of his shirt pocket, tossed it to her. "Password is your birthday. Check my messages."

Harmony punched in the digits. Pulled up messaging. Scrolled down until she found Adele.

Look, Harmony's good, but it was Gwen that made her great. And I'm not gonna raise someone else's kid, so I think we might have hit the end of the road—

"Stop the truck!" Harmony dropped his phone onto the floor.

Bo braked hard, swerving onto the shoulder of the highway. Harmony flung the door open, unlatched her seatbelt, and bolted out. There was a green field next to them. She ran through the tall grasses until she was far from the truck.

Then she collapsed.

Adele didn't want her?

That's not what she had said.

She had told Harmony that Bo wouldn't allow her to stay in New York. That's why they couldn't continue with lessons.

Seconds later, she felt Bo beside her. He pulled her into his arms, holding tight. *"The moon finds the night, and the sun meets the day. You'll find your way, just like they find their way…"*

And then she couldn't help it. She cried, soaking his shirt.

After a long while, Harmony finally lifted her head and looked him in the eyes. "I'm sorry, I'm a terrible daughter."

He tucked damp strands of hair behind her ears. "You're absolutely perfect. I'm the one that's a failure. Couldn't even go to Gwen's funeral when you needed me most."

"It's okay," she said. "I understood it might be hard."

They sat for a moment in silence, listening to vehicles pass on the highway. Harmony rubbed her nose against her arm. "I love classical music."

He smiled. "I know. And maybe I can figure out some kind of job in New York. Get you back studying under Adele."

"But I think I like country better."

He raised his brows. "Seriously?"

She shrugged. "It's the source, the story, the song."

Bo laughed, brushing the tears from her cheeks. "I have no idea what that means."

Harmony glanced back at the highway. "I don't suppose you could turn the truck around? Get me to Nashville?"

Bo got to his feet, held out a hand. She took it and he hoisted her up. "Hold onto your strings."

And then the two of them ran back to the truck.

IT WAS ALMOST impossible for Harmony to stop watching the clock. They had driven through without stopping, but they were still cutting it close.

And as far as Harmony could tell, Luke hadn't read her message.

Or if he had, he didn't feel like responding.

Bo pulled to the curb along Fourth Avenue. "I gotta find someplace to park. You get inside. Find your group."

But Harmony couldn't move. "What if they don't want me back?"

"Then I guess you cross that bridge when you see them."

She swallowed hard and nodded. Got her instrument from the footwell in the back seat. Bo placed a hand on her arm. "Just in case I don't make the performance. Make Gwen proud."

"I will."

Bo's eyes grew shiny. "See you inside." His voice sounded hoarse.

She opened the door and got out, running up to the doors of the Ryman Auditorium. Harmony entered the red brick building and found a woman at a table. She had a stack of paper and seemed to be directing students. Harmony stood in line, waiting until it was her turn.

"Harmony Ward, No Strings Attached," she said.

The woman looked up. "They're on in five minutes. You'd better hurry."

She pointed down a hallway. Harmony sprinted off, making her way around to the back of the stage, where she was directed to a set of stairs. The sound of country music was all around.

She spotted Luke first. Then the others.

For a moment, she thought about leaving.

But then Jessa saw her and ran over, throwing herself at Harmony. "I knew you'd make the right choice."

Tanisha followed. "I wasn't worried in the slightest. We're way cooler than those New Yorkers."

Harmony laughed.

"Are you sure?" Jenny asked. "We wouldn't want you to miss out on something you really want."

"I'm sure," Harmony said. "And there's nowhere I'd rather be."

She wanted to talk to Luke next. But there wasn't time.

"No Strings Attached," a woman in black said, herding them to the stage door. Applause filled her ears. Harmony got out her violin, quickly warmed it up, and made a few adjustments.

And then they were walking up to the stage.

And out.

The auditorium was full.

The spotlight caught them right away.

There was silence while they got into position.

And then –

They were off.

And it was like magic.

The music flowed through Harmony like water. And she was caught in the sound. Spinning and playing. She caught Luke's eyes and grinned. He glanced away, his fingers stiff.

This was fun.

So much fun.

She twirled, poked Luke with her bow. He laughed. And so did the audience. It broke the tension and their strings danced, held together by Tanisha's vocals.

Harmony caught sight of Bo in the aisle. He waved, and she smiled at him. And knew she wasn't playing for Gwen. Not today. Nor was she playing for him. This time, she was playing for herself.

We're Not Eating Sam

SKYE RILEY

We're Not Eating Sam

SKYE RILEY

THE ONLY BAD THING ABOUT STARTING WINTER BREAK WAS
realizing that Maya still had a whole semester left before
getting out of her hell hole of a high school.

The end of senior year was drawing near, but nowhere
near enough, especially not with assholes like the ones
who'd been following her since she cleared out her locker
for the end of the term, taunting her from just a few feet
behind.

"Yo, Maya! If I failed my art midterm, will you retake
it for me? I'm sure I'll pass since Mrs. Conaway is in love
with you," one taunted, snow crunching underneath his
heavy boots. His lacrosse stick dragged through the dirt
slush at the side of the road, making an awful squelching
sound that indicated he was *way* too close to Maya's
personal space.

"Nah, she'll probably paint some lesbo shit and get you
in trouble," his friend cackled right before getting punched
in the arm.

Tyler and Nathan had been two of the biggest recurring assholes in Maya's life since first meeting them in second grade. But it seemed like they'd somehow only grown more obnoxious with age. Weren't people supposed to mature as they got older?

"Whatever, man, you're not gonna fail art anyway. It's such a nothing class," Nathan said.

"Shit, like that's probably how losers like Maya keep their GPAs out of the gutters. Anyone can do it," laughed Tyler.

Maya knew it was probably best to just keep her head down, keep silent, and keep walking towards home. Focus on her beat-up combat boots and the snow beneath them, watch her breath in the cold air, and wait for this moment to pass. But there was something about the way they spoke about her, nonchalant as if they had no idea she was there while still being so intentional with their words. Sure, Maya's grades weren't the best, but to insult her artistic skill was another issue altogether. She'd probably won more awards for their school's art department than either of the two had for Lacrosse combined. Not that either of them would know that, let alone care.

She tried to keep her temper at bay, visually and internally. Snapping back would let them know they'd succeeded at provoking her, and she didn't want them to have the satisfaction. Not only that, but these guys could easily fuck her up if she stepped out of line.

But she was officially on break. She could make peace with the fact that she would have to spend the break reflecting on whatever words she was about to unleash. And maybe the repercussions that would come with them.

So she glanced over her shoulder and said with a lot more nonchalance than she felt, "If you think my GPA is gutter adjacent, yours must have been rotting in the sewer for ages now."

"What was that?" Tyler demanded. "I know you didn't just say what I think you said."

Maya heard both boys stop in their tracks, and assumed they probably expected her to do the same. But she kept walking, not even turning to look back. And then she utilized her newly bestowed confidence to push just a *bit* farther.

"What, you're allowed to say whatever you want about me, but the second I make a joke, I'm the bad guy?" She wasn't stopping herself now. "It's bold of you to be making these jokes when it seems like you're not clear on whether or not you'll be repeating senior year for a third time."

Before she could even piece together what was happening, Maya felt herself lurch back faster than a carnival ride coming to a full stop. Before she could even figure out how Tyler had gotten ahold of her backpack straps, she felt the icy shock of the snow hit her face like a reverse snowball. One of the boys pushed her down into the lawn while the other cackled like a hyena. Maya clawed the ground to find any kind of purchase she could. But she could hardly breathe, the snow stung her face with a fury so frigid that breathing was the last thing she could think about. And then she wasn't thinking about anything really, face numbing as her head emptied, the sound of the boys' laughter fading into the background along with her vision...

"Nate, don't be an asshole!"

Why would Tyler say that to Nathan?

It took Maya a solid few seconds before realizing the voice belonged to a girl, the same girl who was now pulling Maya up out of the snow and brushing stray flakes from her face.

"Hey, you okay?"

Ruby Lopez stared back at her, honey eyes warm

enough to melt away whatever snow had stuck to Maya's face. Ruby was about as popular as a true good girl could get. She had the kind of social status that granted you access to most of the parties and hangouts thrown by the school's elites. But she wasn't enough of a bitch to actually get along with most of them. It also probably didn't help that she'd been Maya's best friend since elementary school, that had to have taken her down at least a couple pegs on the social ladder.

Maya's vision was still hazy, but she watched as Ruby turned back towards the two boys.

"You assholes really could have hurt her, you know?"

There was something pitiful about the way Ruby said it, something that made Maya feel more ashamed than protected. It didn't help that neither Tyler nor Nathan seemed to be taking her seriously.

"Yeah, yeah, whatever, Ruby," Tyler waved one hand as he bent down to pick up his lacrosse stick. "It's not like we would have killed her or anything."

Ruby wrinkled her nose. "That really shouldn't be the bar."

Nathan and Tyler ignored her. Once they'd both collected all their things, they were quick to turn in the opposite direction.

"See you at the chalet!" Nathan called out. And then they took off.

"God, those two get eviler every time I see them," Maya murmured.

"This was definitely a low for them, but they've also done much worse," Ruby replied like that was any kind of decent defense.

It wasn't Ruby's fault she sympathized with people like them. Even if she wasn't cruel herself, she tended to surround herself with those who were. Maya always wondered how she managed to stay as kind as she was. She also wondered how many more atrocities her tolerance would allow before she finally put her foot down.

Ruby took Maya's bag, carrying it for her as they walked home. They only made it a couple houses down the block before Ruby finally asked the question she'd already been hounding Maya about all week.

"Sooo... have you made your mind up about the Rockies this weekend?" She asked it with a subtlety that couldn't have been learned from anywhere but a telenovela.

Maya groaned, but Ruby cut in before she had a chance to protest. "I know it isn't your scene, the whole... partying and skiing thing, but I really think you'll have fun. The chalet I rented is huge, fancy enough that I had to use Dad's credit card!"

"It's less the partying and skiing scene that's putting me off and more the Nathan and Tyler scene. Why'd you have to invite them?"

"They're not that bad," Ruby replied simply. Unconvincingly.

Maya raised a brow.

"Didn't you just pull me out of their snowstorm equivalent of a swirly two minutes ago?"

"Well, yes. But I'll ask them to be on their best behavior, and they don't really pull those types of stunts when I'm around anyway," Ruby shrugged.

And that much was true. The more antagonistic characters of their high school definitely tended to lay off Maya whenever Ruby was around. One of the many perks of having Ruby as her guard dog, even if she was more of a chihuahua than a Rottweiler.

"Even if they do pretend to be somewhat tolerable, partying isn't really my thing..."

Ruby's eyes lit up, and a slow smirk spread across her face. "Yeah, probably because you'd rather just stay at home all break chatting with your giiiiirlfriend!"

"Sam and I aren't really using labels like that yet…" Maya said, her blush looking extra red against the snowy white landscape.

"Right, sorry. I forgot," Ruby laughed before correcting herself, "your online-girlfriend-who-is-totally-real-but-you've-never-actually-met."

"Talking to girls in real life is hard!" Maya protested.

"You seem to do just fine with me." Ruby batted her lashes.

"Yeah, because I've had a decade of practice," Maya said with a playful shove. "Besides, *you* try looking for another queer girl in this town! I bet I'd have to cross state borders just to find someone bi-curious, let alone another lesbian."

The only thing worse than the isolation was the ungodly amount of harassment that came with it. Maya wasn't just a lesbian; she was the *only* lesbian in Oakwood. While Ruby had some rumors spread about her after Maya came out, she debunked those pretty quickly after getting together with the high school's star basketball player. Then, the star baseball player. There was a hookup with the captain of the swim team.

"Well, Sam is only a couple hundred miles away." Ruby wiggled her eyebrows. "Supposedly, that is."

"I *promise* she's real," Maya insisted, though it'd be a lie to claim she didn't share any of Ruby's concerns.

"Have you guys even video-chatted yet or anything?"

Just as Maya's flush had started to go down, it immediately came back in full scarlet power. "Oh! Wow, would you look at that— we're already on my street." She quickly took her bag back from Ruby, slinging it over her shoulder and offering her a small parting wave. "Bye, Ruby, see you soon, but probably not until you're back from your faraway mountain ski party!" Her syllables were so rapid-fire they all came out as one long word.

"At least consider coming?" Ruby called out, watching from the sidewalk as Maya took her porch stairs two at a time.

"Bye, Ruby!"

~

FAMILY DINNER HAD JUST AS MUCH PROMPTING as Maya's conversation with Ruby had. If Maya's parents were so worried about her being lonely, what on Earth made them think that spending a whole week in the middle of nowhere with a bunch of popular kids would make her feel any less alone? The idea was ludicrous. She was tired of feeling like a pity case, some kicked dog that needed to be coddled and spoon-fed friendships as if she couldn't make her own. She had all the friends she needed.

The only thing that got Maya through dinner was knowing that Sam was waiting for her afterward. She rushed upstairs as soon as she cleared her plate, hopping onto her bed and opening her laptop with a haste that couldn't be matched by anyone other than a loser lesbian in their first relationship. But the messages waiting on her screen weren't at all what she'd expected. And as she scrolled down through their chat, her excitement quickly crashed into panic.

SAM: hey, i miss you :)

SAM: i know you're at dinner right now but do you want to call after?

SAM: i can't wait for this weekend, ruby just told me

135

everything and i'm bouncing off the walls at the thought of finally getting to see you!!!

Maya blinked. Then blinked again. Her fingers moved slowly, typing out the only thing she could think to say.

MAYA: what?

Three dots floated on her screen as she waited for Sam's reply.

SAM: the trip!

SAM: to the chalet?

SAM: ruby said you were too nervous to invite me yourself

Saying Maya saw red would have been the understatement of the century. She was on the verge of ripping her hair out, slamming her laptop into the wall, throwing herself out the window...

SAM: i thought it was cute :)

Maya's ragged breathing calmed slightly, face flushed from something other than anger as she read the message. But as fluttery as Sam's heart felt, her message did little to quell the rage boiling beneath the surface of her blush. She reached for her phone, pressing it to her ear so quickly that one could have missed her dialing Ruby entirely.

"What the fuck did you do?" Maya spat, but the panic in her voice canceled out whatever vitriol her tone implied.

"Did you talk to Sam?"

Maya could hear the smirk on the other end of the line.

"What do you think?!"

"I *think* it's about time you two met. And what better place for that than my trip? That way, I can meet her and see for myself whether or not she's worthy of my best friend."

Maya wanted to scream. Instead, she settled for teeth grinding so harsh that she'd probably receive comments about it from her dentist at next month's bi-annual checkup.

"You can't just *do* that, Ruby. She's my girlfriend."

"What?" She sounded almost offended. "I thought you guys weren't doing labels."

"That's not the point, and you know it!"

"It's not like you would have ever taken the initiative to meet her yourself."

"I would have when I was ready."

But Ruby ignored her. "You're not backing out of this, okay? Get your shit packed and be ready to go by tomorrow. I'll kidnap you if I need to."

And then she hung up before Maya could protest any further.

~

"I'M JUST SO glad you decided to take Ruby up on her offer," Maya's mom sighed when they pulled out of their driveway. "What got you to finally change your mind?"

Maya's grogginess was at an all-time high after staying up all night packing her bags. As if dressing to impress her first-ever girlfriend wasn't a hard enough task, she had to worry about the trip itself on top of it. What were you supposed to wear on a ski trip when you didn't know the first thing about skiing? What was the dress code for hanging out with your best friend and her snobby bully friends at a chalet for a week? What the fuck was a *chalet*?

"Making friends and meeting new people, I guess…" Maya mumbled in reply, her stomach letting out a loud protest of unsureness as she thought about meeting one new person in particular.

"Well, I hope to hear all about your brand new friends once you're back. And, Maya… I'm proud of you for going through with it even though it's pretty clear you don't want to." Her mom's voice was so genuine it almost hurt.

Maya knew how worried her mom was about her not being properly socialized, given she was about to leave for college. And if lying made her mom feel better about Maya, she'd take all the stomachaches in the world. Maybe if things went well enough with Sam, she could finally tell her parents about her. They'd probably known Maya was a lesbian long before she herself figured it out. That wasn't the problem. But entering a relationship with someone she'd never met in real life before was. If she passed Sam off as a friend of a friend of Ruby's, that was a pretty standard way to meet someone. Wasn't it?

The sickness in Maya's stomach grew every mile they crawled closer to Ruby's house, and she asked her mom to turn around at least three times before they reached her neighborhood. But her mother wasn't hearing it, even when Maya threatened to vomit all over the dashboard. She really felt like she could, too; all it would take was one sudden swerve of the car to get her rice and egg breakfast splattered all over the windshield. If anything, her mother almost seemed to find the whole thing amusing, and Maya had to admit her slight smile made her feel a bit better about the situation, too, as they said their goodbyes.

But the nerves returned as soon as she was on Ruby's porch, waiting to be let in, the doorbell echoing through the entrance hall of Ruby's near-mansion.

"Maya!" She beamed with surprise when opening the door as if she hadn't orchestrated this whole thing.

"Ruby," Maya sighed, unable to keep the slight smile off her face at the sight of her happy best friend.

But the smile fell to a flat line as Ruby opened the front door, revealing a swarm of popular kids from their grade, a handful plucked straight from some of Maya's nightmares. At least half of the room seemed to be made up of ex-bullies of hers. Ruby encouraged her to mingle while they waited for everyone else to arrive before boarding the bus. But Maya found herself slumped in the corner after realizing Sam wasn't even there yet. She couldn't tell whether the rumbling in her stomach was from relief or disappointment. And then her quiet corner was interrupted by a giddy Ruby, who slid down the wall to take a seat beside her.

"Waiting for Sam?"

Maya nodded.

"Nervous?"

Maya stared at her like she'd asked her whether the sky was blue. Was the sweat sticking to her forehead and the color drained from her face not telling enough?

"You know, this is probably the best way to go about things," Ruby said. "You guys probably won't end up at the same college or anything anyway, so this is kind of like, make it or break it. You know? If you don't click in real life, it'll be better to find out now before either of you are U-Hauling to your fancy art school together or whatever."

Maya couldn't help but laugh at that. "You may have a point there."

Ruby pulled herself back up to her feet. Then offered a hand to Maya. "Well, Liza just got here. She's the last person we're waiting on, so we can head out now."

Maya's brow furrowed.

"What about Sam?"

"She's already on the bus, silly!" Ruby replied like it was the most obvious answer in the world as if it had been Maya's turn to ask *her* whether the sky was blue.

· · ·

STEPPING ONTO THE PARTY BUS, Maya was reminded of astronauts taking their first steps outside their spaceship. She'd been one of the last ones to board, so she was fully prepared to scan every aisle as long as it took to find her sort of girlfriend. Luckily for Maya, a familiar face was waiting for her in the very first row of the bus.

Sam's chocolate waves fell past her eyes just like they did in all her pictures, though the deep hazel irises peering from underneath were something her photos never could have done justice. Maya felt like she'd been punched or, better yet, shoved face-first into the snow again. The air had vanished from her lungs quicker than her cool, and she could barely keep herself composed as everything became real. Someone pushed her from behind, and she practically fell into the empty seat beside Sam, who had caught her just in time. Sam turned Maya around so her head was in her lap, and Maya let her, because, what the hell else was she supposed to do?

"Hey," her sort of girlfriend said softly.

And in that moment, with that barely whisper of a wind chime voice, Maya realized that Sam looked just as nervous as her. She could barely hold eye contact, she could barely hold *Maya*, the soft hands underneath her back that had caught her fall were shaking. And was that dewy glow emanating from her actually... sweat? Maya was surprised that none of these things made Sam any less attractive to her, and that if anything, it only drew her closer.

"Hey," Maya whispered back, voice cracking on the single syllable as she watched the warm smile spread across Sam's face.

Maya... you might have won the lesbian lottery.

· · ·

WHILE RUBY and her friends got completely wasted towards the back of the bus, Sam and Maya slowly found their rhythm in the real world. Maya had met online friends IRL dozens of times before, but talking to Sam felt like such higher stakes.

Thankfully, Sam seemed to feel similarly. Their first five minutes were slightly awkward, but soon smoothed to a solid back and forth that felt like picking up where they'd left off on their keyboards. They updated each other about school and their winter break plans and theorized about what the trip would be like.

They got caught up on each other's personal lives and geeked out over the latest update to their favorite webcomic. They talked about what they packed and bonded over how embarrassing of a time they'd had trying to figure out what to bring on a ski trip when neither of them skied.

By the time night fell, they'd already reached hand-holding territory.

The drive was long, with twisty turny roads through huge stretches of forests Maya had never even heard of. She had somehow managed to doze off even with all of the rowdiness at the other end of the bus.

Ruby and her friends' whooping and cheering were no match for the comfort and coziness she and Sam felt in each other's arms. Maya was barely awake when she heard the bus driver warn of an impending snowstorm.

The chalet was by no means small, yet still managed to feel cramped with the amount of people Ruby had brought along. They all split off to pick their rooms, and Maya's heart ached as Ruby dragged her off toward their shared bedroom.

But as much as she wanted to spend the night with Sam, Ruby had made a decent point earlier about how it might be better to wait until they were more used to each other. As they got settled in, a very drunk Ruby was chomping at the bit for updates on how Maya and Sam were doing.

Unfortunately, she immediately passed out as Maya started unpacking, barely two sentences into her update. When Maya later woke in the middle of the night, she was disrupted by howling winds loud enough to make her question the structural integrity of a chalet. And when she looked out the window, she saw more snow than she'd ever witnessed in her life.

MAYA COULDN'T HAVE PLANNED A BETTER setup for the first day at the chalet. Ruby and her friends took off early in the morning to ski, leaving Maya and Sam all by themselves to explore their temporary home. Maya tried to keep her heart from leaping out of her chest every time their hands brushed over a door handle.

The first thing they noticed was the cellar, which was full of even more alcohol than Ruby and her friends had crammed onto the party bus. Just with a little more aged wines and whiskeys, a little less Fireball and peach Smirnoff. The second thing they noticed was that despite the absurd amount of alcohol now in their possession, there didn't seem to be a whole lot of food.

"Maybe Ruby is expecting a grocery drop?" Sam suggested.

"I think you may be overestimating Ruby's ability to properly plan in advance," Maya said.

When her friend returned from skiing, Ruby admitted it was odd. She'd requested that the place be fully stocked upon arrival so that they wouldn't have to worry about navigating foreign mountains in the middle of winter.

"Whatever, we can make a grocery run tomorrow," one of Ruby's friends, Nick, said with a shrug. "Town can't be that far."

Maya didn't like the lack of privacy in this place. She felt like all of Ruby's friends were watching her every move. Sure, none of this was sensitive subject matter, but she still didn't like the fact that anyone could listen to her conversations whenever they wanted.

"Yeah, and we don't even *need* groceries yet. You see all this booze?" Tyler called from the couch.

Maya crossed her arms over her chest. "Yeah? We'll see how you feel in twenty-four hours when you've got nothing but cheap beer sloshing around in your stomach."

"Maya, it's fine. We can go tomorrow," Ruby cut in through gritted teeth.

"With what car? We came here on a bus," Maya sighed, realizing now what an awful idea that had been.

"Chill, My." Coming from Ruby, the nickname felt more patronizing than comforting. "We'll order a cab from town."

Beside her, Sam gave Maya's hand a gentle squeeze. It was the only thing that kept Maya from pointing out the holes in Ruby's plan. Then the hand hold turned into an arm around the waist, and when Maya turned to face Sam, she caught a glimpse of the blizzard through the window.

～

"I JUST DON'T UNDERSTAND how you aren't even a little bit worried," Maya grumbled, fluffing a pillow.

"No use in worrying over things we can't control. This is a tomorrow problem," Ruby replied with a slight slur.

Maya wasn't sure she'd seen her sober since they entered the house.

"Ruby, no cabs are going out in this weather. Did you see that storm?"

"Just some snow," she sniffed.

"Try once in a century storm."

"Okay? And we'll go shopping once it lets up. Jesus, give it a rest." Ruby sounded irritated, like Maya was somehow overreacting for being concerned about the situation.

"I don't know why you're acting like this," Maya said.

Truthfully, she didn't know whether any of this was intentional. Was Ruby just tipsy with a short fuse, or was she genuinely annoyed over Maya's concerns?

"If you don't like how I'm acting, there's plenty of other places in this chalet to sleep," Ruby said.

Maya blanched. Surprise boiled to anger, then eventually soothed itself into relief. If Ruby was kicking her out of their room, so be it. Her friend was right. There were other places she could go if she didn't want to be around this behavior. And that place would welcome her with warm arms.

MAYA RESTED her head on Sam's chest, snuggling a bit closer for warmth to combat the cellar's chill. Sam's arms were wrapped around her protectively, and Maya cursed herself for ever agreeing with Ruby about not spending the night with Sam when they first met. There was nothing awkward about lying down with each other like this, though the bottle of merlot they'd downed together probably hadn't hurt.

"I just don't know where she gets off treating me like that," Maya said.

"Is it always like this between you two?" Sam looked concerned.

"Well... no," Maya said shakily. "I mean, not always. She's really great most of the time; she's my best friend, you know."

"But the other times..."

Maya closed her eyes with a soft sigh. "Sometimes I feel like she just keeps me around to make her feel better about herself. Like I'm a charity case to her. She can feel good for taking the loser lesbian under her wing, knowing I'll be grateful for that, no matter how shitty she treats me."

Guilt gnawed at Maya's core as the words left her mouth. How could she talk about Ruby like that so easily?

"Or maybe she's just drunk," she added.

"You might be, too," Sam said with a laugh that sounded like birdsong.

"Maybe," Maya nodded because it made her feel better about possibly shit-talking her best friend, even if it were all true.

"I'm really glad you're here," Maya admitted softly, lifting her head up to stare at Sam's wine-stained lips while she worked up the courage to meet her eyes.

"Me too... I've imagined holding you like this for weeks now."

That was enough for Maya to meet her eyes. "Really?"

"Yeah." Sam smiled, rubbing circles into Maya's back with her thumb. "I've imagined some other things, too."

Her boldness caught Maya off guard, and she went rigid in her arms.

"O-Other things? You mean like… holding hands, or maybe hugging, or—"

She cut herself off as Sam leaned down to kiss her, her eyes falling shut as her mouth opened to meet hers. She tasted like salt and sweet snow and merlot and everything Maya had spent the past few weeks imagining herself.

~

THE NEXT MORNING, everyone gathered in the living room, lolling on the various floor cushions and plush armchairs as Ruby held the old landline to her ear. Maya weaved her fingers between Sam's, her head on her shoulder as they watched. They'd been inseparable since the previous night, practically attached by the wrists since they'd bunkered down in the cellar.

When Ruby called them upstairs to help her figure out how to use the landline, she hadn't acknowledged anything from the night before, let alone apologized. Maya was disappointed but not surprised.

"I just don't understand. It was supposed to be fully stocked. I paid extra for food."

Maya could hear a confused sound from the other end of the phone, and then a muffled voice. "No, it looks like your reservation was cancelled when you guys never showed."

Ruby swallowed. "Never showed? What do you mean? We're here right now."

"Fuck," somebody murmured from the couch.

"It says here that nobody showed up at the address you put a reservation on. Where are you now?"

Ruby twirled the phone cord between her fingers, and Maya noticed she actually seemed nervous for the first time.

"I don't know…" she said, leaning into the receiver. "Look, can't you just come get us now? We've only lost one day."

"Way too much snow for us to reach you, wherever you are. I'm sorry." The woman on the other end hung up.

Maya stood, approaching her friend. "Ruby?"

"I don't know where we are," Ruby said, "but we're in the wrong place. This isn't the house I rented, which is why there's no food. The bus driver must have driven us to the wrong location."

"Okay, so we'll figure out where we are first and go from there," Maya said slowly as she saw the panic in Ruby's eyes. "Let's call the bus company."

Ruby nodded, then pulled out her cell to get the number. Once again, Ruby explained the situation, and the company was apologetic enough to agree to pick them up immediately. Except when they asked for a pickup address, Ruby had no idea what to say. None of them did. Their phones didn't get a signal this far out, so GPS was a total bust.

Ruby seemed as though she were about to spiral, so Maya took the phone from her. "Can you ask the bus driver who brought us here? Surely he must know where he left us?"

There was a pause, and when the man spoke again his voice was crackly, somewhat garbled like he was traveling under a tunnel.

"Unfortunately, his bus slid off the mountain early this morning, taking him with it."

Maya gasped, and Ruby looked like she was going to be sick.

And then the lights flickered once, twice, and after a third time, the power went out. Now the only light came from the few windows scattered throughout the living room, only hints of brightness sneaking in through the rapidly falling snow.

"Hello?" Maya said into the receiver.

There was no answer.

A WEEK WENT BY, and still no electricity.

The group had started sleeping together around the fireplace in the living room, trying to conserve heat and energy by sticking together. The remaining food was minimal. The alcohol was a lot. Ruby was folding under the pressure of the unknown, and Maya was struggling to lead the group without her support.

And as grateful as she was to have Sam by her side, it's not like the two lesbians in a group full of popular kids would have any kind of social power to sway people in the right direction. The only reason Maya succeeded in her suggestion to divide everything into rations was because Nathan's girlfriend, Amy, agreed and helped convince the rest of the group.

But the same night that they all agreed to ration out the food, Tyler broke into the food storage and ate nearly everything.

"I was starving!" Tyler snarled, baring his teeth at Amy as she tried to snatch the half-eaten bag of jerky from his hands.

"We're all starving," a girl groaned from the couch.

"Yeah, but I'm jacked. I've got more muscle than all of you combined," Tyler huffed. "A couple more days without protein, and my body will stop working."

"That's stupid," Sam said with what could probably be mistaken for bravery, but Maya knew it was just exhaustion.

"Yeah, and what are you gonna do about it now? Jealous because there's nothing left for you now, huh, Big Girl?"

"What's your fucking problem?" Maya scowled. She didn't like the implications of Tyler's weird fat-shamey nickname. Sam was tall, maybe just a head shorter than Tyler himself, but certainly not big in the way that warranted a fat joke. If anything, Maya was surprised that a weight comment hadn't been shot her way.

"Okay, everyone, calm down," Ruby interjected, waving her hands in the air.

Maya wanted to tell her that she didn't *want* to calm down, and she didn't want Ruby to just let this slide like she always did. But she kept her mouth shut, like *she* always did.

"What are we supposed to do now?" Nathan looked down at all of the empty food wrappers left over from Tyler's glutinous excursion.

Sam stared down at the food, too, then gave Maya's hand one more of those signature squeezes. "We need to get out of here."

AND SO IT WAS DECIDED, the three best skiers geared up early the next morning. The blizzard had finally let up, so they could at least try venturing out into the unknown to alert the authorities. The heaping mountains of snow were menacing, but nothing they couldn't handle with their buckets of experience. Graham had a couple skiing awards tucked under his belt. Jackson had been training under an ex-Olympic medalist since the age of four. Maya had no idea what Amy's background was, but she'd trust her with just about anything after she'd sided with her on rationing.

Everyone not chosen to go watched from the windows as they took off. But they'd barely made it twenty feet before a loud rumbling erupted through the mountains. Snow tumbled down, heading for the skiers. And the road.

Jackson disappeared first, then Graham. Amy tried making it back to the cabin, but she was swept away by a large boulder.

They had to hold Nathan back from running out the front door. His loud wail triggered yet another avalanche.

IT STARTED AS AN INNOCENT JOKE – who would they eat first? But as the group huddled around the fireplace, the question became more and more legitimate.

"You have to admit, it doesn't look good for us right now," Liza started cautiously, "we'll probably starve before we're found."

Ruby's jaw dropped. "But surely you're not saying we should?"

"No, no!" Liza quickly interrupted. "Well, not yet, at least…"

The silence was worse than deafening.

"So what, one of us then?" Asked Noelle, a hotheaded girl Maya recognized from AP English.

"What about the skiers?" Someone, a junior named Cade, piped up.

"Absolutely not," Nathan replied firmly.

"If they're already dead, it wouldn't be the worst thing in the world, right? We wouldn't have to, like, actually do anything bad…" Sofia said. She had been going to be one of the skiers before Amy volunteered.

"We'd be eating someone!" Ruby cried.

"Yeah, my *girlfriend*," Nathan said.

"It wouldn't work anyway. The bodies outside will be frozen solid by now," Nick stated plainly, without emotion. "There'd be no way to thaw them, and it's not exactly toasty in here."

The group went quiet for a while.

"If I were to pass while my friends were dying of starvation, I'd want my body to benefit them if it could. I'd just be lying there. I wouldn't know whether they ate me or not," Cade said after a few minutes.

"Well, I'll hold you to that then," Nathan sneered. He looked to Tyler for backup, but he was eerily silent, staring at something in the fire the rest of them couldn't see.

~

MAYA MISSED the privacy of the cellar she and Sam used to share, but it was far too cold to spend nights down there. They still got to cuddle up with each other in the main room and have their late-night conversations, even if they had to be slightly more hushed than before.

"You wouldn't really do it... would you?" Maya whispered.

"I mean, I guess it would depend on the circumstances. Are they already dead, or are we killing them for their meat?"

Maya didn't really like how intrigued Sam seemed by the idea, but some decent points had been made earlier around the fire. If someone was already dead and they were all next, why wouldn't they use an unfortunate situation to put themselves in a more fortunate position? There was something noble about it in a way, a sacrifice made without knowing that's what it was.

She hated herself for thinking about it so much. She

couldn't tell whether the sickness she felt in her stomach was from the thoughts themselves or the starvation.

"I don't think I could ever kill someone…" Maya said.

"Not even if it was essential? What if you were in danger? If they were threatening you?" Sam asked.

"Well, maybe then. But I'm not sure I could kill someone just to eat them." She paused. "Maybe if they really deserved it."

"What if it was me?"

"Kill you?" Maya tilted her head.

"Eat me," Sam clarified, holding back a smile.

"No way!" Maya gasped, then giggled when Sam shushed her. "I couldn't do that…"

"Not even if I gave you permission? Come on, if something ever happened to me, I'd want to make sure I gave you the best possible shot at making it out of here."

"I guess that's… kind of romantic?" Maya laughed, and Sam joined in soon after.

They lay in each other's arms like that for the rest of the night, debating the topic in hushed tones until they eventually drifted off together.

～

MAYA WOKE TO A BLOODCURDLING SCREAM.

She immediately noticed the lack of warmth beside her and whipped her head from side to side, searching for Sam amongst the sleeping (and some now awake) bodies.

Only to see Sam sprawled across the floor, with Tyler standing above her, a hatchet raised in his hands.

"Tyler, what the fuck!" Maya screeched, leaping onto her feet and charging towards him.

He faltered slightly, then lowered the ax as Maya approached. He swayed slightly. Was he… drunk? They had plenty of alcohol left, but there was something else off about him that seemed like much more.

"What do you think you're doing?" Maya demanded, trying to keep her aggression at bay now that Tyler had the ax lowered.

"I don't trust her," he raised an accusatory finger towards Sam on the floor. "I don't trust you either, but that's probably because I don't like you."

"So you're going to kill her because you don't like me? That's crazy."

"Is it?" He raised an eyebrow. "Weren't you two love-birds just chatting about that as you fell asleep?"

Maya blinked, then quickly shook her head. "We were talking about some hypotheticals, other situations outside of here where we would have to—"

"Are you sure about that? Cause you know, I wouldn't blame you for wanting a bit of revenge for some of the shit we've put you through these past couple years...."

"What's going on?" Ruby murmured wearily, sitting up from her pile of pillows. Her eyes widened at the sight waiting for her. "Oh— oh my God... Tyler, I said what's going on?"

"These dykes are scheming against the rest of us," Tyler pointed again, this time at the both of them. "All that shit we were talking about earlier, eating each other for survival and whatever... I have to say, I actually don't see any harm in that. And if we're going to start with anyone, it should be the person we know the least."

"The person *you* know the least." Maya hoped she sounded braver than she felt. "I know Sam, and I trust her."

"I trust Sam too," Ruby added, sounding exactly as confident as Maya wished she did. She made her way over to the two girls, putting herself between them and Tyler protectively.

Maya's shoulders slumped, touched by the gesture. If there was ever a time for Ruby to come to her defense in front of her awful friends, surely it should be when one of them was wielding a hatchet.

Ruby put her hands in front of herself like a warning. "So put the ax down, Tyler. We can figure out an alternative for food that doesn't involve hurting my friends."

"Or eating them," Sam added quietly.

Ruby looked horrified. "We are *not* eating Sam!"

"Oh, don't be two-faced!" A voice called out from the couch, and Maya turned to see Sofia. "You were bashing both of them with us last night. Don't act all high and mighty now."

"Sofia!" Ruby hissed.

Sam turned to look at Ruby. "What's she talking about?"

But Maya really wasn't paying attention. Because she knew that Sophia was telling the truth. And her head was swirling with every single moment she'd had to convince herself that Ruby cared about her. Truly cared about her, not just as an accessory or charity case or token gay friend. She thought about all the times she'd doubted whether or not Ruby talked about her behind her back the same way her homophobic friends did, all the times she wondered whether she hopped right in on the bullying she'd asked her friends to stop the second after Maya left. Her stomach churned, and it was only partially due to hunger.

"I didn't mean it like that, I just meant that... well, sometimes you have to let off steam about your friends, you know—"

"You know, the only thing worse than not actually caring about me is to pull the shit you're always pulling,"

Maya interrupted. "Do you realize how insulting it is for you to claim that you're an ally, to act like you actually give a shit about me and the awful lesbophobia your friends spew at me, only to be totally fine with them saying that stuff when I'm not around?"

"Maya, I—"

"No."

She glared at Ruby, hoping that the harsher she stared, the harder it would be to cry.

"You continually put me into situations with people who *clearly* do not like me. People who would be ready to swing a fucking axe at me and my girlfriend just because they're hungry. If you cared about me at all, you'd be taking that into account while making your guest lists." She choked on her words slightly, blinking back tears before continuing. "Do you know how horrible it is knowing that when you're not busy hanging with me out of pity, you're spending time with people who want me dead?"

"I don't think anybody wants you dead, Maya…" Ruby switched to her consoling voice, that soft Little Miss Perfect tone she shifted to whenever she was trying to get Maya to not just calm down, but back down.

"Open your fucking eyes, Ruby!" Maya nearly shrieked. "The only reason your friends haven't tried killing me before is because they've never had an excuse until now."

"But I protect you. I take care of you. I tell them to stop whenever I see that behavior," Ruby pleaded.

"But they never do stop, do they? You don't actually care about changing their morals. You only care about how bad they make you look," Maya said. "You're a bad friend. You're a *horrible* friend, and I don't know why it took me this long to figure that out."

Maya had completely forgotten about Tyler above

them. She'd even nearly forgotten about Sam until she heard her cry out.

"Guys!"

Maya shifted her gaze upwards just in time to see the hatchet swing down, a still fired-up Tyler staring her down with malice in his eyes. She squeezed her eyes shut as she heard the squelch of metal colliding with flesh, sinking into soft skin with a deafening sharpness. But she didn't feel anything. Not anything at all except the warm droplets hitting her thighs. Droplets that turned out to be red as she slowly opened her eyes. And not only were they red, but they were coming directly from the gaping wound in Ruby's chest.

"My…" Ruby gurgled her shortened name, blood spurting from her mouth with the single syllable.

"Ruby!" Maya let out a piercing scream. Ruby's eyes fluttered shut, barely noticing Sam struggling to stand up behind her.

The chalet broke into immediate chaos around them. Tyler pulled the hatchet from Ruby's chest while Nathan broke open a beer bottle, brandishing the sharp edges like a weapon. Liza grabbed a fire poker, and Cade lunged for a shovel. Sofia held a ski out in front of her like a cross between a baseball bat and an impractical shield. Everyone else ran for cover in opposite directions. But Maya barely processed any of it, too busy sobbing into Ruby's bloody chest as she clutched her body.

"Maya, we gotta go," Sam urged.

She shook her head.

"Come on, come on, come on… please, Maya!" Sam begged, eyes darting around the room.

Before she knew it, Maya was dragged away from Ruby and down to the cellar. She opened her eyes long enough to catch a glimpse of Liza impaling Cade with the fire poker, blood spurting across the wall behind them as Sam slammed the door shut above them.

~

THEY SPENT the next week locked in the cellar, waiting for the violence upstairs to quell. They created an elaborate locking system to keep the trap door shut. And burned old bits of paper for warmth, surviving on ancient tins of food and wine, listening to the screams from above. Maya couldn't shake the feeling of Ruby in her arms, the image of her blood-soaked body coming back every time her eyes fell shut.

Sam tried her best to comfort her, but no amount of convincing would help Maya process that Ruby's death hadn't been her fault.

The guilt was eating away at her. Why couldn't she have just been direct with Ruby before all of this? Why couldn't they have sorted out the kinks in their relationship before her best friend took an axe to the chest?

And how was she supposed to live with herself now, knowing the last words she'd ever spoken to her were those of malice?

All Sam could do was reiterate how glad she was that Maya was safe.

~

TOO THEY WERE STARVING. Their rations had only lasted so long, and the situation was becoming dire. The screams had stopped a couple days ago, but there were still footsteps upstairs. Until today, that is. Nobody had moved as far as they could tell, but then again, their sense of time was shoddy.

And now it was either rot away in the cellar or risk whatever danger lurked above. So they made their way upstairs. The main room looked like an abattoir. There were bodies everywhere, and not just bodies, but parts of them too. Liza's leg had been sawed off and lay a few feet from her body, and part of Cade's arm was missing. Everything smelled of rot.

"This is…"

Maya never heard the end of Sam's sentence because she stopped to spew up a mouthful of vomit.

"Who's missing?" Maya asked, scanning the room.

"There's Sofia, Liza, Cade…" Sam composed herself and started pacing between the bodies. "Nathan over here." And then she peered into the kitchen. "Nick and Noelle."

"Ruby…" Maya murmured, staring down at the rotting body of her best friend. She bent down and picked up the phone lying beside her, clicking the lock button to see a photo of herself and Ruby as the wallpaper. It was on airplane mode and still had some juice. She pocketed the device.

"Tyler," Sam added the name to their list in a tone Maya couldn't place.

She snapped back to focus. "Huh?"

"Tyler!" Sam called out a bit more urgently. "Maya, turn around!"

She did. Behind her, Tyler had crept up with the same hatchet, only now it was stained with blood.

Tyler swung down, and Maya dodged left. The axe got caught in between the floorboards. His head shot up to glower at Maya, his eyes full of something stormy and feral that she'd never seen before.

His chin and the front of his cable knit sweater were both smeared with blood, and the snarl from his lips reminded Maya of a caged predator waiting for its food to be dropped in the cage.

He grunted, pulling the axe from the floorboards, ready to swing again. But not before Sam snuck up behind him, tackling him to the ground with a loud thud.

"Maya, grab it!" She yelled, nodding towards the hatchet.

Maya did as told but trembled as soon as the weapon was in her hands. Where was she supposed to go from here?

"Come on, hurry!" Sam called, pinning Tyler's hands behind his back, shoving all her weight down between his shoulder blades to keep him on the ground.

Maya wasn't sure she could do it. And then she caught a glimpse of Ruby's body out of the corner of her eye. That's all it took. She brought the axe down on Tyler's neck, letting out a loud cry that drowned out the snap of flesh and crack of bone.

Sam stared up at her with wide eyes, blood splattered across her handsome features. Maya would have bent down to kiss her if it weren't for the loud sob that escaped her own throat when she dropped the axe to the floor.

AFTER ONE LAST debate of whether or not they could quite literally stomach eating Tyler, the two concurred that they couldn't handle it. Maya seemed more opposed to it than Sam did, but at the end of the day, neither was willing to go through with the act.

So, just like that, they prepared to die. They retreated to their cellar, opening another bottle of wine, hoping it would help the days pass faster. They fell asleep before getting even halfway through the bottle, their bodies weary and exhausted from lack of sustenance.

Maya woke up a few hours later.

Whatever was digging into her back had made it far too painful to sleep, and her body was mad enough at her to wake her. She dug around the blanket pile to find Ruby's phone. She'd forgotten about it.

She scooted a couple feet away from Sam to avoid waking her, then turned it on. Soft light filled the small room. She punched in Ruby's password and scrolled her photo album. Ruby and Maya at the water park two summers ago, Ruby and Maya at Ruby's first ever annual barbecue. Ruby and Maya at a picnic last spring, Ruby and Maya getting their ears pierced in middle school. Ruby and Maya posed in front of a poster at the theater. Ruby and… Sam?

Maya blinked, then rubbed her eyes just for good measure. But sure enough, there she was. Those same warm eyes staring through that mess of brown curls. She held her finger down on Sam's face, tapping a search button to see what other photos of her were in Ruby's phone.

And it was a lot. Probably more photos than Sam had ever even sent Maya before they met in person. Her vision blurred, mind swirling with confusion and the little bit of wine still in her system. She gripped the phone in one hand as she crawled back towards Sam, shaking her awake. It took a few tries, but eventually Sam yawned and stared up at her groggily.

"Maya? Hey, what's going on?…"

Her voice was sleepy, her guard let down. She was so soft, so sweet, it almost comforted Maya enough to forget the whole thing.

She held the phone up, bringing it inches away from Sam's face.

"What's going on in this photo?" She asked.

"Fuck," Sam breathed.

"Yeah?" Sam's reaction didn't instill any confidence in her doubts about her.

Sam sat up quickly. "Maya, I can explain."

"Great, because that's kind of what I'm asking you to do right now."

Sam bit her lip. "Ruby's my cousin."

Maya wished it didn't surprise her as much as it did. How had she gone this long without noticing any of their visual similarities? The hair, the eyes, the complexion that made them look like they'd been kissed by the sun itself.

"Ruby set us up because she felt bad that in all your time as friends, she's never seen you with a girlfriend. She wanted you to learn how to be in a relationship before the end of senior year so that you could be prepared for college."

Maya's mouth opened, a red tint quickly finding its way to her cheeks. Did Ruby really think she was that pathetic?

"She asked me to start talking to you because..." Sam trailed off; clearly, it was her turn to be embarrassed. "Well, I have a bit of experience."

"You sure didn't act like it," Maya said without thinking. "You were just as awkward as I was when we met."

"Because I liked you!" Sam almost laughed.

Maya didn't know what was so funny about this situation.

"I was supposed to break up with you by the end of the weekend so that you could use your newfound skills to try picking up girls in IRL rather than behind a screen. That's what Ruby said, at least. She hoped that after a two-week whirlwind romance at the cabin, maybe you'd see the importance of pursuing real relationships."

Maya blinked back hot tears, refusing to let Sam see her cry. "And you were just okay with that? You knew going in that you'd be breaking my heart?"

"I didn't know we were going to work so well! I didn't think either of us were going to catch feelings!"

Sam tried to move closer, but Maya shoved her back. Hard.

"What the fuck do you mean you thought neither of us would catch feelings!? You're smart, kind, and beautiful, and you treat me like I might be, too, like I'm something worth wanting. You helped me kill a man, and after we finished, all I wanted to do was kiss you. You told me I could *eat your corpse if you died*, and I thought it was the most romantic shit I've ever heard in my life. Fuck, Sam!"

Maya felt like ripping her hair out. And she was about two seconds away from doing it too, but instead, she stood up and headed for the stairs without another word.

"Maya!" Sam called.

But she pushed open the door and climbed upstairs without turning around.

She didn't know where she would go with all the snow, but she needed to put as much space between her and Sam as possible. She paced the main room, trying to avoid Ruby's corpse. It felt like some kind of cruel joke. Her friend's plan had been well-intentioned, but after everything that had happened, how was Maya supposed to see it that way?

She felt used and misunderstood and pathetic. But most of all, full of rage. Rage she didn't know how to direct.

She heard footsteps behind her. Sam.

"Why didn't you protect Ruby when Tyler attacked her?" Maya asked, turning around.

"Because I didn't want to die first," Sam said. "Better her than me."

"How can you say that?"

"You probably wanted it, too, right? With everything you said about her earlier?"

"You're horrible." Maya's voice was hoarse.

"So was she."

Something inside of Maya finally broke. Everything she'd done to try and remain rational flew out the window and before she knew what she was doing, she was reaching for the hatchet.

But Sam was onto her, and within seconds, she was *on* her.

She grabbed a fistful of Maya's hair and pulled, dragging her away from the axe, reaching for it herself. Maya's scalp burned harder than her tears, and she kicked and yelled until she finally elbowed Sam in the chin with a loud cry. Sam fell back but rebounded quickly, and seconds later, they were fighting for the hatchet yet again.

Then they rolled right on top of the open cellar door. And the two tumbled downstairs into the cellar's pitch-black darkness.

THREE MONTHS LATER, the snow was gone.

Grass had already begun poking through the rich soil surrounding the chalet. A car pulled up into the driveway, and a couple got out, eagerly unloading their suitcases before unlocking the front door.

When they walked through the entryway, the house

seemed clean enough, but it looked like someone else had already been staying there.

And then a girl walked down the stairs, dragging a hatchet behind her. She looked vacant, like a house with no one home. She was far too thin, and her hair looked as though it hadn't been washed in months. She didn't even acknowledge them before she walked right past them and out the door, heading for the forest.

The couple shot each other a look.

The husband pulled his phone and dialed 911. His wife made her way into the kitchen with their groceries. When she opened the fridge, she let out a shrill scream. A girl's head sat on the top shelf of the freezer compartment, brown hair, empty eyes. Beside the head, sat an icy note.

I got permission.

Substitute Student

DAVE PASQUANTONIO

Substitute Student

DAVE PASQUANTONIO

MR. BAGSHAW

Casey Rose. Leaning back in his chair, flipping his long hair, laughing like he doesn't have a care in the world. There's a kid like him in every high school. Smart, but uses his brains for evil instead of good. Gliding through life without any purpose other than to make everyone else's life miserable. A loser who's always winning. And now? Now, he wants to date my daughter, Piper.

He leans forward and whispers something to her, sending her into peals of laughter. She's laughing *with* him when she should be laughing *at* him. Why can't she see that? The other girls in class eye Piper with jealousy, and the other guys in class eye Casey like he's a war hero returning home.

I've dealt with Casey Rose for four years as his teacher. Every year, he takes my English class. Always the same superior attitude. I'd love to take a blowtorch and wipe that smug smile off his face.

. . .

CASEY

Mr. Bagshaw looks like he ate bad tacos. The last thing he wants is for me to hook up with Piper. And if I didn't like her so much, like *really* like her, I'd have already done it, just to see him lose it.

The thing with Piper Bagshaw is that she's the first girl in my four years at Thurber High who I respect enough not to just hook up with. And now that we've only got two weeks left of high school, I need to do something about it before we go our separate ways – her off to college, me off to ... somewhere.

Crap. Am I getting old?

MR. **Bagshaw**

Casey Rose ... Casey Rose ... what do I do about Casey Rose?

"Mr. B.," Casey's voice chimes out. "You teaching class today, or are you dead up there?" The class bursts into laughter. I glance up at the wall clock – I must have been too lost in my thoughts to hear the bell for the start of class.

"All right, all right, settle down," I tell the class. Piper looks at me strangely, then rolls her eyes. Great. Embarrassed in front of my daughter. Again. Embarrassed by Casey Rose. Again.

CASEY

Mr. Bagshaw looks like he's about to burst. I nudge Piper's chair in front of me and whisper, "Your dad is having a heart attack. You want me to call 911?"

Piper stifles a giggle – I can tell by the way she's shaking. She's so cute when she giggles.

"Mr. Rose!"

"Yes, sir!" I reply, looking straight at him.

"Something you want to say to the class?" Bagshaw snaps.

"Just worrying about your health, sir," I say. "You look a little flush."

Chuckles from the class. They've seen this dance before. Bagshaw is trying to figure out if he's just been insulted. He has. But you can't discipline a kid who is worried about your health, right?

"I'm fine, Mr. Rose," Mr. Bagshaw says, then adds, "Since you seem ready to talk, why don't you lead off our discussion of Melville? What are the major themes in *Moby-Dick*?"

He thinks he has me. He's never seen me crack open a book in class. But I've read them. And I understand them. I just don't let him see it.

"Obsession and revenge," I say. "Ahab is obsessed with the whale. All he thinks about is revenge. It'll kill him if he's not careful."

Mr. Bagshaw looks surprised. "Well, very good, Mr. Rose."

I add, "If only he weren't being such a Moby-Dick about it."

The class erupts in laughter.

More importantly, Piper erupts in laughter.

MR. **Bagshaw**

Things quiet down in class after I send Casey to the principal's office for bad behavior. He's been down there so often that they should name the bench after him. Piper keeps her head down for the rest of class. She looks ... well, she looks like I sent her romantic crush to the gulag.

But that's my job. I not only have to teach, I have to discipline. These kids are so close to getting through high school, and I don't need Casey Rose to screw it up for them.

I don't know how Casey has such good grades – heck, he's even got an A- in my class. For acting like he's never done a stitch of work, he always does the work. I just don't know how. Or when.

Piper can do so much better than Casey Rose. He'll ruin her life if they're together. I know that as a teacher. I know it more as a father.

CASEY

"And that's why investing in a portfolio of just a few index funds is your best bet for a solid retirement," I tell Ms. Harwood, the principal's assistant.

"Casey Rose," Ms. Harwood says, beaming. "Thank you. Is there anything you don't know?"

"Only the things I don't know yet," I say. She laughs. Adults love stuff like that, even if it doesn't mean anything.

"You know," she says, "there are only a few minutes left until the end of the school day. Why don't we forget this little visit? I'll tell Mr. Bagshaw that you were duly punished."

"Truly duly," I add. She titters. Now, off to the end of school. I text Piper. *Busy?* She replies immediately:

Free until 6.

I hit her up with:

Adventure time! Meet @ flagpole.

I actually do have a plan. I think it's something she'll like. I just have to make sure Daddy Bagshaw doesn't see us. I leave the office, run to my locker, dump my books, and grab my keys. Then something catches my eye. Was that a bald head poking out of a classroom? There's only one bald head in school. Mr. Bagshaw. He's spying on me. I dart behind a pillar. Game on.

MR. **Bagshaw**

He's up to something. I need to find out what. He's at his locker. He doesn't see me. He's smiling at something … something on his phone. He turns. I duck back into the classroom. I wait … five seconds … ten…

I peer around the door to see—

—he's not there. I look down the corridor. Nothing. I listen for footsteps. Nothing. Where could he have gone? A cough. From behind that pillar. I duck back into the classroom. I wait … five seconds … ten…

I peer around the door to see—

The far door closes shut. How did he do that so fast? I stride into the corridor.

Wham! I slip and fall, right onto my butt, and something, a lot of somethings, skitter across the floor. Marbles?

"Sorry, Mr. Bagshaw," says the voice — that voice — from behind me. I look up. Casey Rose. How did he get behind me?

"I guess I lost my marbles," he says, gesturing at the floor. My eyes go wide.

"Maybe you have, too," he adds.

"Casey Rose, you little—" The bell rings, doors slam open, and then I'm surrounded by students, all of whom start kicking marbles down the corridor and pointing at me, laughing.

"See you tomorrow!" Casey yells over his shoulder as he runs down the hall.

. . .

CASEY

"Always be prepared," no one ever told me because no one ever *had* to tell me. I came out of the womb knowing that. I run down the halls to the exit, too many shouts of "Hey Casey!" to fathom. This place is going to be so dull after I graduate.

I get to the flagpole before Piper, then lean against it, a long blade of grass jammed between my lips like I don't have a care in the world. Because I don't.

Between the walkers and the buses and the cars, the driveway in front of the flagpole is a madhouse, but eventually, Piper walks over, a big grin on her face.

"Hey, you," she says. She tosses her long hair back. "So what's the adventure?"

"The adventure is the adventure," I say, trying to sound enigmatic. She eats it up. From behind Bus 4, a bald head darts out, then back behind the bus. Then I think I see it poking out from *under* the bus. Mr. Bagshaw is on the hunt again.

"Come on," I say, taking Piper's hand in mine for the first time. It's soft, and she squeezes my hand in return. Nice.

"You should tell me where we're going," she says, sounding coy. "I don't know you that well."

"I'll be a perfect gentleman," I reply. And I will. "There's something I want to show you. You'll love it. I promise." We walk to my car — a 2000 Ford Mustang GT convertible, red, looking way better than it drives; I'd bought it with the money I'd earned in a questionable (according to some) pyramid "scheme" — and Piper hops in while I start it up. We drive out of the lot, the cars in front of us parting like a shark swimming through a school of herring. I glance at the rear-view mirror. There's a tan minivan a few car lengths back — and is that a bald-headed driver?

MR. **Bagshaw**

I keep about two hundred feet behind Casey and Piper. I'm sure my minivan blends in enough that Casey won't spot me. All my years of watching TV cop shows are paying off. I'm tailing them, and they have no idea.

CASEY

Mr. Bagshaw's minivan sticks out like a wart on a shaved pig. I crank some Green Day as Piper and I speed to our destination. Piper turns to wave to her dad, then throws her head back and laughs. This day could not get any more perfect.

MR. **Bagshaw**

With my baseball cap and sunglasses, they definitely won't recognize me. Casey's car, on the other hand, is the only ancient red convertible in town. It must be annoying for Piper to ride in that thing — her hair is a mess, and she seems to be waving bugs away from her face.

CASEY

In the center of town, I pull down a side street and park alongside an abandoned warehouse.

"And here we are," I say to Piper. She furrows her brows.

"The old cannery?"

"Much more than that today. Come on." We hop out of the convertible, and Piper offers me her hand as we walk around the side of the building to an adjacent lot.

"Close your eyes," I say to her before we round the corner.

"Hmm," she replies. "Casey Rose, where are you taking me?"

"Trust me." She does that oh-so-cute thing with her lips, twisting them, but her eyes are happy.

"Okay," she says, and she shuts her eyes. I take her hand again, lead her around the side of the building, and stop.

"Open your eyes."

Colorful tents form a U around a crowd of shoppers. Black balloons tip in the breeze, and the scent of burning rosemary and sage mixes with incense. She looks delighted.

"What is this?"

"A pop-up occult market," I explain. "They travel from city to city. It's one of those 'if you know, you know' things. They're here only for a few hours."

"It's amazing!"

We wander the stalls, still hand in hand, looking at beetles in jars, Tarot cards, stones, feathers, and many things I don't recognize. Ten minutes in, I see one thing I *do* recognize — a bald head with a baseball cap poking out from behind a tented stall selling banners with arcane symbols.

MR. **Bagshaw**

So that was the plan. Casey is planning to sacrifice my daughter to a pagan god. I knew that kid was trouble. I creep up behind them as they enter a stall marked only with the silhouette of a raven. I crouch behind a basket of willow twigs and listen.

"Welcome," says the proprietor, an old woman cloaked in purple. "Ask questions with your eyes, and the answers will appear." Her nonsense sounds like a poorly written fortune cookie. But I can see that Piper is entranced, while Casey looks so self-satisfied that I'm surprised he isn't urging the other shoppers to applaud him. I'll admit that Piper looks happy to be with Casey. But it's CASEY ROSE, a kid born wrapped in trouble and baptized in annoyance.

I don't know if that even makes sense, but it makes more sense than Piper falling under Casey's spell. I've got to stop this. Now.

CASEY

"This," says the shop owner, who is bedecked in violet and giving off an aura of wisdom, "is the Orb of Yearning." She holds out a blue-tinged glass sphere toward Piper. "What is it that you want? Think of it. Then touch the orb." Piper shakes her head.

"I don't know," she says, then looks at me. "Maybe you go first. Is there anything you yearn for?"

Now, *that* is a loaded question. Several things spring immediately to mind — most involve me and Piper whisking off to a tropical island — but I bat those away because I want to treat Piper properly. I want to respect her. Huh. This is new for me.

"I'll give it a try," I say. *What I want*, I think, *is to give Piper what she wants*. I reach for the orb, touch the tips of my fingers to its smooth, warm surface—

—just as another hand slaps the orb away, where it

shatters on the asphalt. Something tingles along my spine as the pieces of glass tumble across the parking lot.

MR. **Bagshaw**

"No sacrificing Piper today!" I yell after I swat the crystal ball to the ground. Whoa. That was a weird tingle. Must be the tingle of success. Then comes the yelling from everyone at once.

"Mr. Bagshaw!" Casey yelps.

"Dad!" Piper says. "What are you doing here?"

The old woman shrieks. She sounds suspiciously and irritatingly like a raven.

"Kasbah!" she adds, then claps her hands. The sound is surprisingly loud, and the shoppers in the area fall still. Then she starts chanting. It sounds like she's reciting the state capitals backward. I'm sure it's all nonsense, as is everything here. But oddly, I can't pull away from listening to her, and neither can Casey or Piper, it seems. Thankfully, she soon stops, then thrusts out both hands, pointing a finger at me and another at Casey.

"Comutati rezolva!" she says. Then she shapes her hands into claws and bares them at us. "Until then, go! Now!"

I feel another tingle. Casey has a weird look on his face, probably mirroring mine. Piper turns to me, her face a mix of loathing and disappointment.

"Dad!" she starts. "What have you done?"

CASEY

Piper is quiet on the first part of the way home. Then she breaks into tears as I drive. She's disappointed in her father, who she says is always trying to make decisions for her.

"He told me to stay away from you!" she says. "He doesn't want me living my own life. He's so afraid I'm going to get hurt!"

Part of me wants to say something stupid slash funny to belittle Mr. Bagshaw, who, I must add, doesn't need to change a thing to get belittled — he's a pro. But a little part of me I don't recognize comes out of nowhere and says, "He loves you. He's being protective. It's what all of us parents feel for our children."

Wait — what?

"Wait — what?" Piper says, looking shocked. "You have a child?"

"No!" I say. "I just…" Just what? What is that little part of me trying to say? "Look, Piper," I add as I near the school, "I — I mean, your dad — he's trying to protect you the best way he knows. I would never do anything to hurt you, I promise, but he's just doing his job." *If I were a girl's father, I wouldn't let them date Casey Rose, either.*

Where did that come from? Of course, I would. I'm what girls look for — I take chances, I do what I please, and sure, sometimes that means wounded pride, but I'm not *really* cruel. Am I?

Piper stays quiet until I pull into the school and park alongside her sedan. She drags her backpack out, slings it, then leans over and gives me a quick peck on the cheek.

"Thank you for today," she says, but she doesn't look thankful. She looks sad. "I'll see you in school tomorrow."

"I…" I start. Now, this is where I'd turn on the charm, say something so witty that the girl, whoever she is, throws herself back at me, and we'd take off for a night of fun and thrills. But right now, I have nothing. "Sure. You have a good night. And thank *you* for today."

She gives me a sad little wave and trudges over to her car. I need my backpack, so after she drives off, I use my (stolen) key to a maintenance door and walk through the silent hallways to my locker. Then I head for the main entrance and spot Mr. Bagshaw's minivan. He's sitting inside, alone, his hands gripping the wheel, a far-off expression blanketing his face.

Weirdly — very weirdly — I think I know what he's feeling. And double, weird, I feel the same way. This day is not turning out like I thought it would. A first for me.

MR. **Bagshaw**

At home, Piper locks herself in her room. She's not coming out for dinner. My wife, Marta, raises her eyebrows at me after I knock on Piper's door for the third time, asking to talk.

"Do I want to know what happened?" Marta asks after Piper again refuses to speak with me. I sigh as I plop onto the couch.

"Same thing as always. Casey Rose acted up, and I sent him to the office, so at least *that* was normal, but after school, he picked up Piper, and they headed for … ah, it doesn't matter. I think I really messed up this time."

"You followed them?"

"I didn't want to, but I couldn't *not* follow them. That boy is trouble. Piper shouldn't get involved with him. Especially not this close to the end of the school year."

"Maybe Piper needs to find that out for herself," Marta says, sitting next to me. "Or maybe you need to start thinking differently about this Casey Rose. People change. Kids especially change. If she likes him, let her figure out what's best for her."

"I can't sit by and let something happen to her," I say. "I wouldn't be doing my job as a father."

"Or you *would* be doing your job," Marta says.

I grumble. Mostly because she's right. The rest of the night passes in silence as I stew in my emotions before I head to bed.

CASEY

I race through what little homework I have before I shut out the lights and get into bed. There's the usual chatter on my phone, dozens of texts — *Are you online? Can you break into the teacher's computer system and get me the test answers? Are you up for meeting in the back room of Rosie's for baccarat?* The usual swill. Normally, my night would just be getting started, but tonight, I feel off for some reason. I must really like Piper. She's gotten to me. Hopefully, tomorrow will be back to normal.

MR. **Bagshaw**

Weird dreams kept me restless all night. In them, I was sneaking around the school, laying dozens of marble traps, hoping I would slip on them. Laying traps for myself? Whatever I ate yesterday, I'll pass next time.

I yawn, stretch, and open my eyes to see … a poster of Selena Grimes, a popular teen singer, tacked on the ceiling above the bed.

"Marta?" I ask, turning to her. "When did you—" I almost fall out of the bed. A twin bed. With no Marta in it. What the heck? I'm still dreaming. It's pretty realistic for a dream. I stumble to our bathroom, but there's a wall instead. I need coffee in this dream.

It looks like the bathroom is down the hall, so I walk

there. I shut the door, then grab a cup of water, shaking the hair out of my face. Hair? In my face? I haven't felt hair in my face in twenty years! I look in the mirror. I'M CASEY ROSE! Or at least I look like Casey Rose.

Wake up!

I pinch myself. "Oww!" Pinch. "Oww!" Pinch. "Oww!"

Footsteps from the hallway, a knocking at the door, then the door opens.

"What's wrong, Casey?" It's Casey's mom. I don't know her first name, but I know it's not Mrs.

"Mrs. Rose?" I say without thinking. She clucks her tongue.

"Master Rose," she says. "I heard you owwing. Dad took your car in for an oil change, so find another way to get to school."

Another ...

"What would that be?"

She looks annoyed, then says with great sarcasm, "Think of a time long ago when you didn't have a car. How did you get to school then?"

She tromps away. I turn back to the mirror. This has to be a dream, right? I can't really be Casey Rose. There's no way—

Wait. What did that old woman say before I tingled? Tabula rasa? Domo arigato? Dua Lipa? The crystal ball. The shattering. That weird tingling.

No.

There's no way this can be real.

But if it is ... where is Casey?

CASEY

"Wake up, sleepyhead," a voice beside me says, dragging me out of sleep. Phew. Weird dreams. In one, I was driving a minivan, chasing a red car, and I think I was also *driving* the red car. So, I was chasing myself? I need to lay off the late-night Mountain Dew.

"I'm getting up, Mom," I say, refusing to open my eyes.

"Mom?" the voice says. "We haven't roleplayed that one yet."

Huh? I feel someone's breath on my cheek. I rub my face, but I don't feel any hair. It's like my face goes all the way to the back of my head. Someone shaved my head in the middle of the night!

"Aagh!" I yell, opening my eyes and turning to see—

"Mrs. Bagshaw!" She wiggles her eyebrows.

"Well, hello, *Mister* Bagshaw. Feeling better today?"

She's wearing like next to nothing! And my bed is way too big, and she's way too close! I squeeze my eyes shut. What is happening? This woman is old enough to be my mom. And I don't know her first name. I'm guessing it's not Mrs.

"I feel … like I need to go to the bathroom."

"Well, hurry up," she purrs. "You know what we need to talk about."

I do not know what we need to talk about. I stumble to the bathroom. I'm afraid to look in the mirror. Also, my body hurts all over, and I feel like my weight doubled overnight. I close the door and flick on the light.

No.

I'm Mr. Bagshaw!

I bite my finger. Well, that hurts, so I must not be dreaming. I am definitely nightmaring, however.

This can't be happening.

Wait.

The occult pop-up shop. The shattered crystal ball. What did the old woman say? Commuting revolver? That doesn't make any sense.

I turn back to the mirror, sticking a finger into my cheek, my forehead, my way-too-big belly. I lift my shirt. Eww. I have gray hair on my chest! I really am Mr. Bagshaw. I need to get out of here. Now.

I leave the bathroom, and there's a knock on their — our — bedroom door. I freeze halfway between the bathroom and the bed.

"Come on in, honey!" Mrs. Whatever Her Name Bagshaw says. Piper opens the door.

"Piper!" I say, and without thinking, go to hug her.

"Gross!" Piper says, a look of horror on her face. "Dad, put on some pants, I don't need to see your underwear!" She turns and leaves, slamming the door.

"At least she's talking to you," my "wife" says. "Now get back here." She pats the bed. "We need to talk." Oh, we need to talk, all right. I slide into bed but keep myself on the edge and pull the covers up to my neck.

"A little shy today, are we?" the woman says. "That's definitely one we've played before. So: tonight."

"Tonight," I repeat, nodding.

"When Piper is at her dance class," she says.

"Dance class," I say, nodding some more.

"When we're alone," she stresses.

"Alone," I say, not nodding but shaking my head *no*.

"I was thinking these three," she says, then goes to grab her phone. She hands it to me, but I don't look at it.

"It's Thursday," I manage to say. "You're talking about Thursday tonight night." She looks at me oddly, as she should. I — he — I am an English teacher, after all.

"You need coffee," she says. "Yes, it's Thursday. Our Thirsty Thursday. I told you I'd stop by The Velveteer this afternoon for a new toy. Whichever one you choose from these three."

"A toy?" I ask because The Velveteer, which I know by

name only, isn't a toy store. It's some adult store that sells—Wait. I can*not* have this conversation. With anyone. I want to flee, but I can't make my body move. This is no occult spell holding me back, however — this is fear of whatever Mrs. Wife is going to show me.

"Fine, don't take the phone," she says. "I'll show you instead."

She opens her phone's browser window and scrolls through three pictures, showing me each. The first looks like a blown-up picture of an amoeba, except this amoeba is bright pink and the size of a fist. "This is The Juicer." I can't. The second looks like a bright blue burrito that got attacked by a woodpecker. "The Pompeii," she says. I really can't. The third is … if you took a fork, doubled its size, made it out of rubber, painted that rubber in camouflage, and gave it … are those suction cups? "The Oh My Godzilla," she says proudly. "This is my favorite, but it's your choice."

Then she gives me a wink. My stomach roils like I'm on a Tilt-A-Whirl plummeting off a cliff.

"I can't…" I start. "I mean, you know, you should, or could…" She frowns.

"Get all three," I say out of nowhere.

"Oooh!" my — his — wife says. "Thirsty Thursday and Freaky Deaky Friday!" She leans over to kiss me. No.

"I just remembered," I say. "I need to go throw up."

MR. **Bagshaw**

I've got to get to Casey soon before he screws up my life more than he already has. If I'm him, then maybe he's me. If he's not me, then there are two Casey Roses, and the world does *not* need two Casey Roses.

Thankfully, "Mom" has left me alone. I look around for

a tie and suit jacket, like normal, but I'm Casey, so I dress in an ironic tee shirt and jeans. I look around for my briefcase, but I'm Casey, so I grab his backpack. I go to trim my mustache, but I'm Casey, so I drop a dollop of hair gel in my — his — hair and comb it until I look presentable.

Now, what did Mrs. Rose mean by how I used to get to school? I think back. Casey used to walk. No. Casey used to take his skateboard. Down Puncher's Hill to the school. Too steep. I'll walk.

I glance at the clock in Casey's room. I'm late. On second thought, I'll take the skateboard.

CASEY

Logically, if I'm Mr. Bagshaw, then maybe Mr. Bagshaw is me. Me? He's going to ruin my reputation! He's the opposite of me! I need to figure this out. He won't have his number on my phone — I mean, I don't have his number on my phone — whatever. I know my number. He doesn't know my number.

As Mrs. Bagshaw putters in the kitchen, looking too pleased with herself about her upcoming purchases, I quickly shower, disgusted at the adult body I'm washing, and then dress.

Not much variety in Mr. Bagshaw's closet. White, pressed shirts, some suit coats, some ties. Hmm. You know, I don't look bad in a tie. I thumb through the collection. They're all boring. Then I notice a tie rack lodged far in the back.

I blow the dust off. These are really outdated, but they might be old enough to eventually come back into style. I choose a Christmas-themed one because why not? It's May. Skeletons wearing Santa hats on a garish green background? Perfect. I complete the look with a pair of unmatched blue tennis shoes. Mr. Bagshaw will certainly stick out today. On to the part of the morning I'm dreading, saying goodbye to "my" wife.

"All set," I say as I trudge downstairs. "I'll see you after school."

I head for the door.

"Come here, Tiger," she says, stopping me. "Give me a proper goodbye." In for a penny, in for a pound, as old people say. She reaches for me, and I give her a deep kiss, maybe more than she's expecting. But the way she looks at me after, I think that's their normal goodbye.

Not only am I not hungry for breakfast, I think I'll skip every meal for the rest of the day.

"Gross!" comes a voice from behind me.

"Piper!" I squeak, then remember and lower my voice. "Umm, Piper, honey. I'm sorry about yesterday."

"Whatever," she says.

"Do you want a ride?" I ask, jangling the minivan's keys. The missus and Piper look at me like I've grown horns.

"You never ask if I want to ride with you," Piper says.

"Well, I used to, I know," I say, not knowing, "but maybe we can talk on the way." Something happy briefly crosses her face, but it's gone as quick as it came.

"Thanks, Dad, but I have dance after school, and you'll be in bed before I get home."

Mrs. Bagshaw steals a quick glance at me that says, "He sure will." No eating for a week.

"I've got to go," I say. "See you at school, honey." I head out before I can see her reaction. I sit in the minivan until Piper peels out of the driveway. I want to leap after her and tell her to slow down, but I'm guessing I've done that a million times, and she's never listened to me.

I call me. Ring, ring, ring. "You missed me," my voice-mail says, "but not as much as I miss you." *Beep!*

"Mr. Bagshaw!" I say. "It's Casey. I'm in your body. I'm guessing you're in mine. We need to talk."

He's an adult. He'll know what to do. Right?

MR. **Bagshaw**

There's a ringing coming from my backpack — actually, not a ring, but the heavy beats of a 70s disco song — Casey's ringtone. I've heard it too many times in class, then seen him take calls like he's a lawyer before an important case. The attitude on that kid. But I don't answer the call because I'm too busy trying not to die. Puncher's Hill looks steep from my minivan. It's three times as steep-looking from a skateboard.

I've skateboarded before, back what feels like a thousand years ago, and I'm in better shape now in Casey's body than I ever was in mine, so I crouch and let gravity tug me along.

Whoosh, past a lady walking a poodle.

Whoosh, past a car pulling out of a driveway. The long honk of the horn spurs me along instead of stopping me and making me apologize. Something about this body feels so … carefree!

Now I get into it. *Swerve* around a parked power company truck. *Swerve* around a stopped school bus — the driver shakes her fist at me, and Casey's going to get into trouble for that, but this version of me doesn't care. *Swerve* between a couple holding hands as they walk on the sidewalk, ducking under their arms. I look back to see them shoot two fingers at me.

"Woohoo!" I yell out. This feels like freedom. I hope I beat Casey to school.

. . .

CASEY

Kids, not answering their phones.

I drive like an old person to school on purpose, seeing what it feels like. I stop at every yellow light, I use my turn signal a thousand feet before the turn. I hammer the brake pedal like it's a heartbeat. The traffic piles up behind me. I can be late and not get written up for it. Bonus!

I pull into the school and head for the teacher's lot, purposely taking up four spaces and leaving the flashers on. I grab the Bagshaw briefcase.

"You're late," an ancient teacher, Ms. Cromwell, says as she gets out of her car, eyeing my parking job with suspicion. Ms. Cromwell is mean. *Mean* mean. Crotchety Cromwell, the kids throughout the decades have called her. I think she's been teaching since before there was electricity.

"You're late, too," I say to her.

"I don't have class until second period, Mr. Bagshaw. Which is in twenty minutes."

"You haven't had a period for sixty years, Iris." The horrified look on her face is all the breakfast I need. I strut into the school, then into the office.

"You're late," the office lady says.

"Better late than never," I say, then sit down and grab my phone.

"Aren't you supposed to be in class?" she asks.

"Eh, class. Class, class, class. Everyone worries too much about class. Call the room and send them to the library. They've worked hard all year. They deserve a day off."

"I, uh, I don't know about that," she says.

"Whatevs." I open my phone and look at Mr.

Bagshaw's bookmarks (boring) and apps (boring) and emails (boring) and texts (boring, except for those from his wife — definitely not boring). Eventually, I order a same-day delivery of adult diapers to the school — please rush to Ms. Iris Cromwell.

"Mr. Bagshaw?" the lady says.

"Huh?" I ask.

"What are you doing? You've been here for half an hour."

"Wordle. Gotta keep the ol' mind sharp. Can you call Casey Rose to the office? Wait, not here. Find Casey Rose and send him to the theater department dressing room." She looks befuddled.

"There's no theater class this morning."

"I know that, Jane."

"Brenda. My name is Brenda."

"You old people and your labels. Let me ask you this: are you still sleeping with the gym teacher?" She drops the phone's handset and blushes so hard, so quickly, that I'm afraid her face is going to explode.

"What are you talking about?" she stutters.

"Oh," I say, "This isn't about talking. This is about, well, you know." I get up and grind my hips against the chair. "The old drop down and give me five, you know what I mean, Brenda?"

She puts her head down on the desk and begins moaning, "No one was supposed to find out."

"Casey Rose to the theater department dressing room, remember?" I tell her. "Don't worry, I'll keep your secret. Not that everyone doesn't already know." I open the office door to leave, then add, "Also, whoever's responsible for cleaning this pigsty of a school needs to get fired. There are marbles all over the floor."

MR. **Bagshaw**

"Ooh, Casey's in trouble!" the class choruses as I hear my name called to the office. Wait — the theater department? It's got to be him/me. I gather my stuff and look apologetically at the teacher.

"Sorry, Ms. Cromwell. I don't know what this is about." She doesn't seem to care as she puts her head down on her desk and sobs.

"He called me old and dried up!"

Teachers and their drama. I try to avoid it. Someone knocks on the door.

"I have a package for Iris Cromwell." She sees the package and shrieks. The kids burst out laughing. I slip out of class and head cautiously to the theater department. Once there, I head to the dressing room, and inside, I find—

—me.

"What am I wearing?" I ask, indicating the tie and sneakers.

"Jazzing you up," he says with a big grin. "You gotta loosen up, Mr. Bagshaw."

"Casey, what is going on?"

"I've been thinking about that," he says cockily. "That orb you broke—"

"We broke."

"You broke."

"We broke."

"Enough, young man!" he snaps, then grins. "I always wanted to say that. Anyway, the orb. I think that woman put a spell on us. Caused us to switch bodies."

"Well, I don't want to stay in this body," I say. Casey Bagshaw looks hurt.

"What's wrong with my body?"

"I'm not a teenager, Casey. I'm a married man."

"You sure are," he says. "It's Thirsty Thursday, and your wife is parched. Don't worry. She'll get a tall glass of Mr. Bagshaw tonight."

"You fink!" I say, realizing that no teenager says fink. "If you touched her…"

"Don't worry," he says. "But really … Oh My Godzilla?" *Great.*

"Can we just concentrate on this body switch situation and how to fix it?"

"I've got an idea, but we can't go until after school."

"No," I say. "I need out of this body and back into mine now."

"No can do," he says. "It's the occult pop-up place. It's not in town. There's another one today, but it's ten miles away and doesn't start until three this afternoon."

"No," I moan.

"And to add a cherry to the sundae," he says, "we've got two bigger issues to deal with first. Actually, three."

"Three?" I ask.

He ticks them off on his fingers. "First, I'm teaching your class in fifteen minutes. Second, Piper is in that class. And third, today is the Open Session assembly." Great. At Open Session, the entire school gathers in the auditorium and airs issues and grievances in a safe environment.

"Not that. Not today."

"I have to say, Casey," Casey tells me, "there will be some *very* fresh grievances aired today."

CASEY

"Excellent, Piper," I say after she responds to my question about Melville's use of setting. Well, she didn't exactly volunteer to answer the question. I called on her. She's been avoiding looking at her "father" all class, keeping her head down, but I wanted to get a good look at her from up front here in class. She is *so* cute. Those eyes. Mr. Bagshaw is right. I need to get out of this hairy old body and fast.

"Casey" raises his hand. I avoid recognizing him.

"Mr. Bagshaw?" he finally asks.

"Hmm?" I reply. "Yes, Mr. Rose?"

"Can you explain the ending of *Moby-Dick*?" I start. I hadn't gotten that far. Obviously.

"I read ahead," he says with a smirk — a smirk! The insolence of these students. "I have a question about the ending."

I have no idea how the book ends. I'm assuming badly for everyone. "Ah, no need for spoilers, Mr. Rose," I say. "We don't know if the rest of the class has finished."

"Are you saying, Mr. Bagshaw, that my pursuit of knowledge should be halted because I'm an overachiever?"

"Ooh," the class choruses. Putting me on the spot like … I would? Fine, Fake Casey.

"Do you have something specific, Mr. Rose?" I ask.

"Well," he starts, sounding all too proud, "Ahab and the White Whale … one's fate is known, and one's fate is not. I'm drawn to Fedallah's prophetic dream about hearses earlier in the novel. Is Melville adding a speculative element here that we should fully embrace, treating the story as a fantasy not based in reality, or should we ignore Fedallah's prophecy and treat his dream as a symbol of man's uncertainty and belief in a higher being, subjecting humanity to a deterministic fate rather than forging our own destiny?"

My brain became full from digesting that word salad, full of ingredients I'd never heard of.

"Let's turn that over to the class for discussion," I decide. I glance around the room. Most students' jaws have dropped because the Casey they know would normally have made another *Moby-Dick* joke. "Who else has read to the end?"

Murmurs, of course. Eye avoidance, of course. Then, one hand cautiously raises.

"Yes, Ronald?" I ask the red-haired slacker (and my sometimes partner in crime).

"I only read the end, Mr. Bagshaw," he admits. The class laughs. I let out the loudest, most inappropriate laugh I can.

"Excellent, Ronald! Cutting right to the chase — and saving time to boot." The class falls silent.

"Tell you what," I say. "Anyone who can provide me an excellent title for a never-to-be-made sequel to *Moby-Dick* gets an A for the term!"

That's how you get hands to raise.

Piper looks as confused as she's ever looked. She looks to Casey slash Mr. Bagshaw, who looks like he has no idea what to do. He can't speak out against the teacher — normally, I'd be first in line to try to worm an A this way.

After I hand out some A's for sequel titles like *Moby-Dick 2: Electric Boogaloo* and *Moby-Dick 2: Die Harder,* and *Moby-Dick 2: The Dick Strikes Back*, the bell rings.

"To the auditorium for assembly, kids! Also, there's no homework tonight!" I say as the students leave. Several give me a high-five. I don't think the real Mr. Bagshaw has ever been high-fived. Except possibly by Mrs. Bagshaw after 'Slinky Sunday.' Eww.

Piper remains in her seat, as does Casey. Methinks trouble is afoot. Huh? I'm beginning to talk like a dorky English teacher. I need to get out of this body.

"Mr. Bagshaw?" Casey starts.

"Mr. Rose," I say, "Can you wait in the hall?"

"But," he says, eyeing me, eyeing Piper, eyeing the

floor, "Uh, sure." He slinks away. I close the door behind him.

"What is it, Piper?" I ask. She alternates between looking angry and looking hurt.

"What has gotten into you, Dad?" she asks, sounding like she's going to sob. "You follow me and Casey and make a scene, and today you act like a teenager when you should be teaching, and I heard that you called Ms. Cromwell a wrinkled prune and—"

"Wait," I interrupt. "You've got that wrong."

"Which that?" she asks.

"The part about Ms. Cromwell. Prunes are already wrinkly. There's no need to modify them."

"Ugh!" she says, stamping a foot. "Just leave me alone! I don't ever want to talk to you again!" She marches out of the room.

Casey says to her, "Piper, stop!" but her footsteps slam down the hallway, growing fainter, then disappearing. Casey boils into the room.

"What did you say to my daughter?" he snaps.

"She had a question about fruit. Just one more thing I adore about her." He stomps his feet like Piper did. It must run in the family. I've never seen *me* lose my cool like that before. It's very unbecoming.

"Look," he says, taking a step back and a deep breath to calm himself. "We need to work together. This is no good for either of us."

"We will," I promise him. It's a false promise. I can only hope that finding that occult pop-up market will work. "But first, it's time for Open Session."

MR. **Bagshaw**

At Open Session, the teachers and students sit together

in the auditorium. If you have an issue, you walk to the front of the room and line up for your turn at the microphone. Anyone can say anything — what's working in the school, what needs improvement. What it's not supposed to be is a forum for gossip or finger-pointing.

I usually sit up front, but that's when I'm a teacher. Today, I sit in the last row. Casey is usually surrounded by his entourage, students who either want to be like him or who have helped make him who he is — trouble.

Today, the usual suspects gather around me, but I pop on a set of headphones I'd found in Casey's backpack and pretend to be disinterested in everything around me. In reality, I need to stay sharp. I smell trouble in the air, trouble that smells like Casey Rose. Unfortunately, today, that's me.

Principal Pratt strides to the microphone, lowers it — she's as short as a toddler — and begins the assembly.

"Welcome, students and staff, to Thurber High's Open Session," she starts. "Please raise your hand to be acknowledged, then walk to the front for your turn to speak."

Open Session always starts slowly, with no one wanting to speak, then a teacher or two will prod the kids into action by saying something generic, like "I'm excited to see so many engaged students this quarter." Eventually, a kid or two will say something. It's a waste of time, honestly. Today, a sea of hands shoot up. This can't be good.

Principal Pratt looks delighted at all the hands. "Excellent!" she says. "Let's start with Ms. Cromwell." Iris Cromwell totters to the microphone.

"I have an issue with you, sir," she says, pointing at Casey-me. I'm stunned. Iris and I have always had a cordial relationship. "Mr. Bagshaw," she continues, "is incredibly disrespectful. He accosted me in the parking lot this morning and said something quite unseemly. He also took up four parking spaces, and then he sent me a package of adult diapers." I jump out of my seat.

"I didn't do that!" I yell out without thinking. Heads turn.

"Uh," I say, sitting back down, "I mean, *I* didn't do that. For once, it wasn't me."

"Right on, Casey!" Ronald says. Mrs. Cromwell returns to her seat, shaking a finger at my body. Casey as me guffaws.

"She's only mad because I didn't leave enough room in the lot for her horse and buggy," he yells. The students whoop in surprise.

"Mr. Bagshaw!" the principal barks out as she approaches the microphone. "Harassing a colleague is against Thurber High's code of conduct. You should know better."

"Can someone get Principal Pratt a stepstool?" Casey yells out. "Principal, how are things in the Land of Oz?"

"My goodness!" Principal Pratt says as the room erupts in laughter (students) and shouts (staff). Casey is trying to sabotage my reputation.

I stand, then scan the room for Piper. I can see the back of her head getting lower as she slumps in her seat, obviously embarrassed to have the last name Bagshaw. I force my way out of my row, then run to the front of the room and grab the microphone.

"Mr. Bagshaw is just covering for me," I say to the crowd. "That was me who parked that way, and that was me who said something mean to Ms. Cromwell. I was in costume."

Raised voices from the students — Casey Rose never apologizes!

Ms. Cromwell looks perplexed. "I'd swear that that was

Mr. Bagshaw," she says to the teacher next to her. "But now I'm not so sure."

"You should be sure, Ms. Cromwell. Mr. Bagshaw just made fun of the principal, too," a voice shouts out. "We just heard him."

"You heard him wrong, then," I say.

"He said she was from the Land of Oz," a student shouts.

"Because she's so short!" another student shouts.

"Oh," the first student says. "I thought it was about Dr. Oz."

"No, he said she was from the Land of Oz."

"Doctor Oz is from the Land of Oz? That's cool. I'd like to have a country named after me." Do they think Oz is a *country*? Have we done nothing as teachers?

"Principal Pratt," I say into the mic, "Obviously, geography is one area where our students need more education. I would like to propose an hour of mandatory geography homework every night for all students from now on."

Whoops erupt from the teachers and groans from the students. "I'd also like to propose," I add, wanting to sabotage Casey some more, "that we eliminate student parking. From now on, all students should either walk or take the bus. We have to think about our planet. Teachers, of course, should continue driving. We need to respect our elders."

Now, the auditorium is in an uproar. Piper is shaking her head. Casey-as-me stares open-mouthed.

"I am surprised at you, Casey Rose," the principal says from next to me. She sounds suspicious.

"I am, too," Casey-as-me adds, glaring.

The rest of the session devolves into accusations and gossip-mongering. It's exactly what the school does not need — so why does it feel so good? I may look like Casey, but I'm really a teacher and a good one at that. It's because of this body. It's because I'm feeling young again. Young and stupid.

What Casey doesn't know, and what I've never told him, is that I used to be Casey when I was younger — a rebel, a disruptor, the student that teachers never wanted in their class. It's what attracted my future wife to me. Her love of the "bad boy"… she still sees me like that. Or at least she wants to see me like that. I broke a lot of hearts and caused a lot of misery before I grew up and realized that I was wasting my life. Deep down, I know that's why Casey Rose affected me so much through the years — because I see my old self in him.

Of course, I've never told Piper any of this. To her, I'm a boring father who she's forced to see every day in school. If she knew the real me, maybe that would change. And maybe I shouldn't be so protective of her. Maybe I should let her fly instead of keeping her in a cage so she can't get hurt.

CASEY

Part of me is overjoyed that *Fake Casey* was so disruptive at Open Session. But, weirdly, part of me was proud of *Fake Casey* for proposing things like more homework. I know that Mr. Bagshaw went way over the top, as did I — we are digging at each other like this while we can.

But there's a part of me that feels … wiser. Maybe it's this out-of-shape body. Before this, I just saw Mr. Bagshaw, and most of the teachers, as old adults standing in my way. I never realized until now that someday I will be that "old adult," and the next generation will annoy me as much as I annoyed those who came before me. Stupid wisdom. It was getting in the way of my fun.

As Open Session concludes, Principal Pratt strides over to me and leans in. "My office, now," she says sternly. "And bring Casey Rose."

MR. **Bagshaw**

"We need to work together," I whisper to Casey as we sit side by side outside of Principal Pratt's office, waiting to go in. "We need to get to that pop-up market."

"I know," he whispers back, then adjusts his — my — tie. "How do you wear these things every day? I'm choking!"

"How do you think I feel?" I gesture at the ratty tee I'm wearing. "I'm freezing! I'd have thrown a cardigan over this if I'd found one in your room."

"You're cold because you're old, plus I don't even know what cardigan means!" he hisses. Casey brings out my phone.

"Speaking of good looks, your wife sent you this." He thumbs open my texts and hands the phone to me. In the picture, Marta is—

"Sexy, right?" Casey asks. Inside, I rage, but I can't explode here.

"Casey, if you even think about sharing that picture or telling anyone about it ..." He actually looks concerned.

"I wouldn't," he says, and weirdly, I believe him. "She loves you, and you love her. If anything, I'm jealous. Not of her, but of what the two of you have." He hands the phone to me.

"You keep your phone, and I'll keep mine." I give him his, and then we each disable the face recognition — we'll rely on our passcodes. "I don't want to intrude on your private life, I mean, any more than I have." Ordinarily, I'd snap that he's done more than enough damage, but then I remembered this wasn't his fault. If anything, it was mine for not trusting him with Piper.

"We got into this together. We'll have to get out of it together." The principal's office door cracks open.

"You two," Principal Platt says. "In here. Now." After we're seated and she shuts the door, she turns up the heat. "I don't know what's gotten into the both of you today." She points to me. "Casey, I don't know what you were pulling at the assembly, advocating for more homework and no student parking, but I know you're up to no good."

"But—" Casey starts, then shuts up.

"But what, Mr. Bagshaw?" she says, turning to Casey. "You're defending him?" I never realized how confused I look when I look confused.

"I can explain," he says, then turns to me. A cold shiver runs up my spine. I don't know what he has planned.

"Casey and I have been meeting out of school," he explains, "to help him prepare for his college applications. Yes, he's applying later than he should, but he put off deciding to go until he knew it was the right decision. Last night, we pulled an all-nighter at my house, with his parents' permission, of course. I was overtired — my all-nighter nights were a long time ago, and I was half out of my mind. I've apologized to Ms. Cromwell — Iris — and I was speaking gibberish at the assembly. It won't happen again. I take full responsibility for this."

I'm shocked. Those are words that would come out of my mouth, not Casey's. Is this the start of another devious plan? I didn't even know he was thinking about college. For some reason, I believe him.

"I see," says the principal. She turns to the window, seemingly lost in thought. I glance at Casey. He quickly nods as if to say it'll be all right.

"And Ms. Pratt," he says, "I think Casey and I should dismiss ourselves for the day. Get some rest. Tomorrow, everything will be back to normal. I promise."

"Now that is an excellent idea, Mr. Bagshaw," Principal Pratt says. She turns to me. "You are lucky, Casey Rose, to have caring adults like Mr. Bagshaw in your life. You two can go."

CASEY

Mr. Bagshaw and I both text Piper, but she doesn't answer because she's in class — or, more likely, she wants nothing to do with either of us. Mr. Bagshaw is driving his minivan. I look over at him as me in the driver's seat. Me, driving a minivan? It's not a good look. I've pinned down where the pop-up market is — they've set up in the parking lot of a shuttered strip mall a few towns away.

"Watch the speed!" I say. He turns to me.

"I'm not speeding."

"That's the problem!" I need to get out of this body. It aches constantly. Is this what it's like to get old? I give directions, and soon enough, we slide into the parking lot and race to the market. Mr. Bagshaw beats me by a good thirty seconds — this body is not meant for running.

"Slow down!" I pant.

"Can't," he says. "I've already had two Four-Hour Energy drinks. I had the weirdest craving for them. I couldn't slow down now if I tried."

That's because I live on them. Once at the market, we pace the perimeter until we spot the tent with the raven silhouette.

"Not open," the old woman says without looking up as she places items on tables. She's right — the market doesn't open for almost two hours. But this is an emergency.

"We're back," I say. She glances up, then recoils.

"You!" Then she lets loose a tirade I don't understand. I pull out my phone and pull up my translation app. "Can you repeat that?" She sighs, then says the same thing, only slower. I show the ragged translation to Mr. Bagshaw.

"That's incredibly rude," he says.

"And anatomically impossible," I add. The woman glares at us.

"You are…" Then, she moves her hands in a weird way.

"Switched," I say. Mr. Bagshaw nods in agreement. She shakes her head as if disgusted, then beckons us over and pulls out a metal bowl. Inside are what look like the pieces of the smashed orb. She indicates the bowl, then shakes her head.

"Permanentay." I don't need a translation for that. "It can't be permanentay!" Mr. Bagshaw steps forward.

"Ma'am," he says, "we can't stay this way!"

"What to do?" she says. "The orb, she is…" She picks up a piece, then drops it back into the bowl.

"Broken," Mr. Bagshaw and I say in unison.

MR. **Bagshaw**

I take Casey aside. "Let me handle this." He looks shocked.

"We're going to be stuck like this." I give his shoulders a shake.

"Casey, part of being an adult is dealing with things we don't like, to face them head-on. There's always a solution." He sits, and I lead the woman over to two chairs and pull up my own translation app. I can't pin down her exact language—some Hungarian, Romanian, maybe Italian—but after several minutes, I learn what we have to do.

"So here's the plan," I tell Casey as we walk back to the minivan. "The orb is broken, and that means she can't switch our bodies back herself. No one can."

"But there's no orb!" Casey whines. I've never heard him whine before. I hope he's not getting that from me.

"There's another way," I say, "but it has to be done before midnight, then we'll switch back at midnight."

"I'll do it!" he says. "Whatever it is, I'll do it!"

He looks so joyful that I don't have the heart to tell him that if this plan doesn't work, we won't switch at midnight — and we'll live out our lives in the wrong body.

CASEY

I'm at a loss for words. Which never happens. One of us has to help the other get the one thing they truly need—and do so selflessly?

"Are you sure you got the translation right?" I ask. "Maybe she meant 'selfishly.' Now that I'd be good at."

"We can't scheme, Casey," he tells me. "We have to work together, and we have to do so honestly. Or at least we have to be honest with each other. That's all I could get out of her."

I'm at a loss. I can't *not* scheme. It's how I've gotten through life, along with luck (and great looks and extremely high self-confidence). I don't know if I can do this. We lean against the side of the minivan and talk through it.

"What is it that you truly need?" Mr. Bagshaw asks me.

"Hmm." Honestly, I have no idea. I live life from moment to moment. Why worry about the future? Why care about the past? That, I realize, is what being an adult is. You have to think about the past *and* the future — *and* you have to put other people's needs ahead of your own.

"Maybe this isn't about me," I say, realizing that's the first time I've ever said that. "Maybe this should be about you. What is it that *you* need?"

He doesn't hesitate. "That's easy. I need to heal my relationship with Piper. I'm losing her." He rubs his face, then adds, "She's our only child, so I don't know what it's like to have her leave for college, to leave her childhood behind and become an adult. I have everything else I need — a loving wife, a home, a job I love. I'm happy. But with Piper ... I'm either trying too hard or not trying hard enough. And I'm scared that I won't fix this before she leaves for good."

I think this through as we both stare off into the distance. He knows what he needs, and for us to get back to our realbodies, I have to help him get that.

But what can I do? For all my bravado, I'm a kid. A superlative kid, sure, but a kid. And for this to also be about Piper — who I'm just getting to know, I don't want to screw that up — I have one shot to get this right. Then it comes to me.

"Tell me what Piper is thinking about doing for college."

MR. **Bagshaw**

The plan is simple: I have to trust Casey Rose to save my relationship with Piper so I can live out the rest of my life in my real body. This just might be the worst plan in history.

We head out to a print shop, where we borrow a computer, type out a one-page letter, and print it out. I text Marta to let her know I'll be late, assuring her that

"Thirsty Thursday" is still on — she wonders why I didn't call, and of course, I can't tell her because I have a teenager's voice. Then Casey and I grab some fast food and talk over the rest of the plan.

The problem —a mountain-sized one — is that for this to work, Casey has to do the talking because he's in my body. Casey Rose, the kid who's played dozens of pranks on me over the years, has been disruptive, disrespectful, and all about himself. Can I really trust him? I have to. I also let him know the stakes.

"If you fail," I tell him, "you'll spend the rest of your life in *my* body. And you think you feel old and sore now? That's the *best* you'll ever feel."

He grimaces. "Then I guess I'd better not fail."

Casey texts his mom and says he'll be home by ten. Then it's waiting time until midnight. If this works, we'll be back in our own bodies.

If not — then Casey is going to grow old with my wife and be the father of my daughter, while I'll be Thurber High's most notorious student until I graduate with no future plans. This had better work.

We swing by Casey's house. I use a spare set of keys and grab his car, which is back from the oil change, then we drive to the dance studio, where we wait side-by-side in the parking lot for Piper's class to end at nine.

I've been so bent on figuring out what to do that I haven't given in to just how unbelievable this whole situation is. Can a broken crystal ball and a foreign language curse really make people switch bodies? This world is so much bigger than I'd thought.

At nine, the doors swing open, and Piper trudges to her car. She stops when she sees us standing side by side under the parking lot light.

"I can't even with you two," she says, putting her hands up to block us as she marches to her car.

"Piper, stop," Casey says.

"Remember, you're me," I whisper to him.

"Got it," he whispers back. He jogs over and blocks her path.

"Piper, give me two minutes," he says. She waves him off.

"I don't know what you're doing here with Casey," she says. "You've been acting so weird, even weirder than usual." She points to me. "And so has he."

"It has been an interesting day, honey," he says. I gulp — I don't like hearing him call her "honey." But that's what I'd do. "Just give me two minutes, and then I'll leave."

She looks over to me. "So what is Casey doing here?"

"We've, uh, been working on a project. We're also trying to come to a truce." She laughs. "Casey? A truce with a teacher?" He grins.

"It's the end of the school year — actually, the end of high school. Some things should be left in the past. Tell you what — you listen to me, and I'll leave, then you and Casey can talk, okay?"

She agrees, and they sit in the minivan. Casey's left the windows down so I can hear. I lean against Casey's car and pretend to talk on my phone, but I'm really concentrating on what they say.

CASEY

She looks so pretty. I've never seen her dance, but I bet she's graceful and bold. Okay. I'm the dad, not the smitten teenager. I start.

"I'd like to give you something," I say, taking out the

envelope with the letter and handing it to her. She snaps on the overhead light, then reads it out loud.

"Dear Piper," she starts. "I will pay for your college, wherever you decide to go, however I can. Your mother and I love you. You've been an amazing daughter to us, and we know you will be an amazing adult. Go as far away as you like. Be free. Explore the world. We will be here for you when you come back. I will be here for you when you come back. All I ask is that you and I spend one day together before you leave. Love, Dad."

I tear up hearing her read it. She tears up as she reads it. Even Casey discreetly wipes his face.

"Oh, Dad!" Piper says, leaning over and wrapping her arms around Casey. "Of course!"

"I just want to add that I know I haven't been the best father," Casey says. We'd agreed that he could say that.

"It's not true," Piper says. "You are a great father. You're just, sometimes, well..."

"Overprotective," Casey says.

"That's right," Piper says.

"Clueless."

"Maybe a little."

"Oafish."

"Well, I don't know about that."

"Doltish. Overweight. Bald." Okay, that's enough. I hurry around and rap on the minivan before Piper can respond.

"Mr. Bagshaw?" I say, then point to the ground. "I hate to interrupt, but there's a raccoon chewing your brake cables."

"I guess I'd better get going," Casey says, discreetly rolling his eyes at me. He turns to Piper. "Thank you, honey," he adds. Then he stares at her. "You look so beautiful tonight that I could kiss you."

"*What?*" Piper asks as she recoils.

"Umm, I said you look so grown up, and I'm going to miss you," Casey says. "Sorry, my throat caught. I'm just *so* emotional right now."

MR. **Bagshaw**

Piper gives her "dad" another hug and promises to see him at home, then Casey drives off. We've planned to swap cars at the school so that when we wake up in the right bodies — *if* we wake up in the right bodies — we'll have the right vehicles in the morning. If not, at least I'll have my mid-life crisis red sports car decades before I reach mid-life.

Piper launches herself into the passenger seat next to me in Casey's car and squeals. "My dad just did the nicest thing!" she says. "And said the nicest things." She explains it to me, working her way through joy, tears, and so many other emotions.

I feel them all, too. I want to laugh with her, cry with her, tell her that I meant it all, but I'm Casey right now, so I can't. I look happy for her but keep my distance. When she's done, I say what I hope Casey would say.

"I'm happy for you, Piper. Really. So what are you thinking about for college? We've never talked about it."

"I'm accepted at three schools," she says. "One is local, but I was thinking of that as my safety school. The other two are hundreds of miles away. When I applied, I wanted to get as far away from here as possible." She turns from me to look ahead. "Part of me wants that, still. But I don't know, after what my dad said … maybe I'll stay close to home."

I'm overjoyed. I want to bawl right now. But I can't.

Then she adds, "And if I stick around, and you're still around, then who knows? Maybe we can … get together."

My first urge, as a father, is to say, "I would love it if you stayed close to home!" And my second is to say, "And stay away from Casey Rose! He's nothing but trouble!" But today, I've seen a different side of Casey. I was like him when I was younger; maybe he'll turn out like me when he's older. A little clueless, not always saying the right thing at the right time, but a devoted father and husband. She could do a lot worse.

"I would love it if you stayed close," I say. "And I'm sure your parents would as well."

"So what are you going to do?" she asks.

I have no idea what Casey has planned or what he'd say. But from how he looks at Piper with actual respect and from what has happened over the last two days, I take a chance.

"You know, Piper, if college is right for me, then I'll go," I say. "And if it's not, I'll do my best at something else. But what I do know is that I have to stop thinking of myself all the time and start thinking about others. Be a better friend. A better student. A better person."

"Aww!" she says, then moves in to hug me. It feels very different from how she hugs her dad. I break away.

"I would love to go out with you again," I say. "But a real date. Not to a pop-up market. And we'll talk. About whatever you like. I want to take things slow with you, Piper."

"You do?" she asks.

"Very slow."

"Very slow?"

"Slow like a sloth." She looks disappointed and hurt. Even as Casey, I say the wrong things. "Okay, not like a sloth. I just want to get to know you. You're smart, you're beautiful, you have a great family, and you have a great future ahead of you. I'm lucky to call you my friend, and I'll be even luckier if anything more happens."

Now she looks happy.

"Casey Rose, you are full of surprises tonight."

If she only knew.

CASEY

I hang out at the school for half an hour until Mr. Bagshaw pulls in, driving my car.

"Baby!" I say, getting out and patting the car's hood. "I'm sorry I cheated on you with a minivan."

Mr. Bagshaw frowns.

"I hope this works. Was it enough?" I don't know, but I turn on my inner Casey, since my outer Casey is currently an old man. "You got what you wanted, and I helped. At least, I think. It's gotta be enough."

It's just past ten, so we'll know in two hours.

"Guess I'll drive to your place and wait it out," I say. "Just two more hours to get through."

"Oh, no," Mr. Bagshaw says. "You can't do that. My wife … she's expecting me home. We have, err, those plans…"

"Riiiiight," I say. Yeah, I can't be Mr. Bagshaw in front of Mrs. Bagshaw. And I actually don't want to see Piper right now. I *do* want to see her again when I'm really me. Tomorrow. So, no tricks. No scheming.

"I've got a key to the school," I say. "Several."

"Several?" Mr. Bagshaw says.

"Eh, when you're Casey Rose, it's expected. I'll put all that behind me. After graduation."

. . .

MR. **Bagshaw**

Casey and I make our way through the dark school corridors until we get to my room. He sits behind my desk, and I pull up a chair. And we talk. I tell him about how I was, who I was when I was younger. I was more like him than I like to think. At least, that's how I used to feel. Now, I see a young man who wants to find his way and did so the best way he knows how.

Casey does want to go to college, maybe not right away, but I can see him doing anything and doing it well. He asks me why I became a teacher.

"I wanted something solid, something that meant something," I say. "I wanted to put my wildness in the past. I thought that if I could teach students who were like I used to be, I could teach anyone." I look away. "As time went on, I got set in my ways. I kept the past in the past, but maybe too far in the past. I don't think I did a great job with you, for instance." He shakes his head.

"Mr. Bagshaw, look … I caused a lot of trouble for you. But I know now, and I think I even knew back then that it was because I respected you. I knew you could take it, and I think you understood me." He laughs.

"The marbles?"

"It's a process."

I tell him about the wild stuff I used to pull. Some of them are things even Casey Rose wouldn't do. Soon enough, I look at the clock. Three minutes until midnight.

"I guess we'll know soon enough if this worked," I say, indicating the clock. Casey looks worried.

"I hope it was enough." He sighs. "What should we do?"

"I don't know. I hope we don't have to be asleep. But that woman said midnight. So maybe we don't have to do anything." We stand. I grasp his shoulders, and he does the same to me.

"Ready?" I ask.

He smiles. "Ready. And Mr. Bagshaw?"

"Yes?"

"Thank you. For everything."

"You're welcome, Casey. And thank *you*."

CASEY

WE HOLD each other's shoulders. I look at the clock's secondhand sweep toward the twelve. Ten seconds ... five...

A weird tingle runs up my spine, and everything goes blurry. I feel Mr. Bagshaw shake as I shake, and then we both fall to the floor.

"Ugh," I say. "That was rough." I hear Mr. Bagshaw moan. I open my eyes to see ...

Mr. Bagshaw!

"It worked!" I scream, then I get up and start staggering around the room. "I'm me! I'm me!"

"I can't believe it!" Mr. Bagshaw says, struggling to his feet. I give him a hand and pull him up. He surprises me with a hug, and I surprise myself by hugging him back.

"I feel incredible," I say because I do. "Way less achy."

"I feel *more* achy," he says, rubbing his hip. "I guess we *are* back to normal."

"So that's it?" I ask. It's hard to believe how much I've missed my own body.

"That's it," he says. "Oh, wait, there's something I have to do." He pulls out his phone. "I'm texting Marta. I hope she hasn't fallen asleep yet. We have plans." I shudder.

"Oh, My Godzilla, do *you* have plans."

We laugh.

Then, from outside the class, a flashlight shines through the window. "You two in there! This is the police!" I hear the crackle of a radio. "Two intruders inside Thurber High School. We're going in."

"Now what?" Mr. Bagshaw asks.

"Eh, this is nothing," I say. "This happens to me all the time."

"It does?"

"Sure. Like I'm sure it used to happen to you back in the day."

He chuckles. "Well, there was this one time when—"

"Tell me the story on the way," I say. "First, we need to grab three reams of copier paper and a gallon of olive oil from the cafeteria. Second..."

Frenemy

KIM M. WATT

Frenemy

KIM M. WATT

"Oh, look, Michaela," Keri-Lee said. "Isn't that your grandpa's cardigan?"

She pointed one perfectly manicured fingernail across the school hallway, although there was no doubt who she was talking about. Her voice carried easily, and the girl wearing the cardigan in question hunched her shoulders and scurried on a little more quickly.

"I think it looked better on him," Keri-Lee added, raising her voice a little. "He had better hair."

The two girls with her laughed but without a lot of enthusiasm, and Michaela said, "We should leave her alone. Her mum died."

Keri-Lee glared at her. "That's no excuse for such shitty clothes. I mean, vintage is cool, but it looks like she's been dumpster diving at a charity shop. And does she never wash her face? Or her *hair?*"

"What happened to her mum?" Tina asked. "Do you know?"

Michaela shook her head, her straight, glossy brown

215

hair shivering delicately. "Something weird, though. It wasn't like cancer or anything."

Keri-Lee sniffed and adjusted the front of her top. "Something weird sounds about right. I mean, she called her daughter *Annie*. No wonder she wears old people clothes. Come on."

She turned and headed toward class, long blonde hair swinging, lesser mortals dodging out of her path. Behind her, Michaela and Tina exchanged glances, then hurried after Keri-Lee.

After all, you didn't disobey the queen of Westminster High.

KERI-LEE SAT VERY straight in the hard-backed chair, not listening to whatever the teacher was saying about warfare in medieval England. She had no idea why subjects like this were considered important. It wasn't as if she was going to take up arms against Buckingham Palace or something. So she watched Annie instead. She was seated two rows ahead and one across, twisted over on herself like a caterpillar that had become stuck in its cocoon. She'd taken off the old brown cardigan to reveal a floral blouse stained yellow at the collar. Keri-Lee curled her lip in revulsion. How could Annie just *sit* there, being so … so … she couldn't even find the words. It felt like an affront that a girl like that could even exist in the same world as Keri-Lee. She probably didn't even shave her legs, not that anyone would ever know, thanks to the shapeless khaki trousers she always wore.

Keri-Lee reluctantly tore her attention away from Annie and back to the teacher.

"So," he was saying, with far too much enthusiasm, his floppy hair pushed back like he thought it made him look young and cool rather than old and desperate. "Hot oil was actually very rarely poured onto attackers. Most places just didn't have enough of it. Hot sand, though, was popular and *very* unpleasant to get into your armor. Plus, murder holes allowed water to be tipped on any fires the enemy might start—"

Keri-Lee tuned out again. There'd be no point pouring hot oil onto Annie. It'd probably just join the oil already saturating her face and hair. She pictured it for a moment, then suddenly thought of that movie with the weird girl who had blood tipped over her at the prom. Now, wouldn't *that* be cool? And it'd just serve Annie right for being … *Annie.* Not that they had a prom coming up. But Halloween was.

Keri-Lee covered her mouth with one hand to hide her smile. But the teacher caught the movement.

"Am I boring you, Miss Turner?"

"No, sir. It's *fascinating*," she said, setting off a titter of muffled laughter around the class.

"Oh? Care to tell me three facts from today's lecture?"

"Hot oil treatments were less popular than exfoliation?"

The teacher's response was drowned out by both the class' laughter and the bell. Keri-Lee walked out into the hall with the smile still on her lips. Maybe there was some point to school after all.

IT WAS ALMOST RIDICULOUSLY easy to set up.

A note passed to Annie, inviting her to a Halloween

party at the lake, which was *the* party that everyone wanted to go to anyway. Annie didn't even need to know who had invited her – in fact, it was better she didn't. She might've been suspicious if it had been Keri-Lee, but this way, any one of the other kids going could've taken pity on her. Even getting the blood was easy since Gage's dad had a pig farm. Michaela would help Keri-Lee douse Annie, and Tina had agreed to film the whole thing.

It was lucky Gage was so hot. And indisputably the coolest boy in school, since he was captain of just about every sport going. Otherwise, Keri-Lee couldn't have gone out with a pig farmer's son.

Late on Halloween afternoon, as tiny trick-or-treaters began to come out in force, Keri-Lee drove carefully out to the lake with the bucket of blood sloshing gloopily in the passenger side footwell. She'd put some bin bags down to catch any spillage, but she was hoping to avoid any. The only place that blood was going was all over Annie Hayes. When Keri-Lee threw the blood, the moment would be immortalized online for all eternity.

She was grinning at the very thought of it when she pulled into the parking lot at the lake. She parked with the car's nose to the wooden barriers, and the fading light washed the picnic shelters and kids' climbing frame with soft autumn tones. There was someone here already, standing down on the lake shore where the party was going to kick off in an hour or so. Keri-Lee frowned, then shrugged. It was probably a dog-walker or something. She just needed to take the bucket down and hide it in the reeds; by the time she'd done that, they'd be gone, anyway. She got out, shivering slightly as the cold air cut through the thin, gauzy fabric of her fairy costume. She hauled the bucket out and lugged it down toward the shore. The figure turned toward her when she approached, the setting sun over the lake turning them into a silhouette, featureless and ill-formed.

Keri-Lee tried to ignore the figure's scrutiny, but she could feel their eyes on her when she stepped onto the sand. She raised her free hand to shield her eyes from the sun. The figure swam into focus. It wore baggy khaki trousers and a pink, fuzzy jumper that was as hideous as the brown cardigan had been.

It was —

"*Annie?*" Keri-Lee tried unsuccessfully to hide the bucket behind her legs. "What're you doing here?"

"I'm here for the party," Annie said, her voice reedy and small.

"You're awfully early," Keri-Lee said. "By the way, who invited *you?*"

"You did," Annie said.

And then she was *right next* to Keri-Lee, grabbing her, pulling her forward onto the sand. Keri-Lee yelped, the bucket splashing blood all over her legs when she tried to twist away. She dropped it, stumbling over a line of stones.

The blood surged onto the sand, and Keri-Lee shouted, "Stop! You've ruined *everything!*"

Annie ignored her, still holding her arm with one hand. In the other she had a book, heavy and old-looking, beyond old, *ancient* even. Keri-Lee tried to pull away from her again, but Annie had a surprisingly strong grip.

"What're you doing?" she asked. But Annie was talking over her, nonsense words that didn't mean anything to Keri-Lee. She looked around for help, but they were alone on the beach. The blood seeped into the ground at her feet, and now Keri-Lee saw that they were standing in the centre of some weird design created by stones. It was a star or a pentagram or whatever it was called.

"Let me *go!*" she shouted and shoved Annie as hard as

she could. The other girl finally lost her grip and stumbled back, but she was smiling.

Annie was smiling, which Keri-Lee had never seen. And now the last of the sun was gone, and it was cold, *so cold,* and then she was falling.

~

KERI-LEE WOKE SHIVERING.

Was the heating off? Had she left the window open? She opened her eyes, expecting to see the smooth white ceiling and poster-plastered walls of her bedroom, but instead discovered a curtain of leaves, faintly lit by grey dawn light. She blinked and waited a moment for the illusion to vanish. It didn't, though, and she stretched out a hand, touching the cold edges of glossy green. Was she … was she lying in a *bush?* Why?

She sat up, her body aching from the cold ground, and rubbed a hand over her face. It felt greasy. She must've slept in her make-up. She looked at the screen of bushes around her. *Of course,* she'd slept in her make-up. She'd slept in a *bush.* How much did she drink last night? Or did someone slip her something? She could barely even remember getting to the lake.

Keri-Lee rolled to all fours and pushed through the slim branches of undergrowth, finding herself at the edge of the woods that rolled down to meet the lake. There was no one around, just the blackened remains of a fire on the beach and a jumble of abandoned cans and bottles and crisp packets, as well as a cat mask, one fairy wing, and half a dozen magic wands.

"So predictable," she whispered, getting to her feet. She looked around for her phone, but there was no sight of it. Some asshole had stolen it. She limped toward the car park.

Stopping.

Her car was gone, too.

She was still standing there, staring at the empty spaces, when a council truck pulled in. The driver, a round, bearded man, rolled down his window and looked her up and down. "Rough night?"

"Someone stole my car," she said.

He pointed through the windscreen at the beach. "I don't suppose it's any help my saying, *serves you right for the bloody mess you've left me?*"

Keri-Lee just looked at him, trying her hardest not to cry. "I can't find my phone. I don't know what happened. I don't remember *anything.*"

He returned her gaze for a moment longer, then sighed. "Get in, love. I'll take you home."

KERI-LEE CLAMBERED out of the truck at the gate to her house, still feeling like her body didn't belong to her. The bearded man – who was called Gaz – had given her a cup of sweet, milky tea from his thermos, lectured her about scaring her parents, then told her far more than she'd ever wanted to know about the ecosystem of the lake.

Now, he leaned out the window and said, "Get inside and get warmed up. No harm done this time. But you want to be more careful."

"I suppose," she said. "Thanks."

He waved dismissively as if collecting bewildered teenage girls from the beach was as much a part of his job as collecting rubbish. Then he drove off, the truck coughing exhaust and the bins in the back rattling. Keri-

Lee watched it for a moment, then let herself in the gate, frowning. Her car was in the drive. How was her car *here?* Had she gotten a lift to the lake? No, she remembered driving down. She'd gone early. Why had she gone early?

She touched one hand to the car's roof when she passed as if to assure herself it was real, then headed for the door, patting her pockets. Her house keys were missing. Of course, they were. She dug into the flower-pots by the door for the spare and let herself in, closing the door behind her and slumping against it as the familiar smells of her own home washed around her, both suffocating and familiar all at once. She hesitated, wanting to just go straight upstairs and have a shower, but there were voices in the kitchen. Gaz had been right about worrying her parents. Well, her mum anyway. Her stepdad probably wasn't exactly beside himself.

She pushed herself upright and headed into the kitchen, already speaking as she walked in. "I'm so sorry, I don't know what happened, I just—"

She stopped, the words drying in her mouth. Her mother was standing at the breakfast bar, a cup of tea cradled in her hands, looking at her with a puzzled frown. And sitting at the bar ... sitting at the bar ...

"Excuse me, who are you?" her mother asked. Asked *her.* Asked *her own daughter.* "How did you get in here?"

Keri-Lee couldn't look at her. Because she couldn't stop staring at the other person, who was smiling just slightly, her long blonde hair flowing over her shoulders, one eyebrow raised in question.

"Are you alright?" Her mother set the cup down and took a step toward Keri-Lee. "Do you need to sit down?"

Keri-Lee still couldn't look at her.

The girl at the bar took a sip of her tea, her smile

widening. "Mum, that's Annie," she said. "I don't know what she's doing here."

Keri-Lee looked down at herself, noticing for the first time the fluffy pink jumper and the khaki trousers, the new heaviness of her limbs. She turned stiffly toward the oven set into the wall, the stainless giving her a distorted reflection. She raised a hand to her face, feeling the grease under her fingertips. She turned back to the other girl, the one wearing her clothes, her hair, her *face*.

"What did you do?" she said. "What did you *do?*"

THINGS WERE a little muddled after that. Keri-Lee knew she'd tried to attack the girl wearing her face, and her mum had pulled her off, shouting for help. Then her stepbrother had come running in and restrained her while she pulled away from his touch, screaming for her mum. The other girl filmed the whole thing on her phone, grinning.

By the time Keri-Lee could think straight again, she was being forced out of the house by a tall, thin man in a police uniform, who was saying, "Thanks, Mrs Turner. I was worried when she didn't come home last night. We'll be having a serious talk, won't we, Annie?"

Keri-Lee stared at him. He was looking at *her* and talking to *her*.

"I'm *not Annie!*" she screamed. "I'm *Keri-Lee!* This is *my home!*"

The police officer shook her, not hard, but not gently, either. *"Annie.* Stop that."

"It's alright," her mum said, her voice gentle. "It must be hard after her mother … well."

Keri-Lee felt the police officer stiffen. "Yes," he said, the word clipped. "It is."

And then he was bundling her out and into a police car. She was still crying when he pulled up outside a scruffy bungalow with stained white paint and an overgrown garden. The police officer turned the engine off and opened the back door to let her out, taking her arm as if afraid she might run off. When he escorted her up to the house, a woman popped her head out of the house next door.

"Daniel! You found her!"

"I did, thanks, Ruby," he said, not stopping.

"I'm so glad. You worried your father terribly, Annie," Ruby said, waggling a finger at Keri-Lee.

Keri-Lee ignored her. She *wasn't* Annie. She couldn't be! She tried to brace herself against the door, but Annie's father – Daniel – pushed her inside with a sigh and locked the door behind them.

She turned to face him. "This is kidnapping!"

"That's enough, Annie." He rubbed a hand over his face, his shoulders slumping with exhaustion. "I was looking for you all night. *All night.* What the hell happened?"

"I'm *not Annie!*"

He grabbed her shoulders even as she flinched, examining her eyes from close quarters. "What did you take? Who gave it to you?"

She pulled away from him, taking in the gloomy hall with its threadbare green carpets and worn wallpaper. "*Nothing!* I'm telling the truth!"

He looked at her for a long moment, his face grey in the low light. "Go to your room. We'll talk about this later."

"I want to go *home!*"

"*You are home. Now go to your room!*" He bellowed it, pointing down the hall, and Keri–Lee retreated in fright, stumbling through the nearest door. School books were piled on a desk in the corner, and photos crowded the walls. She collapsed onto the single bed in one corner, sobbing into a hideous crocheted green blanket.

This couldn't be happening.

It *couldn't.*

But it was.

～

KERI-LEE DIDN'T KNOW many phone numbers by heart. Who needed to? But once she'd done crying, she went digging through the schoolbag hanging on the back of Annie's door and found the other girl's phone. It was some dismal knock-off of a knock-off, a brand Keri-Lee had never even heard of, but it had credit, so that was something. She punched in her home number, holding her breath while it rang and rang. No answer. She closed her eyes and lay back on the bed again, thinking. She needed help. But who would believe her?

Michaela. And she did know Michaela's home number by heart, from the days before they'd been allowed phones. She dialed it quickly and held her breath until Michaela's mum answered.

"It's Keri-Lee. Can I speak to Michaela?" she asked.

"Oh, hello, love. Do you have a cold? You don't sound quite right."

"Um, yes," Keri-Lee said, wishing she'd just get off the phone. "Is Michaela there? It's important."

"Why aren't you calling her mobile?"

"Mine's dead, and I don't know her number."

"You girls and your toys," Michaela's mum said, the smile clear in her voice. And then, thankfully, she was gone, shouting for Michaela.

A moment later, Michaela said, "Hello?"

"Mik, you won't *believe* what's happened—"

"Annie? Is that you? Mum said it was Keri-Lee."

"It is—"

"I'm so glad you didn't go to the party last night after all. That was a really mean trick Keri had planned."

Keri-Lee stopped, her stomach suddenly feeling even more hollowed out than it had all morning. "What?"

"If she finds out I told you about it, she'll kill me, though. So you can't say anything, alright? She takes things too far sometimes."

Keri-Lee squeezed her eyes shut against the tears. "Oh?"

"Just stay clear of her for a bit. She'll move on. I've got to go."

The line clicked dead in Keri-Lee's ear, and she dropped the phone to the floor, pressing both hands to her face. Michaela had betrayed her. Michaela thought she was mean, that she went too far. *Michaela.* Her best friend since she'd even known what a best friend was. She'd chosen Annie over Keri-Lee.

Keri-Lee heaved a whooping, painful sob, curling back into the bed. It smelled of long nights and dark days and loss.

KERI-LEE DIDN'T MOVE AGAIN, not even when Daniel put his head around the door and asked her if she wanted some shepherd's pie for dinner. She didn't respond, but he came back with a plate anyway. He put it on the desk. It smelled of rich, dark gravy and fat.

"Annie," he said, sitting on the edge of the bed and putting a hand on her hip.

Keri-Lee scrambled away from him, curling herself into the corner where the pillow touched the wall, her heart going too fast, her back to him. He was silent for a long moment, then the bed moved as he got up.

"What happened last night, Annie? Did someone do something to you?"

She wanted to shout *yes, yes, they stole my life!*, but instead, she just shook her head, still with her face pressed to the corner. It was safer there. After a moment, the door closed, and she slid back down into the grip of the bed again, looking at the photos and staring down at her from the wall. They were all of the same woman, never quite looking at the camera, except in one where she had an arm around a young Annie. They were both laughing, hair disheveled by the wind, eyes alight with life. Only in that photo, though. Keri-Lee couldn't see the same light in any of the others, and she wondered why Annie kept them all. Because she certainly didn't like looking at them.

At some point in the night, she slept, and the next morning, she rushed past Daniel as he buttered toast in the kitchen.

"Annie!" he shouted after her. "Have breakfast before you go!"

"I'm not hungry!" Then she was out into the grey Monday morning, hurrying toward school. She'd had enough moping. It was time to *do* something.

At school, Keri-Lee went straight to her locker, knowing everyone would already have arrived. Michaela and Tina were leaning over a phone and laughing about something. Gage had his arm around Annie's shoulders, his lips almost touching her ear as he whispered something that made her giggle and squirm in a way Keri-Lee would *never* have done.

"You," she snapped, pointing at Annie. "Take it back!"

Annie looked her up and down. Her make-up wasn't applied very well, the mascara globby and the lip gloss too heavy. "What do you want, pig-girl?"

"Take. It. Back," Keri-Lee snarled, grabbing Annie's bag – *her* bag – and pulling it off her shoulder.

"Back off," Gage shoved her away.

Keri-Lee staggered back a couple of steps, hand going to her shoulder where he'd shoved her. "Don't you touch me like that!"

"Then keep your hands to yourself!"

"Annie," Michaela started, stepping forward.

"No!" Keri-Lee rounded on her. "I'm *not Annie!* I'm Keri-Lee, which you'd know if you were a *real* friend!"

Annie whistled and circled her finger by her ear. "She's gone nutty like her mum."

"*Keri,*" Michaela said, her eyes wide.

"Her mum was nuts?" Tina asked. "I suppose that explains some things."

Keri-Lee glared at Annie. "You know I'm telling the truth."

Annie's smile was stiff and stretched, and her hand was shaking just slightly. "Stay away from me, you crazy bitch."

Then she turned on her heel and walked off, not waiting to see if the others would follow. Gage snatched Annie's bag off Keri-Lee, making her stagger. Michaela mouthed *sorry* and then followed Tina, who was already trotting along behind them.

Keri-Lee watched them go, taking deep breaths against the tears threatening at the corner of her eyes. Then she turned and headed for the doors, her prize in her hands. Keri-Lee always put her keys in the inside pocket of her bag. Annie, she knew from the bag in her room, clipped hers to the outside. And that made them very easy to steal.

Keri-Lee's car was parked badly on the street outside

the school, and she got in, taking a moment to breathe in the familiar, lingering scent of her own perfume, disturbingly overlaid by a whiff of sugar. Annie better not be eating *doughnuts* in her car. She needed to get her body back as soon as she could before that monster ruined it. And if Michaela wouldn't help, then Keri-Lee's mum would. Every mother recognizes their own daughter, no matter what they look like. Surely.

She drove straight to the accountancy firm downtown and hurried into reception. "I need to see my— Mrs. Turner," she said before the receptionist could say anything. "It's about her daughter."

"I'll call her," the receptionist said, tapping the phone and turning slightly away from Keri-Lee.

"Can I not just go through? I know where her office is."

"She's in a meeting," he said, smiling at her. "Just take a seat for a moment."

"It's *urgent*," she said.

"I'll be sure to tell her." He pointed at the seats.

Keri-Lee didn't move. "You're not calling her."

"I have."

"You—" she stopped suddenly as she saw the security guard moving across the lobby toward her, his face serious. "You called *security?*"

"Sorry," the receptionist said, and he did actually look a little apologetic. "Mrs Turner told us you might turn up. Something about stalking her daughter. You have to leave, or I'll call the police."

Keri-Lee stepped back as the security guard loomed over her. "Fine. *Fine!* I'm going."

The door spilled her back out onto a bare grey pavement on a cold grey day. A light drizzle hung in the air. Keri-Lee stood in the shelter of the building's overhang for a moment until the security guard cleared his throat behind her, and she scowled at him.

"My dad's a cop," she told him. "A proper one, not a bloody make-believe one like you." Well, *Annie's* dad was, but close enough.

The security guard didn't respond, and Keri-Lee headed out into the drizzle with a sigh, wondering what to do next. If no one was going to help her, she was going to have to fix this herself. But *how?* She didn't even know how it had happened. How did *anything* like this happen? It had been Annie, Annie at the lake …

She could almost grasp the memory, but not quite. There was no logical explanation for this. She had to look elsewhere for answers.

"Like shitty bloody magic," she muttered to herself, bouncing her keys in her hand, then suddenly thought of something. That grungy shop Tina always liked going in to buy crystals and such rubbish. But it didn't just sell crystals. It sold Ouija boards, sage bundles, and spell books. It was ridiculous to think they might be able to help, but what had happened was ridiculous, too. And it wasn't like she had an awful lot of options. Go back to school?

Live life as Annie Hayes?

No bloody *thank* you.

BELLS TINKLED over the door when Keri-Lee let herself into Tarot & Tales. She was greeted by a waft of incense. The interior was dimly lit, the permanently scungy windows letting in little of the dull day. She threaded her way inside, past shelves of dog-eared books on astrology and numerology, stacks of rune stones, tubs of crystals and silver charms on strings, and candleholders made out of what she assumed were fake animal skulls. The counter was at the very back, and a woman with long dark hair sat on a stool behind it, reading a book with a werewolf on the cover.

"Can I help you?" she asked, barely looking up. "Love spell? Zit-banishing charm? Nose ring? I do piercings out the back."

"How would someone swap bodies?" Keri-Lee asked.

The woman lowered her book, examining her. Her face was older than her hair suggested, lined and creased with evidence of a long life. "That's serious magic."

"But you know how to do it?"

The woman nodded. "Sure. A pentagram, some wild water, some blood—" she broke off when Keri-Lee pressed a hand to her mouth. "Are you alright?"

Keri-Lee nodded jerkily.

She remembered.

Remembered all of it, like a punch to the gut that was half rage, half horror, and she could barely breathe for either. The lake. The pentagram of stones. The bucket of blood splashing across the sand.

She swallowed hard and finally managed to talk. "Can you reverse such a spell?"

The woman frowned. "I mean, if I had the right book, I could. That's seriously dark magic, though. There are only a handful of books that hold the right incantation, and I don't have access to any. They're dangerous."

Annie had had the book. Which meant she'd still have it – probably in Keri-Lee's bedroom. "What if I could get one?"

"How would *you* get a book like that?"

Keri-Lee lifted her chin, scowling at the woman. "If I did, could you do it?"

The woman laughed, a little coughing sound. "You find a book like that, I'll do whatever you want."

"Get set up," Keri-Lee said. "I'll be back in an hour."

She marched out of the shop, and was almost running by the time she got back to the car. There'd be no one home. She could fix this *now*.

~

THE HOUSE WAS quiet when she let herself in, and for a moment, she just savoured being there, breathing in the familiar scents, the warm light, and the soft decor. But she didn't have time to linger. She needed to find the book.

Upstairs, she dug through her own bedroom, feeling both at home and like a stranger. She discovered her make-up neatly stacked rather than spilled across her dresser and books straightened on the shelves rather than thrown all over the place. "This is how the three bears felt," she said, shoving her hands beneath the mattress, finally meeting the hard edges of a book. Not her diary – that had vanished, and for a moment, her stomach rolled slickly, wondering if Annie had read it. But she couldn't waste time worrying about it. In an hour or so, everything would be back to normal.

She hauled the book out, heavy and textured, and caught a whiff of old blood and secrets that set the hair on her arms shivering. She shoved the book in her bag, then hesitated, thinking of Annie in here, believing she'd won some sort of lottery by swapping lives. Of course, Keri-Lee was going to change it back now that she had the book, but what if it took some time? What if it was another day? Another *night?*

She grabbed a pen off her desk, scrawled a note hurriedly on the back of some scrap paper, then shoved it under her pillow and jogged out the door. She had just made it to the bottom of the stairs when someone called out behind her.

"Hey!"

She froze. Her stepbrother's voice lit a chill on her spine. She turned back to him. "What're you doing home? I thought you'd be at school."

"Study day," he said, walking down the stairs. "You're that chick from yesterday. What are *you* doing back here?"

She held up her bag, shaking slightly. "An— Keri-Lee asked me to get something for her. A book."

"Yeah? After you attacked her?"

"It was a joke. Halloween prank."

"She didn't seem to think so." He stopped too close, examining her. "And you don't look like her usual friends."

Keri-Lee managed not to squirm under his scrutiny, backing away down the hall. "Well, she gave me her keys." She held them up to demonstrate.

He followed her, broad-shouldered and slouching. "Show me what you took."

"I have to get back. I'm going to be late." She fled down the stairs and threw her bag into the car, trying to get in without taking her eyes off the door. He didn't follow, though. Not when she looked like Annie.

Keri-Lee drove too fast back to the magic shop, parking badly outside and running in with her bag clutched to her chest. The woman looked up, startled. "Are you ready?" Keri-Lee demanded, fumbling the book out.

"You didn't..." the woman trailed off, staring at the book, then held her hands out. "Give it to me."

Keri-Lee did. The woman turned the book over, examining the cover, then opened it carefully, biting her lip.

"Well?" Keri-Lee demanded. "Can you fix this?"

"Um, sure." The woman looked up. "Where did you *get* this?"

"From a friend. Can we do this now? I *need* to get back to my own life."

"Sure, sure." The woman was still caressing the pages. "How much do you want for it?"

"If you can reverse the spell, you can keep it."

The woman looked up sharply, searching Keri-Lee's face, then got up so hurriedly she knocked her stool over. "Come on. I've got a pentagram in the back."

Keri-Lee expected something more dramatic from a witch's back room, but it was just a small, book-crowded space, with a sofa pushed up against one wall and a TV on the other. There was a big rug on the floor, topped by a coffee table. The witch pushed it away, then rolled up the carpet, revealing a pentagram drawn on the floor, sigils marking the points.

She went to a cabinet and pulled out a bag of sand, which she poured onto the floor, following the lines of the pentagram. Then she took some candles and lit them, placing one at each point. They looked less occult and more like they came off the bargain shelves at TJMax.

The woman gestured to Keri-Lee. "Get in."

"That's it? I just get in?"

"Almost." She handed her a pin. "Stab your finger and put a few drops of blood on the sand once you're inside. I'll do the incantation, and Bob's your uncle."

"Bob's your *what?*"

"It'll be done," the witch said, leafing through the book. "Here, we go. To reverse it, I just have to do it backward."

Keri-Lee stepped into the circle, staring at the pin dubiously. Finally, she stabbed it into the meat of her thumb, hissing at the pain, then squeezed a few drops out onto the sand. "Alright."

"Brace yourself," the witch said and started chanting.

Keri-Lee sat down in the centre of the pentagram, closing her eyes and waiting for the cold to return, for that awful sense of falling, but there was nothing. Just the hardness of the wood floor beneath her, and the witch's rising and falling voice, and Keri-Lee's rumbling stomach reminding her she hadn't eaten since lunch the day before. After a moment, the witch fell silent. Keri-Lee didn't move, waiting for something to feel different. Finally, she opened her eyes.

"Is it still you?" the witch asked uncertainly.

"Do I still look the same?" Keri-Lee asked, touching her face.

"Yes. Maybe it takes a little time to kick in."

"It didn't before."

"You might wake up in your own body tomorrow."

Keri-Lee stood up. "I didn't feel anything."

"I think it's a little colder in here," the witch offered. "And the candles flickered."

"They're *candles*," Keri-Lee said. She stepped out of the circle and wrested the book away from the woman. "You don't know what you're doing at all, do you?"

"I do," she said. "I might just need to read up a bit—"

But Keri-Lee had stopped listening and stormed out of the shop and back to her car. She threw the book in the back. It hadn't worked. The only person who knew how to make it work was Annie, and she wasn't going to do anything because she *wanted* this.

She pressed her hands against the wheel and screamed as loudly as she could, ignoring a startled man passing on the pavement.

Keri-Lee was stuck.

She was going to have to be Annie forever.

~

KERI-LEE WAS WAITING for Michaela when she came home. As soon as she saw her, she scrambled out of the car to meet her at the gate.

Michaela stared at her. "What're you doing with Keri-Lee's car? She's going to kill you!"

"I *am* Keri-Lee!"

"Annie, this is silly." Michaela shook her head, opening the gate. "I know she's really being a bitch to you right now, but how's this meant to help?"

Keri-Lee swallowed hard. "She's being a bitch because *she's* Annie. She's stolen my body!"

Michaela snorted, walking up to her front door. "Are you high? It's not Freaky Friday."

"I know it sounds impossible, but—" she grabbed Michaela's arm, stopping her. "When you were six, you stole your brother's tooth and put it under your own pillow so the Tooth Fairy would give the money to you, and you were really upset when she didn't."

Michaela stared at her. "Who told you that?"

"When we were eight, we shoplifted an entire box of Cadbury Creme Eggs from the corner shop and made ourselves so sick your mum said it was the best punishment we could have, but *my* mum made us go and scrub the floors in the shop for Mr. Patel for the next three months."

"That was kind of common knowledge."

"You had such a crush on Liam Jennings when you were eleven that you vomited in your schoolbag when he spoke to you once. It got on his trainers, and he called you Vomley for the next two years."

"I mean, yes, but—"

"I spiked my stepbrother's protein shake with ground-up laxatives, and he had the shits for an entire month and never bought that brand again."

Michaela didn't reply for a long moment, then she said, "This isn't possible. Are you playing some joke with Keri-Lee?"

"*No.* Michaela, I *need* you to believe me. It's me!"

Michaela examined Keri-Lee for a long time, her bag clutched in front of her like a shield. "But it's *not possible.*"

"I know," Keri-Lee said, and this time she couldn't stop the tears. "I wish it wasn't."

Michaela put her arms around her, and Keri-Lee breathed in the familiar scent of her friend, lip gloss and fruity shampoo and mints.

Finally, *finally*, everything was going to be alright.

KERI-LEE AND MICHAELA sat in the living room, eating ice cream straight from the tub, when the doorbell went. They looked at each other, startled, and Michaela said, "It's probably just the neighbour. I'll be back."

She left, and Keri-Lee took another spoonful of ice cream, savouring the security of having her friend back. It had been so damn *lonely* being Annie, everyone looking right through her as if she didn't exist at all. Now that Michaela was on her side, everything was going to be okay. They'd tackle Annie together and *make* her change them back.

And then Michaela returned.

Only it wasn't.

It was Annie's dad, his face drawn and tired.

"What're *you* doing here?" she asked.

"Michaela called me," he said. "She's worried about you, and I can see why."

Keri-Lee scrambled up. "Michaela. *Michaela!*"

"I told her to go upstairs," he said. "Come on, Annie. We're going."

"I'm *not Annie!*"

He sighed. "Sweetheart—"

"I'm not your sweetheart! I'm Keri-Lee Turner! That's *my* car outside! *Your daughter stole my body!*"

He rubbed his face, and for a moment, she thought he might cry, but then he just stepped forward, grabbing her arm before she could move away. "Enough, Annie. Enough."

"Don't *touch me!*" She was screaming, but she didn't care. She didn't stop, even as he collected her bag and propelled her out of the house, putting her in the back of the police car where she couldn't get out. "*Let me go!*"

He didn't reply, just pulled away from the curb, and she could see his jaw working as she grabbed at the back of his seat.

"Don't you want your daughter back?" she demanded. "You should be helping me!"

"I do want my daughter back," he said quietly. "I won't lose you too, Annie. We'll get through this."

"I'm *not Annie!*" she screamed and pounded her fists against the seat. "I'm *not! I'm not! I'm not!*"

She was still screaming when he stopped the car, and someone opened the door from the outside, and she screamed even louder when firm, unyielding hands pulled her out. She screamed loudest of all at the sudden spike of a needle in her arm, and she kept screaming until, quite suddenly, she was falling again.

Oh, she thought. *Maybe it's working.*

And then she was gone.

TWO WEEKS LATER, Keri-Lee sat in the psychiatrist's office, her hands folded in her lap, her hair freshly washed. The hideous khaki trousers and shapeless green cardigan Annie's dad had brought in for her felt scratchy and strange after days spent in pajamas and hospital gowns.

"Now, "the psychiatrist said, her own hands clasped on the desk. "How are you feeling?"

"I think it must've been stress," Keri-Lee said. "I was … confused." She looked at Daniel, sitting in the chair next to her, one booted ankle resting on the opposite knee, his foot jiggling restlessly. "I'm sorry I worried you, Dad."

It was a hard word to say, but not as hard as it might've been. It wasn't as if she'd ever called anyone else in her life Dad.

The psychiatrist smiled. "These sorts of breaks aren't out of the ordinary. Adolescence is a difficult time of life, and the added stress of losing your mother and starting a new school is a lot."

Keri-Lee nodded. "It was. But now I know to ask for help before it gets to be too much."

The psychiatrist looked at Daniel. "Mr Hayes, it's our opinion that Annie is well enough to go home. I'd recommend that she comes back for sessions twice weekly for the next few months."

"That'd be great," Daniel said, smiling at Keri-Lee. There were dark shadows under his eyes, and he'd missed a patch of stubble on his cheek. It was coming in grey. "Are you ready to come home, sweetheart?"

"Yes," Keri-Lee said, with feeling. "Very ready."

"Good." He stood up, extending a hand over the desk. "Thank you, doctor."

"My pleasure. Annie has been a model patient. She really does want to get better."

"That's a relief to hear," Daniel said, and Keri-Lee let him rest his hand on her shoulder. Then they walked out into the thin winter sunlight, away from the stink of cleaning liquids and boiled vegetables and stark, primal fear.

"Do you want to stop for doughnuts?" Daniel asked, opening the car. It wasn't a police car this time, just an old Volvo with a dent in the door.

"Anything but boiled potatoes and dry chicken," Keri-Lee said, getting in. "I mean, would it have killed them to give us some gravy, at least? What were we going to do, weaponize it?"

Daniel gave a startled laugh, then covered his mouth with one hand. "Sorry. I know it must've been awful for you. I wish I hadn't had to do it."

"Me too," Keri-Lee said. "But now you can make it up to me." She plucked at her trousers. "Can I get some new clothes?"

"Really? You always ..." He swallowed. "You've not worn anything but your mum's old stuff since ... Well. Since."

"New start, that's what the doctor said," Keri-Lee said, looking at the cardigan. She'd never thought about why Annie wore them before.

"I think that's a good idea," Daniel said quietly. "For both of us."

He reached out and rumpled Keri-Lee's hair. Then she let him give her an awkward hug in the confines of the car.

It shouldn't have felt as warm as it did.

He wasn't *her* dad, after all.

～

KERI-LEE WALKED into school with her head up and her shoulders back, her stride sure in new boots, her skirt sweeping Annie's surprisingly-toned thighs and her jumper just low-cut enough to flatter without drawing any teacher's disapproval. She walked past Michaela and Tina without acknowledging them, and stopped in front of the girl wearing her body.

Annie stared at her, and Keri-Lee flicked her softly curled hair over one shoulder. "What did I miss?"

"Um," Michaela started.

Keri-Lee held a hand up imperiously. "I'm not talking to you. I'm talking to Keri-Lee." She smiled at Annie. "How's life?"

Annie straightened up, scowling. "Where's your cardigan?"

"I felt like a change."

"I don't like it."

Keri-Lee tipped her head. "What? Feeling a little threatened there, Keri-Lee? Worried you can't hold onto your crown?" She looked Annie up and down. Her make-up was looking better, but she definitely hadn't been keeping up with Keri-Lee's morning hundred crunches and evening 5km run. "Takes work, you know."

Annie grabbed Keri-Lee's arm and dragged her down the hall, out of earshot of the others.

"Where's my book?" she hissed. "I want it back."

"Only if you reverse this," Keri-Lee said, her voice low. "Because I want my life back. Or I'll steal yours." She indicated herself. "I can work with this."

Annie shook her head vehemently. "I found your diary. I'll tell everyone how you make yourself throw up your dinner every night. How you cheated on the physics exam. How—"

"They're *your* secrets if you're me, you dick," Keri-Lee snapped. "How d'you think that's going to help?"

Annie hesitated, then leaned in close, her fingers digging into Keri-Lee's arm. "*Get my book back.* Or I'll tell Dad you're still delusional, and you'll be back in that hospital forever. And I know how to make him believe it, too."

Then Annie turned and strode down the hall, the others trailing after her and shooting anxious little glances at Keri-Lee.

Keri-Lee ignored them, a sick taste in her mouth. She wasn't going back to the hospital. No way in hell. She'd take the book to Annie and barter with her some more. Her dad was kind of cool. Surely, if Keri-Lee promised to be friends with her, Annie would rather be home with her father than at Keri-Lee's house?

Keri-Lee would if it was her.

ANNIE! WHAT ARE YOU DOING? Daniel stood in the doorway of Annie's room, staring at the devastation. Every drawer had been emptied, the closet contents strewn across the floor, the bookshelves overturned.

"The book," Keri-Lee said, standing in the middle of the chaos. "I've lost a book."

"What book?" he asked.

"It was in my schoolbag when I went to the hospital. I need it, Dad. It's not even mine."

"Well, I'm glad to hear it wasn't yours, but it's gone."

"*Gone?*"

He crossed his arms. "You don't need things like that around, Annie. Magic isn't real, and books like that are just going to give you strange ideas."

"Where is it?" She stepped toward him. "What did you do with it?"

He shook his head. "It's gone."

"What do you mean, gone?"

"Annie! There were things in there about *raising the dead!* Why the hell did you even have it?" His face was pale, drawn in tight lines, his hands clenched into fists. "What were you *thinking?"*

"I need it!"

"Stop shouting!"

They glared at each other, both of them breathing hard, and Daniel shook his head. "We need to talk to Dr. Hasan again."

"No," Keri-Lee snapped. "I'm *fine.* But that was my book, and you had no right—"

"You just said it wasn't yours."

"Why did you take it? How am I going to fix this now?"

"Fix *what?"*

"Everything!" she waved wildly, almost crying, taking in the dingy little room and the dingy little house and this dingy little *life* that she was never going to get away from now. How could they fix *anything* without the book? *"Everything is awful!* I'm going to be Annie *forever!"*

"I'm calling the hospital." He turned away from her, already pulling his phone out, and Keri-Lee shoved past him, sprinting for the front door. *"Annie!"*

Keri-Lee didn't stop. She didn't even pause, sprinting down side streets and alleys, dodging through footpaths and shortcuts. She didn't stop until she was outside her own house, panting, her legs stinging from where she'd run through nettles somewhere. She hesitated on the street, then let herself quietly in the gate and edged up to the big windows that gave onto the open plan living area. The kitchen was brightly lit, the table piled with plates and dishes, and Annie was laughing.

Keri-Lee's mother had one hand on Annie's arm while they shared some joke that should've belonged to Keri-Lee. *All* of this should've belonged to Keri-Lee. The warm, light house, the meal that was more than a one-pot wonder, and her mother's hand on her arm. Her gaze drifted to her stepfather and stepbrother, and she stepped back from the window. She wanted all of it, for better or worse.

But with no book, there was no hope. None at all.

She didn't go back to Annie's straightaway. She didn't go anywhere that she remembered. She just knew it was late when she finally walked back to Annie's house. She tried the door. It was locked. She knocked. Wished she'd thought to take her key.

There was no answer, and she knocked again. Still nothing from inside, but the door opened next door, and the woman — Ruby, her name was Ruby — said, "Annie, love?" in an odd, gentle tone that made Keri-Lee's stomach turn over.

"Yes?"

"There's been an accident."

THE HOSPITAL WAS raw and loud, too bright and too crowded. Ruby kept one hand on Keri-Lee's shoulder, steering her through the chaos. If she hadn't, Keri-Lee thought she would've run back out into the cold, empty night, back to where things were still awful but not *this* awful. There was no escaping, though, and before long, she was sitting in a hard plastic chair, cradling a paper cup of tasteless hot chocolate, while Ruby prattled on about something utterly irrelevant, but that was okay because Keri-Lee didn't want to have to talk, or even listen.

It had been a drunk driver.

Daniel had been out in the car, searching for her, and the driver had plowed right through a stop sign and into the side of the old Volvo. And it was her fault. She shouldn't have run off. She shouldn't have scared him, shouldn't have let him think his daughter was losing her mind.

She should've been *better*.

Someone stopped in front of her, and she kept her eyes on the hot chocolate, which was rapidly becoming tepid chocolate.

"I called a couple of your friends, Annie," Ruby said. "I thought you might want them here."

Keri-Lee looked up.

Annie stood before her, tears smearing her mascara. "Is he—"

Keri-Lee screamed a wordless, wounded sound that turned every head in the waiting room toward them. "*Get her out,*"she yelled as soon as she could form the words. "This is *her fault! Get* her *out!*"

"Annie—" Ruby was fussing, trying to calm her, but Keri-Lee shook her off, surging to her feet and shoving Annie away.

"Don't you come near me. Don't you come near *him!*"

Annie backed away, her hands held up and her mouth working in strange shapes. Then she turned and hurried out, a security guard following her. Keri-Lee slumped back into her seat. Ruby put an arm around her, and they sat there silently, waiting.

It seemed to take half the night before the doctor appeared, her face tired but her smile genuine. Keri-Lee scrambled to her feet.

"He's banged up," she said. "And he's not going to be on his feet for a bit, but he'll recover just fine. Do you want to see him?"

"Yes," Keri-Lee said immediately and followed the doctor into a shared ward. Daniel was in the bed nearest the door, and he gave her a lopsided smile.

"There you are," he said.

"You were the first person he asked for," the doctor said to Keri-Lee. "You've got about five minutes before he's out from the meds." Then she was gone.

Keri-Lee approached the bed cautiously. "I'm sorry. This is all my fault."

"No, no," he said. "I should've talked to you, not just got rid of the book like that." He hesitated. "Did you really think you could bring your mom back?"

"No," Keri-Lee said truthfully. "It wasn't for that." But then she wondered exactly why Annie had the book.

"Your mum loved you so much," Daniel said, his words already starting to slur. "But the world … it was just too much. It wasn't your fault. No one could have helped. No amount of love could have stopped her doing what she did."

Keri-Lee took his hand, finding her chest tight. "It wasn't your fault either."

"I suppose," he said. "Maybe if I'd loved her just that bit more—"

"No," she said. "Like you said, no amount of love could have stopped her."

He nodded. "I love you so much, sweetheart."

"I love you too, Dad," she said and hugged him as gently as she could, keeping her head on his chest as his arm slipped off her and his breathing grew slow and regular. Only when she was sure he was asleep did she straighten up and walk back out into the waiting room, where Ruby led her back out into the night.

KERI-LEE WASN'T SURPRISED to find Annie sitting in the kitchen when she got home. She'd washed her face, but mascara still spackled the area under her eyes, and she had the old brown cardigan wrapped tightly around her. She stood up when Keri-Lee entered, her eyes haunted.

For a moment, they stood staring at one another.

"He's going to be alright," Keri-Lee said, walking in and opening the fridge, staring at the contents. "Does your dad not keep *any* booze in the house?"

"He has a whisky stash behind the sofa," Annie said.

"Gross. But better than nothing." Keri-Lee found the bottle and brought it back to the kitchen, pouring them each a shot into stained mugs. "Why would you leave, really? I mean, he's such a *dad*, but he's alright. He loves you."

Annie waved slightly, indicating the house. "It's not him. It's her. It was like living with a ghost. All the time. I didn't even know how to stop wearing her clothes."

Keri-Lee looked at the photos on the walls, all the same woman, all not quite looking at the photographer, already stepping out of the life she'd ultimately leave behind.

"I'm sorry," she said. "That's shitty. And I'm sorry I was so mean to you. That we all were. We didn't know."

"Shouldn't have had to," Annie said, sipping the whisky and making a face.

"That's fair," Keri-Lee agreed. "Were you really going to try and bring your mum back with the book?"

"No," Annie said with a sigh. "I think I wanted the *possibility* of being able to. But she was too sad. I mean, she was *always* sad. Why would I make her live through any more of that?"

Keri-Lee looked at her mug and took a mouthful. It burned, but it wasn't bad. Annie was a lightweight. "The book's gone. Your dad got rid of it. So I guess we're stuck."

"No," Annie said, and Keri-Lee looked up sharply. "I know how to reverse it. I don't need the book." They looked at each other for a moment, then Annie added, "Do you want me to?"

Keri-Lee bit her lip, then said, "Life on the other side's not so great either, right?"

"Thank you for the note. For telling me to lock the door." There was a wobble in Annie's voice. "I'm sorry. I always thought you had it so easy. That you were so *perfect.*"

Keri-Lee snorted. "I think that's what they call a defense mechanism at the hospital."

Annie winced. "That must've been *really* bad."

"Not super-fun, no." She looked at Annie sideways. "Were you … was it okay? Was the lock enough?"

"Pretty much."

Keri-Lee didn't ask for details. She didn't need to. *Pretty much.* The passing too close in the hall, the press against the sink, the hand on the thigh under the table.

"You should tell someone," Annie said.

"He'll be moving out next year for school."

"What if he does it to someone else?" They were both silent for a moment, then Annie said, "I can tell your mum. While I'm you, I mean."

Keri-Lee looked at her, her throat clicking as she swallowed. "You'd do that?"

"Of course."

They fell silent again, then Keri-Lee shook her head. "No. I need to do it. But perhaps you can come with me when I do tell her?"

"Sure. Anything you want." Annie got up. "I'm going back to yours, and I'll reverse everything. It'll all be back to normal tomorrow."

"Not quite normal," Keri-Lee said and got up, too, putting her arms around Annie. The other girl stiffened, catching her breath, then relaxed, and for a moment, they stood there holding each other in the mellow light of the kitchen.

They were both as hurt and scared and scarred as the other, although in a thousand different ways. But they were also just as full of hope and strength and endless, wild potential.

Which was more magic than any book could offer.

Retargeted

SKYE RILEY

Retargeted

SKYE RILEY

"NOBODY EVEN CARES ABOUT PROM QUEEN ANYMORE. What is this, the 80s?" Natalie sighed, two seconds away from an eye roll. "There are far more important elections we could be talking about."

The four seniors had been discussing prom court nominations for longer than anyone should have been able to tolerate, let alone Natalie.

Benji raised a brow at her declaration, plucking a french fry from his lunch tray and popping it into his mouth.

"Well, Nat, I'll have you know that Brianna is supposedly the only one running."

"Shit!" Shay's eyes darted from Benji to Natalie.

Kayla let out a mix of a hiccup, a snort, and a laugh at Shay's reaction.

"Okay, so she has no competition. That just makes this all worse, these are all of the ingredients for a boring election."Natalie crossed her arms, leaning back in her seat, daring her friends to question her. "Again, why would I care?"

"Maybe because she used to be your *best friend?*" Shay said, stating the obvious that their other two friends were clearly too nervous to share.

Natalie's blasé front faltered slightly. She uncrossed her arms, reaching for a fork to pick at the gelatinous spaghetti sitting atop her plate.

"Not since the ninth grade." She shoved a forkful of noodles into her mouth.

The library tended to stay deserted during their lunch period, leaving Natalie and her friends with the perfect home base in their hell hole of a high school. Most seniors chose to eat lunch off campus, but with Benji being the only one among them who could drive, it was difficult for them to coordinate a successful lunch trip before the bell rang. Especially since Kayla's wheelchair could barely be squeezed into the trunk— at least a quarter of their rare lunchtime field trips were spent getting the thing in and out. They hadn't attempted an outing since the disastrous Five Guys Fiasco of Winter 2024 when Shay spilled a milkshake all over the backseat. Benji's hysterics nearly caused them all to crash on the freeway, and then he pulled over and refused to start the engine back up until his baby was spotless.

None of them made it to class that day on time.

"Well, maybe you don't care about her being your ex-best friend, but what about the rest of her whole deal? The girl's a total bitch!" Shay said. Kayla nodded in agreement.

"Shay's right; it's not like you to not have an opinion about something," poked Benji.

Natalie's shoulders tensed, and she would have taken another thousand milkshake spills just to get out of this conversation.

Luckily, Kayla swooped in at just the right moment,

her voice as comforting as always. "Well, Benji said it's only a rumor anyway …"

"A rumor from a very reliable source!"

"Since when is Instagram a reliable source?"

Their voices faded away and Natalie initiated a staring contest with her spaghetti, not even processing that the bell had rung until everyone else had their bags half packed and ready to go.

~

WHEN BENJI DROPPED Natalie off at home after school, she lasted a grand total of eighty seconds before succumbing and digging out the old suitcase of memories from the depths of her closet. And then she tried to hold back again; she really did, but it only lasted twenty-two seconds before popping the lid off and rummaging around inside.

She sorted through various memorabilia with a scowl, cursing herself for breaking her promise to never again touch the Brianna Box.

Her fingertips skimmed across various photos and scraps of paper, the memories flooding back with each one.

A charred firecracker wrapper from the time they'd found a pile of wet fireworks on the side of the street and decided to put them to use. It had been Natalie's brilliant idea to dry them off in the microwave, which inevitably set them all off in Bri's tiny kitchen. Her mother looked like she would have throttled Natalie herself if she'd been her own daughter, but instead, Stacey opted for some harsh language that introduced a whole new set of vocabulary to an eight-year-old Natalie.

There was a lollipop wrapper from Brianna's trip to the

emergency room after the two girls had scooped up a dead possum and plopped it into Natalie's bag for safekeeping. Only the possum wasn't dead, and the very much alive mammal was so startled that he bit the tip of Brianna's pointer finger clean off. Brianna had thought it made her look cool.

A wrinkled photo from their middle school's Career Day celebration sat next to the lollipop wrapper. A twelve-year-old version of Natalie stared back at her with a grin wide enough to claim half her face. Brianna stood beside her with a sheepish smile of her own as Natalie pointed to the sash draped across her body. Brianna had shown up dressed as a Prom Queen, to which Natalie had argued that was no career at all, let alone a career for someone as bright as Brianna. She crossed out the word *prom* with a Sharpie, leaving just *Queen* for a giggling Bri. However, that moment was spoiled hours later when Natalie learned that the sash belonged to Stacey. Her vocabulary was more advanced than anyone else in her grade at that point, and yet she still managed to learn a new word or two from the earful she got that day.

Natalie continued to sort through the suitcase, brow furrowing with frustration. And then she held it upside down and shook the contents out onto her bed.

The flood of memories turned to a hurricane, violent flashbacks souring any joy she'd felt from the earlier mementos.

She glared down at the pair of matching Tokyo Mew Mew shirts splayed across her bed. She'd bought them the summer before freshman year so that she and Brianna could match on their first day of high school.

Only Brianna never showed up at the bus stop. Instead, she'd gotten a ride from her new best friend (and previous tormentor) Madison. They both ignored Natalie for the entire day. Or at least ignored her when they weren't busy making her day a living nightmare. One of the shirts was stained with blue raspberry Slurpee, and Natalie could still feel the cold rush of slush down the front of her shirt from when Brianna had dumped it on her during lunch.

Natalie still had no idea what caused things to go so sour between them. They had been inseparable since the third grade, up until something shifted in Brianna the summer before freshman year. She'd left for school without Natalie, and was all of a sudden besties with the biggest bully on campus.

Maybe all it took to get on Madison's good side was to look the part. She'd always had the makings of a popular girl. Brianna was practically a living doll. But there was a stark difference between the "weird girl with hidden potential" and the "this whole school worships my looks" switch that had happened between the end of eighth grade and the start of ninth.

Brianna showed up at school with hair extensions that had to have cost at least two hundred dollars, paired with a full face of makeup and a new wardrobe. Natalie probably wouldn't have recognized her if she hadn't spent practically every single day with her over the past half-decade.

She didn't know why Brianna decided to drop her for Madison without a word or what had compelled her to spend the next four years torturing Natalie and her friends the same way they'd been tormented all of middle school.

Natalie didn't know a single thing that was going through Brianna's head, just that she was no longer the bashful sweetheart she used to be proud to call a friend.

But Natalie *did* know that it was about time someone took Brianna down a peg after all the havoc she'd wrought on her heart. Somebody needed to make her feel just as small as she'd made Natalie feel over the years.

And there was only one person with enough insight — and vocabulary — to get the job done.

~

"I'M RUNNING FOR PROM QUEEN," Natalie slammed her hands on the library table, chest puffed with pride.

Kayla's jaw dropped while Shay let out a cackle.

Benji didn't look up from his English homework, barely acknowledging Natalie before he spoke. "What happened to all that junk about there being far more important things to care about than prom?"

"And something about how it's not the 80s anymore?" Kayla reminded her.

"That was all before I saw the prom royal court for what it really is," Natalie said, pausing for effect.

The group waited with bated breath, except for Benji, who seemed focused on his assignment due next period.

"An election," Natalie finished. "It's an election, it's politics. I'm *good* at politics."

"Not the social kind," said Shay.

Natalie glared at them.

"Although we can work on that. Though I'll be real, Nat, I don't like your chances. I can't really see you winning this thing." They slung an arm around Natalie like a coach talking to their most promising player. "But give me a shot at this campaign, and I swear I'll get you to the top."

Benji finally looked up from his paper, if only to give the two an eye roll before returning to his work.

"I'm not saying this is all about Brianna being my ex-best friend because it's *not.*" Natalie paused to shoot an individual glare toward each of her friends. "But I do think it would be crazy to let Brianna simply walk away with the crown just because everyone else is too scared to run."

"It's not … a *bad* idea," admitted Kayla, putting emphasis on *bad* that made it sound like a question more than reassurance.

"We'll get you on that ballot, Natalie," Shay said. "And I'm sure Benji would feel the same if he hadn't waited until the last possible second to start his assignment that's due today."

"Huh?" Benji snapped his head up at the mention of his name, just in time for Shay to swat him on the back of his head.

THE NEXT DAY, Natalie and her fellow students shuffled into homeroom with a mix of anticipation and stark indifference. Some of them seemed to care about prom nominations even less than Natalie had before she'd decided to run, while others buzzed with excitement.

Some of the excitement was being shared in voices a little too painfully familiar.

"It'll be a total sweep! You've got no competition," Madison practically giggled, leaning over Brianna's desk. "I mean, literally, no competition. No one else is running! And even if they were, you would crush them for sure."

Natalie held back a smile at that last bit.

Part of her wondered why Madison hadn't run for Prom Queen herself, it's not like she was any less popular than Brianna. She was their school's Queen bee — if anything —the one making the rules and starting the trends that Brianna had climbed to the top by following.

But maybe that's exactly why Madison couldn't be Prom Queen; she was already a Queen in her own right.

She was so big that a title referencing literal royalty was somehow too small for her.

"Umm, hello?"

Madison's snooty voice brought her back to reality.

"The freak's staring at us…" she stage whispered to Brianna.

"Does she know she looks constipated when she holds her face like that?" Brianna whispered back, holding eye contact with Natalie while the words left her perfectly glossed lips.

The PA crackled to life before Natalie could interject, and Principal Ryder began listing off that day's announcements.

There were plenty of nominees for Prom King, the list so long that Natalie practically fell asleep. But hearing Shay's name caught her off guard enough to resurrect her interest, and she sprang from her seat with a loud cheer despite the scattered stares from her classmates.

Shay grinned at her.

"You slip your name in while you know —"Natalie dropped her voice to a proper whisper — "nominating me?"

"Of course!"

"And finally, the nominee for Prom Queen," Principal Ryder gave a loud sigh. "Er — well, nominees."

Natalie resumed her seat at her desk.

Brianna perked up with interest, along with a handful of other students.

"Just for future reference, I would really prefer that you all get your nominations in before the absolute last possible second of the final day to submit them," Ryder said, not even trying to hide her annoyance. "Not that any of you seniors will be around for another one of these elections, thank God. So Juniors, take notes."

"And the nominees are … Brianna Finch …"

Madison squealed and wrapped her arms around Brianna in a celebratory hug, wiping mock tears as though they hadn't already known her nomination was secured.

"And Natalie Foster."

Their was a buzz of confusion from the students, but Natalie couldn't hear a word over the slamming of Brianna's hands against her desk when she stood, turning toward Natalie.

"What the fuck do you think you're doing?" She stomped over toward Natalie's desk with a scowl.

"Just exercising my right as a member of our beloved student body, of course," she said, offering a small shrug.

"Ha. Ha!" Brianna scoffed, rage slipping into a laugh that didn't quite match the venom in her eyes. "You just have to try and ruin everything, don't you? Always swooping in to have the last word?"

"You used to love letting me have the last word," Natalie sighed with artificial nonchalance, not wanting Brianna to know how painful it was for her to think about their past at all.

"Ohh, you little—"

Brianna looked like she was about to snap for real, but Madison clamped her hand on her forearm. "Come on, this isn't worth it."

Brianna scowled, but it looked more like a pout. Madison's gesture seemed to have pulled all the steam from her performance.

"Who cares if the ugliest girl in school wants to run? There's no way she can win," Madison said.

And with that, Brianna seemed to finally relent.

"Right, yeah." She blinked, shoulders loosening as she un-tensed her body. Then she took a deep breath, cooling herself down before meeting Natalie's gaze again.

"Well, good luck then. You'll need a lot more than that to win, though."

Seeing how little of a threat she considered Natalie to be was infinitely worse than any of her rage. It was enough to turn Natalie into the fiery one, enough to make her view this as a competition and not a game.

Natalie wasn't just going to run for Prom Queen. She was going to *win*.

"DO you really need to stand on top of the table for whatever this is?"

Natalie frowned at Benji's question, taking her final step up onto the wooden picnic table in the courtyard.

"Well, yes, of course."

"This is about the election, right? Are you sure it's a good idea to talk strategy where our opponents can hear it?" Kayla whispered.

Natalie scanned the empty courtyard. The lawn was so empty they'd probably be hearing crickets if it was a different time of day.

"I think we're fine," laughed Shay.

"It doesn't matter to me anyway," Natalie said, chest puffed, "let Madison hear, for all I care! She was right. I won't be able to win because I don't have a wide network of friends." She stomped her foot on the picnic table for emphasis, then paused. "Not that I'm unhappy with you all, of course."

"Charmed," Benji said, with a shake of his head.

"But despite my slight setback, I'm going to come up with a plan to take the crown for myself."

"You can't steal it though, remember?" Kayla said with

such sincerity that made Natalie wonder if Kayla really thought she could ever stoop so low.

"It's all legal, Kayla. I'm going to get elected. And I'm going to do it by being sooo friendly to everyone, they won't know what hit them. I know I don't have a lot of time, and I know I'm not off to a great start ..."

Natalie could tell from the spectrum of expressions that each of her friends was likely reminiscing on a different time she'd sunk her popularity in the past.

"But I'm thinking if we can organize some kind of event that'll get everyone's attention, it would be the perfect way to swoop in and prove how capable of having fun I am." Natalie spread her hands wide, then sat on the picnic table, leaning towards her friends. "How do you all feel about paintball?"

~

NOBODY SHOWED FOR PAINTBALL.

It was obvious word of mouth hadn't worked, and neither had the flyers that Benji so carefully tucked under the windshield wipers of every car in the senior parking lot. The problem was that most of the graduating class didn't even know who Natalie was. Now, time was running out, and they needed to come up with another plan ASAP.

"I don't think I quite understand," Benji shook his head. "How can you win an election through targeted ads?"

"*Re*targeted," Natalie said. "Branding is important, my dear Benji. We're retargeting here, redirecting their opinions on Brianna by giving them hyper-specific ads that will remind the Class of 2025 of how awful she's always been."

"Won't that get expensive?" Kayla asked.

"Can't be more than fifty cents an ad, right?" Shay piped in.

"And how do we get all the information for those ads?" asked Benji. "Don't you think people would get suspicious if we just started approaching random students to ask about the times they've been bullied by Brianna?"

Natalie whipped out her phone and slid it across the picnic table, screen up. "Lucky for us, Brianna and Madison have never been shy about sharing their successes."

"Smug bitches ..." Shay murmured under their breath, eyes locked on Natalie's phone. A video whirred to life of Brianna and Madison playing Monkey in the Middle with an asthmatic kid and his inhaler. "It's about time they get what's coming to them."

Natalie closed Madison's feed and cracked her knuckles. "Let's get to work then."

COLLECTING information wasn't a quick process, but Brianna and Madison's endless need to gloat definitely made the job easier. Within a handful of hours, Team Natalie had gathered a list of offenses long enough to execute their plan twice.

Then, they got to work on creating the ads, using the atrocities committed against their fellow students to craft individually tailored slogans favoring Natalie.

In sophomore year, Brianna had bullied Jenny into overstuffing her bra right before the opening night of their school play, leading to a complete humiliation when the padding fell out on stage during the performance: *Don't believe the body-shamer, you're perfect. Vote Natalie!*

Junior year, Brianna filmed Eric sitting by himself,

singing a song he had written about his cats. He couldn't go anywhere for a full year without the taunting choruses of "Sauron, you're fluffy, and Gandalf, you're sweet, but little old Gollum has six toes on each feet" everywhere he went: *Some people don't get music, but Natalie does!*

Just a few months before, Sarah had arrived to homeroom and found a basket of toiletries on her desk. A note awaited her, telling Sarah that she needed a good wash, signed "from the class" despite Brianna's obvious handwriting: *Brianna stinks— literally! Do you really want a smelly Queen? Vote Natalie!.* And then Natalie hit submit. Soon, everyone in 12th grade started receiving them. Even some of Brianna's most loyal followers (out of fear, but followers nonetheless) were starting to wonder whether they really wanted to elect *this* person as Prom Queen.

After all, a vote for Natalie was a vote to punish Brianna for any shade she'd sent their way, and the people (i.e., the voters) seemed eager to finally have a way to get back at her. Anti-Brianna sentiment quickly swelled, and kids who used to be afraid of her and Madison were now standing up to them.

Natalie practically cheered when she saw the Costco-sized bottle of revenge-scented body wash sitting on Brianna's desk before homeroom just a few days after the retargeting campaign started. Not only that, but Natalie was actually starting to make headway in Kayla's election polls. Her win was no longer hypothetical. When her campaign team decided to host a water balloon fight in celebration of Natalie's sudden shift, *everyone* showed up.

Everyone, that is, except for Brianna and Madison. Who had planned their own little party the same day to compete — only nobody went.

When Natalie showed up at school the next day, Brianna was waiting for her. Arms crossed and foot tapping against the tile, her mouth a flat line — full confrontation mode activated.

"Look, you may have managed to pull off … whatever the fuck this is, whatever you've been up to. But there is *no way* you are going to win the crown." Spittle flew from her mouth.

"And what makes you so sure of that?" Natalie asked.

A somewhat lazy reply, but it still held more than enough power to rattle Brianna.

Her mouth searched for words but found none, arms slowly uncrossing and falling to her sides.

For the first time, Natalie saw doubt in her eyes.

"WE'RE in the home stretch now, baby!" Shay said, spinning themself around and around in a creaky office chair that had maybe five more spins in it fell apart.

"We've just gotta get you through your speech, and then it's pretty much a guaranteed sweep at this point," Benji said with confidence. "I've read over what Kayla's written for you so far, and it's *good*."

Kayla looked down at the notecards sheepishly, letting a small smile escape before passing the speech over to Natalie.

Natalie scanned the cards, speed-reading. Benji was right, it was … good. But she had a better idea of what to say.

"I love what we've got so far, but I think I might make a couple changes," she told Kayla, trying to figure out the nicest way possible to tell her it wasn't enough. "I'm going to add a bit of flair."

"Care to share?" Shay asked, trying to take a peek at the notecards while Natalie scribbled away.

"It's a secret."

Benji's brow furrowed, and he leaned forward. Not to read Natalie's notes but to meet her eyes. "Nat, those cards were perfectly fine."

"Right, *fine*." She emphasized the word. "Just fine. That's why I'm embellishing them."

"I think you might be taking this a little too seriously."

Natalie let out a sharp laugh. "Trust me, you'll *know* when I take this too seriously."

NATALIE SHOULD HAVE KNOWN there'd be trouble as soon as she heard Brianna's shrill voice screeching behind her.

"Natalie!"

But Natalie ignored her, continuing her stroll to the gym where she'd be delivering her final speech prior to the vote.

"I know what you're up to!"

Now, that was enticing.

Natalie came to a stop, turning on her heel to meet Brianna, who was striding toward her in a fury. She bumped into several students on her way, grabbing their phones from their hands.

"Vote Natalie: Because she won't make fun of you for playing the tuba?" Brianna read. "Vote Natalie: Because she won't bully you for loving cats?"

"Good copy, right?" Natalie smirked.

"This is illegal," Brianna said, pointing a finger at Natalie's chest like she'd just uncovered enough evidence to lock her up for good.

Students walked around them like nothing was happening at all.

"I don't think that's true," Natalie replied, sounding bored while she brushed Brianna's accusatory finger away. "I didn't do anything you couldn't have done yourself. Assuming you were smart enough to ever think it up in the first place."

Brianna looked like a tea kettle. Maybe worse. Closer to a boiler about to burst. But her expression quickly softened, gaze shifting to follow whoever had just passed Natalie in the hall.

"Oh, Principal Ryder!" Brianna called out before chasing after Ryder with feigned distress and puppy dog eyes.

"Not now." Ryder didn't even turn in their direction. Instead, she pushed the doors to the gym open.

"I have to tell you something about Natalie!" Brianna said.

"And I have to keep this circus on schedule," Principal Ryder sighed, making her way over to the podium. "Talk to me after?"

Brianna huffed but reluctantly made her way toward the candidate seating section of the gym.

THE NOMINATED KINGS made their speeches first. Shay's speech not only brought the house down but caused so much applause and enthusiasm that the following speech needed to be shaved by thirty seconds. After a tirade hopping from gender roles to bullies to performative kindness, Shay had managed to weave together a narrative that seamlessly connected the social hierarchy of their high school's misery. Natalie could only listen in awe, amazed at how, despite all the social deterrents stacked against them, Shay was somehow charismatic enough to make her wonder who else anyone was supposed to vote for.

By the time Natalie took the podium, the class seemed bored. But Natalie was ready to change that and rile them up just like Shay had before.

"You have before you today two choices for Prom Queen," she said. "Over the past few months, I have gotten to know so many of you. Which is more than Brianna can say."

Brianna stiffened upon hearing her name.

"I think we can all agree that, as new grads, the future is uncertain. But one thing we know as a class that is certain? Brianna Finch is a bully."

A handful of gasps filled the gym.

Brianna's jaw dropped and she spun toward Principal Ryder, saucer sized eyes screaming *SEE?! This is what I was talking about!*

Natalie continued. "Brianna doesn't care about anyone but herself. She'll call the prettiest girl in the school — Parvati, that's you — ugly."

Across from her in the gym bleachers, Parvati slumped.

"And the smartest girl, Ellen? Dumb. The funniest boy, Ari? A moron."

A soft *What?* could be heard from the audience.

"She'll target those she considers lonely — Eric, Jenny, Sasha, Stella, Rupert —or meek — Tom, Krista, Kenji …"

Natalie pounded the podium. Ryder stood.

"She laughs at your insecurities. And for what?" Natalie paused for emphasis, this was really the finisher: "To make herself feel better because she's simply a scared little girl who failed second grade."

"Alright, Natalie—" Principal Ryder took a step toward the podium, looking ready to confiscate the mic.

"I'm almost finished!" A loud whine of feedback was

heard from the mic when Natalie turned from Ryder back toward the audience. "So in conclusion ... a vote for Brianna is a vote for a bully. And you all deserve someone better for Prom Queen. You deserve me!"

She raised her right fist in the air, dropping the mic with her left.

"Vote Natalie!"

Not a single wisp of applause.

The gym was deadly silent. Even Natalie's friends were staring at her from the bleachers with their jaws halfway to the floor.

But Natalie did not factor in a single one of these things. When she hopped down from the podium, shoved the mic against Brianna's chest, and took her seat with a whisper of *"Top that."*

Brianna slowly got up and took the podium, staring out into the audience with unblinking eyes.

It took what felt like hours for her to do anything. She just stared, eyes even wider than Natalie's ego. But when she did finally open her mouth, all that came out was a loud sob.

"Alright," Ryder said. "My office, you two — NOW."

"SHE'S BEEN BULLYING ME ONLINE!" Brianna cried, her accusatory finger making another appearance.

"It's not bullying if I'm just telling the truth," Natalie said.

"Show me." Principal Ryder sighed, burying her face into one hand while her other stretched toward the girls, palm up.

Brianna placed her phone down, revealing dozens of snapshots featuring Natalie's ads.

"Jesus Christ ..." Ryder murmured. "Every student got one of these?"

They nodded in unison. Brianna's gesture was eager, but Natalie's nod was one of admittance.

"This borders on harassment, Natalie."

"What?" She blanched. "That's so unfair! I've been bullied and harassed for years by Brianna. How was any of that acceptable, but this isn't?"

"You could have come talk to me at any time," Ryder softened just slightly, barely enough to notice.

"I prefer to solve my own problems," Natalie huffed.

"Clearly," murmured the principal. "Alright, Natalie. I'm going to have to suspend you for a day."

Natalie's heart dropped like a falling elevator. "You can't do that."

Ryder laughed. "I can."

Brianna stuck her tongue out when Ryder turned around to grab a suspension slip.

Natalie was seeing scarlet by the time Ryder faced her again. "So I'm being punished for standing up for myself?"

"For harassment."

"This is BULLSHIT!" Natalie yelled, throwing her arms up in the air.

Principal Ryder slid a piece of paper across the desk towards her. "Now it's two days."

"WHAT HAPPENED?" Kayla asked, her voice filled with concern.

"Suspended for two days," Natalie said through gritted teeth.

"Fucking hell," said Shay.

Benji's frown deepened. "Went a little far, don't you think?"

"I know," Natalie sighed, running a hand through her hair. "Brianna's allowed to do whatever she wants, but the second I stand for *anything*, I'm too much of a problem!"

"I meant the speech."

"Oh," Natalie's shoulders slumped. "You ... didn't like it?"

"It was a little much," Shay admitted.

"It's one thing seeing all that stuff digitally. But hearing it out loud ...? You made it real, Natalie," Kayla said softly.

"It's always been real."

"But *you* were the one saying it this time around. What if someone else had stood up there and bellowed all your biggest insecurities out to the entire senior class?" Kayla tried to place a sympathetic hand on her shoulder, but Natalie pulled away.

"Nat, come on," Shay sighed.

"If it was so bad, why didn't you stop me?" Natalie turned toward them. "You were right up there with me."

"I had my own speech to worry about," they defended.

"I thought you didn't care about that!" Natalie scoffed. "Nominated yourself as a joke."

"I thought you didn't either. What's this about for you now, Natalie? Is it really just about getting Brianna back?"

Natalie vented a shocked laugh, the kind that escapes in anger when there's nothing else to say. "You know what, I'm done with this. And I'm done with you all."

"Natalie," Benji started.

But by the time he'd figured out what to say, she was already out the door.

~

WHEN NATALIE'S mom arrived home, she found her lying facedown on her bedroom floor in a pile of tears and shredded Brianna memorabilia.

She scooped her into her arms like Natalie was six years old all over again, brushing the hair away from her tear stained face with a gentle hand.

"Speech didn't go as planned?"

"No."

"Want to talk about it?"

"No." Natalie sniffed.

"How could she do that to me? After everything?"

"Brianna?"

Natalie gave her a weak nod. "She just … tossed me out like I'm some toy she didn't want to play with anymore. Like she outgrew me."

"I know," said Natalie's mom with a reassuring pat.

"I loved her."

"I know."

"And I think I went too far."

"When have you not gone too far?"

Natalie grunted.

"I think you have some leftover hurt that never got resolved. And even though she dumped you all those years ago, you still let those hurt feelings get the better of you."

"Yeah. I fucked up."

"Whatever happened between you and Brianna back then wasn't your fault."

"No, I mean with my friends. The way I treated them, I'm no better than Brianna."

"Okay," her mother sat up a bit straighter, reaching to give Natalie's hand a firm squeeze. "So what are you going to do about it?"

NATALIE SPENT a good chunk of her suspension deliberating the best way to make it up to her friends. Clean Benji's car? Rig the votes so Shay won Prom King for sure? Let Kayla take her place as Queen?

The more time she spent deliberating on what grand gesture to perform, the simpler that answer became.

"I'm sorry," Natalie said, staring at her three friends with a jumbled mix of regret, embarrassment, and humility. She'd invited them to the coffee shop, then spent the whole night worrying that they wouldn't come. But they did.

"Wow, I don't think I've ever heard those words come out of your mouth before," Shay said with mock shock. "Could you repeat that real quick ...? You're... sow- sah ... saaah-ree?" They chewed on the pronunciation.

Natalie turned a shade of red so bright that Benji gently punched Shay on the shoulder.

"I truly am. Sorry, I mean. I'm sorry," Natalie repeated. "I only wanted to hurt one person, but instead, I wound up hurting everyone. You guys specifically."

Shay still looked a little pissed. Benji looked sympathetic, and Kayla was looking anywhere but at Natalie.

"I don't want to go to prom anymore, this whole election bullshit has made me lose sight of what's important. Which is you three."

"Oh no, you're *going* to prom," Benji said.

"Huh?"

"You owe your classmates a pretty big apology, don't you think?" Shay raised a brow.

"And you've never been one to run away from accountability," Kayla said, finally looking her in the eyes with what Natalie could have sworn was almost a smile.

THE SAME HIGH school gymnasium that hosted her disaster of a speech just days before had transformed to something straight out of a movie. Color coordinated streamers mingled with delicate fairy lights throughout the gym. A refreshments table in the corner looked like it was probably professionally catered.

Shay had organized a group trip to their local thrift store to pick up outfits for the big night. Benji had already rented a tux, and Kayla'd had her dress picked out for months, but they were happy to come along as Shay and Natalie hunted for their perfect finds. Shay finally settled on a snazzy vintage suit, and Natalie opted for a flattering pantsuit. More presidential than prom, but nobody complained.

They'd all driven over together in Benji's car and spent the whole first hour of prom dancing the night away like nothing had ever gone wrong between them at all.

But as the night stretched further and they got closer to the crowning, Natalie began to worry. Brianna was nowhere to be seen. And she may have still been pissed as hell, but that didn't mean Brianna deserved to miss celebrating her own graduation.

Had she not come because she knew Natalie would be there? That bothered her. So, without a word to any of her friends, Natalie slipped out of the party and walked towards a house she knew all too well.

She ran a spectrum of possible scenarios for what might happen when she knocked on the door of her former friend's home. Brianna would answer, in some sort of hazmat suit, because she'd contracted a horrible contagious illness that prevented her from making it to prom.

Stacey would answer and cuss Natalie out for whatever unresolved issues she had with her.

Or maybe the house wouldn't be there at all, a long-gone figment of Natalie's childhood that only existed in her memories.

But she never expected to see Brianna standing in the door with a black eye, busted lip, and swollen nose.

"Jeeeesus, what happened to you?" Natalie said.

Brianna was quick to startle after realizing who was at her door, and even quicker to slam it shut.

But Natalie wedged her foot in right before it closed and pushed Brianna back to force herself inside.

"Hey, hey, stop," she said more gently, raising her hands in front of her like a white flag. "Brianna, I'm serious. Drop the antics for a second. What happened?"

Brianna's bloody lip quivered, and the tears came soon after.

"Stacey," was all she could get out, tears spilling.

"Stacey?" Natalie repeated, face scrunching as images of Brianna's unpleasant mother flooded back. "Why?"

A flash of frustration took Brianna over so suddenly that she nearly quit crying altogether. "It's obvious, isn't it? You won."

"Prom Queen?"

"Yes."

"We don't know who won yet. And why should that matter? It's not that serious."

Brianna let out an exasperated sigh. "It is to her. Her mom won, she won, *I* was supposed to win."

"And you still might!" Natalie said, the strangeness of the whole *comforting your ex-best friend who hurt you in ways you didn't know you could ever hurt* situation slipping into her tone.

"You made sure I wouldn't," Brianna replied. "You should leave now, Natalie. They're probably announcing the winners soon, and you wouldn't want to miss that after all your hard work."

Brianna's resentment swallowed her sarcasm.

She turned toward the stairs, but Natalie grabbed her shoulder and spun her around.

"Why did you stop being my friend?" She surprised herself with the question. Probably looked almost as caught off guard as Brianna did.

Brianna stared back at Natalie in silence.

"Just tell me, and I'll leave. You won't have to see me again."

"I always wanted to be your friend, Natalie. But Stacey thought you were too weird," Brianna said.

"I'm not weird!" Natalie almost yelled.

"You blew up our kitchen."

"Okay, maybe a little weird. But Brianna, so were you."

"I was, yeah. And Stacey didn't like that, so she made me stop seeing you. I didn't know how to tell you. It seemed a hell of a lot easier to just pretend we were never friends in the first place."

Natalie breathed out a long sigh. "That's fucked up."

"Tell me about it. I've spent all of high school working so hard to live up to exactly who Stacey wants me to be. I don't even know what I'm doing after any of this because all she ever wanted was for me to win Prom Queen. And I failed at that."

Brianna wiped her eyes. A loud chime sent Natalie digging for her phone.

SHAY: *coronation in half an hour. where are you?*
NATALIE: *Can you meet me at Brianna's house?*
SHAY: *who's house?*
NATALIE: *Brianna.*

SHAY: *sorry, i thought i read that wrong*
NATALIE: *88 Elm Street*

THEN SHE DRAGGED Brianna upstairs and got her dressed. Makeup over the bruises. Hair done. And minutes later, when Benji's car pulled up, they were ready to go. They piled into Benji's car alongside Shay and Kayla and made it back to the school with exactly two minutes to spare — just enough time to make it inside the gym when Principal Ryder took the stage.

"The votes have been cast... we got a great turnout this year, even you last minute slackers pulled your weight."

A few people laughed. Some of them sounded nervous. It didn't take long for the room to still for Ryder to continue.

She began opening a weighty envelope, the gym so silent you could hear every single crinkle of paper.

"And the Class of 2025's prom king is..."

The room went still.

"Shay Davis!"

The stillness erupted into applause, and Shay's friends had surrounded them within seconds with the loudest cheers of all.

"Not so fast! We still have the queen," Ryder grumbled, with a tone that all but said she couldn't wait to finally get this drama over with.

"Your Class of 2025's prom queen..."

Natalie sucked in a breath.

"Is... also Shay Davis!"

Ryder sounded more impressed than confusion or shock, but Natalie felt enough surprise for the both of them. But a good surprise, near relief. She joined the rest of the gym as their cheers crescendoed into a roar.

Natalie glowed with pride, slapping her friend on the back with excitement.

Shay turned to her, breathless. "You're not mad?"

"Hello, no! Long live King Queen Shay!"

The last syllables of Natalie's sentiment were drowned out by cheers and chants from their fellow classmates, demanding a speech from their newly crowned prom royalty.

"SPEECH! SPEECH! SPEECH!"

Shay bounded up the stage steps two at a time, grabbing the mic from Principle Ryder with a photo perfect smile.

"Listen up, all you Kings, Queens, Jokers, Aces, and every other card in the deck. In a world where you can be anything …?" They paused, looking out into the audience expectantly.

"Be kind!"

"Hell no! Have you learned nothing? Be yourself!"

The class laughed, and Natalie beamed with glee.

"Unless you're an asshole. Don't do that."

The crowd erupted with laughter and cheers. There's a reason Shay won, and Natalie couldn't be any prouder to call them her friend.

"Now," Shay gestured toward the Prom King crown, "this one is all mine." They plucked the Queen crown off its decorative pillow held by Principal Ryder. "But I'm giving this one to a friend of mine who earned it. Come on up, Natalie!"

Natalie tried to hide her shock. The entire row of students turned to stare at her. She shook her head.

"Oh, come on. I know you've got something you wanted to say to everyone …" Reluctantly, Natalie took the stage. For all her earlier big talk of winning and coming out on top, she was nervous as hell, turning to face what

279

felt like millions of glares from her prom-clad classmates. Her usual *halfway-to-Senator* confidence had been toned down to more of a *let's just get this over with* class president, vulnerability leaking through her thin veneer of courage like a broken faucet.

She blinked, taking a shuddery breath, trying to focus on anything but the bubbling feeling in her stomach that threatened to spill out onto the stage underneath her.

The soft glow of the gymnasium's fairy light and electric candle combo did little to calm her nerves, but combined with the streamers hanging limply from the basketball hoops to her left and right, Natalie found her way back to reality.

This was only high school. A high school *prom*, of all things. If she was letting herself get this worked up after everything that had already happened, how was she going to handle Congress?

Her eyes flickered toward the banner commemorating the *Class of 2025* before returning to her audience.

The room waited, the previous excitement over Shay's presence melting to impatience.

If she took any longer to get started, they'd probably shove her off the stage themselves.

Natalie drew a deep breath, grip tightening on the microphone, and inhaled.

"I know you all must hate me by now, after everything I've done ..." she started, ignoring the sharp digital whine let out by the mic as she wrapped the cord tighter around her fingers, "but I thought it'd serve us all best if I were to explain."

Somebody in the front row rolled their eyes. Another one sighed.

Natalie's breath hitched, scrambling her thoughts up into something new.

"No. Forget that. I don't want to explain. I want to ask for your forgiveness."

A few students looked at her in surprise, a few with a *well, it's about time!* expression. She sorted her three (potentially four) friends into each category, meeting the gazes of Shay, Kayla, Benji, and Brianna. Her eyes settled on Brianna.

"I only ran for Prom Queen to get revenge on a friend who dumped me."

Then, her gaze drifted away from Brianna's baby blues and traveled around the rest of the gym.

"But I had no idea what else was going on in her life. And there are a bunch of cool kids at school — Eric, Jenny, Frank, Lee, Parvati, Stewart, Elijah, Murphy — kids I never got to know over the years. I regret missing out on your friendship."

Natalie stared down at the crown, loosening her grip to allow the color to return to her knuckles. "This crown belongs to the entire class, and everyone should get a turn with it."

She extended a hand toward the audience, inviting Brianna to join her on stage from the front row.

"How about you start?"

Brianna froze. Natalie leaned down to press the microphone in her trembling hands and the crown atop her head.

"I want to apologize too," Brianna finally said into the mic, turning back to face the rest of their class. "Nine years ago, I braved bullies with a fearless girl who taught me how important it was to be myself. To be ... weird." She smiled to herself. "But instead, I ended up becoming no better than the people who used to make our lives hell."

She turned to face Natalie one last time. "It deprived me of your friendship. And for that, I'm truly sorry."

Natalie gnawed at her lip to hold in the torrent of tears that threatened to spill down her face. Shay, noting Natalie's reaction, nabbed the mic from Brianna.

"Class of 2025, let's get this party back on track!"

Natalie gave Shay an appreciative smile, which earned her a wink in response.

She hopped down from the stage and turned to Brianna, offering her hand in a gesture that reminded her so fondly of their third-grade introduction.

"Wanna dance?"

"I thought you'd never ask."

The two girls grinned, making their way out onto the dance floor with linked arms.

Natalie didn't know what it meant for the status of their friendship, what it meant for their remaining week or so of high school. They didn't know what would happen with Stacey once Brianna got home or what they'd do about Madison glowering at them from the corner of the gym.

But none of that mattered because they'd picked up right where they left off. Smiling, laughing, and embracing each other with equal parts of overwhelming weirdness and love.

And they'd learned it the hard way, sure, but both girls now knew there was *nothing* in the world worth losing that again.

How To Train A Murder

CAMERON STONE

How To Train A Murder

CAMERON STONE

THE WOMAN SITS ON THE PICNIC TABLE IN OUR BACKYARD. It's made of pale white wood that hasn't been painted, so it looks like it's fresh off the lot at Home Depot or something. That would be because it is. Mom and Dad can't be bothered to paint it, schedule someone else to do it, or even pick up the paint for me to do it for them.

The woman pulls out a tape recorder and, when she sees my expression, says, "It's far more reliable than phones." Her name is Aileen Mira, and if you've ever paid attention to the late-night news, you've seen her reporting on location, talking about how the suspect got away or how the police are now looking for tips.

Aileen's blonde hair could use another round of bleach around the edges. Dark circles surround her eyes, and she seems uncomfortable. The skies are gray, but they're a light gray, so there isn't any real threat of rain. What she's worried about, and won't admit to, is the crows. She wants to see the real reason she's here, but she's also afraid.

I took a seat across from her, sipping a glass of water because I didn't want to be seen drinking anything else on

285

camera. The asshats at school are going to say that it was vodka, and they'll have a new reason to make me hate their guts. But the producer of the piece, who refuses to even be on the property because birds creep her out, says to me through Aileen's earpiece that it seems more relaxed if I have water. It's more like a conversation and less like an interrogation.

Aileen pushes the tape recorder closer. I can read the words SONY across the bottom. There's a red button at the top that's already been pressed. It has no mechanical motions, but it hums. Maybe that's just my imagination. Maybe it's the birds.

Aileen leans forward and says, "It's okay to be nervous. I'm just going to ask a few questions. Don't worry about the cameras."

"I wasn't until you said something," I say and laugh. She laughs, too.

"I think I've seen you a lot on the news lately. My parents still watch it. You reported on that boy who went missing a few months ago." Maybe if she thinks I like her, she'll go easy on me. Aileen's face turns cold. Maybe I'm wrong. She looks down at her feet for a split second, then turns to me with a shy smile.

"They were good friends of mine. They lived right down the road there." She points, but I'm not sure exactly where she's pointing to. "Maybe you know about them?" I shake my head.

"I know there were signs up all over the place, but they came down after a few good rains, and then they were replaced by the garage sale signs."

Aileen mutters, "Got to love those garage sales, right?" She's good at pulling down your guard at first. But her eyes dart from point to point. She's not actually talking to me or the producer. She's talking to the fence post behind me.

She's talking to the giant evergreen across the yard. She's talking to the garage we have at the back of my house for some reason. Anything and everything but me. It's like this with my parents. Aileen does it so well that I want to call her mom and ask for my allowance.

Something bangs around in the kitchen. Mom pretends to do the dishes suddenly: metal pots and pans bang in the deep metal sink.

We haven't had our house cleaners in for a week now, and I bet Stella will wake me up tomorrow and ask me to get up so she can clean my sheets.

"Is that going to be a problem?" I say, pantomiming the pans and pots and banging on the counter. Aileen waves it off.

"It's good for the cameras," she whispers. "It makes it feel like a real American home."

"Oh, we're American, all right." I smile and nod. "My family is tragically disconnected from the real world." She raises an eyebrow. I try to wave it off.

"You believe Americans are disconnected from the real world?" she asks.

"They don't tend to see what's right in front of them."

"Fair enough," she whispers back, but she still seems confused. One camera is set up behind me, and one camera is behind her. We're supposed to ignore them, but it's like a big, dark, shiny eye staring at me over her shoulder. Someone is behind it, keeping track of what I'm saying. How am I supposed to pretend like he's not judging me? I can see a hat and a nose, and sometimes a cheek and chin when the man looks off to the side at the banging noises. Other than that, it's legs and cameras everywhere. The producer is, who knows where.

Aileen doesn't wait for anyone to tell her what to do. Seasoned professional that she is, she just starts asking questions. "So, tell us, Noah, when did you first meet the birds?"

"They're crows," I say. "Not birds." Aileen smiles and nods like she's really listening.

"They were hopping around my backyard, eating worms and hanging out on the wires that go from my house to the garage." I point from one thing to the next. I wait for the cameras to move along with my finger, but Aileen shakes her head.

"Please don't look at the cameras," she reminds me. I put my finger down.

"Anyway, they were always hanging out. Did you know they have their own social media account? I guess people post pictures and videos of them flocking into the trees by the nature reserve."

"They've been around for quite some time," Aileen says. Her smile and eyes never change.

"We're new here. I never had a lot of friends before, so I figured, why not make friends with these little guys." As I end the sentence, T hops onto the gutters, just behind where Aileen is sitting. His feathers are black and shiny, reflecting the ambient light around him.

"There's one," I say.

Aileen turns around, and T stares at her for a moment. When the cameras spin around to catch a glimpse, he flutters off. "Did you catch that? Guys? Tell me you got that." Both of the camera dudes shrug.

"Goddammit," she says. She catches her language and says, "I mean, sorry about that." I figured she was going to ask sooner or later. "Can you call them? Make them come here?"

I nod. "Of course."

"You're their master."

"I'm their friend," I correct. "Master implies that I

own them. But these little guys and gals are just little black birds trying to eat and sleep and fu—" I stop myself. "You know, find love."

She laughs politely. "Nice catch."

"Too much?" I ask.

"No, we can always bleep it out later." My shoulders relax. T appears again, this time a ways back on the roof. He's hiding in plain sight. He knows the humans won't look for him there, but if he wanted to be completely hidden, he'd be invisible.

"The one you saw," I tell them, "Is named T. I named him that because he has that big black feather that sticks up along the top of his head like it was ruffled together. There was that movie from, like, ten years ago about the spy team, and there was a guy named Mr. T. He had that mohawk."

"The movie based on the TV show?"

"Huh?" I ask.

"It's based on a TV show."

"Oh, well, I don't know about that. I just liked the guy with the mohawk. I guess on him it's a *mo-crow*?" My heart stops. I am frozen in the critical eyes of the camera.

The cameraman behind me chuckles a bit but controls it. I lean forward.

"Can you edit that out?"

"Why?" she asks. "It was cute. It's human."

"It's stupid. Do you know how much I fear for my life at school?" I pause again. I'll never be able to go back. "I mean, that's hyperbole. It's not that bad."

"Hyperbole?" she asks. Aileen looks back at the notes on her phone. "Our school systems aren't failing after all?" Aileen smiles. I get the joke. I don't think it's funny.

"I just read. A lot." I point to myself. "No friends.

289

Remember?" *Why am I like this?* I keep digging the hole deeper and deeper. I wish the crows could take me away.

"Anyway," I stress as loud as possible. "I'll call them. No time like the present?" I stand up and can't help but notice that Aileen is pushing the recorder closer still.

"This might get a little loud," I say. Aileen doesn't make a sound. She barely flinches. I go over to a shiny metal pan I stole from Mom. She didn't approve of my intended usage, but after she saw crows standing in it, she decided to let me keep it.

If I'm being honest, she hasn't touched the sheet pan in at least a few months, if not years. She doesn't cook so much. Instead, she adds garnish to frozen lasagna and calls it homemade. She's trained us not to make jokes about it.

Aileen shifts her body, following me with her eyes as I walk down the stairs, about three feet from the deck and out to the sheet pan.

"I have to wipe out the pan at least once a day because of the rain and bugs and stuff."

"That's nice, but don't crows eat bugs?" Aileen asks. I could have told you before, but now my brain is as empty as the sheet pan at my feet.

"Sure," I mutter. I pull out a handful of seeds and dried fruit. I go for something that's going to be heavy because the noise is the most important part.

"What do you have, exactly?" Aileen says.

"Just bird seed," I say, "But I touch it up with heavier seeds and some yummy foods. Mostly fresh fruits like apples and some dried fruits as well."

"You spend extra money for this?"

"It's not that expensive," I say. "It's no more than some people spend on their toy poodles." Aileen smirks.

"Fair enough." She looks away to keep from laughing. I hold my hand over the pan, making a tight fist. If you look carefully at the crevices between my knuckles, you'll see bits of dried apples and brown seeds peeking out.

"Are you ready?" She nods. I open my hand and let the seeds trickle down like rain onto the sheet pan. They bang loud enough to echo above the scarce street traffic. Aileen stays on the bench, but I can see that she's holding her breath. She looks up, searching. There's a question in her eyes, but I don't have the answers she craves. Not yet.

"It takes a minute," I say. I take a seat next to Aileen, and we wait.

She leans in, almost whispering, and says, "What are we waiting for?"

"The crows, right?" I don't bother to whisper. The crows know me, but I forgot that they aren't familiar with her.

The crows line up on the branches of the giant evergreen. They pack in tight, some of them almost disappearing between their bigger brothers and sisters. If you squint hard enough, you can see the shine of their eyes as they watch us.

Aileen stands up. Her hand clutches her chest, and she steps back from the bench.

"That's impressive," she says.

"That's not all of them." I run my finger in the air as I count. "There's only eight." Aileen's eyes widen, and her jaw slacks. "How many are there, usually?" I try to make it like I don't already know the number.

"This is about half."

"Half?" Aileen says. She leans into the recorder on the table. "You have about fifteen each time?"

"It's a pretty big murder," I say with a slick smile.

"I don't think," she says as her vision fixes on the crows. She doesn't seem aware of where she is. "That, um." She coughs into her hand. "You should use the word murder like that." She tries to smile. "It's a news show, and we use it for other things."

"Like an actual murder," I say. "Right."

The first of the crow to approach is the smallest. She leaves the branch quietly, landing just before the sheet pan. She's the runt of the family.

"That one's name is Flower. I didn't expect her to come out first." Aileen takes a slow, careful step closer to me. "How do you know it's a she?"

"You can't," I say. "Not really. From what I've read and seen on YouTube, there's not a clear-cut way to tell." Aileen grabs the recorder off the table. She doesn't think I see it when she holds it up by her elbow, closer to my face.

"So, you decided to give her a female name?"

"It feels weird to call a living creature an 'it,' you know?" Aileen says nothing. Instead, she watches Flower watch us. Or, more accurately, watch her. Flower's eyes are fixed on Aileen. The other crows keep to the safety of the branches. They observe quietly to see how we react to Flower's presence.

"They don't trust you," I say. Aileen grabs her chest again in mock offense. "I'm sorry. I can go. If that helps."

"Just give them a minute," I say. "It'll be fine." I kneel and pat the ground near my toes. "It's okay, Flower. She's with me. No worries." Flower tilts her head. The feathers on top ruffle, and she steps back. Then, she looks over her shoulder and caws three times like she's speaking to the others. It reminds me of Morse code.

"I'm convinced all of that means something, but I don't where to start as far as deciphering it." Flower hops toward the cookie sheet and stares at Aileen. When Aileen doesn't move, Flower hops again. Then again.

"Food is a big motivator," I say. The rest of the flock comes down off the branch, landing about two feet away from the pan. It takes about four tiny hops for them to line up and peck at the seeds.

"I used a metal sheet pan because it draws the most attention. That way, they know it's feeding time and can hear it from some distance away."

"How far can they hear?"

"Some records include up to thirty hectares, I think." She blinks. I try not to roll my eyes, but withholding my disdain isn't easy.

"Um, sixty acres, I think?" Aileen's eyes widen, and she nods. The number doesn't mean anything to her. Like when you hear that six million Jews died in the Holocaust. The number makes sense, but to understand the magnitude and emotional impact is another matter. We know it's a big number, but we have no reference for how big it really is. Not that sixty acres is the same as six million people.

"They can hear us?" Aileen asks. She leans in close.

"Yes," I say and take a slight step back. She had Mexican for lunch, and cilantro hangs on every syllable.

Aileen watches, but her camera guys don't. They start to shift around the table, not bothering to pick up their feet. The scraping of their shoes is enough to scare them off. Flower and the others return to the branches.

"I'm so sorry," the guy says. He's built like a lumberjack, with a beard so thick it crunches when he moves his head. The camera atop his shoulder points down at the empty silver tray. "I didn't realize."

My shoulders drop, and I look up at the sky. Thick gray clouds are moving above as the flock heads over to the neighbor's yard.

"It's fine," I say. Aileen and the cameraman look up. We're all staring at the sky. I'm trying not to lose my shit. These people are clueless. Fucking clueless.

"Can we get them back?" Lumberjack asks. I want him to shut up.

"No," I whisper.

"Will they come back?" He asks, but louder this time.

"I heard you the first time," I say. "And no. They'll come back when they want to." I sit back down at the end of the picnic table and watch as the crows shift their weight to the thicker parts of the branch closest to the trunk. They seem to move in shiny unison, keeping safe in the shadows.

"That's cool, though," Lumberjack says. He smiles and shakes his head like he can't believe what he saw. His hand is now on his thick hips, a black shirt pulled taut over his belly. I heard that black is slimming, but there's only so much it can do.

Aileen returns to the table and holds out the microphone at the end of the recorder. "Do they all have names?" she says. "And do they answer to them?"

"I don't think they intentionally answer to them. But I think they know when I'm talking to them." I look to the neighbor's yard and call, "Don't you, Flower?"

Flower's head turns and then nuzzles into her brother's wing. It's cute, and probably why she's my favorite. There are only six of them there because crows are much larger than you'd think, and the branch would certainly crack under their collective weight if too many perched there.

I point and go down the line. "That is Smurf, Edward, Penny, Flower, Flower's brother Zoomer, and Sally."

"Sally?" Aileen says with a smile. "Some of those names are kind of normal."

"I guess. I let my mom name them." I peek over my shoulder and lower my voice. "She's not very creative, but please edit that part out." Aileen laughs.

"No worries." Suddenly, something slaps the ground just next to the sheet pan. I already know it's an offering. I stand up to see what it is. There's a glimmer on something bluish, with dark streaks down the side.

"Fuck," slips out of my mouth. "I mean… Sorry." Aileen peeks over the edge of the deck to see my gift. Thankfully, she doesn't have great eyesight. I cough into my hand to turn her attention back to me and wave her away from the end of the deck. "You should see some of the nests they've made." It's pure bullshit. The nests aren't low enough to see much of, but they won't know that.

"Did I hear something land over there?"

"The crows like to flutter around sometimes." I peek at the birds, and they're all together except the one on the branch above them. He is bigger than the others.

"Oh, look," I say. Aileen lets out a sigh and gives me a fake smile. "There's T."

I try to block her view, taking small, measured steps to position myself between her and the sheet pan so that they won't capture a human body part on camera.

"T?"

"Over there," I point at him. Aileen closes one eye to focus on where my finger is pointing. "See that feather up on his head?" Aileen kneels so her head is the same height as mine.

"What feather?"

"On his head." I tap the top of her head, and she pops up almost immediately. "Sorry, but on his head. That feather reminded my mom of Mr. T's mohawk."

"Oh, my goodness. I can see it." She laughs.

"T is the leader of the group. He's the one that everyone else follows."

"He's also bigger."

"Absolutely. I think that puts him at the top of their social ladder, but I honestly don't know that much about this group's dynamics."

"Have you always wanted to study birds?"

"I never once considered being an ornithologist." I wait for her to reply. Nothing. "A bird scientist."

She nods.

"But corvids are just so damn..." I stop. "Can you say damn on television?"

"If your mom is okay with it." I'm fifteen. Damn isn't the worst thing I've ever said, but I don't exactly want a permanent record of it. I glance over at the recorder. Aileen immediately catches the drift.

"Understood."

I smile and edge myself, step by step, over to the end of the deck. She keeps her eyes on the birds, and the cameraman follows her lead. I've almost reached the shiny thing when she starts talking again.

"What else do the birds bring for you?"

"Bring?" I lean down and snatch the mystery object with the finesse of a magician. Now you see it, now you don't. It's a finger. Or it used to be. There isn't a fingernail anymore, and the edges have gone so blue they're almost black. It's otherwise pale and drained of blood. I can only presume the dark black streaks protruding out, hardened and thick as yarn, are muscles or tendons or something. The whole damned thing is stiff, and yet the skin still gives like pressing on a rubber tire.

With my right hand, I palm the finger into my left and then take up the cookie sheet for cover. I need to move it somewhere Aileen won't see it.

"I know that the birds engage in some kind of transactional economy," she says. I stare at her. She needed me to define ornithologist, but then uses phrases like "transactional economy." Have I been played?

Her lips curl into a smile—just a little. The camera doesn't see it. What it does see, while the dark eye of the lens peeks over her shoulder, is my mouth agape as I analyze just how much I've been talking down to her. I'm going to look like an asshole on TV.

"I don't know," I tell her. "Sometimes I get shiny little things. It's usually just cheap costume jewelry."

"And other times?" Did she see something? My hand grips the pan a little tighter. I bite my lower lip to keep from panicking,

"Do you need help with that?"

"What?" I say, clearing my throat. "With this?" I pretend to laugh it off while I low-key die inside. "I'm fine. It's good. I'll just put it over here."

Here, being the table. It will take some maneuvering, but if done right, I should be able to slip it into my jacket pocket while I'm setting the pan down. This is a time for looking cool and confident. I set the cookie sheet down as nonchalantly as possible, but I'm overselling it. I feel the finger slip from my sweaty palm onto the ground below. Aileen's eyes and mine meet for a split second before I have to look away. I pretend to look at the trees, but my feet roll in tiny circles around me. Now, I have to find the finger before she does.

It's a race that she doesn't even know she's in. Suddenly, someone comes around the corner. Never before had I wished we had a fence separating our backyard from the front. The person is wearing a pink shirt with darker pink buttons and a coordinating vest. Her pants are, for some uninspired reason, the same color as the rest. The monochromatic nightmare draws my eyes to her instead of the ground. Finding random body parts just feels like a bad way to end an interview. I mean, great TV. Wonderful TV. But it's not how I expected this to go.

"We can go inside and take that in if you need to." I sit down instead, hoping that Aileen will follow my lead. She doesn't. Aileen goes over to the woman, who's tapping her ear. Aileen shakes her head.

"I'm not wearing that."

"Why not?"

"The buzzing is ridiculous." Pink comes over and extends a hand. The hand is a wrinkled contradiction to the youthful face above the hideous shirt.

"Hi," she says. "I'm Jodie Miller."

"Noah."

"Yes," she says. "I know. It's so good to finally meet you. I've been talking to your parents." She looks around the big yard, putting her hands in and around her pink pants until she finally finds her pockets. "I'm so excited to finally meet you."

"What took you so long to get here?" Aileen says.

"I got lost," she says a little too matter-of-factly.

"You don't say," Aileen says. She looks at me like I'm supposed to understand what's going on beneath the surface. I don't know what the deal is with … I've already forgotten her name, but I get the sense Aileen's mocking 'Pink Pants.'

"I'm the producer," she says. I stay seated at the table, hoping the others will sit down and I can focus on the ground. Now it's a party. We have a cameraman, a reporter, and a walking bottle of Pepto Bismol, along with a whole murder of crows watching from the sidelines. 'T' must think this is fucking hilarious. It's not. Giving me the finger must be his idea of a prank.

I'm tapping my feet nervously under the table when my toe brushes against something squishy. My eyes shoot open. 'Pink Pants' misreads my expression to be that of a starstruck teen.

"You must be wondering what a producer does." She sits down because, of course, she does. Now that she's sitting close to me, I can see that she's tried to hide silver streaks in her hair with black that shines dark blue in the waning sunlight. Not unlike the feathers of our avian audience.

"I was the one that called when I heard about the crows," she says. Aileen takes a seat next to her. She sits uncomfortably close.

"I believe you mean I was the one that called," Aileen says as she taps herself on the chest. "But we can discuss that later."

'Pink Pants' looks at me and smiles. Now I see the wrinkles and the caked-on makeup between the folds of her face.

Hands. The hands never lie. Speaking of hands, I need to grab what's just underneath my foot, but both of them are watching me. I point over at the branches.

"The crows are over there if you want to take a look."

Both of them lean to the side and peek at the branches. As the dipshits are staring, I pop my head under the table, but the finger is gone.

My forehead starts to itch from the sweat, and my fingers shake. To keep still, I grab the table's edge and squeeze until my knuckles crack and my fingers grow limp. Aileen is the first to look back at me.

"You seem flushed," she says. "Do you need some water?"

"No, no. I'm good." I glance at the birds. "Just a little tired. School has been…" I look for the right words. "Trying. School has been trying."

"I'm sorry to hear that," she says. "Exams? It was the exams that got me."

"No," I say. "It's just the amount of homework. Then there's these little guys and gals." Flower caws at me. Then Zoomer.

'Pink Pants' slaps her wrinkled hand down in amazement. "They know you're talking about them," she says. "That's fantastic."

Aileen holds out her hand. "Fine," she says. "I'll take the earpiece if it means I get to finish this interview."

I don't know where the earpiece comes from, but it's the same color as Aileen's skin and shaped to fit her ear perfectly. Aileen shoves it inside with a gentle press of her index finger.

'Pink Pants' stands up, presses her hands against her side in a weird bow-like motion, and mouths, "Thank you."

She disappears behind the cameraman, but not before slapping him on the shoulder. "Thanks for being out here, Doug." Doug presses a finger against his lips.

"Shh." I smile and turn away. Aileen's shoulders barely move as she stifles her laugh. When the producer disappears, Aileen's shoulders finally relax.

"You were telling me about the things they give you?"

"I was?" My voice cracks like I'm back in middle school again. "I mean. I was."

"Last I remembered, you were talking about costume jewelry."

"I was, yes. Old stuff. You know." Her face is unmoved.

"Right, so sometimes it's anything that catches their attention."

"Do they ever try to feed you back?" I thought of the cold appendage beneath my feet. Yuk!

"No. I think they just think they're paying for food. My guess is they understand transactions like you said." I smile and wave at Flower, who is the first to hop off the branch and land at the base of the tree. She looks over where the tray once was and turns her head to the side. 'T' sits just above the tree, but he's no longer watching us. He's watching Flower on the ground.

"She's hungry still," I say.

"Can you feed them again?"

"I can, but I don't know how much to feed them. I don't want to make them get too reliant on me."

"Money?" Aileen pipes in.

"What? You're offering me money?" For a split second, I imagine her pulling a check from her pocket. But no. That's not what she meant. What she meant was, do the crows bring me money?"

"Oh, just coins. Sometimes, they're big coins because that's what gets their attention. I've gotten money clips before, but there was nothing in them."

"Wow," Aileen says. "Who has those anymore?"

"I know, right?" I slap the table as my shoe slaps the deck. I need to find that finger. It has to be somewhere around me, but it occurs to me as I tap my foot around that the finger must have rolled away from me. And the reason why Aileen sat so close to 'Pink Pants' earlier was to claim the finger for herself. That bitch. If I pretend to tie my shoe, I can survey the situation. Deep breath. It's all fine. I smile, "Excuse me."

My head barely fits underneath the tabletop, and I have to suck in my gut to even bend over that far. When I get to my feet, my hands reach around, and my fingers sweep over the deck. My fingertips graze across splintered shards of wood that serve as a warning that what I'm doing is a very, very bad idea.

But we're talking about a human finger. On TV. I cannot, and I mean I cannot, be the kid with random body parts in his backyard. I'll never be able to step foot in that school again. I'll have to move to a different state. A different country. Hell, a different planet if it goes viral. Even then, Martians will probably point at me.

"See that guy over there? They found a severed human finger in his backyard. That sick fuck."

"Are you okay down there?" Aileen's head peeks under the table as well. I jump, hitting my head against the table. The crows caw at the sudden noise, but they don't flee. Aileen laughs. I rub my head.

"Are you okay?"

I don't speak because 'T' hops out of the tree. He's on the ground, turning his head to keep an eye on me.

"They're so cute," Aileen says.

T's mohawk stands up taller, almost like someone ran their hand through his feathers backward.

"What's he doing?" Aileen says. She turns to the cameraman. "Are you getting this? Please tell me you're getting this." The cameraman nods, putting a finger to his lips. But it's Aileen's job to talk and narrate. So she does.

"The crow that Noah calls 'T' is coming toward us, alternating between hopping and taking short steps that make him waddle. He keeps his eyes on Noah, who just hit his head. I can't help but wonder, does 'T' know that Noah is hurt? Is he coming over to check up on Noah?"

"No, he's not." Aileen turns to me.

"What?"

"He's not checking up on me."

"What's he doing, then?"

"I think he's watching you." I point over at T's head. The head is turned toward me, sure, but the eye that's facing forward isn't looking at me. It's looking at Aileen from across the table. Aileen shifts her weight. She even slides back a little down the bench.

"I don't think I understand." Oh, but she does. She really, really does.

"He might be thinking that you hurt me," I say.

"That's adorable," Aileen says, but without the softness in her tone. Like when you talk to a little child after they do a goofy trick. When you talk to dogs and squirrels, you raise your tone and soften your voice to appear non-threatening. None of that happens when Aileen speaks now. She even drops the tone of her voice, and her shoulders go up to make herself look bigger.

None of that really matters to 'T' and his group.

'T' stops about three feet from the edge of the deck. A railing separates us, but to a bird, a three-foot railing is nothing. His dark eyes, which look shiny and wet, keep their focus on Aileen.

"Listen," she says to 'T'. She raises her hands before lowering them and then raising them again. I can tell she's wondering what is considered threatening and what's considered actual "crow-speak" for "I surrender" or "I come in peace."

"I didn't mean anything," she says. "I didn't do anything." Flower and Zoomer are the next to come up behind 'T'. They form a little black triangle, feathers shining.

"Oh," Aileen says. "There's more."

"It's fine, guys," I say. "We're okay." I stand up and put my hands out to the birds. "I'm good, okay?" From the corner of my eye, I glimpse Smurf coming up behind Aileen. He picks at her jacket, draped over the edge of her seat. Aileen pulls the jacket back.

"Excuse me."

"They don't understand words," I say, "But I'm pretty sure they can figure out your tone."

"They're being very rude right now." She uses the pronoun *they*, but she's really talking to them directly. Trying to be politely rude back to the birds.

"Again, tone is more important. And I don't think they're afraid of you. I saw them chase off a German shepherd-mastiff mix just a few weeks ago."

"Mastiff?"

"Mix. So it wasn't as big. But you're missing the point. These guys have no fear." Aileen stands up and steps back from the picnic table, inching toward the door to the house.

"Not even of you?"

"They don't have any reason to be afraid of me." Zoomer creeps closer to Aileen's feet and pecks at the ground right before her. He's not trying to hurt her. He's only testing the waters. He takes a hop back. He's toying with her. It isn't unusual. He loves to pick on Flower, too. The movements are mostly the same: peck and move, peck and move. That's partially why I named him Zoomer. The boy's funny, but he's a pain in the ass to anyone he's around. Aileen pushes her back against the door, and Smurf hops down next to Zoomer as if they are guard dogs—uh—birds between me and Aileen.

"What are they mad about?" Aileen asks. Her mouth twists like a frown, but her eyes almost smile at the moment. Zoomer moves closer, then closer still. He's within pecking distance. Young bird that he is, he makes a quick jab with his beak, digging into her shoe. Aileen lets out a small scream. Then, as if checking to see just how much pain she's in, Zoomer peeks up at her and turns his head. Smurf hangs back, but he's watching the pockets in her pants. He knows something's in there, and he's not letting her leave with it. Zoomer goes in for another peck, but this time, Aileen kicks at him. Zoomer hops back and caws intensely. The cameraman peeks his head out and eyes the scene.

'T' comes directly to the railing and rests on the broad

wooden beam. He keeps his dark eyes on Aileen but says nothing. This is T's personality. Like my dad used to say, quoting some long-dead president: "Speak softly and carry a big stick."

That's 'T'. Except he is the stick. He knows how to throw his weight around. Even now, though he's a full four or five feet away from Aileen, he's a big boy, and he's letting her know that if it comes down to it, he will throw down with the best of them. Zoomer, out of respect, hops backward and rests by the stool.

"What did you take?" I ask. Aileen's eyes widen and she turns to me like a child with their hand in the cookie jar.

"Nothing," she says. Smurf doesn't buy it. He caws at her, screeching three times, then turns to 'T.' 'T' moves closer to me. I reach over and pat him on the head. When I stop, his feather mohawk flips back up again. Clouds cover most of the sun at this point. The edges of the sky turn pink and orange.

"If it's nothing, then the birds are freaking out about something you did," I say.

"Call them off." Aileen's eyes are pleading now.

"I can't just call them off, Aileen."

"Do something." Her hand goes to her pocket. She made the mistake. Smurf flaps up to the height of her waist and pecks at her pockets.

"What is that?" I ask. Aileen manages to throw herself into the house and closes the glass door behind her. We lock eyes, and she takes a step back. My mom comes out from behind her and asks her something. I don't know what.

I go to talk with 'T' and see how he's feeling, but the entire flock hops over my head and onto the rooftop. They line up with 'T' in the front, staring at the car Aileen drove here.

I go around the house, and God, I wish we had a fence. The cameraman stands there, watching me and the crows.

"Dude," he says, "That's fucking crazy."

"Please don't show any of that?" I ask.

"To be fair, Aileen's kind of a bitch." He presses something on the camera.

"It should get erased soon, my dude." He lowers the camera down to about chest-high and bows at the birds. Not a single one of the corvids saw him, but I'm sure they would have appreciated the sentiment. "Be excellent, my friends."

He hustles around the corner with me, pushing past me to a blue van with a white circle outlined in yellow with a black number six in the middle. Channel Six news. A little red Camaro sits on the edge of the property. That must be Aileen's car. The cameraman gives me a little salute and then backs out of the driveway. Aileen's only chance at protection just left. She comes out of the front door and stops as our eyes meet.

"They don't always do that, you know," I say just loud enough for only her to hear. She pretends like she doesn't know what I'm talking about. She stares at me, keeping her hands up on the doorframe. She digs for something and pulls out her car keys. The silver jingling isn't helping.

One of Penny's favorite gifts is lost keys. I think she likes the feeling of metal in the ridges of her beak.

Aileen steps out of the front door with such careful steps that she looks like a cartoon character sneaking past guards in a bank. Her knees go high, her steps slow and careful. But the birds can see ultraviolet light. They can hear her steps no matter how quiet she is. Crows, if anything, are amazing hunters and clever creatures. Aileen could never hide from them.

"It's okay," I tell Zoomer and Penny. They coral Aileen where they want her to go. They're leading her to the edge of the grass. I don't know why. When I take a peek along the roof of the house, everyone is there except for 'T'.

Suddenly, the wooden bench at the front of the house, the one feature that my mom "absolutely fell in love with" — her words — darkens as 'T' flaps over and lands. His claws tap along the painted wood. He watches Aileen try to retreat back towards the house. When she gets too close, he opens up his wings in an impressive display of his size. Aileen gasps and takes a step back.

"I didn't do anything," Aileen says. "I didn't do anything, I swear."

"They think you took something. Something they dropped."

"For you?" Aileen says. She gets closer to me, and 'T' caws as loud as he can.

"It's the shiny ring they wanted to give me. The other part. The finger. That's just birds being birds."

"Your birds are picking apart dead bodies," Aileen says. Her eyes start to water. "They can show us things. Help us find people."

"What do you mean by 'us'?"

Aileen wipes a tear from her eyes. She takes out the finger and holds it up like a chicken nugget. The thought that it once moved and bled and belonged on a human hand seems to be lost on her.

"If they're bringing it all to you, then you must know something." I shake my head. My heart beats so hard I have trouble breathing.

"I don't know anything." My hands shake, so I shove them behind my back. "I swear." Aileen tosses the finger into the grass. 'T' looks at Aileen, then the finger, then Aileen again. He hops off of the bench and flutters over to the finger. He picks it up, tossing it in the air to get a better grip. His tail feathers go up like he's happy to finally retrieve it.

"You know something," Aileen says. "You have to know something. We'll find out. I swear to God I'll find out, and when I do." But she doesn't finish the sentence. It fades into empty threats that only my mind can fulfill. I wonder if they can convict me of a murder I never committed because of a bird. Then, for a split second, I imagine animal control coming to contain the whole murder of crows.

"You're insane," I say. "I didn't do anything, and you're basing your evidence on crows?" Aileen stumbles toward her car. The red Camaro's door opens wide as she climbs in. I watch her through the windshield. She seems too shaken to even start the car. I know what she thinks she knows. She wants to find her friend's son. I get it. I really do. But don't you think if I knew anything, I would tell them?

Aileen lowers her eyes for a moment. The car's engine whirs into a full roar. Lights come on, nearly blinding me. 'T' and Zoomer hop between me and the car. Maybe they're trying to protect me. Maybe they just want to see the crazy bitch leave. God only knows what the fuck they're thinking.

Aileen backs out of the driveway and disappears down the road. As soon as the lights fade into the shadows around the corner, 'T' and Zoomer disappear up onto the roof of the house. Penny, Flower, and the gang watch me go back into the house, but just before I close the door, something drops from the roof. It's a dry slap, something small. I peek down. It's the finger.

"Honey," Mom cries out. "What was that? Did she leave already?" I pocket the finger.

"Yeah, she said she had everything she needed."

"What about us? Did they need to interview us?"

"Did you train the birds, Mom?"

"You don't have to be an ass about it, Noah."

"I have something to do first," I shout back, ignoring the comment. Sometimes, I am indeed an ass. "I'll be back soon."

"Don't play with the birds for too long. It's a school night."

"Don't remind me."

I close the door and go back out to the front yard. The murder keeps me in their line of sight as I go around the house, past the deck, and behind a light blue shed behind our house. Inside the shed are boxes of stuff we'd normally shove into a garage, along with our lawn mower and a bunch of empty boxes for the new speaker system my dad had installed with the house.

But just behind that, where no one else will look, is a pile of dirt. I kick at the dirt pile that's as big as a literal ant hill. There's still some space for the things the other crows have left for me. Rings, earrings, sometimes shiny gold caps of teeth. The money and the coins I keep for myself. But these kinds of things I can't just go to a pawn shop and hand over. People will ask questions. So, I pretend I'm a pirate and bury the treasure. Sometimes, this means I have to bury the body parts.

If it weren't for the crows, a stray cat or raccoon may have already dug up the pile and tossed the fingers, toes, and earlobes all over the place.

For now, it's a safe haven. I drop the finger into the hole and kick the dirt back over it. When I'm confident that the entire hole has been covered, I shove my foot down onto the mound to pack the dirt in tight. Maybe I'm paranoid. Maybe it's just common sense. Either way, I don't want anyone—or anything—else to know that it's all there.

Mom shouts from the backdoor. "Noah, it's getting dark. Your father and I are going out tonight. Please come back in and finish cleaning up for dinner." I slam my foot onto the pile one more time.

"Okay, Mom." My teeth grind as I take a step back from the mound. The fragrant smell of grass and moist soil is alluring, but Mom's voice is an irritation I don't want to deal with again.

I hear the tippy-tappy of T's claws touching the roof of the shed. I walk just underneath him. His toes tap along as he follows me from above, watching me go into the house.

When I get inside and turn around, his dark figure sits like a shadowy statue above the shed. I wave to him.

As soon as he sees my wave, I watch in amazement as he leaps off, flaps his strong, quiet wings, and lands with the rest of his murder in the trees. If I didn't know any better, I'd say these birds actually like me.

Ding Dong Bitch

BRYON CAHILL

Ding Dong Bitch

BRYON CAHILL

I KNOW COLLEGE ESSAYS ARE SUPPOSED TO BE STRUCTURED. But I actually don't care whether you accept me into your prestigious school. How about that?

Mr. Shepherd, my guidance counselor, told me not to be overly verbose.

"Try to keep it under 1,000 words, Mr. Bradley." *Ppbbt-thh! Fat chance of that, Sheppy!* I don't mean to be a jerk about this. I just want to be upfront with you, whoever you are—'Sir or Madame or Mademoiselle' or whoever is forced to read this. I don't expect to get in, not with my track record. I've never been college material.

You see, my parents were at the top of their class and have always expected me to follow in their footsteps at Rainier. I'm sure you've received their letters about me by now. Did my dad go on about my steadfast, gentlemanly qualities? Bah. I know he did. It's always been their dream for me to attend their alma mater, so here I am applying. Don't ask me why. I've no earthly idea what I'm doing anymore.

313

My parents met and fell in love, etc., at Rainier. Sometimes, they joke that they even studied a little. I know. Gross. Dad seems to think I'll fit right in up there — that I make friends easily and keep them easier. He doesn't get that maybe that's the problem. Maybe I'm *too* loyal.

Lou (sorry, Lewis) and me are neighbors. Or we were, anyway—our whole lives, in fact, up until quite recently.

Dad used to say (back when he was prone to saying stupid crap for laughs), "Nathan and Lewis are like peanut butter and jelly. They mix well but can also stand alone." Forget it. It's just something he used to say.

One of my earliest memories of Lou and me wasn't of anything we did together but of a thought I'd had. I remember wishing I had been born a year earlier so we wouldn't have to separate at school. I don't know why it stuck with me, except that Lou got to do everything first. When he got on the bus for kindergarten, I was probably soiling myself in front of the TV. I don't know. When do kids stop wearing diapers? In Pre-K, yeah? Doesn't matter. Everything between then and now has been about living in Lou's shadow and tempering my jealousy. My jealousy.

Lou's off to college now. But he wasn't the only one with brains. It was my idea to copy Sammy's notes that day in the library. No, I'm not proud of cheating. But if it weren't for that nexus event, Sammy and Abby would have destroyed us in the debate. If it weren't for my sheer lack of morals, the girls never would have sought their cold-hearted revenge. None of my ensuing pranks would have happened, and Lou and Abby wouldn't have gotten together. The last I heard, they're still going strong. As strong as a couple can, hundreds of miles from one another. Distance makes the heart go fonder or whatever.

Do I need to hear a "Thank you, Nate?" No. I'm only telling you where I'm coming from. High school is all about being immature. It's true. There's not one kid in my class I'd call 'mature.' Then again, you don't find many mature adults out there either, so what does that say about the world? Incidentally, no one else is going to tell you this stuff. The truth is much easier to deliver when you don't care about your future, but save your applause for someone who deserves it. I'm no hero.

Lou got straight A's, across the board. The only exception was when he came in direct competition with Abigail Brown, and that rarely happened since making grades at John Jackson High was seldom (if ever) based on a curve. Debate was the only class where peers (freshmen through seniors alike) were literally judged against one another.

It would have been obvious to anyone with two working eyes in their head that those two just needed a push. So yeah, I became my man's pusher, so to speak. It was just my luck that Sammy was such an over-preparer that she took extensive notes on more than Mr. Lindert's proposed subject matter. Abby thoroughly studied every imaginable counterpoint, jotting down every argument she could conceive that Lou and I might rebut.

I was daring, yes. I was bold, of course. But mostly, I was slick. Sitting at the far end of the table that day in the library, I clocked Sammy's trip to the bathroom, slid through the stacks to her quiet, unguarded table, and took quick pics of her notes with my phone. If anyone saw, nobody mentioned it. Maybe that says something about our generation's withering morality. Maybe not. I dunno.

The next day, Lou and I trounced Abby and Sammy in the big debate. Booyah! We destroyed those suckers with Abby's own words. They never had a chance. I admit wholeheartedly here, for the first time. I was a cheat. And I dragged Lou along with me. If anyone cared enough to listen to Abby and Sammy's accusations, there might have been a scandal. But guess what? Nobody cared— no one except Lou.

"I knew you weren't smart enough to come up with those counterarguments! She's not lying, is she? You stole her notes! Didn't you?"

"So what?"

"So what?!" He was beside himself with the qualms of his unintended misdeed. "I don't want to win valedictorian that way."

"Win it?" I asked him. "Is that all this is to you? A game? This is life, Lou. This is about the rest of your life. Get with the program. Get on the bus. Yale doesn't want second-best. You may have gotten in, but they'll shun you when you get there if you're anything less than perfect."

I was talking out of my ass, for sure. And maybe stealing Abby's notes was a shameless thing to have done. But I'd done it. And with *Lou*, at least, I took responsibility, but we suffered no repercussions. The girls had no proof. After an uncomfortable half-hour in the principal's office, they gave up shouting into the void, folded up shop, and walked out.

"This isn't over," Abby muttered.

"This never started," I muttered back. The two of them were likely more pissed about our cunning than our cheating. As she left, I could feel Abby seething, like the poisonous drip on a viper's fangs. They were bound to take revenge. But how? It didn't take long to find out.

The girls were smart about their plot in so many ways. Later (much later) that night, instead of splitting up and nailing us both, Abby and Sammy pooled their efforts against Lou.

This is where I must interject: if foul language offends you, turn away. The rest of my story can't be told by sticking to proper, 'High school appropriate' vernacular. I won't apologize. You've been forewarned.

Abby and Sammy unleashed a systematic fury of ringing doorbells, playing *Ding Dong Bitch!* to perfection. The key to the game, you see, is to space out your interruptions just enough to absolutely destroy someone's slumber. The *Bitch* of it all differs slightly from its tamer predecessor, *Ding Dong Ditch,* a game our forefathers played (yes, even Rainier elite, of which you may or may not be aware).

In the original version, the Ding Donger rings only once, in the dead of night, then hauls ass out of Dodge. The updated version is much dastardlier. If well-timed, a perfect game of *Ding Dong Bitch* will render your victim utterly sleepless and unable to focus on anything come the new day.

Lou and his parents were spooked and woken too often to count through most of the night. Maybe he got a wink or two, but hardly enough to keep him mentally stable for his Advanced Bio final in the morning.

No, Lou didn't fail, but he was exhausted and botched just enough of the exam to give Abby and Sammy the lead (and eventual co-win) in their stupid valedictorian race. I'm no genius, but one B+ didn't affect Lou's promising post-high school collegiate career. It only pissed him off. Royally.

Why do colleges have to be so hung up on grades, anyway? There's so much more to a person than their report card. Yeah, I see the irony. I've attached my grades to my application. You think you know what kind of student I am, but you don't. Not really. My senior English teacher, Mr. Jared (he insists we call him that), convinced me to apply despite my grades.

"You have lots to offer, Nate." His words. Not mine. "In the real world, grades don't make the man. It's quite the other way around, and you could turn it around at the drop of a hat."

Honestly? Why does every adult in my life insist on spouting superficial nonsense? If I had a thousand dollars for every cheap, unremarkable piece of so-called wisdom I've been dealt, I'd be one rich bitch, but you haven't yet heard the half of it. I am nothing if not creative.

What's the next logical step in an escalating war? If you're thinking we went straight to the classic dog shit in a paper bag routine — well, you're half-right. Because that's just what she was expecting, you see. Anyone would, right? When dealing with a couple of feeble minds (as I'm sure Abby considered ours to be), retaliation resembles a flaming bag of doo-doo on the front lawn. It's so classic, it's undeniable! Ding dong, bitch! Come and put the fire out!

From behind a nearby distant shady tree, I spied her through a porch window. Abby burst through the front door before her parents could drag themselves out of bed and after a quick laugh at what she surely considered the most asinine prank ever conceived.

"Is that the best you've got, Lewis?!" Abby ran to the far side of the garage to retrieve the hose. She wore blue bunny slippers and an unprovocative robe. She should have hesitated.

She should have considered her actions. But she didn't. Why? Because it was hella late, and her brain was fried from being woken by a doorbell and a fire? Because, in her heart, she felt superior to Louie (A kid who had absolutely nothing to do with this, for the record), and she was sure she could one-up him just by *not* stepping on hot shit. I don't know. If I were her, I might have done the same thing. Sometimes it's too damn easy to second-guess your opponent *and* lose sight of yourself. That's what makes what came next so fucking genius. When she hosed down that bag... holy shit, man. Pfoom! Minor grease fires exploded across Abby's lawn. Thankfully unharmed, she stood there for a moment, entirely flabbergasted, searching the dark street for Lou's shadow.

All right. Let's take a step back here, just for a second. In hindsight, yes, of course, I can see how childish my behavior was, but I was there to scream a warning at her had it gone the other way. On the slim-to-zero chance Abby had come barreling out of her house, intending to stomp out a grease fire, I would have stopped her. I swear it. I'm not insane. I'm just really, really good at mental chess.

I waited until she got the fire extinguisher and returned to... well, extinguish, before tearing off into the night, laughing my fool head off. With the harmless prank in my rearview, I'd be a liar if I didn't cop to enjoying it.

That, whoever this may concern, is among so many other despicable reasons Nathan Bradley is not "Rainier material." If you haven't chucked this essay across the room in disgust, you may be looking for that inevitable turn. The one Mr. Jared so deftly put in my head. Well, maybe it's coming. Probably not. The next day, Abigail Brown marched right up to Louie at school and slapped him hard across the side of his face. She struck him so forcefully, even *I* felt it.

"Was that your idea of a joke?" She shouted between third and fourth period. It was the last week of school, and we had an exam-free day that Tuesday. Everyone was in the halls, pointing, laughing, and tittering over what looked to have the potential to be a smarty scrap — a proper battle of brainiac brawn.

"I apologized for the debate," Lou said, shocking me.

When had he talked to her? Why had he apologized? We were supposed to be in this thing together, him and me.

"I'm not talking about the stupid debate!" She yelled. "I'm talking about the bag of flaming grease you left on my lawn last night! I could have gotten hurt, asshole!" She was wrong about that, though. I'd been three moves ahead of her from the start. I've already mentioned she was never in any real danger, so let's skip that bit.

"Wait," Lou said. "Someone set fire to your lawn last night?" Abby, still convinced Lou was the culprit, slapped him again. This time, her smackeroo knocked him down.

"Get ready for retaliation," she said, towering over him, then stormed away. As he got to his feet, I tried to shield him from lingering looks.

"Was it you?" I was stupefied into silence. "Why am I even asking? Of course, it was you."

"It was just a stupid prank, Louie."

"Yeah. You said it. Stupid."

"Why do you even care? She's fine."

"You know her and Sammy are going to retaliate."

"I could not let her heinous slight against you stand, Brother."

I admit I was putting on airs, hoping to rekindle a glimmer of good humor in my friend.

"You're a tool." He bent, though he did not break — not under my stupidity, anyway. "It's already been decided. My last two exams won't matter. Even if I ace them both, Abby and Sammy are going to be co-valedictorian. It's all in the math… Brother."

"I'm sorry to hear that," I told him because I was. Deep down, though, our enemies' victory gave me all the more reason to finish what I'd started. "Forget it. There are only so many days left before all of this is in the past. You might as well make the most of it."

"By relentlessly harassing the smartest girl in school? That's grade school shit, Nate." This was the first inkling of my best friend's true feelings. He'd left Sammy out of his equation.

"'Smartest *girls*,' you mean. Plural."

"Right."

"Oh my God, you like her!"

"Shut up."

"You do! You like the queen of the nerds! That's why you're so upset!"

"No. I'm upset because you could have set Abby's house on fire or worse." The bell for fourth period rang just then, and our talk was put on hold.

"I've got an idea," I told him as he slammed his locker shut. "Meet me at the toy store after school. I've got the perfect thing to make Abby swoon." He huffed and walked away, but I knew he'd be there. As tough as he pretended to be, Lou had always been a romantic at heart. Plus, I could tell my proposition intrigued him.

So yeah. The toy store. That's what an esteemed Rainier education will get you. But not to own outright! No. Dad is the humble (read: proud) co-owner of *Macabee's Toys* here in town. That he didn't have the foresight to insist they add his name to the lease, the storefront, the grand opening, or the tax forms only led his supposed friend, John Macabee, to steamroll him, hustling fifty-one percent of their forever-struggling venture. But forget it. I'm not talking about that. For the purpose of this story, I only want to share how six dozen dolls, made irrelevant by time, sat in the back of my father's toy store (forty-nine percent his, anyway) for well over a year.

Maybe you recall the Dear Abby craze of 2025? If not, I won't hold it against you. This fad came and went in a heartbeat. By the time Dad got around to ordering a batch wholesale, little girls all over the world had decided they were over it. Or, more likely, their parents didn't want to shell out the extra bucks for a set of *the same doll.*

What can I say? Dad gambled on the wrong horse, leaving him stuck with all these creepy plastic dolls that would only activate if a clone was nearby.

"Abby, Abby, Abby, Abbbbby...." OK, the stupid chant-like song doesn't translate to the page. The point is that they had all these dolls just sitting around, collecting dust.

When Lou showed up, he immediately got what I was laying down — the surface value of it, anyway. Of course, he disapproved.

"This is beyond any game, Nate. We can't do this."

"We have to. Your honor depends on it." I spoke again in the code of our youth. My mindset was simply: If I could divert his thoughts of 'This is wrong' to sappy memories of playing chivalrous knights out in the woods behind Castle Way's cul-de-sac, maybe he wouldn't notice the burdensome sheath of Cupid's arrows I was slinging.

"Honor?" he asked. "The days of storming the castle are over. We're not eight."

"You've always been so hung up on age. I get it. I'll never be as mature as you." Lou hung out his palms, face front. Then he left. The bastard wouldn't even help me load the truck.

You're wondering if my dad knew I was taking those worthless dolls, aren't you? If he approved of the use of them for a well-intended prank, just to get them the hell out of his store? Well, what do you think? Does that sound like something a Rainier man would be cool with? I told him I'd haul the six dozen Dear Abbys to the dump or something. It doesn't matter. Fast forward.

I waited until long after dark. With the nonexistence of

light on my side, I was forever patient. At long last, the lights in Abby's house went out. For all her daytime gusto, Lou's nemesis and burgeoning love interest appeared to have gone to sleep. Whatever she was planning for her 'Big retaliation' was going to take more than one evening to plan. Amateur.

Lou was, I presumed, sleeping peacefully in his room. Perhaps dreaming of the day he might have the guts to profess his true feelings. I know. I'm speculating. I'm not an idiot. Just a sucker for a happy ending. What can I say?

Six. Dozen. Dolls. It's even more exhausting than it sounds. Had even *one* car passed in the two hours it took to set it all up, I would have bailed. Lucky for me, Abby lived on a dark, quiet street.

Under the cover of a cool pre-summer night, with the lonely breeze as my only guard and a new moon hidden to keep my cover, the Abbys were finally in place. From the truck, I retrieved a Santa sack full of D batteries — thanks again, Daddy — and went about the tedious work of inserting them, careful not to set the damn things off. I had read the instructions thoroughly, and in fine print, near the end, the manufacturer claimed:

Though Abbys are designed to harmonize with one another upon hearing their name, it is possible they may infer other sounds as their given moniker, thereby pronouncing and repeating their name in song.

OK, batshit toy corporation. Whatever you say. I didn't so much as whisper. Not until I was ready.

"Abby." I exhaled the word. The lawn lit up with a— a — a cacophony of cooing! I'm sorry if that sounds trite; I assure you, the dolls' chirping chants-turned-most-foul was anything but.

As I ran from the warbling madness of seventy-two

robotic voices serenading Del Rey Court with Abby's sing-song name upon their synthetic lips, did I consider my true motivations? Was I really trying to win the girl for the boy who so deserved her? Did I actually think it could work? More importantly, why did I care so much? Why?!

I left that waking nightmare of matchmaking trickery in my dust. Imagining Abby emerging from her house (perhaps clad in purple pajamas and panda slippers this time) to behold the intricate love letter I'd strewn across her partially scorched lawn was nearly enough to set my own heart ablaze with the grotesque romance of it all. With a head full of self-importance and feeling a little like Cyrano de Bergerac on speed, I spent the rest of the night basking in my deviant nature, unable to close my eyes.

"And they lived happily ever after," I spoke softly to the sheets. Sheets don't smirk, you see?

The next day, Abby didn't go anywhere near Lou. Anyone could plainly see she despised him all the more.

"I don't get it," I confided in him at lunch. "I was sure she would have warmed to you."

"Huh?"

"Nothing." I retreated, snapping my big mouth shut. In the light of day, six dozen Dear Abby dolls in chorus proved the wrong way to win her heart for Louie. If that didn't do the trick, what could? Then, it hit me — the perfect ploy.

When my last exam was done, I tore out of the parking lot and headed straight for the local pet store. I knew they sold mice — the sort that Frankie Vasquez's ball python, 'General Slaughter,' ate. I also remembered how Abby led a protest against dissecting mice in biology class last year. She'd made a debatable argument that fetal pigs, rabbits, rats, some birds, garter snakes, crayfish, perch, earthworms, grasshoppers, and especially mice gave their lives each year, all in the name of well-documented science.

"It's not right we should contribute to the unnecessary death of these animals when we can learn all about their insides from a book!" No one wanted to debate her. So, that was that. When all was said and done, Abby's big hullabaloo didn't change school policy regarding the dissection. However, she *did* force their hand to allow students the option of whether to pick up the scalpel. She took the win, snagged an A in Bio for 'Organizing a worthy cause' (What a crock!), and successfully escaped slicing up poor Mickey.

I tell you all this only so you understand that Abby loves all creatures, great and small. Buying out the pet store's supply of skittish snake food was a no-brainer. It was a gesture I was sure she would appreciate. The amiable lady who rang me up thought so, too —it wasn't just me. She even gave me a couple of shoeboxes with well-placed air holes for transport. Bonus.

Later that night, I parked three blocks away and high-tailed it through the woods under cover of the fully waned new moon. Not being an astronomer, I couldn't tell you how many nights the moon stays in one phase or another. At least, for one more night, I was golden. I didn't have to set up a bunch of dolls for this gesture. Behind what was becoming my favorite tree, I waited. When the last light went out in Abby's home, I knew I was in the clear. Whatever spell she'd been concocting was still not ready for prime time, apparently.

I ran up to her door, half expecting a booby trap, but no such gadget presented itself. I quietly slid the two shoeboxes full of rescued mice at her front stoop, rang the doorbell twice, and hauled ass.

Behind the cover of her neighbor's fence, I crouched to

watch my love trap get sprung. It wasn't Abby, but her mother who came investigating. Beneath the faded glow of the porch light, she bore witness to my gift and… oh man, did that old lady scream!

"Ahhhhhh!" Abby's mother flew into a terrified fit upon seeing so many tails wriggling through those well-placed air holes. With a swift kick, her bare foot nailed the side of one of the shoeboxes. It went flying, soaring through the air on a tremendously unsuspected trajectory. Abby's father stuck his face through the front doorway. The fucker was smoking an old-fashioned pipe when he got a face full of rodents. He flailed and fell while his wife tried to climb over him to safety. Abby soon arrived and was assigned the hopeless job of collecting and re-caging the skittering 'Innocents.' With all the chaos surrounding her, I'm afraid I was completely unable to ascertain what her feelings were on the matter. Suddenly, a police siren cut through the thick of the night like a raven through smog.

I ran as if the wind at my back owed me a favor, one I was cashing in. I dove into the truck and drove home. No interruptions. Just a brain load of too-late doubts and concerns that hung around until the wee parts of the morning.

"Nate?" Mom was calling. It wasn't even six yet. Why was she up? "Nate! There's some girl here!"

I must have tripped and fallen half a dozen times getting dressed, but I was somehow able to leave my bedroom and bound down the stairs in under a minute. The light from the tree-line-shielded sunrise struck Sammy's hair, igniting her downcast eyes. She stood there in our doorway, hiding something behind her back.

"Good morning, son of mine," Mom said. "Glad you could come. This young lady was going to place something on our welcome mat. Weren't you— What did you say your name was?"

"Mom!"

"She might be!" Mom exclaimed. "This young lady has got a goddamn positive pregnancy test! Nate, what the hell were you thinking?"

"How did…" Sammy began.

"I see everything. Don't think I don't know what goes on. And now… proof! There, behind your back!"

It is a miracle that I didn't sink through the carpet, melt into the earth, and become nothing.

"I'm…" was all Sammy said. She was Abby's best friend. No doubt, placing a positive pregnancy test on my porch would get me into trouble. Now, *she* was the one who was in trouble! Big time!

"You're pregnant?" I asked dumbly. What else can one say when confronted with such a bizarre scenario? And before I'd had a chance to wipe the sleepy time crust from my eyes, too.

"It's not…"

"Zip it." Mom cut her off. "Get in here and sit down. Do you drink coffee? No, of course not. Not in your condition."

"But I'm not…"

"You too, Jackass." Mom kicked my butt into the kitchen. "We're gonna sort this out." (I've omitted that she also slapped me upside the head only because of the picture I find myself painting. I don't want you to think my parents are abusive. Just so we're clear. My folks are Rainier folk. Always remember.)

You know what? I don't need to revisit the most awkward conversation of my young life. Mom talked to us as if we were curious kids asking about the birds and the bees. Sammy should have run for the hills. I told her several times. I think a part of her felt like she deserved the torture.

"Thank God it was a misfire this time, Lewis! What have I told you? Time and again! Wear a rubber!"

"Sammy. Please. Go. I beg you." Maybe she was sticking around because she saw my torture as worse than her own. Was that it? Talk about sadistic!

"Got any more exams?" I asked when Mom finally gave up on our souls, stormed upstairs, and slammed the bedroom door behind her. Probably to go pray.

"Just Calc. Easy peasy."

"Free and breezy."

She laughed. Why did she laugh? It wasn't that funny?

"Your Mom thinks she's going to be a grandma."

"Yeah," I said. "I'm going to have to talk her off the ledge."

"It's a stupid game anyway," Sammy said.

"What is?"

"Ding Dong Ditch. Right? I mean, what's the goal? To get away scot-free? What's the fun in being a winner who can't bask in the glow of the credit?"

"I think you got more credit than you deserve for that thing you're holding," I said. Why was she still holding it? "How'd you get a positive pregnancy test, anyway?"

"Blue dye," Sammy said, all too fast. She bounced up to leave, only about twenty minutes too late.

"Truce?" she asked at the door. She's so naïve. If only she'd known the stakes.

"Truce." I offered her my hand, and when she reached out with hers, I zapped her with static.

"Plush carpet," I said in the way of an excuse. She smiled and went to her ladybug of a car, idling barely two homes away.

Amateur, I thought, then rushed back to the mental

gymnastics of plotting my secret romance. Nothing short of the greatest of all-time grand gestures would suffice. This time — this last time — I'd burn with honeyed lightning from the heart. Of course, rodents and smoldering grease fires wouldn't win Abby ... because Abby was never the right girl.

I should have been targeting Sammy. She'd always been there, right in front of my eyes, since we were kids, whispering in Abby's ear, making her do whatever it was Sammy Atwood wanted done. If Abby had a thought in her head unrelated to schoolwork and/or studying, it had been put there by my unrealized rival. The amateur needed to be taught a lesson. Because who brings a prank to someone's front door first thing in the morning? There's very little chance of success in that!

I'm sorry. But you can't just say, "Blue dye," and think anyone's buying it. So, who was the mother-to-be? It didn't matter. Sammy wasn't preggo. That's all I knew for sure. She probably just found it in the girls' bathroom or something.

I rolled past her house later, after school, looking for inspiration. Something to destroy her with. The true and only way for Lou to steal Abby's heart, I had learned, was to go through her BFF. And Sammy was... Sammy was...

Coming my way. She was holding the car door open for her sister. I stopped and was idling dumbly by her mailbox. She spotted me. I couldn't escape.

"What the fuck, Nate? Stalk much?"

"Sorry," I said. "I was worried about you." And I was.

Sammy's older sister had the puffy eyes of someone who'd been crying. With that mystery solved, I felt awful for intruding but incredibly lucky for my impeccable timing.

"No need to worry about me," she said. "Didn't you hear? Me and Abby are co-valedictorians."

"Yeah, I heard."

"Sammy, we have somewhere to be," her sister said, and Sammy nodded. She got in the car and pulled out, stopping only to tell me one last thing.

"Stop being such a dick, Nate. It doesn't suit you."

Graduation came and went, and I managed to refrain from any more games. I let them have their night. The girls made their valedictorian speeches, Louie made his saluta-torian one, they turned their tassels, and that was that. Lou and I spent the fleeting days of June getting into whatever trouble we could find, making up for lost time.

During the town's annual fireworks display, the girls found us. They forgave me for my misdeeds. I later learned that Lou had spoken to them on my behalf. He never told me what he said — but whatever it was must've been a whopper of a fish story. In life, he's always been my best advocate.

Surprisingly, the four of us... we just clicked. We had an absolutely unreal July. It was like... sometimes I wished I could freeze time so those days would never end.

Then came August, and it was bliss—sheer bliss marked by undeserved love and friendship. If a person could die from being happy, I would have. But then the Ding Dong Bitch of it all came back around, and Louie and Abby and Sammy... they scattered to the winds of academia.

Sure, we've promised to stay in touch and all that stuff. But I gotta be realistic, you know? I have to be me. Who exactly is that? I'm not quite sure, but I can tell you that there's this kid named Cooper in my grade. The guy is so smug and totally deserves a serving of Ding Dong Bitch, but I'm not going to go there. You know why? Because if I pretend to evolve, then I am evolving. Fake it 'til you make it, right?

So yeah, I'm still here. And yeah, I'm currently alone. That's just the way of the world. I've always known it was inevitable. I don't understand why shit's always gotta change, but it does, and so should I. Maybe I have.

So, to whomever this may concern, you can either accept me or not. Either way, I'll be fine.

The incessant, untimely bells of my future are ringing. Come what may. Peace.

I Dream of Zombie

AUGUST NIEHAUS

I Dream of Zombie

AUGUST NIEHAUS

CORNFIELDS ARE AS VAST AND UNEASY AS THE SEA.

I remember my father first taking me to the Atlantic Ocean when I was a few years old. It looked just like this field. At the time, I had been so sure there was a storm brewing *inside* of it.

There's a storm in this cornfield, too. One of fate and coincidence. It's the first obstacle between us and the freedom of a secluded island. And by us, I mean me, my true love Samantha Blair, and the nine hundred and ninety-eight other zombies at our back.

We seek a future where we're not terrified that the next headshot is coming from behind a nearby concrete pillar. There are a thousand of us, and we've only been zombies for a day ... but it's still so lonely.

I reach for Sam's hand, weaving my fingers through hers.

Her ring finger falls off in my palm.

But she doesn't notice.

I tuck it into my pocket, reluctant to let any part of her go.

Tear ducts I didn't know I still had fill with toxic water. My dream of slipping a ring onto that finger tumble away. I know in my heart that was once our fate, but now I'll never wed her properly.

A deep sadness swells in my chest, or maybe that's just hunger. I'm horrified by it, but I can't deny it: I'd do anything for another bite of Dr. Tony.

God, what a horrible thing to crave. I shouldn't want it, but I do. *I want flesh.* I wonder if all people are more delicious when they run or if that was just because he was my first taste of human meat.

This is who I am now. I'm Nicholas Grey, a zombie — and I really could use another bite of that doctor we chewed through on our way out of Hope Hills General Hospital.

Sam squeezes my hand with her four remaining fingers, and I remember her beautiful face, her long, shiny hair gleaming in the hospital lights. We'd huddled together dreaming of a beach vacation together, should the treatment take...

The treatment took, all right.

It took everything.

Everything except my feelings for Samantha.

Now, a thousand escapees of Hope Hills stand huddled against a cornfield in North Londonberry Township, Pennsylvania. There's no missing a crowd of a thousand. Someone is surely on our trail by now.

I shuffle in a half circle and raise my free arm, swaying on my feet, gesturing, and groaning. I hope that somehow, my wordless communication will tell the horde what I need them to know: that today, we have our freedom, our first taste of it — and if we want to keep it, they have to follow me.

They seem to know what I'm groaning about because a

ragged cheer rises from their throats. It sounds like what would happen if you stepped on hundreds of rubber chickens all at once.

And then, my hand still intertwined with Sam's, we plunge into the corn.

The moon winks at us from above. I keep my hand raised in front of me, fully aware I look like the stereotypical zombie. I don't feel an urge to moan for brains, but the posture *does* make it easier to navigate the sea of half-grown corn.

Eventually, the stalks thin out.

I stop abruptly. Three dozen zombies bump into me.

I turn and shush the one behind me, who in turn shushes the one behind her, and so forth, until a ripple of hissing slides through the cornfield like a snake. I take a hesitant step forward, then another, certain that someone or something else is here.

I part the golden stalks with my decaying fingers and come face to face with a large, doughy, red-ball cap-wearing man. He takes one look at me. "Who the *fuck* are you?! What the fuck are you?"

I grab the man by the shoulders, then bite his neck. *Two birds, one stone.* Whoever this guy is, there's no way he's got zombie best interests at heart. And I need a snack.

Blood gushes from the artery I've opened. The man's limbs flail out of control. He's holding a scythe, and as the others gather around to eat, he chops off zombie heads with his ungainly, uncoordinated death throes.

Somewhere in the distance, I hear more voices. "Did you hear that?"

"I sure as fuck did. Sounded like some punk kids."

"Let's get the fuckers!"

Truck engines turn over and rumble low. No question: there's a group of redneck farmers close by. They're sure to look at a bunch of zombies as a fantastic opportunity for free sport.

My hearing — supernatural after the transformation — catches the sound of booted feet crunching corn stalks. The trucks draw closer, too. But there's another sound—

I shove Sam aside just in time.

A chainsaw howls, the blade seizing at the air where Sam's head was a second before. The man wielding it stumbles past Sam, turning his blade sideways. With a few expert sweeps, he decimates several of our horde before our sheer numbers overwhelm him. Zombies throw themselves willingly on the chainsaw blade so others can sink their teeth into his flesh. He dies shrieking.

I turn away, unable to watch. This is inhumane … but I'm not human, am I? I'm also a lost man … because I can't find Samantha.

Sawed-off shotguns explode in the not-so-distance, one discharging after another. Clearly, this is a coordinated attack and not a random meeting. I hear several trucks mowing down zombies amidst the corn. They've figured out some kind of driving pattern, and my zombies are too dull to realize what's going on.

I try to form Samantha's name with my mouth, but even to my own ears, it sounds like a meaningless warble. To disguise my fear, I issue commands to each dazed zombie I pass: I point, I direct, I command. They can't seem to track what I'm saying. I'm like a general with an incompetent army. I gesture for them to attack from the flank — *no, not that flank, the other kind!*

Suddenly, there's a new machine sound. This one sounds like a hundred demons rising up through the earth. Metal blades. They roar towards us with murderous intent, corn crumbling in its wake.

I close my eyes and concentrate. I can tell the machine

is coming straight for me because of the way the ground rumbles. I pivot and shamble back into the corn, out of the path carved by the trucks, but I'm too slow.

One of the rednecks, half-turned into zombie form now, grabs my ankle and tries to gnaw on my calf. The dead weight slows me just enough.

Now I can clearly see the yellow flash of metal in the moonlight: the machine is a combine, and it's almost on me. The blades circle, slicing through the corn in the same way they'll cut my body to ribbons.

I'm too slow. This is it.

I close my eyes again and let my mind float free. If this is the end, I'll die happy, thinking of Samantha. She stands before me in my mind's eye, healed from being a zombie, reaching towards me with both five-fingered hands and imploring me to stop…

And then the real Sam's palm slaps my face, and a chunk of my cheek goes flying. She bellows at me before lumbering towards the combine with twenty other zombies. Shotguns blazing, the rednecks riding the combine try and kill us. But it's too late. We swarm the machine.

Zombies crawl up the doors and push themselves through the windows, chewing hands and ears. Sam puts her hand on the window. One of the rednecks raises his gun and blasts a hole in Sam's wrist.

Sam shimmies through, her mouth gnashing until it finds the neck of the combine driver.

The machine groans and shudders to a stop.

Sam crawls onto the roof of the massive machine and scans the ground. My heart skips as I realize she's looking for me. The way she's glowing up there in the moonlight, I can think only about her in a wedding dress, rotting away into our future.

When she catches sight of me, Sam flashes her teeth in a bloody smile, then climbs down and lumbers over to me. We embrace. She's warm, a bit warmer than me—but still as ice-cold as any of our half-dead bodies are.

Throughout the flattened field, the bodies of the redneck party lie cooling. Most of them won't rise again because the Hope Hills zombies are hungry, and they're cleaning the meat from the bones like piranhas. It's not that they can't — there won't be enough of them left.

I do a rough count of the heads bobbing to take bites. We've lost nearly a hundred and fifty of our number, so many people I *almost* knew. I hadn't met a lot of the other patients at Hope Hills besides Sam.

Now, their bodies are still, heads and brains damaged beyond reanimation. They're just sacks of steaming organic matter, hardly the people they once were before they were infected.

A great wash of sadness knocks me backward. I think of the families who will never know the fate of someone they loved. God knows the powers that be will pretend this all never happened, and Hope Hills will close, and they'll put the story on ice. The experimental research will be burned or buried.

I try hard not to think about my family and how little they'll know and how much they'll wonder if there was anything they could have done.

I tip my head back, trying to stop the grief from spilling toxic tears again, and stare up at a gradient of a night sky. There's hardly a cloud over the crescent moon, but the night feels heavy.

I sense things rustling in the corn. We risk so much, staying in the open: deadly headshots, more angry rednecks, opportunistic animals. So many things want us dead. As much as we might not feel pain — and as much as it might be a challenge to truly kill us — there are plenty of ways to take a zombie down. After all, we *are* slow and clumsy.

All I want is to eat and live.

I grunt and gesture to the rest of the zombies. Still stunned by the combat they just survived, they shuffle aimlessly towards me. I look at the amassed horror and think about those who might be in pursuit. There are probably a lot of people who will find destroying us quite profitable.

Maybe those who accidentally engineered us. Maybe more people like those rednecks, protecting their homes from something they see as a threat or just hunting us for sport. And, of course, there's always the military. I would really, *really* like to avoid the military.

Just as I think this, the *put-put-put* of a helicopter bats at my skull. I slowly turn my neck an unnatural number of degrees and stare at the bladed beast on the horizon.

It's definitely not the kind of helicopter my dad flew us in when we traveled from our summer home back to New York City. It's a military helicopter, no question: it's black, imposing, and heading towards us like a dragon.

I up the urgency of my growling, grabbing Sam by the shoulders and shaking her. And then I remember her ring finger falling off. I do *not* want the same to happen to her head. She stares me down and lets her jaw hang slack. Clearly, she's not impressed.

But the helicopter gets closer, and the sound gets louder, and now all the zombies look up and stagger where I direct them.

The helicopter swoops close to us, and a man who looks like Gaston leans out the side, howling with primal insanity, his face red and popping with veins.

If I'm a zombie with human intelligence, that right

there is a human with a zombie's intelligence. Beyond bro. All the way up to "beefcake asshole."

"Sergeant Suffox! Don't lean out so far."

The beefcake asshole, presumably Sergeant Suffox, barks back, "Dyin' killin' zombies? Sounds fine to me! Chop 'em up, pilot!"

The helicopter tips suddenly, angling the blades so they slice through zombie heads like a lawnmower on overdue grass. The night fills with the squelch of blood and guts, along with the whine of sawed bones.

I grab Sam's wrist and break into a run through the corn, a mass of Hope Hills zombies following. Helicopters might be slow, but zombies are slow, shambling messes. Suffox's metal beast slides back and forth across our number, tearing us into bits.

There's a dark tunnel entrance straight ahead of us, probably an abandoned transportation project. It's the only way forward I can see — but if we go in, we could easily be trapped.

Suffox howls with glee as his helicopter decapitates another round of zombies. Our numbers shrink by the second.

I have to lead them to safety.

I have to save Sam.

By the time we get to the tunnel entrance, only half our number remain. I step under the concrete arch and turn to see the helicopter blades whirring dangerously close. The horde shuffles frantically, bouncing off one another in their clumsy haste to enter the tunnel.

I gesture wildly as if my summoning can bring them faster into the temporary sanctuary. This tunnel is not for the humans who abandoned it anymore — it's for us now. Zombies stream past me, moaning with relief as they stagger into the safety provided by sturdy concrete. The helicopter hovers right outside, but it can't get any closer. And then it rises.

The ground shakes under my feet. I scan the horizon and spot it: a tank. The long gun swivels, and it's as if I'm staring down the single eye of death.

Before I can breathe or think, Sam shoves me. I stumble fully into the tunnel just as a projectile slams into the arch. The tunnel entrance collapses into rubble, dust, and smoke. I can feel the heat of the explosion on my calves. And can smell the sharp, sweet scent of taxpayer dollars burning.

I clamber to my feet and stand in the dark. Darkness is a strange thing now that I'm a zombie. It doesn't really matter if there's light; I just *sense*. I'm not even sure which of my sensory organs are providing the signals because something about being a zombie mashes them all into one *sense of being*.

Pre-Zombie Nicholas would have been livid in the face of all these injustices towards the American people. But Post-Zombie Nicholas is sad about things that *won't* happen: the children Sam and I won't chase around the yard; the little house we'll never get drunk in and clean together; and that beach vacation we'll never take, lying side by side on perfect sands, dreaming and planning for when we come back.

That's it. We're going to the damn beach. My anger and determination rallies me.

I start to usher the zombies through the tunnel, but Sam grabs my shoulder and grunts something about the humans easily calculating how long we'll take to get to the other side. I gaze into her earnest face, and my deepening love makes me smile. She really does have the street smarts that I lack. We're a perfect match.

She's right, of course. I consider where the tunnel

might go. Hershey is a short distance behind us, west of Hope Hills. It's likely this was intended for trains or an early attempt to connect the town to New York City via subway. If we go straight through, chances are high it will dump us in the heart of civilization.

I think hard about the kinds of projects my dad's blue-blooded friends would trick small municipalities into funding. Often, to multiply the potential funds they'd eventually siphon off, they'd offer cheaper sub-tunnels to small towns whose future elected officials wanted to run campaigns on a platform of mass transportation.

I suspect Sergeant Suffox will go straight to the other end of the main tunnel, getting there in plenty of time to destroy us. In which case, we should probably take a turn as soon as we can. Preferably, it'll be a turn that leads to an exit … but if we have to, we'll dig our way out. Who cares if we lose a few arms in the process? We're going to lose them anyway. It's the docks or death.

I need time to strategize.

I push to the front of the horde and signal for them to stop moving for now. They comply, grumbling with confusion, and break off into small groups — probably the cliques that formed in the hospital before any of us went in for our treatments.

As they settle for a moment, I nod in satisfaction. I may not be able to make everyone happy, but at least they'll stay alive a little longer with me in charge.

A warm, bloody scent makes me flare my nostrils and exhale excitement. It's the smell of human flesh. The news murmurs through the ranks of zombies: someone was smart enough to bring the remaining redneck bodies along.

I slump, relieved. We need all the sustenance we can get, and I have no interest in sending out a hunting party to kill more innocent humans. But those rednecks weren't innocent; they sure as fuck tried to kill us. I thank whatever divine forces might have our backs for this small miracle.

The burly zombies who clearly carried the corpses divvy them up, piece by piece, making sure everyone gets a bite. I take a proffered thigh, then search for Sam in the crowd.

But she's not there. She's sitting by herself on a concrete bench and looks downtrodden. I carry the thigh over and set it beside her, seating myself awkwardly against the wall.

I lean forward, my eyes locked on Sam's beautiful face. Without blinking, I take an *almost* sensual bite of the thigh.

Sam bursts out laughing, her spittle flying into my eyes. The spit stings, and so do her hiccups of laughter. But it's infectious, and I start to laugh, too. Soon, the laugh catches and echoes until the whole horde is huffing like a bunch of wounded bears. It's so comical to our human intelligence that we collectively can't stop laughing — laughing and eating, laughing and drooling, laughing and crying.

When her laughter is spent, Sam finally leans over to take a bite of the thigh. She chews thoughtfully, looking out into the nothingness. Suddenly, she vocalizes a clear note of sadness for everything we'll never do and how meaningless the things we worked so hard on when we were alive are now dead to us. Her world has shrunk to just me and eight hundred of our closest distant cousins. Plus, some beach port somewhere that she's certain we'll never see.

She looks so small and lost. I try to reassure her, but she stares at me, demanding to know what *I* thought was important before all of this.

I quickly take another bite of the thigh to buy myself some time. I know my answer might bring more scorn. Since waking up to find my days and choices numbered,

I've made my decisions based only on what's most important to me. My inner compass points so straight that I
always follow it without asking where it's pointing.

Finally, I look Sam in the eye and explain: love. Love is
what was important before, and it's what's important now.

Sam rolls her eyes and snorts, but I smile and keep
going. I tell her about my parents, who love each other
very much. They've always had it so easy. They never
fought, never even argued, at least not that I saw. And
that was how I knew that when you find true love, it's
easy.

And now I've found it. I rest my hand on hers.

Sam looks down at our skin, gooey with rot, bubbling
where we aren't blistered or bruised. She shakes her head.
Her eyes make it clear: she's sure you have to fight for love
because the good stuff never comes easily. Her moans
convey that if you don't have to fight for it, can it really
matter that much?

My heart breaks as I listen to her. To hide my pain, I
tease her: she must say this to all her boyfriends.

She tosses her head and holds up two fingers. She's
clearly a little proud of that low number, or she's
pretending.

Now, my smile is genuine. One of her boyfriends could
have been in elementary school, for all I know. I trace a
whorl on the top of her hand and wonder what kind of
guy Samantha Blair dates.

I must have wondered aloud because Sam flashes her
rotting teeth. It's exactly what I feared. She dates bad boy
athletes from the wrong side of the tracks, boys, exactly *not*
like me.

I consider this. Then I smile and gesture around us,
because this sure feels like a date. Sam's gaze follows my
gesture, taking in tunnel, the food, the bizarre and horri-

fying scene of zombies munching on human parts as if we're dining at some restaurant in Hell.

She busts up laughing again, but this time, it's a laugh that means warmth and agreement, not scorn and derision. It soothes my fear and makes me want to reach out and caress her cheek, but I hold myself back.

A whisper runs through the zombie ranks: someone managed to keep a phone, and they've found a live stream of reporters crowding into the other end of the tunnel — exactly where I thought Suffox would end up. We'll have to go another way, or we'll be trapped in here for sure.

The decision tree of my choices narrows to a single branch, with a shadowy force chasing me to the precarious tip. My choices are being made for me.

Free will is a human thing, they always say. Now I understand why.

I get up and take my place at the head of the horde. Some of Sam's sadness clings to the backs of my eyes in the same way some of her flesh now sticks to my hand. I want to cry, but I don't want toxic fluids running down my face.

Besides, I refuse to give in to these baser instincts. I'm still Nicholas. I will rise to the level of logical thought.

I think about our next move as if we are collectively the queen on a crowded chessboard. Zombies are obvious (we think with our stomachs), and we're weak. We might be able to overpower a defenseless human, but one with any kind of weapon has our head off in a matter of moments. We can only survive if we hide or blend in, perhaps at some kind of large event.

As we trundle along, I keep an eye out for where the various side tunnels lead. Finally, I see a worn hand-painted arrow on the concrete that reads OUTLET MALL, NEW JERSEY.

I do the math. New Jersey is probably a three days' slow walk away.

It smacks me like a hand on my decaying cheek. The large event we need is also three days away: Black Friday. My tainted blood is evidence that I got exactly what I paid for by opting for discount services over Thanksgiving week. Discount needles jabbed into my arm by discount nurses, while discount doctors wrote discount evaluations with discount pens...

But maybe the black eye of the capitalist's year can be our salvation.

FOR THREE DAYS, eight hundred and fifty of us flow through the slowly narrowing tunnel. A few fall to the wayside, too starved to go on. Sam lets some distance grow between her and I as we walk, though she's still never more than a few bodies away.

After a mind-numbing eternity, we spill through a double door into the Tanger Outlets in Atlantic City.

The doors open into a side entrance near a bathroom, the kind with inexplicable exits no one ever uses. Now I see why. They must all lead to some strange experimental promise of easy, cheap mass transportation.

The mall smells bad, like poop on the floor. But it also smells good, like fried meat: chicken, fish, even beef, deep-fried in ancient oil.

I'm drooling like crazy. Though I might crave human flesh, some old patterns can't be overridden. My base cravings are so strong, and I have less willpower to resist them. Despite my better judgment, I lumber towards the food court with the rest of the horde.

We must look a sight: almost a thousand diseased

people descending before nine in the morning on this smattering of hapless, part-time high schoolers who don't give a shit about the angle of their hat, much less serving a bunch of insatiable undead mouths before they're even technically open.

Every zombie moans in anticipation of the feast they're about to consume. The sound turns the heads of the few patrons waiting in the food court for stores to open.

I push to the front of the line for Southern Fried Heaven and pantomime that we're a group of foreigners hoping to experience some American hospitality, and we don't speak any English. I fold my arms as if to say, *I hope you can accommodate our cultural differences.*

The young woman behind the cash register stares at me, smacking a wad of gum in the corner of her mouth. "Cash or credit?"

I hold back my grin because I know my rotting teeth will be terrifying, not charming. A second later, credit cards make their way to the front of the line through the ranks. Apparently, some of my group managed to keep their wallets.

The woman takes the cards and swipes them, and through some miracle, the transactions go through.

I wonder how long before they shut our accounts off. I'm sure "undead" isn't a value you can fill into any form for online banking.

As the orders are prepared, zombies take the food from the wide-eyed employees and find seats in the food court. Then, they stuff their faces with a lack of manners that would make pirates cringe.

I perch with some discomfort on a sticky plastic chair. This is not the level of hygiene and quality I'm used to in my dining furniture. I pick at the basket of droopy fries, mostly stuffing the deep-fried drumsticks into my mouth, bones and all.

A middle-aged man in a Burrito World uniform sidles over after we've finished most of the food. He squats down next to the elderly zombie on my right, his expression leery but with a genuine streak of compassion. "Hey, ma'am, you don't look so good. Can I call you a doctor?"

The zombie is still busy stuffing her face with a fried fish sandwich and doesn't answer. I tug on the employee's shirt to draw his attention away and gesture to inform him that this one's with me and he doesn't need to worry about her at all.

The man reluctantly pulls away from the elderly zombie. But when he finally looks at me, his brow creases. "Uh, you don't look so good either."

Now he's looking from one face to another, growing horror dawning on him as he realizes the extent of what he's looking at. "Are *all* of you okay?"

I grunt that we're fine and he can leave us alone.

The man stands up and takes two steps back.

"Okayyyy. I'm gonna see if somebody else wants to, y'know, maybe talk to you a little bit. I'll … I'll be right back." He staggers away as if drunk, then bolts to the other side of the mall, jabbering into a smartphone and pointing in our direction a few times as if the person on the other end of the call can somehow see us.

They're on to us. We need to leave.

I stand up and motion for the other zombies to do the same, but not everyone is finished licking their baskets clean.

And now it's too late. The double security doors fly open, and seven burly mall cops strut through with their batons.

The Burrito World guy must have identified me as the

ringleader because the mall cop in charge makes a beeline to my chair.

"Excuse me, son. You look like a little *young* to be in charge of … these people." He puts his hands on his hips and studies my face, his disgust deepening as he takes in my rot.

Swallowing down fear, I attempt once more to explain without words that I don't know English and can't communicate with him.

"Oh, uh, I don't speak your language. Sorry about that. *Como se dice* 'your language'?" He scratches the back of his head, revealing yellowed sweat stains under his arm. "I think your friend should come with me. Let's make sure she's not spreading some disease the rest of our patrons won't be able to shake."

He places a hand on her shoulder, and his squad descends.

I turn around in my seat, irate, then feel my torso start to come undone and stop cold.

The old zombie looks back at me as they lead her away, and one of her eyeballs pops out and rolls down her cheek.

The zombies and the cops disappear into the back room, and the door clicks softly closed behind them. Sam squeezes my knee, and I realize I'm holding my breath.

Then I catch the unmistakable sound of a zombie snarling and cops shrieking. Clearly, they were caught entirely unaware. Now, the looks exchanged around the food court tables are filled with envy. Why does she get fresh meat?

The snarling and slobbering get quieter and quieter, and my stomach rumbles in the silence. I mouth another piece of chicken, trying to sate my rising saliva. Seven cops for one zombie? That's a lot of sustenance to go around.

It *is* painful to hear how brutal we are from afar. Those

mall cops were just doing their jobs. I swallow down my jealousy with the chicken.

After a few more minutes, the back doors swing open again, and the zombie shuffles out, wiping her chin. I take the opportunity to stand and instruct the horde to scatter before someone finds the abandoned uniforms. I point towards a correspondingly mysterious pair of doors on the other end of the outlet mall, then towards the clock, raising nine fingers.

Nodding, the zombies drift away in ones, twos, and fours. Sam scoots her plastic chair closer and hugs my arm in an uncharacteristically affectionate gesture. As I watch all the other zombies trickle away, I feel the heavy mantle of leadership settle on my shoulders. No more am I simply one of the crowd.

Sam tugs my wrist and gives me a charming smile, clearly reminding me that *she's* sticking with me.

Her face is so close I could nibble on her nose. The idea sends a rush of heat through my groin.

With a gap-toothed grin, Sam bounces towards Forever 21, pulling me after her. We've got half an hour to burn, so we might as well go shopping. We enter the store side by side, and I can feel her excitement raising my mood. It's so funny how she can be so sad one moment and completely set it aside the next. If I was feeling as low as she was, I'd be feeling that way for days.

Sam touches each dress, shirt, and pair of pants we pass, leaving a thin trail of zombie slime on the cheap fabric. We pass a pair of middle-aged women, clearly locals, who cast a judging look at us before turning away and pointedly returning to their conversation.

"What a strange buncha people this morning."

"I don't like 'em. Look like they're out-of-towners, certainly not from around here."

The first woman, as polite as the Queen of England, glances over at me and Sam. "Well, those two look alright, boyfriend and girlfriend. At least *they're* normal."

Boyfriend and girlfriend. I try the thought on for size. I don't hate it, but now I'm blushing again. I grab a polo shirt and some khaki pants off the nearest rack and pat Sam's shoulder, ready to move on.

She flips a coy look at me, one eye rolling loosely, and then proceeds to browse. I shuffle a few steps behind her, uneasily watching the clock. Finally, Sam snatches a floral sundress off the rack and holds it against her body with a beaming smile, striking a pose to indicate how perfect it is for her.

Then she motions for me to join her and heads for the changing rooms. There are only two, and they're not marked by gender. One of them is already occupied.

I freeze and swallow nervously.

Sam gives me the coy look and holds open the door to one of them. I find I have no sounds. Sam raises a brow at me and pats her torso. I realize that she means *we both look like this, the same everywhere now, dead flesh.*

But I can't help but think of Sam in a *different* way, just for a moment. I force the thought out of my mind with great effort … and follow her into the changing room.

I walk straight to the opposite corner, facing the wall. Sam faces the mirror, which means she'll be able to watch me. I sure hope the pants I grabbed make my ass look good.

I let my old jeans fall down around my ankles. Whatever I've got left back there, I hope Sam thinks it's cute. I grimace, feeling like a middle schooler. Here I am, Nicholas Grey, rowing stern for the champion crew team a year ago. My ass looks just fine.

I pull up the khakis too hard, tweaking my hand. It

dangles loose, the fingers swinging independently of my palm, which I hold very still. I can still feel my extremities, and when I wiggle them experimentally, it seems the electric impulses are still flowing.

I continue to dress, more deliberate now. But as I zip up the pants, I set my foot down too hard, and my big toe falls off.

As I stare at my toe in numb disbelief, an entire dismembered foot of Sam's wobbles against my ankle.

She starts to snort helplessly. I fumble with the buttons on my shirt, not wanting to be in any state of undress but needing to make sure she's okay. With my half-severed hand, I can't seem to find my fine motor skills.

Sam clears her throat and spits something wet onto the floor of the changing room. My shirt in shambles, I turn around.

The sundress tightens at her waist and cascades down her legs, making her hips strong and full. Though she's leaning against the wall for support, she holds her head and spine as regally a movie star poised to take a photo on the red carpet.

I bleat my enthusiasm.

Sam giggles and spins around on one leg. Being so close to death seems to have given her some freedom, maybe peace. She stands there, glowing with inner light.

My lips twitch. I want to kiss her so badly. No other thought can find space in my mind for a long moment.

But then logic floods back in, and I remember that I must be a gentleman because, if this is my true love, when the time is right, we'll both be ready for the kiss. Nobody ever said that to me in so many words, but my parents' relationship and all the movies I watched told me so very clearly. I restrain myself and give her a smile and a small clap instead.

Sam's face falls a little, and she seems about to say something — but then we hear a zombie commotion outside. The sounds of biting and snarling and swallowing fill the air.

The horde is eating someone.

I burst out of the changing room and hobble to the small, worn-down carousel in the center of the mall.

Humans and zombies grapple against the wide-eyed painted horses. I push through the crowd, shoving zombies off the humans and bellowing at them to leave.

One winter-bundled customer raises a broom over her head and smashes a zombie away from a television in a beaten-up box. "Die, you monster! The TV is miiiine!"

Sprawled on the polished mall floor, the zombie gurgles and expires. The shopper stands over him, spit flying from her bright red lips. "That's right, $250 for a 46-inch, in this day and age? This is *legendary*, bitches!"

The other zombies look dangerously close to eating the gleeful woman. I push them away, placing myself between the horde and the enraged humans. I pantomime that we don't really have a use for TVs — where would we put them, anyway? If they'll just let us go, they can keep the goods.

The customer crows, reenacting her zombie murder and hugging her hard-won television box. I slowly back away. Best not to eat her anyway. She's clearly poisoned.

The zombies follow me through the largely quiet mall, shuffling on feet as fast as we can manage. Sam leans on me for support, hobbling on one foot. The clocks we pass show 8:49 a.m.

We make it to the mysterious double doors at the other end of Tanger Outlets. I push one open and peer out to find a massive, empty concrete parking lot. Supply trucks idle with their back ends against loading docks. It seems safe enough.

I motion for a zombie to slip out, one at a time.

Then, the air thumps distinctly right over our heads, and Suffox's helicopter swoops in for a smooth landing on the flat mall roof. Suffox whoops and swears up a storm, words I quickly shut out of my brain because they're so offensive.

Every fiber of my undead being screeches. Without thinking, I turn and shove Sam as hard as I can. She keels into the safety of the mall, just in time.

Machine gun fire sounds: *rat-tat-tat!* Zombie guts splatter everywhere from those who were unlucky enough to crawl out after I said it was safe.

I pull the door shut behind me, and the zombies barricade the door, shoving display racks through the handles. Suffox won't get in this way ... unless he's got that tank. I pray he didn't bring it all the way to Atlantic City.

But we can hear soldiers thundering above us on the roof, more helicopters touching down, and boots crossing the building towards the opposite entrance.

We're outside of a party store. I snag as many masks as I can find and put one on, handing another to Sam. She slips it over her face, becoming a cutesy panda. I dish out the masks to the closest zombies, gesturing for them to don the disguises.

Everyone scrambles to camouflage themselves as best they can, grabbing clothes, props, wigs, sunglasses, anything they can find. Some disguises are better than others, but hopefully, a few of us will slip through.

The doors on the other end of the mall bang open.

"Let's go, men! They're in here somewhere. Inspect everyone and shoot on sight!" Suffox shouts.

There will be no mercy for us now. They're on the hunt.

Sam pulls me into a hallway. Her steps are surer, if slow. She leans against me while the other zombies cluster behind us. It's obvious what we are, but maybe the disguises will buy us some time.

Rat-rat-tat! They've found some zombies.

"Fuck you, you nasty undead motherfuckers!" Suffox bellows.

I imagine a death counter. We would have been at barely five hundred when we entered the mall, and now we must be less than three hundred.

Sam's hobbling becomes more urgent, and she pulls me down a passage that leads into the Nike outlet. The doors are still closed. Outside, shoppers swarm with their arms outstretched.

They groan like zombies. "Deals! Deals!"

"Gaaaains!" roars a man wearing a Bitcoin hat.

The gunfire behind us picks up speed, and dying zombies roar in agony. I charge the door, wrestling with the lock. Several other zombies throw their shoulders against the glass, and we manage to break them open.

The mob of shoppers swarms in, providing cover for us to leave the building. I let out a tiny breath of relief because even Suffox won't shoot innocent civilians on purpose … right?

Blinking against the sudden morning sunlight, I rip off my mask and scan the world outside. Signs indicate that the dock is a few blocks from here, but standing between the two hundred or so of us and our freedom is a traffic jam on Atlantic Avenue.

Agony and ecstasy course through me in equal amounts. I reach for Sam's hand, then close my fingers tightly around hers. I look at her. She looks at me.

Again, I nearly kiss her.

Then, the signal changes. *Beep boop, beep boop, beep boop.* The crosswalk is clear since those in traffic haven't caught up to the fact that a horde of zombies is in their town. They're not trying to smash us; they're politely letting us through. Well, as politely as New Jerseyans ever do.

I step out onto the big white stripe, then into the street. Stripe, street. Stripe, street. I never let go of Sam and she never lets go of me. We make it to the other side and travel two more blocks towards the dock.

And then the helicopter swoops right above us.

The last of the humanity in me despairs. This could be the end. The end of me, the end of Sam, the end of everything.

I envelop Sam in a tight hug. I close my eyes to savor the sensation of her pressed against my chest, just this once.

Sam pulls away from me slightly, then takes my cheeks in her hands and kisses me.

I lose myself in her rubbery lips, oblivious to everything that wants me dead because this is what it feels like to live.

A nearby car explodes, zombies moan, people scream — and I'm back to the now. I break off the kiss and shamble-run. There's no longer a polite allowance for zombie crosswalkers. Drivers are trying to dodge explosions, mowing down anything in their path, even fellow humans.

Suffox's helicopter circles in a tight loop overhead, raining down explosives on everything that moves. As I roll to avoid a flying fender, I catch a glimpse of Suffox's demented grin as he hangs out the side of the helicopter

He shakes the massive gun in his hand at us. "Yeehaw! Here we go!"

I drag Sam into an alley just before a huge truck explodes behind us. I shelter her with my body. Hot metal rains down on my back, and something takes off my kneecap, but I don't feel any of the wounds. It's simply intellectual pain.

Another rocket lands. Another ten zombies down. Then fifty. Our numbers are dwindling to double digits, fast.

But then the helicopter runs out of fuel. It stops circling and drops low on the shore near the dock, coming to an ungraceful stop at the water's edge. Suffox leaps out, rolling for no reason, cradling what appears to be a massive rocket launcher against his chest. When he gets to his feet, he looks like a veritable Rambo.

Suffox puts the weapon to his eye and aims toward the crosswalk. But he hasn't seen Sam and me. Not yet.

While Suffox is distracted, Sam and I hobble towards the dock. I summon the few zombies left alive with my free arm, and they roll with me like a foul, dripping, desperate river.

Suffox empties his rocket into the crowd. Human blood and zombie matter paint the walls with equality. He bellows, sounding like a video game character.

Sheltering Sam with my body, I half-drag her towards the dock. If we can make it onto the water, Suffox won't be able to follow. The helicopter appears grounded. We could be out of here before he can get another ride.

But then, from right behind us, Suffox shouts, "Well, well, well, do I spy a couple of zombie lovebirds?"

I spin around, putting Sam behind me. I look for help, but there's only one other zombie left standing. He's wringing his hands at the end of the dock, uncertain about jumping into the rickety boat he's found.

No matter. It's Sam and me against the world. I point to the boat and nudge her.

Suffox puts his rocket launcher to his cheek and pulls

the trigger. There's a distinct click and no explosion. "Shit."

He dumps it into the water, then pulls a massive blade off his back. The machete glints in the cold sunlight.

I sidle towards Sam, elbowing her again, hoping she'll make a break for the boat. I narrow my focus to how hard I'll have to row — just like it used to be every morning when I rowed for school. I think about which muscles I'll have to engage and which muscles will burn.

My memory is interrupted by the flash of Suffox's blade. "God damn you, motherfucking zombies, America is gonna thank me! YE-AAAAAAAAA!"

Suffox slashes.

Suddenly, Sam is between me and him. She takes the brunt of Suffox's steroid-fueled blow right through the middle.

Her body tumbles in half. Rolling up in the ragged sundress fabric, her legs slide into the sea. Her face blinks up at me from the rotting boards.

I scream.

Suffox raises his machete again. His next blow will decapitate me.

I fling my hands in front of me and close my eyes. I don't want to see the final blow. I want to imagine Sam's face — not lying dead on a dock, but leaning across the pile of well-worn magazines in the lobby of Hope Hills, alight with the dream of an island we'll lie on together.

Suffox screeches. I open my eyes to see Sam gnawing through his Achilles tendon. He misses it, and my hands close around his neck.

I pull the mountain of a man to me with one adren-aline-fueled yank and sink my teeth into his throat. Without hesitating, I rip out his esophagus and shove him so he tumbles into the water.

I limp to the edge of the dock and stare at him leaking blood into the gray sea. I feel relief, but only for a second. Then, the fear rushes in.

I rush to Sam's side and cradle the top half of her in my arms. I check for a pulse, but of course, there isn't one.

This isn't true love — it can't be. It isn't easy. It's *breaking* me.

I try to engage the part of my brain that took meticulous notes for my biology classes, but nothing prepared me to heal the undead. Sam isn't bleeding; she's not spasming or showing signs of broken bones. She's just ... half of her.

But I have to save her. I *have* to revive her, to stop whatever's killing her, even if it takes me the rest of my entire undead life.

A hand touches my cheek.

I open my eyes, and Sam smiles the most beautiful smile I've ever seen. She pulls me down for another kiss.

It's a perfect kiss. I don't lose myself in this one — I take note of every detail, tucking them away in my memory so I'll never forget.

We kiss for long enough that I hear screams coming from the far end of the dock. I raise my head to see a small throng of bloodied, bruised people pointing and shrieking. That's our cue to get out of here.

I cradle Sam against my hip and make to walk towards the boat. But Sam shakes her head and points to the helicopter.

I grin. We'll have to find some fuel, but I can *definitely* fly a helicopter.

∼

LIKE SOME KIND of blood substitute, exhilaration flows through my decaying limbs. I crouch behind lush, wet-smelling foliage, creeping forward to ensure I don't startle any stray tourists who might be soaking up this remote island paradise.

Clinging to my chest, Sam pushes her nose into the crook of my jaw. She's still very much undead, and there's only half of her now, so we're literally inseparable now that we've left the helicopter behind.

Life could be great here. The island is small, and its population stays on the other side, rarely venturing to where we are now. Hunting is as easy as catching the plentiful fish from the sea, which is where I'm headed now.

I push past tropical plants until I can see the telltale gold of the beach. I set Sam down so I can use both hands to clear the leaves and get a good look at the shore.

I had expected to find an empty beach, as I have every day for the past week — but instead, it's dotted with ugly white pop-up tents. There are trucks, too, the run-down kind that live here on the island. Overworked people unload boxes of soda, bottled water, and airplane pretzels.

A sign fluttering in the warm wind catches my eye: *COMING SOON: FYRE FESTIVAL.*

A festival? Intriguing that people would come all the way out here for a music celebration. It's such a remote place. If someone goes missing, maybe it won't be so strange. Maybe they won't even notice for a while.

I smile at Sam.

It's dinner time.

The Sundance Kid

SEAN PLATT

The Sundance Kid

SEAN PLATT

Carmen stood behind the Cinemark concession counter, staring absentmindedly at the popcorn popper while buttery kernels exploded against the glass. A slow Thursday night so far, with only a handful of patrons trickling in to see Galactic Baristas. But then again, watching a movie about space-traveling baristas saving the universe one coffee at a time (yes, the poster actually said that) wasn't exactly her thing. Nor did it appear to be anyone else's. She was about to sneak her phone out to check for updates from the Sundance committee (again) when an all-too-familiar but never (ever) welcome voice jarred her to attention.

"Are my eyes deceiving me? Or is that Carmen Ruiz I see directing the popcorn and sodas? Though I must say, it suits you more than the camera." Natalie Sinclair laughed like the bitch she was while leaning against the counter, her perfectly glossed lips curled into a smug smile. She was wearing an oversized pastel hoodie, the sleeves just long enough to cover her hands. A plaid skirt peeked out from beneath the hoodie and was paired with knee-high socks. The whole look seemed thrown together. But it probably cost more than Carmen made in a month passing Junior Mints across the counter.

Carmen resisted the urge to roll her eyes. "What can I get for the Nepo-baby?"

Natalie glared at her. "I'm not here to ingest empty calories. I was just wondering if you've heard my good news about the Emerging Artists program?" Her eyes gleamed with barely concealed glee. "I got my official acceptance letter yesterday."

"I haven't heard anything," Carmen said in a level voice.

Natalie offered Carmen a performative shrug. "I guess my film really must have resonated with the selection committee."

Carmen had been checking her email obsessively for days now, waiting for any update on the status of Jaguar Woman, the short film she had poured all the lights and magic she had into over the past year. But it had been radio silence so far.

Carmen provided her own shrug. "The submission deadline was just last week. I'm sure they're still reviewing all the entries."

"Of course," Natalie said. But there was a slight tinge of pity in her tone.

Carmen felt her cheeks flush with heat. *Of course*, Natalie's film got in. Her daddy was a prominent studio executive at Warner, and her mommy was a well-known casting director. Every summer since turning 15, she had landed prestigious internships at major studios and production companies thanks to her parents' connections. For her sweet sixteen, Natalie got a state-of-the-art RED cinema camera package worth over $50,000.

For her sweet sixteen Carmen got the book *Making*

Movies by Sidney Lumet. And she wouldn't have traded it for anything.

"It's not like you have a massive leg up with Mommy and Daddy opening all the doors and waiting for you to walk through them." Carmen winced, but she couldn't help herself.

Natalie turned her nose up. "Some of us actually have talent, Carmen. Unlike you, I don't need to rely on cheap gimmicks to get noticed. I *earned* my spot in the program, fair and square."

Carmen's blood boiled. Jaguar Woman was not a "gimmick." Her short film was a raw, fearless exploration of identity and belonging. The magical realism Natalie thought was a gimmick was essential to the story. And it was all anchored by a magnetic lead performance from her girlfriend, Alana. Carmen had written, directed, and edited the entire thing for less than a grand — all money made from tutoring, babysitting, and this job — enlisting her friends for help with the production. God, she even learned how to use AI tools to animate certain sequences and enhance the practical effects.

"Still waiting for you to congratulate me," Natalie cocked her head. "It's the polite thing to do, you know."

"Congratulations, Natalie," Carmen said through gritted teeth. "You must be so proud."

"I am." She smiled, tossing her head, then walked off, leaving Carmen seething.

"Excuse me."

"What?" She turned to look at the pimply boy standing on the other side of the counter, pointing to the popcorn machine.

"Please." It came out as a squeak.

God, her bitch vibes must be strong tonight. "I got

you," she said, softening her tone, then giving him an extra large for the price of a medium.

By the end of her shift, she was emotionally drained. She checked her phone a half dozen more times. How come Natalie had heard but she hadn't? She clocked out and shuffled to the parking lot to meet Alana, who was waiting to walk her home, same as every Thursday night.

"*Uh oh.*" Alana took one look at Carmen's stormy expression and frowned. "What happened? Was that guy back? The one who always tries to pay for his large popcorn with a bag of pennies while bitching about the price?"

"Natalie happened," Carmen said, kissing Alana's cheek. They walked along the cracked sidewalk towards home. "She stopped by to gloat about getting into the Emerging Artists program."

Alana looped her arm through Carmen's. "Don't let her get to you. Natalie was sucking on a silver spoon even before she started sucking at making movies."

Carmen laughed.

"Her 'success' doesn't mean anything. It's bullshit. I've told you before, nepotism will only take her so far."

"I know." Carmen sighed. "It's just frustrating. We worked so hard on our short while Natalie coasted along on her family name and fancy equipment — I mean, she even got a Don Crews cameo in her film. The whole system is rigged."

Alana shrugged. "Most systems are. That's why your parents lied about your address to get you into North Hills. Because they knew you deserved a great education. You deserve a fair shot with your film, too, Carmen. If Sundance doesn't give you that, then screw 'em. You'll find another way. *We'll* find another way."

Carmen gave her a grateful smile. But doubt still

lingered like that one flickering fluorescent light in the theater bathroom that never quite went out. She didn't want to rely so heavily on Sundance as her way out of a dead-end life. But getting accepted could be Carmen's ticket to turning her passion into a viable career.

She loved filmmaking.

But Carmen also felt the weight of family responsibility. Her dad hadn't worked in six months. He'd fallen on a piece of rebar, and his leg simply wasn't recovering. And even though her mom juggled multiple housekeeping gigs, they were simply to keep food on the table. College was barely a dot on Carmen's horizon. Assuming she could scrape together the money for tuition, her parents would never understand pursuing film. Not when a steady paycheck mattered more than anything else.

They walked the remainder of the way in silence. When they finally reached the sagging porch of the cramped bungalow that Carmen shared with her parents and three younger siblings, Alana squeezed her hand.

"No matter what happens, you have to believe in yourself. Jaguar Woman is special. The right people will see that."

"I hope so," Carmen said.

Carmen gave her a parting hug, then watched Alana disappear around the corner to her house. A second later the light in the back went on. Their signal that Alana had got home safely.

Carmen drew a deep breath and entered the house. The TV was blaring, of course, with her little brothers arguing over the remote. Dirty dishes were piled high in the sink. It looked like a restaurant kitchen after a busy Saturday night, minus the industrial dishwasher.

"Mija, there you are," said Mom, wiping her hands on her apron. "How was work?"

"Same." Carmen pulled a chair out from the kitchen table and sat. A cold tortilla sat on a plate. She tore a piece off and chewed it. Still delicious.

"Any word from that fancy film festival of yours yet?"

"Not yet." Carmen shook her head. "But I'm sure it's coming soon."

Mom set a plate of reheated chicken and rice in front of her. "Don't get your hopes up too high, Carmen. You know how competitive those things are."

Carmen picked up her fork. "Yes, I know exactly how competitive—"

"It's good to have a backup plan. That's all I'm saying."

That's all you ever say. Have a backup plan.

"I know, Mom," Carmen said, pushing food around on her plate.

Mom threw up her hands and turned to the dishes while Carmen ate in silence. Resisting the urge to check her phone. Sundance wouldn't be notifying applicants at midnight. Or would they?

Maybe she'd check once more.

Nothing.

Later that night, after the rest of the house had finally gone quiet, Carmen retrieved her battered laptop from the hand-me-down desk in her room and curled up in bed with her favorite movie. *The City of Palaces* always brought her comfort. Lush cinematography and a lyrical score that won the composer an Ariel Award. The eye of the camera panned lovingly over the misty canals and baroque palaces of St. Petersburg, a dream world unto itself. The city's ethereal beauty leaped off the screen, every frame a masterful composition of light, shadow, and color that transported her far away from her cramped bedroom and the leaden weight of her worries.

Directed by the visionary Anton Acquilino, The City of Palaces had ignited her passion for film. Carmen had seen the movie more times than she could count and had memorized every line. She closed her eyes and imagined her own name flickering on the screen: *Directed by Carmen Ruiz.*

During every spare moment over the last year, she channeled that dream into reality and made Jaguar Woman. Now, her proudest creation was out there in the world — her heart laid bare and awaiting judgment.

And not just any judgment. Anton Acquilino was on the jury this year.

Carmen hugged her knees as the credits rolled, surprised to find herself fighting tears. All she wanted was a chance to prove what she could do, to show everyone — her family, her town, even herself — that she had more to offer than they ever gave her credit for.

She took out her phone and opened her email for the hundredth time. Spam and industry newsletters with big promises were all that had arrived. She plugged it into the charger, then closed her laptop with a sigh, setting it on her nightstand. Then she burrowed under the covers.

Soon, Carmen told herself as she drifted off to sleep. The news would come soon.

But even as she succumbed to slumber, a taunting voice drifted into her dreams.

You'll never make it, Carmen. You're not good enough. And you never will be.

The voice sounded suspiciously like Natalie's.

~

TWO WEEKS LATER, it was still radio silence.

The anxiety was eating Carmen alive. She couldn't

focus on anything else — job, homework, school — constantly refreshing her email with a mix of anticipation and dread.

Alana remained the voice of reason, incessantly trying to soothe her nerves. "Stop worrying, Carm. I bet your letter got lost in the mail. These things happen." And when she couldn't take the complaining anymore she said, "Call the festival and check on your application status."

God. How come Carmen hadn't thought of that?

So she steeled herself and finally dialed the Emerging Artists program, her heart pounding when the line rang. Surely, they would view her as passionate, excited and enthusiastic? Not as worried, anxious and a nag?

"Sundance Institute, Emerging Artists program," a pleasant voice said. "This is Melissa, how may I assist you?"

"Hi there, Melissa. My name is Carmen Ruiz. I submitted my short film to Emerging Artists, but I haven't heard about my application status. I was wondering if you could check on that for me?"

"Of course, doll."

Carmen almost collapsed with relief.

"What's the name of your short?"

"Jaguar Woman. Thank you." Carmen listened to clacking keys on the other side of the line. She was about to get an answer. But the typing continued, then silence. "I'm just gonna put you on hold. One moment."

Carmen felt a chill go down her back. One moment? That couldn't be good, could it? Don't panic. She told herself. But she couldn't help it. She was panicking.

And then Melissa came back on the line. "I'm sorry, Ms. Ruiz, but I don't see any record of your application in our system."

Carmen froze. "That can't be right. It was submitted

along with several others from my school. And they've all received their acceptance or rejection letters already. How could mine be the only one missing?"

"It's possible it might have been erroneously entered into the system. But I've checked spelling variations on both title and director."

"I don't understand," Carmen said, trying not to cry.

"Tell you what," Melissa said, her tone sympathetic yet professional. "I'll do a thorough search of our records. Give me your contact details, and I'll give you a call back as soon as I have more information."

"Thank you."

Carmen provided her phone number and then ended the call. A knot of anxiety twisted in her gut.

She paced her bedroom, trying to make sense of the situation. If everyone else's submissions had made it through, then why was hers the only one unaccounted for?

Had Sundance lost it, or had she done something wrong?

An hour crawled by with no further word from the festival. She called into work and said she wouldn't be coming because she felt sick. And it was true. Her stomach churned like her life depended on it. Carmen was about to text Alana when her phone buzzed. Utah area code.

"This is Carmen speaking." She dropped onto the edge of her bed.

"Ms. Ruiz, this is Melissa. I've done an extensive search, and we still can't locate your application. It seems that Jaguar Woman never reached us."

"That's impossible! I sent it in with everyone else's submissions."

"I'm sorry."

Her vision blurred with sudden tears. "What can I do?"

"Nothing this year, I'm afraid. But–"

"Can't I just send in my submission right now?" Her throat was closing up. Even forming words was becoming difficult.

"I'm afraid our submission window has closed, and the judging process is underway. Your best bet would be to reapply next year."

"Next year?" Carmen felt hollow. Reality hit her like a physical blow. She'd be graduated. No longer eligible for Emerging Artists. "But … Anton Acquilino is judging *this year's* competition. He's the whole reason I submitted my film … the reason I even made it. He won't be on the panel next year."

"I understand your disappointment, Ms. Ruiz." And it did sound like Melissa was sad. "But I'm afraid there's nothing more we can do. We wish you the best of luck with your future projects."

We?

What did that even mean?

The line went dead. Carmen threw her phone onto her bed and crumpled onto the mattress. Jaguar Woman was supposed to be her big break, Carmen's chance to prove to everyone — including herself — that she had what it took to make it as a filmmaker.

Her phone blipped.

Alana.

She tried texting her. But couldn't. She felt ashamed. Embarrassed. Stupid. She buried her face in the pillow, wanting to scream. But not wanting to scare her family. So her voice stayed trapped in her throat.

She told her mom she was sick. Her period. Otherwise, she'd be subjected to an abundance of fussing. Eventually she managed to text Alana.

Sundance didn't receive my entry. Don't know what I did wrong.

And then she cried.

Not even thirty seconds later, Carmen heard the front door opening. Dad coming home from his new part-time security job. But moments later, there came a soft knock at her bedroom door.

"It's me." Alana.

"Come in," she said, not moving from the bed.

Alana peeked her head in, her brow creased with worry. "I came as soon as I got your message. I'm so sorry, baby."

Carmen sat, wiping her eyes. "I don't understand how this could have happened. We worked so hard on that film. And I was so careful with the application …"

"You're *always* careful." Alana entered and closed the door behind her. She perched on the edge of Carmen's bed and took her hand. "But I think I might know what happened to your submission."

Carmen frowned. "What do you mean?"

"I got off the phone with Javier just before you texted, and he told me something weird."

"Weird, how?"

"He saw Natalie alone in the room where the festival submissions were being collected. And get this — she was holding a film when she came out. He didn't think anything of it at the time because he thought it was probably hers, but now …"

A cold dread washed over her. "You don't think …"

"I do." Alana's jaw tightened. "I think that jealous bitch sabotaged you. Natalie knew your film was better than hers, so she made sure the festival never even saw it."

The pieces fell neatly into place, including Natalie's smug attitude at the theater.

"That conniving little—"

"I know." Alana squeezed her hand. "But we can't let her get away with this. We have to do something, Carm."

Carmen shook her head. "There's nothing we can do. Melissa at the Emerging Artists office said submissions are already closed, and the judging process has started."

"Then fuck Sundance."

Carmen sucked back air, and they both crossed themselves.

Then Alana grinned. "What I actually mean is that I'm sure we can find some other way to get your film in front of Anton."

Carmen met her determined gaze. Maybe this wasn't the end of the road. Maybe there was still a chance to make her dream a reality.

"What's our first step?" Carmen asked.

"How do you feel about confronting that bitch?"

CARMEN GRIPPED the steering wheel so tightly that her knuckles were bone white. Her jaw clenched with barely contained rage. She had been pickling in her anger the entire drive to Natalie's sprawling mansion, rehearsing exactly what she would say to the backstabbing harpy when she confronted her.

Alana sat in the passenger seat, fidgeting with the hem of her jacket. "Maybe we should wait. I mean, we don't have any actual proof that Natalie sabotaged your submission."

"This was *your* idea," Carmen reminded her.

"I figured we would come up with a plan. Take our time. Be smart about—"

"This is smart. I *know* she did this. I feel it in my gut."

"Instinct isn't proof."

"No, but I'm going to make her admit it to my face." Carmen parked haphazardly in Natalie's circular driveway, then got out of the car and marched up to the front door. Alana trailed behind her.

Natalie's home was an opulent, three-story estate with towering columns, expansive windows framed by luxurious drapes, and a grand entrance flanked by meticulously manicured hedges. There was even a fountain out front.

She jabbed the doorbell with her thumb and listened to the obnoxious chime of Beethoven's Fifth Symphony echoing through the cavernous foyer.

A moment later, a woman wearing an apron answered the door. "Si?"

Carmen had intended to be rude. But she couldn't. Not to the help. So, some of her anger dissipated. "Natalie, por favor."

The woman smiled. "Un momento."

She then disappeared. A few moments later, Natalie arrived, dressed head-to-toe in brand new Lulu Lemon, Dewey from a workout.

"Carmen, what a surprise," Natalie said in a voice dripping with saccharine. "To what do I owe this pleasure?"

Carmen stepped forward, intentionally invading her personal space. "Cut the crap. I know what you did."

A smirk. "And what did I do?"

"You stole my film from the Sundance submissions package."

"I have no idea what you're talking about." Natalie laughed, a practiced look of innocent confusion swallowing her face. "Why would I do that?"

"Because you're a jealous, conniving bitch who can't stand the thought of anyone being better than you," said Carmen.

She felt Alana's hand on her shoulder. A silent subliminal message to calm down.

"*Please.*" Natalie scoffed, tossing her sweaty yet still perfectly styled hair over her shoulder. "I don't need sabotage to get ahead. My film speaks for itself."

"Javier saw you."

Something flickered in Natalie's eyes — a flash of panic, there and gone before her mask slid back into place. "Javier is mistaken. I would never get my manicure anywhere near your amateurish little project."

Carmen's hands balled into fists at her sides. "You lying sack of—"

"Okay, I think we're done here," Alana said, digging her fingers into her shoulder. "Come on, Carm, she's not worth it."

Natalie stepped back and slammed the door.

The house reverberated.

Carmen let Alana lead her back to the car. She got in and slammed her own door before screaming in frustration, pounding her fists on the steering wheel. "All that effort. A hundred late nights and all those long weekends … and for what? For Natalie to just erase Jaguar Woman like it never even existed? And you— you were sublime. Everyone needs to see you act."

"I'm so sorry, babe. I know how much this meant to you." Alana pulled her into a reluctant hug. "There's always next year, right? You can submit again, and—"

"It won't be the same," Carmen said, her voice thick with unshed tears. "Anton Acquilino is judging *now*. This year was my one shot to get my work in front of my idol, and now it's gone."

And then she finally let the damn go. Bursting into tears. Alana held her tight. Until a security car pulled up behind them.

"We should go," Alana said.

Carmen nodded and wiped her face, then pulled out of Natalie's driveway. How could a person crush another's dreams with so little remorse? Who even thought of doing that in the first place?

"I should sneak the film into the festival myself," Carmen said, wiping her eyes with the back of her hand.

Alana laughed. Then, in a serious tone, she said, "How exactly would we do that?"

Carmen looked at her. "You serious?"

Alana shrugged. "Why not?"

Carmen thought for a moment. "Like a reverse heist or something. We slip Jaguar Woman into the lineup, and BAM! — it's there on the screen. Can you imagine Natalie's smug face when it starts playing in the packed theater? *Priceless*."

"That would be pretty epic. But it's not like we can just waltz into a projection booth at Sundance and splice the film into the reel."

"No …" Carmen chewed on her lower lip, thinking.

"What if we signed up as volunteers for the festival? We'd have access to all the behind-the-scenes areas, including the screening rooms. All we'd need to do is befriend the projectionist, and then when the time is right—"

"We make the switch," Carmen finished, her heart now pounding with the thrill of possibility. "It's risky as hell, though. If we get caught, I could be blacklisted from Sundance for life. Not exactly great for my career."

"True," Alana said. "But consider the payoff. If we *can* pull it off, Anton Acquilino will be watching your master-piece on the big screen just as was intended."

Another long silence before Carmen laughed and said, "Fuck it. Let's do this."

OVER THE NEXT FEW WEEKS, Carmen and Alana threw themselves into their new roles as Sundance volunteers. They completed hours of online training, learning everything from crowd control to emergency protocols. They specifically requested working the Emerging Artists screening and were approved. By Melissa herself, who no doubt felt sorry for Carmen. She sent them maps of the facility and they identified every exit, hiding spot, and potential route to the projection booth.

They befriended the festival's projectionist on the Facebook group, a laid-back film school grad named Barrett, bonding with him over a discussion of whether any prints of London After Midnight still exist. Carmen felt a twinge of guilt for exploiting his kindness, but she shoved it down, deep, reminding herself that *this* was her one shot to make her dreams a reality.

And then what after felt like an eternity of preparation, and a long drive to Park City, Utah, the festival date finally arrived.

Even with Alana by her side, Carmen's stomach was a mess of knots when she reported for her first shift. They assumed their positions in the theater lobby, with Carmen scanning the arriving crowd for any sign of Natalie.

But then she caught a glimpse of Anton Acquilino himself — looking every bit the brooding auteur in his black turtleneck and Buddy Holly frames that were slightly too big for his face. She almost stopped breathing.

Carmen's palms were slick with sweat.

This is really happening.

No turning back now.

A shrill voice cut through the buzzing crowd. "What are you doing here?"

Carmen froze. Then, she turned to see Natalie striding toward her with a snarl on her glossed lips. "I knew you were desperate, Carmen, but I never took you for a gate crasher."

"I'm not crashing anything," she replied through gritted teeth. "Alana and I are volunteers. We have every right to be here."

"Volunteers? *Please*." Natalie rattled out a disbelieving laugh. "I know you're up to something." She leaned in close with a venomous voice. "And if you think you're going to weasel your way into meeting Anton to bad mouth my film to him, think again. I'll be stalking you like an ex on Insta."

Then she spun on her heel and marched away.

"Ignore her," Alana said, giving her arm a reassuring squeeze. "Focus on the mission."

Carmen nodded, drawing a deep, steadying breath. Alana was right. She couldn't let Natalie get under her skin, especially not now that they were so close to pulling off their plan.

When the house lights dimmed, and the first film of the showcase began to play, they slipped away from their posts. They made their way through the deserted hallways toward the projection booth. Carmen was about to knock on the door when she hesitated. "I can't."

"Why not?"

Carmen looked at her. "What if he gets fired? Because of me? I couldn't do that to him. How am I acting any different than Natalie?"

Alana nodded. "Alright, let's reconsider. Maybe we should just make a meeting with Anton. Ask him to watch it."

Carmen nodded.

Then the door opened. Barrett stood there, holding an ancient issue of Fangoria.

"I thought I heard voices. What are you two doing here?"

"Nothing," Carmen said, shaking her head.

He glanced down at her hand. Spotted the flash drive. "What's that?"

Carmen didn't know what to say.

Alana snatched it from her fingers. "This is Carmen's film for Emerging Artists. Only a jealous classmate sabotaged it and so her film never got submitted. It's an homage to Anton."

Barrett stared at them. "It's a London After Midnight?"

Carmen blinked. "Kind of."

Barrett grinned and held out his hand. "Give it to me.

Alana handed it over.

"I don't want you to get in trouble," Carmen said.

Barrett stared at her. "How? I don't know where it came from. It just showed up. I thought I was supposed to run it."

Carmen blinked back tears, then gave him a hug.

"Go on," he said. "Before the Cinema police get here."

"I don't think that's a thing." Carmen wiped her eyes.

He grinned, tossing the drive in the air. "Your short will play right after the next one ends. Better get back out there before anyone notices you're gone."

But they did as he said, skedaddling.

Carmen threw her arms around Barrett again. "Thank you so much — I won't forget this."

Then she and Alana raced back to the theater, giggling like preschool kids. They slipped into the theater just as the lights came up for intermission.

Carmen directed guests to the washrooms, her heart

pounded like a drum major's solo. It seemed to take both forever and arrive in the blink of eye. And then the lights finally dimmed again and there it was. Jaguar Woman, in all her glory, playing for the world to see, or at least everyone here in the theater at Sundance.

Carmen thought she might die of happiness.

Or terror.

Carmen watched, transfixed, listening to the audience gasp and laugh and sigh in all the right places. She'd positioned herself so she could see Anton's face, loving the way his eyes widened and his lips quirked with appreciation.

She had no idea where Natalie was, and she didn't care.

This was Carmen's moment of triumph. And nothing, not Natalie's sabotage or the festival's rules or the world's expectations, could take that away from her.

Alana gripped her hand. And Carmen turned and kissed her. She couldn't have done it without her.

Then, the final scene faded to black. And a shrill voice rang out over the applause. "This isn't fair!"

Carmen froze. That was Natalie.

The lights came up. Natalie stood in the lower aisle, her face contorted with rage. "That film wasn't approved for the showcase!" Natalie jabbed an accusing finger at Carmen. "She snuck it in, like some kind of … of … cinema terrorist!"

A murmur rippled through the crowd. Eyes turned to Carmen. She felt the blood drain from her face, her triumph evaporating like mist.

A woman in a headset approached Carmen: Melissa, flanked by two burly security guards.

Carmen's legs felt like jelly. "I can explain."

But Melissa said nothing. Carmen walked toward the

exit, and Alana trailed close behind. Out in the lobby, Melissa turned to face her. She looked disappointed.

"I'm afraid I have no choice but to ban you from Sundance, Carmen."

"For this year?" Her voice was shaking.

"For life."

Carmen felt like she had been punched in the gut. Banned? *For life?*

But … this was her dream. Her chance to…tears spilled from her eyes. "She sabotaged me."

"And you sabotaged the festival."

True.

Melissa turned to Alana. "Look after her, will you?"

Alana nodded and took her arm. Carmen let herself be led out of the theater in a daze, past the gawking crowds. No sign of Natalie or Anton.

She had blown it.

The long drive home was a blur of tears. Carmen barely remembered stumbling into the house. She ignored everyone. Going straight to her room and collapsing onto her bed.

Carmen lay staring at her ceiling for Lord knew how long before she heard a soft knock at her door.

"Mija? Can I come in?"

Carmen didn't answer, but the door creaked open anyway, then the mattress dipped as her dad sat beside her.

"Alana told me what happened …" He set a callused hand on her shoulder. "I'm so sorry, sweetheart."

"*I ruined everything*," Carmen said, her voice choked with tears. "I had one shot, and I ruined it. I'll never be a film-maker now."

"Now, you listen to me, Carmen Ruiz." His voice was firm but gentle. "This is a detour, *not* the end of your dream."

Carmen opened her eyes, red-rimmed and swollen. "But Sundance ... the ban ..."

"Sundance is not the only film festival in the world, and certainly not your only path to success." He smoothed a strand of hair from her forehead, just like he used to do when she was little. "You have a gift, Carmen. A true talent. And nothing, not some snotty rich girl or a bunch of stuffy festival rules, can ever take that away from you."

She sniffled, sitting. "You really think so?"

"I know so." He smiled, his eyes crinkling at the corners. "Your abuelo came to this country with nothing. No money or connections. Barely a word of English. But he had a dream and determination. Look at our family now."

He gestured around at the modest but comfortable room. "We may not have much, but we have each other. And I have faith in you, mija."

A fresh wave of tears sprang to her eyes, but for the first time all night, they were tears of gratitude. She buried her face in his shoulder. "Thank you for believing in me."

"*Always*. Now, get some sleep? We'll sit down as a family in the morning and figure out our next steps. Together."

Carmen nodded with a watery smile, "*Together*."

He kissed her forehead and stood to leave, pausing at the door. "Remember what you always say to me: if the story isn't ending, then it's only a plot twist."

Carmen laughed. But when the door clicked shut behind him, Carmen found hope fading. Maybe it was time to face the cold, hard truth that she simply wasn't cut out for this.

Not everyone was meant to chase their dreams.

~

CARMEN TRUDGED INTO CINEMARK, adjusting the collar of her uniform.

When she clocked in, Dave waved her over. "I need you to cover Theater 7 today. We have a private screening — I want you on the door in case the attendees need anything."

Carmen nodded. They usually didn't have private screenings so early in the day.

She made her way to Theater 7, her mind still sorting through the last few weeks since Sundance … it all felt like a terrible dream. Only she couldn't wake up from it.

She pushed open the theater door, surprised to find the lights already dimmed.

A film began to play.

With a familiar soundtrack.

Wait. Was that …?

No. It couldn't be.

She walked in further so she could see the screen.

Somehow, Jaguar Woman was playing. And the theater was far from empty. In fact, every seat was taken.

And standing in the front row, waving at her …

"Mom?" Carmen said though it sounded more like a croak.

"Surprise, mija!" Carmen walked over and was pulled into a bone crushing hug. "We wanted to do something special for you, after everything …"

"But … how? I don't…"

"*Shhh*," her father, took her hand, pulled her to the empty seat between them. "Watch the movie Carmen. We'll explain after."

So she did. Sitting between her parents, watching her movie. It had never looked so good. She'd watched it countless times, of course, but never with family.

When the final scene faded to black, the theater

erupted into thunderous applause. Everyone was on their feet, clapping and cheering for her. *For her work.*

She spotted Alana next to her father, a cheeky grin on her face.

Then the house lights came up and she saw him. Sitting right behind her with his signature turtleneck peeking out from beneath a leather jacket.

He leaned forward and extended his hand. "Carmen Ruiz, I presume? Anton Acquilino. It's a pleasure to finally meet you."

She took it, squeezing his fingers. "I … I don't understand. What are you doing here? How did you…?"

His eyes crinkled at the corners as he smiled. "Melissa contacted your school, who confirmed your film had indeed been part of the original submission package. And if it wasn't in our possession, well … it doesn't take a genius to connect the dots. So she got a hold of your parents and together they arranged this."

"And *Natalie?*" Carmen breathed.

"Disqualified."

Her mom patted her shoulder and gestured to the audience. Teachers, classmates, friends, neighbors. They were leaving the theater. "You talk. We'll meet you in the lobby, Carmen."

She nodded, then turned back to Anton. "I can't believe this."

"Believe it," Anton said, his tone turning serious. "Now … in your application, you listed The City of Palaces as your favorite film. And yet, Jaguar Woman is nothing like it. Most young filmmakers, when citing an influence, tend to imitate it in some way. But you … you went in a completely different direction. Why is that?"

Carmen felt her throat tighten with emotion. "I do love The City of Palaces. That movie taught me what magic filmmaking could be. But I guess I wanted to find my own voice, my own style. To tell the kinds of stories that resonate with me."

"Can I let you in on a little secret?" He chuckled and lowered his voice, "*I can't stand The City of Palaces.*"

"What?" Carmen stared at him.

He grinned. "Oh, I know it's supposedly my masterpiece, but honestly? I think that film is pretentious drivel. I was young and trying so hard to be profound." He shook his head ruefully. "But you, Carmen … what you've created with Jaguar Woman … that is truly something special. Raw, honest, and utterly unique. You have a voice that deserves to be heard."

"I … I don't know what to say. Thank you." Carmen felt tears prick at the corners of her eyes. "Thank you so much."

"No need to thank me." He waved off her gratitude. "You did all the hard work. I just had the good sense to recognize talent when I saw it. Now, I believe there's a reception in your honor being held out there? Shall we join the others?"

Carmen nodded, still half convinced she was dreaming.

Just before they left the theater, Anton paused and turned to face her again. "I meant what I said, Carmen. You have a gift. I'd like to help nurture it. How would you feel about a position as a production assistant on my next film? It's long hours, and the pay is reflective of our smaller budget, but you would be up to working directly with me—"

"Yes, of course." Anton didn't need to finish. "I would be so honored."

He smiled. "Excellent. And in return, I would love to

help you develop Jaguar Woman into a feature. I think it has the potential to be something truly extraordinary."

Carmen felt like she might faint. This couldn't be real. It was too much, too fast.

But looking into Anton's eyes she saw only sincerity. He believed in her. Saw something in her work worth investing in.

"I don't know how to thank you." It was all Carmen could manage.

"By creating. By telling your stories. That's all the thanks I need. Now, go celebrate. My assistant Noelle will be in touch with all the details tomorrow morning."

Carmen nodded.

Then he gave her parents a wave and headed toward the doors.

Carmen watched him go, her heart full enough to burst. And then she was enveloped in a tight hug and Alana was planting kisses all over her face. "Your dream came true!"

Carmen closed her eyes, committing every detail of the day to memory. The laughter, the tears, the triumphs — all of it would fuel future stories. She was ready for whatever came next.

Carmen Ruiz, director.

Storyteller. Trailblazer. Filmmaker.

The Sundance Kid.

Family Tied

KIM M. WATT

Family Ties

KIM H. WATT

Family Tied

KIM M. WATT

"I DON'T KNOW IF I CAN DO THIS," DINA SAID.

Natalie looked at her and squeezed her arm. "You don't have to. But we're almost there, so we may as well see what she looks like, at least."

Dina took a deep breath, then looped her arm through Natalie's. "Good idea. And thank you so much for coming with me. I just couldn't tell my mum."

Natalie leaned her head against Dina's. "Hey, we're not best friends for nothing."

Besides, she understood. Being adopted was one of many things that bound the two together.

Although Natalie's mum, Alison, had never told her. She'd been less than happy when Natalie had done a DNA test and discovered the truth. The fallout had been spectacular, involving lots of accusations regarding trust and love and the lack thereof on both sides.

So far, Natalie hadn't even suggested trying to find her birth parents.

And while Dina's mum had always been open about her adoption, Natalie understood that this — what they were doing today — was something Dina didn't want her mum knowing about just yet.

This being the fact that Natalie had given Dina a DNA test for her seventeenth birthday, and now they were five minutes away from meeting Dina's sister for the very first time. A twin sister.

"Come on," Natalie said. "Let's find the restaurant. Then you can decide."

"Alright."

They walked down the street arm in arm, just as they'd been doing since their first day at kindergarten, Natalie with her long, dark hair loose over her shoulders and Dina's blonde hair bundled into a messy knot at the base of her neck. Walking hand in hand across the school playground, proclaiming themselves best friends from the moment they met.

So of course she was going to be here to support Dina today. In a way, this felt like meeting her own sister.

The restaurant was a small place with an outside terrace with patio heaters looming over the tables. A blackboard on the pavement proclaimed a quinoa bowl special. The two girls stopped on the corner and Natalie could feel the tension strumming off Dina.

"You don't have to do this now," she said. "Or at all, even. Just send a message saying the bus was late. Or you were grounded. Or you changed your mind."

Dina looked at her. "I've never been grounded."

"I know that," Natalie grinned. "But Madeline doesn't."

Dina's smile faded slightly. "What if she doesn't like me?"

"What if you don't like her?" Natalie said.

Dina made an uncertain noise at that and unlinked her arm from Natalie's. She rubbed her hands on her jeans and took a deep, shaky breath. "Alright, I can do this."

"I know you can," Natalie said. "And I'm going to wait right here for you."

Dina looked around at the corner. "What? Here?"

"No, silly," Natalie pointed across the street to a coffee shop where metal tables had been set out on the pavement. "There. So if you sit on the terrace, you'll be able to see me."

Dina bit her lip, blinking hard, then hugged Natalie, holding her tightly. "Thank you so much. I don't think I could do this without you."

Natalie grinned. "Of course, you couldn't. But I can't do anything without you, either. So, go on and meet your sister."

She gave Dina a nudge, pointing her across the street.

"Alright, alright." Dina made her way to the restaurant, looking back twice. Once when she reached the pavement on the other side and again when she hesitated in front of the door.

Natalie waved her on enthusiastically, her chest tight and hot. Dina looked child-like against the unrelenting black and red colors of the restaurant.

Someone stood at one of the tables.

Natalie's breath caught in her throat. She had the same long, thick blonde hair as Dina, the same slight frame and air of trying to pass unnoticed through the world. For a moment, neither moved, then they stepped towards each other. It would have been like seeing two reflections colliding if it wasn't for the fact that Madeline's hair was loose, tumbling down her back, and she was wearing a summer dress with a little cardigan over her shoulders, whereas Dina was in her usual uniform of jeans and trainers. They stopped a few paces from each other as if on some unheard signal, then gave very similar, awkward waves.

Then Dina's shoulders dropped, and the two girls came together.

Natalie grinned and crossed to the coffee shop, claiming a table. By the time she went in to order a coffee, the sisters had sat down, leaning towards each other, their blonde heads shining in the sun.

It was going to be alright, Dina thought. Everything was going to be perfectly fine.

THE TEXT CAME in almost an hour later while she was contemplating ordering another iced coffee and wondering if a second brownie was entirely reasonable.

Her phone vibrated.

Dina.

It's going great. You can head home. I'll tell you everything tonight.

Natalie looked at the text, feeling an odd mix of happiness for Dina and a little stab of discomfort (that edged unpleasantly close to jealousy) at how easily she was being dismissed. But of course, she was – Dina had just met her sister. They would have lots to talk about. She'd only come to support Dina anyway. This was a good thing.

She texted: *Awesome! So happy!* with a few hearts thrown on the end for good measure.

She still got another iced coffee and brownie, though, to go. She needed a consolation prize.

But Natalie didn't hear from Dina that night, which was weird. There wasn't a day that passed where they didn't talk in the evening. However, she put it down to the excitement of the day. Maybe Dina was saving up the details to tell her in person.

By Sunday lunchtime, Dina still hadn't texted. Natalie gave her until the afternoon and finally sent a message. *How did it go?*

Nothing.

Until a couple of hours later: *Yeah, good, studying. Catch you tomorrow at school.*

Natalie frowned. She'd expected some sort of blow-by-blow account of exactly what Madeline had been like, where she went to school, if she had a boyfriend or a girl-friend or neither or both, whether her favourite cakes were the same as Dina's, who her parents were, everything. But instead, it was just, *yeah, good?*

She tried to calm herself down. Dina was just processing the experience. Natalie's stomach tightened with that odd little twinge of rejection again, and she pushed it down. Maybe if she ever went looking for her birth family, she'd need space. Maybe it was just one of those things that needed to be held a little close to start with. She'd find out more tomorrow, anyway.

She wound up going to bed early.

Monday couldn't come soon enough.

But when Natalie showed up at Dina's house to walk to school with her, she wasn't at the gate waiting. Maybe she was running late? She knocked on the door.

Dina's mum, Cass, answered and gave her a puzzled look.

"Sorry, Nat. She's already gone in. She said she was going early to study – I thought she was with you."

"Oh," Natalie said, trying not to let the hurt show on her face. "Right. I forgot."

She wanted to ask how Dina had been since Saturday, but she didn't know if Dina had told Cass anything yet or not. So she just headed towards school. The lack of Dina walking next to her made her feel like she'd forgotten something vital.

When she finally found Dina at their lockers, she almost didn't recognize her. She was wearing a skirt, and her hair was brushed loose and straight over her shoulders. Only the T-shirt and trainers were the same, and they seemed somehow out of place as if she'd forgotten how to wear them.

Natalie leaned against the lockers, looking at her. "Is everything alright?"

Dina glanced at her. "Everything's fine. Why wouldn't it be?"

"Well, how did the rest of the lunch go? What was Madeline like?"

"Oh, you know." Dina shrugged slightly, not looking at Natalie. "It was alright, but we don't have that much in common. I don't think we'll meet up again."

Natalie frowned. "You looked like you were really getting on."

"It was cool to meet her, but that was all." She closed the locker and said, "We shouldn't get too close."

"Yeah," Natalie said, straightening. "So, are you stealing her style or something?"

Dina looked down at herself and laughed. "I just thought I'd try something different."

"Okay." Natalie took the lead, heading off in the direction of English class, and Dina fell into step with her.

It must've really shaken her up, Natalie thought. Because there was definitely something off about Dina today.

But then again, meeting your birth family for the first time would shake anyone up. Especially a sister that you hadn't even known you had a week earlier, and discovering the mirror image of yourself.

By lunchtime, Natalie was more convinced than ever that Dina was much more upset by the meeting with Madeline than she was letting on. She fumbled easy questions in classes, acting as if she didn't remember which book they'd been reading in English, and when the geography teacher asked her to read a section from the textbook, she stumbled over the names of places they'd been studying the week before.

"Are you sure you're alright?" Natalie asked for the five hundredth time when they queued together in the canteen.

"Stop, Natalie."

"Well, you just seem a bit … off."

"I'm fine," Dina said, placing a piece of chocolate cake on her tray.

Natalie stared at it. "What's that for?"

"Lunch," Dina said, her voice sharp.

"But you don't like chocolate."

Dina took a deep breath. "I'm allowed to try different things, Natalie."

"I know, but —"

Dina snatched up her tray and stomped away, choosing a table over in the corner.

Natalie followed her and sat down across from her. "We're trying a new table today, too, then?"

Dina scowled at her. "Honestly, Natalie, embrace change."

Then she turned her attention to her salad, and ignored Natalie, who poked at her sandwich without much enthusiasm. It was ham and cheese on wholemeal bread, so hardly inspiring, but that wasn't the problem.

The problem was the sick, rolling feeling in her belly that simply wouldn't go away and only got worse as she watched Dina dig into the chocolate cake. This was more than shaken up. This was *wrong*.

~

AS THE WEEK WENT ON, it became clear that whatever had happened, Dina wasn't getting over it anytime soon. Every morning when Natalie arrived at the house to walk to school with her, she was already gone. No matter how early Natalie tried to be. On Friday she finally said to Dina's mum, "Is she okay?"

Cass rubbed her hands on her jeans and sighed slightly. "I don't know," she said. "Have you two fallen out?"

"I didn't think so," Natalie said, and they looked at each other, awkwardness filling the silence between them.

"Is it a boy?" Cass asked, her voice hopeful.

Natalie shook her head. "Not that I know, anyway."

Cass took a deep breath. "You girls haven't been experimenting with anything, have you?"

Natalie almost laughed at that. She'd tried a sip from her mum's Bacardi bottle three years ago and had promptly spat it out in a potted fern. Then had to eat half a dozen custard creams to get the taste out of her mouth. Dina had laughed so much she hadn't even been tempted to try.

"No," she said. "I'm certain it's not that."

"Alright." Cass rubbed her forehead. "Well, she won't talk to me. But I'll try again tonight. If you find something out, you'll tell me, yes?"

"Of course," Natalie said, her cheeks hot. Technically, it wasn't a lie, as she'd only promised to tell Cass anything she found out, not any of the things she already knew.

At school, she couldn't find Dina before class, but when she walked into biology she was already there, sitting at their normal bench. Dina gave her a tight smile when she sat down. She was wearing a little summer dress that looked new, a cardigan over her shoulders.

"Are we not walking to school together anymore?" Natalie asked, pulling her book out.

"I'd just rather leave early and get some study in," Dina said.

"We could both do that."

Dina sighed. "Honestly, Natalie, we don't have to do *everything* together, you know."

She went back to her book, shifting away from Natalie with a finality that turned the uneasy feeling in Natalie's stomach into something deeper and sicker. She swallowed against it, her mouth dry.

An odd conviction raised its head, something that was wildly implausible yet made perfect, horrible sense. "Do you want to come over to mine tonight? There's a really cool new Japanese horror that's just come out."

Dina wrinkled her nose in disgust. "No. I hate horror movies."

"Oh, right," Natalie opened her book as the teacher arrived. "Of course. Well, come over anyway, and we'll watch something else. You can choose."

"I'll see," Dina said, not looking up.

Natalie left it for the rest of the day. She didn't argue when Dina picked her salad and chocolate cake and took the last seat at a crowded table or when she left the canteen without saying bye.

Natalie just ate her own lunch quietly and spent the rest of the break in the library, staring at a book without seeing the words and listening to that slowly solidifying certainty. She walked home alone, and when her mum asked what she and Natalie were up to that night — because they always did something every Friday — she had to shake her head and say that she didn't know.

She didn't have an answer when her mum asked why not, but she took the bowl of salted caramel ice cream her mum handed her and sat through a truly terrible rom-com with her. It didn't stop her thinking about Dina, but it made things feel a little more bearable.

~

THE NEXT DAY, she went over to Dina's early. Cass opened the door and smiled when she saw Natalie.

"Are you alright, love?" she asked.

Natalie nodded. "Dina?"

"Upstairs." Cass stepped back from the door, and Natalie headed for the stairs, the way as familiar to her as if it were her own house.

Dina's bedroom door was shut, and Natalie knocked lightly. Dina opened it, dressed in another skirt, this time paired with some sort of blouse that the actual Dina would have laughed at.

The dismissive look she gave Natalie left her momentarily breathless.

"I didn't know we were meeting," Dina said, not moving from the door.

Natalie found her voice. "Can I come in?"

Dina rolled her eyes – actually *rolled her eyes* — and Natalie's stomach did that sick, swooping thing again.

But she stepped back, allowing her in.

Natalie stared at the room. Because everything was gone. Old toys, Dina's extensive collection of photos — many of her and Natalie — the posters from the walls. Every last piece of clothing was gone from the floor.

"What happened?" Natalie asked.

"Just making some changes," Dina said, sitting down in her desk chair. "What's up?"

Natalie crossed her arms, planted her feet wide, and said as firmly as she could, "Where's Dina?"

Dina stared at her for a moment, then burst out laughing. "What're you *talking* about?"

"You're not Dina," Natalie said.

"*What?*" Dina was still laughing.

Natalie didn't move. "You're dressing differently, you won't spend time with me, you're eating chocolate cake, and you suddenly don't like horror movies? You're not Dina. You're Madeline. And I get it; you're doing the whole parent trap thing or something. You want to try out each other's lives. But this is enough. Where's Dina, really?"

Dina finally stopped laughing and shook her head. "I don't know what's wrong with you, Natalie. Are you jealous because I've found my sister, and you haven't found your family?"

"I just want to know where Dina is."

"I'm right here," Dina said. "God, people do change, you know."

"Not overnight, they don't. I know you're Madeline."

"I'm not Madeline," Dina said. "Meeting my sister just made me rethink some things. And, yes, okay, I'm making some changes. If you can't deal with that, then maybe we can't be friends anymore. People do outgrow each other."

Natalie glared at her. "Dina would never say that."

"Well, I just did." Dina got up. "Look, either deal with it and move on, or stop being so *weird*, and maybe we can still be friends. But I won't deal with this bullshit anymore."

Natalie didn't move. "Just admit you're not Dina."

"I can't admit I'm not Dina because I *am* Dina." She crossed the room and pushed Natalie on the shoulder, not very gently. "Get out."

Natalie scowled at her, not moving. "I'm not getting out. I want to know what's going on."

"What's going on is that you're being a child," Dina

said. "We're too old for this *bestie* stuff. I take back what I said. There's no way we can be friends anymore. Now get out."

Natalie still didn't move, struggling to hold onto her tears and find the right words to fling back. But this time, when Dina pushed her, it was hard enough to send her staggering into the door frame. She caught herself and straightened, trying not to let the hurt show on her face even though she felt like she was going to throw up at any moment.

"I know you're not Dina," she said again, but even she could hear the wobble in her own voice. Maybe she wasn't convinced. But she was certain enough. She may look and sound like Dina. But this *couldn't* be her.

"Go," Dina said. "I don't want to see you anymore."

Natalie wiped her mouth with the back of one hand, took a breath, and said, "I know you're Madeline, and I'm going to prove it."

Then she turned and marched out, clattering down the stairs, running for the front door, ignoring Cass calling after her, asking if everything was okay. She hurried down the street, catching tears on her fingertips before they could start and trying to slow her heaving breaths. She had an idea that if she started crying now, she wouldn't stop until she was crumpled in a heap somewhere, hollowed out and broken.

There's no way we can be friends anymore.

No way Dina would ever say that.

Right?

~

AT HOME, Natalie went back through the messages Dina had sent her after she'd found Madeline, all the long back and forth discussions, and Dina's building nervousness and excitement leading up to the meeting.

The person who wrote those texts would never have said she didn't want to be friends with Natalie anymore.

That thought settled Natalie a little.

Dina was still out there somewhere. She *had* to be. Most likely, she was wherever Madeline should be, although Natalie was a little hurt and hadn't been let in on the scheme. Dina should've told her rather than let Madeline be so cruel to her.

But there was no fixing it now, so she had to find where 'Madeline' was. There was nothing in the texts that gave her actual address, and Natalie opened her laptop, going to the DNA testing website.

She hesitated, fingers over the keys. This was a massive betrayal of trust, and if she was wrong, it was a terrible thing to do. Unforgivable, really. But she was sure she wasn't wrong. Dina wasn't Dina anymore. There was no getting around that.

She entered Dina's email address into the login box, then clicked onto the password. She took a deep breath, and entered *Nat+Dina4Eva*, then hit enter. The website logged on immediately, and Natalie smiled slightly.

Dina always used the same password for everything, and somehow that made this seem better as if Dina were giving her permission to snoop.

The messages from Madeline were still in the inbox, and Natalie scrolled through them, looking for anything that might offer a clue as to where the real Dina might be. But no addresses had been exchanged, which made sense. Meet in a public place for safety and all that.

There was the mobile phone number, though, and Natalie entered it into her own phone. It wasn't much, but it was something.

She was just about to close the browser when she noticed another message. It had been opened but not answered. She hesitated, then clicked it. She'd come this far. She may as well do *all* the snooping.

The message was an automated notification of a match with a woman named Megan, and the system suggested that she was likely to be Dina's birth mother. Natalie stared at it.

Her birth mother.

There was nothing else. Megan hadn't gotten in contact with Dina, and Dina hadn't sent her a message either. It was just the match, sitting there laden with possibility. Natalie hesitated, then hit answer, feeling like she was watching herself from a distance. This was beyond snooping. This was something else entirely.

But her fingers typed, *Please contact me via mobile only*, and added her phone number. She hit send, and deleted the copy from the site's sent items. She just had to hope Megan would want to talk to her. And that she'd be of help when she did.

Natalie rubbed her forehead and messaged Madeline. There was no point in saying she was worried about Dina because if Madeline really *was* impersonating Dina, then she'd simply not reply. So instead, she wrote, *This is Frank from the flower shop down the road. We have a delivery for you. But the address seems to be wrong. Could you please let us know your full address?* Hardly inspired, but it might work.

A message dinged back almost immediately. *Is this Natalie? Dina said you might try and get in touch.*

Natalie sighed. *I'm worried about her*, she wrote.

The response was nearly instantaneous again. *We had nothing in common. We're not seeing each other again. Don't contact me. It's weird.*

Natalie sat there and stared at the message for a while,

more sure than ever that Madeline was the one walking around in Dina's shoes. The wording was too similar to be a coincidence. Wasn't it?

~

OVER THE WEEKEND, Natalie checked the DNA site regularly. But the inbox remained resolutely blank. It was mid-morning Sunday, and she'd almost decided that Megan wasn't going to reply when a text message came from an unknown contact.

She opened it up.

Megan.

This is Megan. Should we be talking off the site like this? I'm not sure I'm comfortable with it.

The site's really glitchy, Natalie texted back, fingers shaking. *Sometimes it doesn't send me notifications. Can we meet?*

There was a long pause, so long she was almost certain Megan wasn't going to reply, then, *This afternoon?*

Natalie blew out a breath, then texted the address of a coffee shop in town, somewhere nondescript and easy to be overlooked in. *Three p.m.?*

Another long pause, then, *Yes.*

That was it, nothing else. Natalie sat there for a long moment, her hands still shaky. This was it. She was going to meet Dina's birth mother, and it felt like the worst sort of betrayal to be doing. But if she couldn't *find* Dina, what else was she meant to do?

At three o'clock that afternoon, Natalie was sitting in the coffee shop with an empty iced coffee in front of her and the last few crumbs of a cookie littering her plate. She'd been here half an hour already, looking up nervously every time someone walked in the door. She wasn't even sure if she'd recognise Dina's birth mother and kept fiddling with her phone, waiting for a text to cancel.

But when a woman walked in the door, Natalie knew it was Megan instantly. The same long blonde hair. The same easy way of moving. The same faint scattering of freckles across her nose. She looked around the coffee shop, frowning, and Natalie raised her hand, waving. Megan frowned.

Natalie got up and hurried over. "Megan."

Megan shook her head flatly. "You're not my daughter."

"Um," Natalie started.

"No," Megan said. "I've met one of my daughters already. You don't look anything like Madeline."

"No," Natalie said because there was no point arguing about it. "I'm not your daughter, but I'm the friend of one of them. Not Madeline. Dina."

Megan didn't give any sign of recognising the name, but she said, "That's who I matched with. Dina. You're using her account?"

"I did. I'm worried about her. Can we sit down?"

Megan's gaze went to the door as if marking her escape.

"Please?" Natalie asked, not having to fake the tremble in her voice. "She's my best friend, and I'm scared for her."

Megan hesitated, then nodded. "Alright. This was shitty behaviour, though."

"I know. But it's important." Natalie ordered another iced coffee while Megan ordered a latte, then she led the way back to the table in the corner of the shop.

"What do you want?" Megan asked, setting her bag on the chair next to her.

Natalie opened her mouth and shut it, and then everything came out in a rush. "Dina met with Madeline, and they both said they didn't want to meet again, but now I think they've swapped places or something because Dina's not acting like herself. She's eating chocolate and dressing like Madeline was the day they met, and she doesn't like horror anymore, and something's just gone *really* wrong." She managed to stop herself somehow, eyes prickling.

Megan grimaced. "I don't know how I can help you. I've only met Madeline once."

"Do you know where she lives or anything?"

"No." She paused when her name was called by the barista, then went to get the coffees and sat down again. She slid Natalie's across the table. "You're Dina's best friend?"

"Since our first day at school."

"That's nice." Megan ripped a sugar sachet open and tipped the contents into her coffee, stirring absently. "I had three daughters. Triplets."

Natalie's mouth fell open. "Triplets? Have you met the third one?"

"No. But Madeline did. Right before she found me. Said they didn't have very much in common."

Natalie fell silent, looking at her iced coffee. She probably shouldn't have ordered a second one. She was feeling jittery already. "She said they didn't have much in common?"

"Yes." Megan nodded. "She said her name was now Jennifer, and her adoptive family wasn't great." Megan sighed, rubbing her face with long, slim fingers. "What about Dina? Is she alright? Does she have a nice family?"

"Yes," Natalie said. "And she's really good at school, and she wants to be a teacher. But since she met Madeline, it's all changed. She's not good in class, and she won't even talk to me. She says she doesn't want to be friends anymore." She hesitated, then added, "I really do think she and Madeline swapped places."

Megan bit her lip slightly, looking down into her coffee cup as if hoping to read an answer in the foam, then shook her head. "If they did, I don't know anything about it. I'm not in touch with Madeline."

"Do you know where she lives at least?"

"No. It's not my place to know. I didn't want to give up my daughters, but I had to. So the least I can do is let them have their privacy. Their lives." She looked up at Natalie. "You must be about the same age as Dina. Seventeen?"

"Yes."

"I was a year younger than you when I had my girls. I couldn't have given them a good start. And once I gave them up, I couldn't *do* anything. I had no control over where they went or the way they were split up. I think Jennifer didn't have … she didn't go to a good place. But I hope Madeline and Dina did." She stopped, pressing her fingers under her eyes, then reached for her bag. "I'm sorry. I don't think I can help you."

"No, wait. Are you sure there is no way you can help me get in touch with Madeline?" Natalie asked, getting up as Megan did.

"I can't," she said. But she didn't quite look at Natalie.

"Please. I'm so worried about Dina. If they've swapped places, then I need to find her. I need to know that she's okay."

Megan hesitated, her fingers so tight on her bag that her knuckles were white.

"Please. To help Dina."

Megan looked away, blinking hard, then pulled her phone out. She swiped through it, and a moment later, Natalie's phone dinged. "That's her parents' address. It's all I can do."

"Thank you." Natalie grabbed her phone, and by the time she looked up, Megan was already gone, the door swinging shut in her wake.

But she had something.

She had somewhere to start.

NATALIE WENT STRAIGHT to the address, taking two buses to get there. It was in one of the fancier parts of town, all big detached houses and well-kept gardens, with two-car garages and quiet, tree-lined streets.

Madeline's house was made of gray stone, roses rambling up a frame around the door, and a cat watching from the windowsill when Natalie rang the bell. It echoed somewhere inside, and before long, a woman opened the door.

She was in the sort of slacks and blouse that proclaimed *Sunday casual but make it designer*.

She smiled at Natalie, her forehead expressionless but her face friendly. "Yes?"

"I'm looking for Madeline," Natalie said, and the woman's smile vanished.

"Who are you?" she asked.

"My name's Natalie. I'm a friend of hers from school."

The woman snorted, an oddly inelegant sound. "I doubt that very much."

"I'm sorry?"

"I know all of Madeline's friends. And you aren't one of them. So, who are you really?"

Natalie hesitated, wondering whether to keep the lie going. Then she sighed. "My best friend is Madeline's sister. She found Madeline through a DNA match, and since they met, she's been acting really weird. I'm just trying to figure out what's going on."

The woman took a deep breath and looked at the sky, her arms folded tightly across her chest. "We haven't seen Madeline for about two years."

Natalie blinked. "What?" *Two years?* Since she was *fifteen?*

The woman looked back at Natalie, her face drawn tight. "We did everything we could to help her. *Everything*. But she just kept getting worse. She was violent, she ran away, she … Maybe it was drugs, or the wrong sort of friends, or … We *tried*. We did. But in the end, we had to let her go back into care. We have another child, and I honestly thought she might hurt him."

Natalie swallowed hard. *She was violent?* "So Madeline doesn't even live here?"

"Not anymore." The woman started to step back from the door.

"Wait! Did you know about the other sister?"

The woman hesitated, looking back into the house.

"Please?" Natalie said. "I'm worried about my friend."

The woman sighed, her shoulders slumping, then nodded, the movement stiff. "We knew about one. Jennifer. She found Madeline somehow, and we think that was what set everything in motion. She didn't come from the best family, and after Madeline met her …" She trailed off, looking into the house again as if listening for something. "I have to go. I hope your friend's alright."

Then she shut the door, not giving Natalie the chance to say anything else.

Natalie just stood for a moment, staring at the smooth white wood, then turned and walked back to the street.

She was on autopilot, her legs stiff and unfamiliar. There were buses, but she couldn't seem to think of how to find the right one. She just kept walking, barely seeing the road in front of her, trying to put the pieces together in her head.

Madeline had met Jennifer, then things had been *set off*, and she'd ended up back in care. Now Madeline had found Dina, and Dina wasn't acting like herself.

She was violent.

Natalie rubbed her mouth and suddenly turned, and some instinct prickled at the back of her neck. But there was no one behind her, just cars passing on the road, people coming home from Sunday movies or shopping trips, and she felt suddenly, impossibly lonely.

She'd usually be with Dina or sprawled on the sofa, eating crisps and laughing at the bad effects in old horror movies. Not out here alone, jumping at shadows. She pulled her phone out, found Madeline's number, and wrote, *I know about Jennifer.*

She hit send and kept walking, looking over her shoulder every now and then. That prickling sensation of someone behind her persisted, but she never saw anyone, and Madeline didn't answer. Natalie didn't really expect her to, and she couldn't think of anything else to do except go home.

THE NEXT DAY AT SCHOOL, Natalie confronted Dina at their lockers, not bothering with any niceties. The time for that was gone. "I know about Jennifer."

Dina just looked at her blankly. "Who?"

"Jennifer. Your other sister, *Madeline*."

Dina shook her head. "Honestly, this is getting boring."

Natalie sighed. "You're Madeline. You used to live in this big fancy house, and then your parents put you back into care. I can see why you'd want to swap with Dina. But you have to let her come back, or at least tell me where she is."

Dina closed her locker, put a hand on Natalie's shoulder, and leaned forward until their foreheads were almost touching. "*I am Dina.* Stop this, or I'll get you expelled for harassment." Then she dropped her hand and headed down the hall. "Don't sit with me anymore."

Natalie watched her go, that now-familiar sickness heavy in her belly. She was sure she was right, *sure* of it, but she couldn't prove anything and couldn't figure out where to go from here. That feeling of being followed was persisting, too, making her feel exposed and vulnerable even at school. What was she expecting? Madeline sprinting after her with a butcher's knife?

She'd watched too many horror movies.

Natalie tried calling Megan again when she got home, but she didn't answer, which wasn't surprising. Natalie had the idea she was lucky Megan had talked to her at all. She still tried a couple more times through the afternoon, then eventually flopped on the sofa next to her mum, who was watching the news.

"You alright, love?" Alison asked. "You don't seem to be spending as much time with Dina these days."

"No. I don't think we're friends anymore," Natalie said and heard the break in her own voice.

"I'm sure that's not the case. You two will always be friends."

"I don't think so," Natalie said. "I think maybe it really is over."

Alison put an arm around her, and Natalie snuggled into her as if she were a little kid again. They sat there as the news began a story about a house fire. Natalie stared at the TV blankly, not really taking it in, until a photo flashed up on the screen. She sat up straight, pulling away from her mum. "That's *Megan*."

"Who's Megan?" her mum asked.

Natalie didn't answer, leaning forward slightly. *Woman tragically dead in house fire*, the bar ran along the bottom.

"Just … just someone I met," she said, thinking of the way Megan hadn't quite answered the questions, the way she looked away when she was talking. Natalie had thought she was just uncomfortable, but maybe it had been more than that. Maybe she'd been afraid, afraid like Madeline's adoptive mother.

But there was no way of finding out now.

NATALIE SKIPPED school the next day. There was no point trying to talk to Dina/Madeline, and she only had one lead left now. She needed to go back to Madeline's house, try to find out more about Jennifer.

She wasn't about to walk that distance again, so she headed for the bus stop, standing on the edge of the curb. While she waited, she pulled out her phone and scrolled through news stories about the fire that had killed Megan. A gas explosion was being suggested, but the investigation was ongoing.

She was just skipping across to another article when something hit her back, hard. She stumbled off the curb, losing her footing and falling painfully to one knee.

Just as a truck bore down on her.

She looked up at a scream of brakes and the blare of a horn, and everything felt drawn out and in slow motion. She couldn't seem to get her legs moving under her, couldn't even roll away. All she could do was stare at the bright metal grill growing bigger and bigger and the horrified face of the man at the wheel. The smell of burning rubber filled the air.

And then someone grabbed her around the waist and hefted her up and around, and suddenly she was crumpling to the curb, and the truck was gone. She was silent and stiff with the fright of it all.

"Are you alright?" someone asked, and she looked up to see a large, bald man, his eyes as wide as the truck driver's had been. He still had both hands on her waist as though he were afraid to let go.

She tried to say something, but nothing came out, and he released her, pressing one hand to his chest as if to hold his heart in place. She understood how he felt. Her own heart was going far too fast, and there was a cold sweat on her arms.

"Are you hurt?" he asked, and she shook her head. She didn't think so, anyway. He helped her to her feet, a big, hulking man with tattoos on his head and sweat standing out on his face.

"What happened?" she asked.

"Some bloody madwoman bumped into you."

"A woman?" Natalie said.

He frowned, his face a map of concern. "Yeah, I didn't get a decent look at her. She was on a bike and went straight behind you. Almost looked like she pushed you."

"Okay," she said, her voice raspy. "Thank you."

"Just bloody happy I was here. Stay further back from the curb next time." He checked the traffic, then stepped into the road, coming back with her phone. She hadn't even realized she'd dropped it. The screen was cracked but still working. He handed it to her, then stayed with her until the bus arrived, making sure she got on safely. "Be careful now."

She nodded, giving him a weak wave, then fell into the

nearest seat, covering her face with both hands. A woman on a bike? Had it been Madeline? Had it been Dina? What about Jennifer? Did it all start with her, somehow? Getting her sisters to … what? Abandon all their friends? Burn down houses? That was ridiculous, wasn't it?

She opened her phone and tried to log onto the DNA website again, but the account had been shut down. She rubbed her face with both hands, wincing as she discovered grazes on both, then became aware that one knee was stinging as well. She'd torn the knee of her jeans, and there was blood dotting the fabric.

Well, she could still walk, at least. It wasn't that bad.

She got off at her stop and walked toward Madeline's old house, knee twinging with every step. She could smell smoke in the air, and at first, she thought it was just someone burning cuttings in the backyard.

But it grew stronger and stronger, and by the time she turned the corner onto Madeline's street, she already knew what she was going to see. Fire engines outside the house, the stone blackened, and the beautiful roses burned entirely away. The windows were shattered, and the roof crumpled in places as if some monster had been taking bites out of it. The property was cordoned off, and she walked up to the edge of the barrier and just stared, one hand over her mouth.

There was a neighbour out in the garden, poking at some weeds in a desultory manner but mostly watching the police as they milled around the front of the house.

"Terrible, isn't it?" the neighbour said.

Natalie looked at her. "What happened?"

The woman straightened, her trowel still in one hand. "I think it was the gas or something like that. We heard the bang, and by the time we came out …" She waved, encompassing the devastation.

"Was anyone hurt?" Natalie asked.

The woman's face twisted. "We saw two bodies being taken out, all covered up. Did you know them?"

"Not really. I was a friend of their daughter."

"Oh, that was a shame as well. Such a tragedy."

"What was?" Natalie asked.

The woman cocked her head. "Haven't seen her for a while?"

"No," Natalie said. "I moved away. Just got back to the city."

The woman nodded understanding. "Well, they were quite a perfect little family, you know. Madeline was so sweet, *such* a good girl. Doted on her little brother. Then, her whole character changed. She tried to hurt him a couple of times. And there was that incident with her father."

"Incident?"

"He fell on the stairs. Never walked again. After that happened, they sent Madeline away." She trailed off, looking uncomfortable. "I imagine that's why he couldn't get out of the house. And poor Stella wouldn't have left him to burn. At least the boy survived, but it's tragic, really."

"Tragic," Natalie echoed. She turned and headed down the road, away from the house again. That feeling of being watched was back, and she kept well away from the curb, her shoulders itching in anticipation of another push.

She was going to have to confront Madeline. It was the only option she had left. She couldn't find Dina and had no idea if Jennifer was even still around, so what else could she do?

Tell Cass?

As if she would be believed.

She went straight to Dina's house when she got back.

Cass was at work, but Natalie knew where the spare key was. She let herself in and went up to Dina's bedroom, sitting on the bed to wait. She wasn't surprised when, less than ten minutes later, she heard the door open downstairs and footsteps on the stairs.

Dina stopped in the open bedroom door and glared at her. "What are you doing here?"

"What are *you* doing here?" Natalie said. "Shouldn't you be setting fire to someone else's house?"

Dina gave a short laugh. "You don't know what you're talking about."

Natalie pressed her fingers into her thighs. "Where's Dina?"

There was silence while the girl in the doorway looked at her. "I'm Dina now."

"And before that, you were Madeline."

"Doesn't matter who I was before."

"What about Jennifer?" Natalie asked and saw the girl shift uncomfortably. "Are you actually Jennifer?"

"I'm Dina."

Natalie got up. "But you're not really, though, are you?"

"No one would ever believe that I wasn't her."

"Why?" Natalie asked. "Why do this? You *are* Jennifer, aren't you?"

The girl shrugged, her long hair flowing softly over her shoulders. "It doesn't matter who I was. Just who I am now."

"But why do this to your *sisters?*"

Jennifer – because Natalie was sure it was her now – scowled. "Because they got *everything*. And I got …" She shook her head. "The things that were done to me. The places I was sent. Meanwhile, Madeline had her bloody mansion, and Dina had *this*…" She waved an urgent little

419

movement. "It's not a mansion, but she's so loved. *By her family.* Even by you. You love her."

"Where *is* she?"

"Right here," Jennifer said. "You'll just have to accept it. I'm just like her, after all. And we can be best friends again."She smiled, and it was so much like Dina's smile that Natalie's heart twisted.

"What did you do to Dina?" she asked.

"I am Dina," Jennifer said again and stepped further into the room.

Natalie stiffened.

Dina was holding a knife in one hand, the blade long and slim and ugly. "Now either you're my best friend, or you're a problem."

"Jennifer—"

"*Dina.* I can't have you running around telling people I'm not who I actually am."

"You can't just *stab* me," Natalie said, her eyes on the blade. It had to be fake, a movie prop. Nothing like this could really be happening, not in her best friend's bedroom, with someone wearing her best friend's face. "You can't!"

"I'll do whatever I need to." Jennifer launched herself forward, and Natalie didn't even think about what she was doing. She just grabbed the desk chair and swung it, hard. As fast as she moved, she still almost wasn't in time. The knife flashed towards her, getting past the legs but hitting the seat. Jennifer staggered, falling sideways, and Natalie shoved the chair at her even harder, pushing her back against the wall.

Then she dropped it and sprinted for the stairs.

"*Natalie!*" Jennifer screamed.

Natalie heard her close behind. She sprinted straight

for the front door, running as hard as she could, almost falling on the staircase.

Jennifer was right behind her, and Natalie was still fumbling with the lock when the other girl grabbed her hair, pulling her away.

Natalie screamed, expecting the bite of the knife.

She snagged an umbrella from by the door and shoved the tip into Jennifer's stomach hard enough to make the girl yelp. Her grip loosened, and Natalie ripped herself free, still clutching the umbrella. She slammed it onto Jennifer's knife arm.

She screamed but still kept her grip. "You *bitch!*"

Natalie made for the door again, unlocking it and flying through, leaping down the steps to the front yard. A car pulled up at the gate. Dina's mum flung the driver's door open, tumbling out and racing to meet her. "Natalie, *run!*"

Natalie sprinted for the car while Jennifer charged out of the house, knife at the ready.

"Go back!" Natalie shouted at Cass. "She's not going to stop!"

But Cass grabbed Natalie and dragged her into the car, then made a run for the other door. Jennifer reached her as she did, taking a wild swipe with the knife. Natalie threw her door open again, catching Jennifer in the belly and driving her back. Cass scrambled in, slamming the door and hitting the locks.

There was a moment's sudden silence, broken only by their wild panting. Jennifer got up, her hair wild and her skirt torn. She looked at the knife in her hand as if suddenly becoming aware of it, then dropped it and covered her face with both hands.

"*Mum!*" she wailed. "Natalie attacked me! I was just defending myself!"

"I didn't," Natalie said.

"I know," Cass said, holding up her phone. It showed security camera footage from inside the house, dim and shadowy.

"I knew something was wrong," she said, her eyes tearing up.

"How?" Natalie asked, staring at Jennifer. She was watching them both as if trying to determine her next move.

"Because Dina was my daughter," Cass said.

NATALIE WAS CURLED into the sofa with her mum. They weren't watching the news this time, though. They were watching a terrible rom-com from the 90s, which had some very questionable gender politics, but the clothes were kind of retro and cool.

"Are you alright?" Alison asked, lifting a lock of hair away from Natalie's face.

"Yeah," Natalie said, not looking at her. After a moment, she added, "I don't think I really want to find my birth mother."

Her mum smiled. "You can, though. You can do it any time you want. I'm sorry I didn't tell you about being adopted, and I'm even more sorry I didn't handle it well when you found out."

Natalie shrugged. "I kind of understand after all this."

Alison pulled her closer, a hug that would've felt suffocating a month ago but now felt like home. "If you want to find her, we'll do it. But we'll do it together, okay?"

"Okay," Natalie said and stayed curled into her mother's side. She couldn't even imagine it. Her heart hurt too much as it was.

Dina was gone.

Just as Madeline had vanished years ago after Jennifer had tracked her down. The police still hadn't found the bodies, but they had enough evidence between the arsons and Natalie's testimony that Jennifer would be tried as an adult.

She'd likely end up in a psychiatric facility, but at least she couldn't do any more harm. But none of that was going to bring Dina back, not ever.

Natalie thought the hollow inside her would never be filled again.

It wasn't just Dina, either. Or Madeline. It was Jennifer herself. Natalie couldn't help wondering what sort of person she might've been if she'd been adopted by a different family or if they'd never been separated.

Would it have mattered?

Had she been broken from the start, and it would've come out in another way? Or had life broken her?

Those were the things Natalie thought, staring at her ceiling that night, watching the shadows of the trees tracing secrets across the plaster.

Everyone breaks, after all. But some people never get a chance to heal. She turned her head to catch a glimpse of the sky through her window, featureless and dark. Did psychiatric facilities allow visitors?

And, if they did — and she went — who was she hoping to heal? And did it really matter? As long as one of them did?

About The Authors

Sean Platt has always been an entrepreneur, but knew he'd rather tell stories. When his wife bought him a laptop for his birthday in 2007 he dropped everything to start writing fiction.

Since making the leap, Sean has written hundreds of novels (including the international best-sellers Yesterday's Gone and Invasion), penned dozens of scripts, and founded the IP Incubator Sterling & Stone where more than thirty storytellers work together to create world changing IP. Sterling & Stone's stable of writers come to Sean for ideas, mentorship, and "better words."

Cameron Stone has been telling stories since he was four, always looking for ways to capture the world as he saw it. When his mom politely reminded him in a scathing yet honest review of his first book that bats aren't birds, the four-year-old Cameron doubled down and wrote another book. This time with rainbows and flying snakes.

Cameron writes thrillers and the supernatural for the "weird" and "queer" kids, with the hope that they will see themselves in stories he never had when he sashayed out of the closet. He lives in Southern Arizona with his husband.

≈

Brea Bolton (She/They) is a screenwriter and novelist based out of Oklahoma City. Along with Sterling & Stone, she is currently working with SYFY, LMN and freelance as a TV screenwriter. When she's not writing, which is seldom, she is producing her own short indie films and attending film festivals and comic conventions. Brea's stories are a mirror of real world authenticity while capturing the magic and wonder in everyday situations, bringing bold characters to life with just a hint of the fantastic. Her stories are the essence of hope and resilience in the human spirit, shouting love conquers all over the den of doubt. They are about triumph and poetry in the smallest of man.

≈

Kathryn Cottam spent over ten years writing screenplays before turning to novels, penning multiple books with her co-writer sister. In 2022, her dream of joining Sterling & Stone came true and she has been able to expand her creativity by exploring more genres and ideas than she ever thought possible. Kathryn currently lives with her two cats in a one-traffic light town on Vancouver Island, Canada. Home is tucked between a mountain, the lake, and the ocean. Which is exactly how she likes it.

~

Skye Riley has always wanted to know what makes people tick. Why does that person look at the world in the way they do? How could someone bring themselves to make that devastating decision? What drove them to that desperate act? Thus began her lifelong love of origin stories and coming of age tales. Skye lives in a small mountain town in Colorado with her husband and a prickly and persnickety pet hedgehog named Mrs. Tiggy-Winkle.

~

Dave Pasquantonio Weird, sarcastic, and thrilling — the first two words describe Dave, and all three describe his fiction.

Dave is a freelance editor who's helped over a hundred authors get their work out into the world. As a freelance writer, he's written hundreds of newspaper features, columns, and articles. He also works behind the scenes at Sterling & Stone to help get our stories ready for publication.

When he has time to write, he loves twisty mysteries, serial killers, quirky speculative tales, and forcing his characters to triumph with wordplay instead of swordplay.

He lives just south of Boston, Massachusetts, where he grudgingly puts up with winter while listening to 80s music and dreaming up bizarre situations to drop his characters in. (Yes, you **can** end a sentence with a preposition!)

~

Kim M. Watt Originally from New Zealand, Kim (she/her) now inhabits a slightly different world, crafting funny fantasies and off-beat cosy (or cozy) mysteries in which tea-drinking dragons collude with resourceful ladies of a certain age, baking-obsessed reapers run petting cafes for baby ghouls, and cats always bring the snark.

Kim's stories blend myth and reality in small and spectacular ways, where the Apocalypse comes on a Vespa, and the healing magic of tea and a really good lemon drizzle cake is unquestioned. But most of all, her tales are about friendship, loyalty, and people of all species looking out for one another. Because these, above all things, are magic.

Bryon Cahill is an author for all ages, also a stay-at-home dad by day who dreams up stories by proverbial candlelight in the wee weird hours of morning. His phantasmagorical stories tend to steer off-course, alighting on the wings of the fantastical to land in the land of impossibility. The words he writes are his ultimate joy as well as his voodoo curse. All the better.

When not writing, Bryon summers, springs, winters, and falls on delightful beaches and boardwalks at the Jersey shore. There he thrives with his loving family, painstakingly penning for their ultimate delight. He constantly strives to live up to his playful craft's unwavering motto: *Fiction is stranger than truth.*

August Niehaus keeps trying to write serious books, but it's no use. She grew up on Star Wars, The Lion King, Redwall, and other fantastical tales of unlikely heroes, which influence what she writes today. When she was five, she typed up her first story, "The Hoppers Go on Vacation." It was love at first inkjet-printed page.

As a writer, August's brand is anchored in talking animals and other un-human characters, as they help her (and her readers) explore complex human issues without all the meatspace baggage. Her stories commonly touch on themes of hope, reluctant leadership, and found family, and occupy the space in and around the science fiction, fantasy, and other speculative genres.

Cambridge, MA

www.ingramcontent.com/pod-product-compliance
Lightning Source LLC
Chambersburg PA
CBHW011141100726
47899CB00010B/3123